Once again Ingermanson takes us on a stunning journey to the nexus of science and faith. *Premonition* is an imaginative and compelling read.

— Brandilyn Collins, best-selling author

Traveling back in time to first-century Christianity with Randy Ingermanson is a delight indeed. . . . He provides a dynamic reading experience you won't find anywhere else in Christian fiction today. I have only one request for Ingermanson upon reading his work: "Write faster! I'm ready for my next dose!"

— Lisa Samson, author, *The Church Ladies*

Premonition firmly establishes Randall Ingermanson as a first-class storyteller and makes you hope he won't keep you waiting too long for the next one.

— Sylvia Bambola, author, *Refiner's Fire* and *Tears in a Bottle*

Be prepared for an intense, spellbinding journey into first-century Jerusalem and the lives of its Christian and Jewish inhabitants. The characters are consistently well-drawn and compelling, their personal and spiritual conflicts authentically heart-wrenching.

— Kathleen Morgan, author, *Consuming Fire* and *All Good Gifts*

W9-BUP-190

PREMONITION

CITY OF GOD SERIES

RANDALL INGERMANSON

ZONDERVAN™

GRAND RAPIDS, MICHIGAN 49530 USA

Premonition
Copyright © 2003 by Randall Ingermanson

Requests for information should be addressed to:
Zondervan, *Grand Rapids, Michigan 49530*

Library of Congress Cataloging-in-Publication Data

Ingermanson, Randall Scott.
    Premonition / by Randall Ingermanson.
        p. cm. — (City of God series ; bk. 2)
    ISBN 0-310-24705-5
    1. James, Brother of the Lord, Saint—Fiction. 2. Bible. N.T.—History of Biblical events—Fiction. 3. Church history—Primitive and early church, ca. 30–600—Fiction. 4. Christian saints—Fiction I. Title.
    PS3609.N46P74 2003
    813'.6—dc21

                                                                2003010003

Published in association with the literary agency of Alive Communications, Inc. 7680 Goddard Street, Suite 200, Colorado Springs, CO 80920.

Interior design by Nancy Wilson

Maps: Jane Haradine

Printed in the United States of America

03 04 05 06 07 08 09 /❖ DC/ 10 9 8 7 6 5 4 3 2

ACKNOWLEDGMENTS

I thank:

- My friends, Don Williams, Jamie Wilson, the Beckers, the Kasdans, the Lundgrens, the Magees, the Poages, the Walkers, the Wearps, and many others at the Coast Vineyard and Kehilat Ariel.
- My fellow writers/artists, John Olson, Brandilyn Collins, Kathy Tyers, Mike Carroll, John DeSimone, Rene Gutteridge, Angela Maust, and my many friends in Chi Libris.
- My consultants on certain details, Ruthie Pletcher and Mike Heiser.
- My agent, Chip MacGregor.
- My editors, Dave Lambert and Lori Vanden Bosch, and the wonderful team at Zondervan.
- My first readers, Brandilyn Collins, Jan Collins, Ellen Graebe, Tracy Higley, Ruthie Pletcher, and Jamie Wilson.
- My mom and dad.
- My three girls, Carolyn, Gracie, and Amy.
- My Eunice.

AUTHOR'S NOTE

In October 2002, the world was stunned to learn of the discovery of a first-century Jewish bone-box inscribed with the extraordinary phrase "James, son of Joseph, brother of Jesus." If authentic, this ossuary would be the earliest archaeological evidence for Jesus.

History tells us that "James, brother of Jesus" (Yaakov the *tsaddik* in my story) was illegally tried and executed in A.D. 62. We know only the barest details of events in Jerusalem in that year — only four years before the ill-fated Jewish revolt. Nobody knows exactly what happened, or why, or what influence the murder had on the revolt that followed. But both Judaism and Christianity still bear the scars of those terrible years.

It is fertile ground, then, for liars, misfits, rogues, halfwits, lunatics, novelists, and other delusional types to invent a tale. I would be charmed if you would listen to mine.

First-century Jerusalem is bound to induce culture shock in any modern person with a lick of sense. I invite you to experience that shock through the eyes of my friends, Rivka and Ari, whom I marooned in Jerusalem in my time-travel novel, *Transgression*. You don't need to have read *Transgression* to enjoy *Premonition*. In fact, I recommend reading *Premonition* first, because . . . it's a better book.

Many of my characters are real historical persons. Therefore I am stuck using their real names, which all sound maddeningly alike. If you get confused, please consult the list of characters at the end of the book.

I benefited from reading scores of books as research for this novel. My two dozen favorites are listed in a bibliography at the back. Translations of biblical passages in the text are my own rough paraphrases, unless otherwise noted.

You can write to me through my Web site at www.rsingermanson.com. I hope to see you there.

But first, let's take a little vacation to ancient Jerusalem, city of God . . .

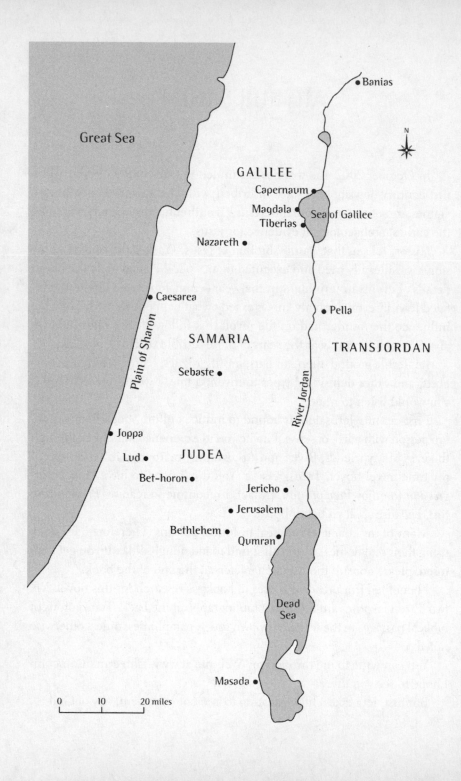

Great Sea

Banias

N

GALILEE

Capernaum

Magdala

Tiberias

Sea of Galilee

Nazareth

Caesarea

Pella

Plain of Sharon

SAMARIA

TRANSJORDAN

Sebaste

River Jordan

Joppa

Lud

JUDEA

Bet-horon

Jericho

Jerusalem

Bethlehem

Qumran

Dead
Sea

Masada

0   10   20 miles

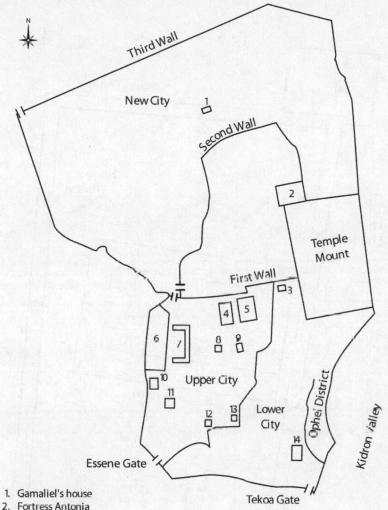

N

Third Wall

New City

1

Second Wall

2

Temple
Mount

First Wall

3

4   5

6   7

8   9

10

11

Upper City

12   13

Lower
City

Ophel District

14

Kidron Valley

Essene Gate

Tekoa Gate

Hinnom Valley

1. Gamaliel's house
2. Fortress Antonia
3. Chamber of Hewn Stone
4. Eleazar's palace
5. Hasmonean palace
6. Herod's palace
7. Upper Market
8. Ari and Rivka's house
9. Baruch and Hana's house
10. Yoseph's palace
11. Hanan's palace
12. Yaakov's house
13. Synagogue of The Way
14. Pool of Siloam

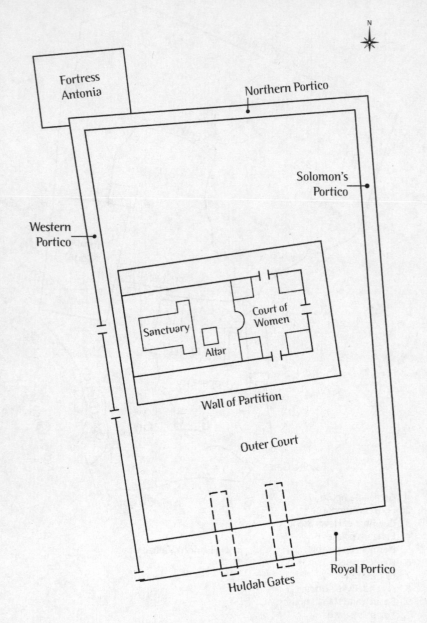

Fortress Antonia

Northern Portico

Solomon's Portico

Western Portico

Sanctuary

Altar

Court of Women

Wall of Partition

Outer Court

Huldah Gates

Royal Portico

N

0   100 yards

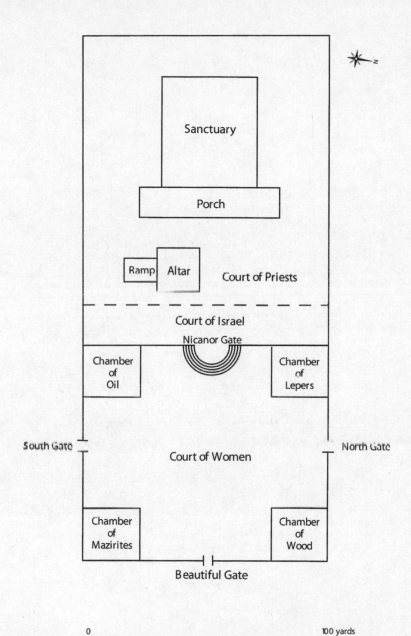

Sanctuary

Porch

Ramp | Altar | Court of Priests

Court of Israel

Nicanor Gate

Chamber of Oil

Chamber of Lepers

South Gate | Court of Women | North Gate

Chamber of Mazirites

Chamber of Wood

Beautiful Gate

0   100 yards

PREMONITION

CITY OF GOD SERIES

PART ONE

SHARDS

Winter, a.d. 57 – 58

For now we see him as in a brass mirror,
but then we shall see face to face.
And now we know him in riddling shards,
but then we shall know him in whole.

— Saul of Tarsus,
1 Corinthians 13:12, author's paraphrase

ONE

Rivka

Rivka woke from a light sleep, her heart thudding. Had she heard a child scream? She listened, her whole body taut, absorbing the sounds of the sleeping city. Jerusalem, city of white stone. City of God. City of fear.

Nothing.

She must have imagined it. Rivka snuggled herself into the warm hollow of Ari's body, willing herself to relax. So much had changed since she'd left Berkeley last summer. Now with Hanukkah coming —

A thin, reedy voice screamed outside in the street. "*Imma! Where are you, Imma?*"

A rush of adrenaline shot through Rivka. Good grief, some little kid was out there in the cold, shrieking for Mama.

Rivka waited, listening. She and Ari were camped out in a small house with their hosts, Baruch and Hana. It was horribly unprivate. Back in America, her friends would just *freak* to hear she'd gone off and gotten married and was sleeping on the floor in the same room with another couple. But this was Jerusalem, another world. She couldn't go back. She had chosen to live here and —

"*Imma!* I'm cold, *Imma!*"

This was getting ridiculous. She would just have to go see what was wrong. Rivka reached for her heavy cloak and pulled it inside under the covers. The air in the unheated room chilled her arm.

"Rivka! Did you hear something?" Hana's voice, a sleepy whisper.

"I'm going downstairs to see what's wrong." Rivka wriggled away from Ari, pushed her covers off, and yanked her cloak around her, shivering. It must be freezing outside, and if that little kid was lost —

"I will come also." Hana rolled out of her bed and stood. A thin shaft of moonlight lit up her belly bulging inside her thin wool sleeping tunic. Hana was a regular Barbie doll — six months pregnant and she still looked fabulous.

"No, Hana, stay here. I'll call if I need help." Rivka slipped on her sandals and tiptoed to the door. From a shelf on the wall, she grabbed a ceramic oil lamp, spiced with cinnamon. They'd lit it earlier that evening, before *Shabbat* began. She sniffed deeply. It smelled delicious. She stepped onto the stairway. Behind her, she heard Baruch's muffled voice. Great, she'd woken him too.

"*Imma!* Help me, please, *Imma!*" The child outside sounded desperate.

Rivka scurried down the stone stairs to the first floor. She opened the wooden shutters and peered out of the high, narrow window slits.

A ragged girl in thin clothing stood in the moonlight, her face awash in terror. "*Imma!*"

Anger kicked Rivka hard in the gut. Some ... *jerk* had gone and abandoned their kid in the middle of the night! It happened all the time and Rivka hated it.

She rushed to the barricaded door, lifted the heavy wooden bar, unlatched the crude iron lock, and pulled open the door.

Upstairs, Baruch shouted, "Sister Rivka, wait!"

She stepped into the street. "Come here, little girl. I'll help you."

Fear twisted the girl's face. She backed away. "*Imma!*"

Rivka followed her. "I won't hurt you! I'll help you find your *Imma*."

The child backed up further, stepping into the shadows of the narrow street.

Rivka hurried forward. "I won't hurt —"

A shadow lunged toward her.

Rivka screamed, spun, stumbled. Her oil lamp flew against the wall, broke into a thousand shards.

The shadow fused into a grubby, bearded man with a very dirty face. Strong hands pinned her arms to her sides.

"Get away from me!" Rivka kicked furiously. "Ari! Help! Baruch!" She twisted her head, trying to butt the man. Several men emerged from the shadows and surrounded her.

Strong hands grabbed her hair and yanked back, stretching her neck painfully. A cold metal blade pressed against her throat.

"Sister Rivka!" Baruch staggered out of the house, rubbing his eyes, squinting into the dark.

Upstairs, Hana screamed.

"You will give us money, sir, or the woman will die," said the man holding Rivka. Three other men stepped in front of her, brandishing crude handmade blades. They blocked the way between Rivka and Baruch.

Dagger-men!

Rivka felt like an idiot. She ought to have smelled a trap. Ought to have been suspicious of a child abandoned in the middle of the night. Ought to have —

Ari's muffled shout filtered out through the window slits above them. Feet thumped down the stairs. Baruch spun to look. "No, Brother Ari!" He disappeared into the house. Then a shout and a terrific collision.

Ari and Baruch tumbled out into the street, sprawling in the dust. Ari rolled to his feet, his eyes black with rage. He stood to his full height, six foot three, glaring at the dagger-men. They were short men, but they had weapons and he had none. Ari pointed at them. "You will give me back my woman."

Rivka saw from Ari's probing eyes and tightening muscles that he was going to jump the men, fight them. *Please, God, no!*

Baruch put a hand on Ari's shoulder. "They will kill Sister Rivka if you make a fight, Brother Ari."

Ari's face tightened and he peered past the men. "Rivkaleh! Are you hurt?"

"I'm f–fine." Rivka had never felt so scared. "They're bandits. They want money." She switched to English. "Ari, it's okay. Just . . . give them some money and they'll let me go." *I think.* The dagger-men were both revolutionaries and bandits, killing the rich and robbing the poor.

Ari turned and whispered to Baruch. Baruch pointed upstairs and spoke in a low voice.

"Be quick, tall one," said the man holding Rivka. "Give us money and we will not hurt your woman."

Ari raced into the house. Baruch stood in the street, arms at his sides, a statue of calm.

"I do not trust the tall one," muttered the man holding Rivka. "He will make some trick on us." The dagger-men backed down the street away from the house. Baruch moved to follow.

"Stay!" shouted one of the men. "You will tell the tall man to remain in the house. When he brings the money, you will throw it to us and we will return the woman!"

Baruch nodded and stepped into the doorway. Ari thumped down the stairs.

Rivka waited, fear clogging her throat. Would the dagger-men keep their word? Would Ari . . . go berserk?

Baruch backed outside, his eyes boring a hole into the house. "Brother Ari, please, you will obey me. You will stay inside. I will give the men the money, and they will release her." Baruch had a way of talking quietly that made people trust him. Ari stayed in the house.

Baruch turned to the dagger-men, holding a long piece of cloth bound in a knot. "This holds all our money." He studied them, his face untroubled. "Now you will release the woman."

"Throw us the money," said one of the dagger-men.

Baruch underhanded the bundle to the one in the middle.

The man peered inside and let out a low chuckle. "It is good." He stuffed the bundle under his arm. Together, he and his companions backed up past Rivka. "Release the woman."

A hand shoved Rivka hard in the center of her back.

She staggered forward, tripped, caught herself, and ran.

Ari raced out of the door and smothered her in his strong arms. "Rivkaleh."

Rivka hugged him, letting her fear drain out in a long sob. "Ari! You were so brave." She pressed her face into his chest.

Ari rocked her gently, stroking her hair. "Rivkaleh."

After many beats of her heart, Rivka heard Baruch's voice. "Brother Ari, it is cold in the street and the night is yet dangerous."

"Of course, Brother Baruch." Ari guided Rivka into the house.

Baruch followed them in, shut the door, lowered the bar. "You are frightened, Sister Rivka. Come, we will pray to HaShem and the fear will leave you and then you will sleep. We have lost only money, and you are restored to us. Blessed be HaShem!"

After Baruch prayed for her, Rivka did indeed feel better. The deep quivering in her belly stilled to peacefulness.

In the darkness of their communal room, Rivka lay awake, listening. Soon Hana's steady, even breathing and Baruch's light snores told her they were asleep.

Ari held her in his arms, tickling her neck with his beard, his breath warming her ear. "Are you well, Rivkaleh?" he said in English, their private language.

Rivka tensed. "I . . . think so." She waited for him to tell her how foolish she had been. And he would be right. She should not have gone out, child or no child. After dark, the streets were a jungle. She could have been killed.

"HaShem took care of you." Ari squeezed her tightly. "And Baruch kept me from being a foolish hero. Sleep, Rivkaleh."

Rivka gave a deep sigh. "Ari, I . . . I want to go home."

"We are home."

"I mean *home* home. I want America. Are you sure there's no way to go back? They can't rescue us somehow?"

"No." Ari's gentle voice cut through her like steel. "I am sorry, Rivkaleh."

Rivka wanted so desperately for Ari to be wrong. He had made mistakes in the past. Like the one that brought them here last summer. Then, she had been sweet little Rivka Meyers from Berkeley, grad student, archaeologist, linguist, Messianic Jew on the run from God and Ari Kazan. He had been a physics professor at the Hebrew University in Jerusalem, a hard-nosed Israeli, an agnostic with a crazy crush on her. They had met at the dawn of the twenty-first century and somehow — thanks to a physics experiment gone awry — they had ended up on the wrong side of a busted wormhole.

In the year A.D. 57.

Married.

And stuck here permanently.

Rivka bit her lip, wishing it were all a movie, but it was just . . . too crazy, even for Hollyweird. Even the dumbest screenwriter knew better than to leave the good guys stranded, with no way back to the future.

Ari's muscles slowly relaxed. Rivka decided he must be asleep. Dear, sweet, opinionated, gentle, infuriating Ari. He was the one good thing that had happened to her in this whole awful adventure. At first, she'd thought him cold, distant, judgmental. And he was all that, but as she'd gotten to know him, she realized that he was like the desert cactus, prickly on the outside, sweet and tender on the inside.

And he had come so far. He believed in God now — she wouldn't have married him otherwise. Someday, he would get it that Yeshua really was the messiah. *Mashiach*. She wanted that. Wanted it even more than she wanted to go home. In the last six months, Rivka had given Ari as much truth as he could handle. Every time she did, it ended in a fight, and she had finally realized that she was making things worse. She had done her part. God would have to do the rest. Ari was stubborn but he was honest. He would come to Yeshua in his own time, not hers. Maybe that was why God had brought them here — so Ari could learn the truth.

Rivka shivered. Yes, God had brought her here. How could she deny it? Last summer, she had saved the life of a man who would change the world. The man they called Renegade Saul. Paul of Tarsus. Rivka had nearly gotten herself killed, and she had made the terrifying decision not to go back before the wormhole was destroyed, just to make double sure that she saved Paul.

According to Ari, she hadn't really changed anything. He said it was impossible to change the past. Instead, she had simply intervened in the past in just such a way as to create the future they had known all along must happen. It was all self-consistent. Something about single-valued trajectories through phase space.

Whatever. It sounded like fatalistic mumbo jumbo, and Rivka wasn't buying it. Without her, Paul would have been cosmic roadkill. She had fixed things once, and she would fix them again.

A slow tear burned down Rivka's cheek. She knew what was coming. Had read the history books. Memorized them, in fact. She had an eidetic memory, never forgot anything she read. The horrors to come made her heart ache.

In just a few years, the Jewish revolt would begin — with easy victories over the Roman legions. Nero's suicide would kindle hopes in Jewish hearts for a final triumph over the great dragon, Rome. But then the dragon's resolve would stiffen, while Rivka's people wasted their strength fighting each other. The city of God would fall, the Temple would burn, the Jews would be decimated, enslaved, deported. The last holdouts at Masada would commit suicide rather than submit. If she survived the years ahead, Rivka would see this whole terrible history.

And that had to be why God had brought her to this forsaken city. To make things right. According to Ari, there was a theory of quantum mechanics that there were infinitely many parallel universes. In some universes, things happened one way. In others, a different way. Ari didn't believe this theory.

But Rivka did.

God had given her free will and intelligence and a knowledge of what had happened in one particular universe. That was a warning — like a prophecy bundled up in a great big *if*.

If you do this, *then* that will happen.

But if you knew the future — one possible future — you could change it. Had a responsibility to change it. Must change it.

Rivka was not going to accept some stupid fate, just because a history book somewhere said so.

Phase space be hanged.

TWO

Ari

The next morning, a *Shabbat*, Ari woke before dawn. Rivka lay sleeping, her mouth slightly open, her silky black hair hanging over her face. She was all that a man could want.

And yet he wanted more, something no woman could give him. Ari awkwardly dressed himself in bed, pulling off his sleeping tunic, wriggling into his four-cornered tunic. He touched the blue-and-white threaded *tzitzit* — ritual fringes exactly like the ones he had so despised growing up as a boy. His stepfather, a harsh and rigid man, a Hasid of the Lubavitcher sect, had made life miserable for Ari. The kosher laws, the rules for *Shabbat*, the endless prayers — all of it was *meshugah*. Crazy.

By the age of thirteen, when he took his *bar mitzvah*, Ari had already read Darwin. Einstein. Russell. The universe was not 5,700 years old; it was fourteen billion. Man had not been molded from the dust of the earth; he was the random endpoint of a long sequence of chemical reactions. And if there was a God, he was not a personal God; he was a First Cause, a Ground of Being, infinitely remote. Or so Ari had believed until he came here.

Ari heard Baruch pulling on his own clothes under his covers. "Brother Ari, it is time."

Ari slipped out of bed and plunged his feet into his sandals, throwing his thick goat-hair cloak around him to ward off the chill. Baruch followed him out of the room. They tiptoed down the stairs to the doorway. Ari wrapped a long, very broad cloth belt around his waist several times. Baruch did the same with an old and worn belt — he had given the bandits his usual belt last night. With many *dinars*.

Anxiety weighted Ari's spirits. Baruch, a scribe, had recently been paid for copying a Torah scroll. That was all the income they would receive until Baruch completed his next scroll.

Baruch snugged his cloak around his shoulders. "Courage, Brother Ari. HaShem has shown us mercy."

Ari felt relief. That was Baruch's way of saying that the bandits had not gotten all of their money. On the way out, both men kissed their fingers and touched the *mezuzah* on the doorpost. In the street, Baruch latched the door with a heavy iron key, put it in his belt, and they set out for the synagogue.

And therein lay the central paradox of Ari's life.

Not in a thousand years would Ari have imagined that he would ever be going to daily prayers, like the foolish *Haredim*, who had made his teenage years a torture. He was a man of logic. Reason. Physics. But that was before he came through the wormhole. Before he met Rivka. Before HaShem gave him one small shard of belief to clutch.

They walked in silence through the streets of white stone. The walls boxed them in tightly, so close that Ari could stretch out his arms and touch both sides at once. He loved this city. It was primitive. Alien. Superstitious. Home.

This city of God was in his bones, in his blood. He had known it from the day he came through the wormhole, that this was home, that he had been made for this city, and it for him. The language had been a problem at first, but first-century Aramaic was not so very different from twentieth-century Hebrew, and that was soon solved.

Jerusalem was a city of infinite wonder, and Ari loved it, despite its strangeness. But he must somehow learn to put together the shards of his life, and this seemed impossible. Yes, he believed in HaShem, a personal God, who had intervened in his life one fine day in a way that could not be explained. And yet neither could one explain ten thousand years of archaeological ruins, or four billion years of fossils, or fourteen billion of light pouring in from the universe, except to conclude that the Torah was not the history book that the *Haredim* said it was.

How to believe in the HaShem of Torah, if one did not believe that the Torah was given by HaShem? HaShem had made a puzzle for him, and Ari's life would be incomplete until he solved it. But he would not give up his reason, and neither would he release his tiny shard of faith.

Fifty paces from their synagogue, Baruch suddenly stopped and held up his hand. "Brother Ari, you will not speak of the matter of the bandits to anyone, please."

Ari narrowed his eyes. "As you say." He rubbed his hands together against the morning chill, remembering that Baruch would not be paid again for several weeks. "How many *dinars* do we have left?"

Baruch gave him a strange look. "None."

Ari stared at him, feeling a huge emptiness open in his stomach. "But . . . how will we live?"

Baruch smiled. "HaShem will watch over us. You will say nothing."

Which was typical foolishness. Baruch made a career of walking a fine line between faith and craziness, and some days Ari wished to strangle him.

"Brother Ari, I see what you think in your heart, but you are wrong. The evil men took only our money, but we have still our honor. Honor is all."

More craziness. This whole city believed such foolishness about honor.

Baruch put a strong hand on Ari's shoulder. "Think, my friend, if they had stolen Sister Rivka instead."

A cold knot formed in Ari's belly. If anything had happened to Rivka . . .

"You see?" Baruch smiled. "You have still your honor and it is worth more than many *dinars*. So be glad, and wait to see what HaShem will do for us. Only say nothing!" He turned and continued walking.

Ari hurried after him. They reached the synagogue and went in. They were almost late. Half a hundred men waited there already for the early morning prayers to begin. This was a heavy irony to Ari. He prayed every day with men who followed a man they called Rabban Yeshua. In plain language, Jesus—a name Ari had been taught all his life to despise. Because of Gentile followers of this Jesus, millions of his people had been murdered. Flogged, burned, decapitated. Forced to convert, then tortured to test that their conversion was true. Their women were violated, their homes burned, their children stolen.

In the name of Jesus. That was a name Ari would never love.

But of course, that was yet future, and these men of The Way of Yeshua would never know of it. Would never believe if Ari told them. He had not even told Baruch. Some horrors were best left unsaid. No, these men could not imagine the evil to be committed in the name of Jesus. They followed Yeshua, the Righteous One—the *tsaddik*—of *Yisrael*. He had done no evil. Instead evil had been done to him, by the hand of Roman soldiers, at the command of a chief priest named Hanan. And his followers continued until now, praying to HaShem in the name of Yeshua, whom they believed to be *Mashiach*. Ari respected Yeshua as a good man, a wise man. Not *Mashiach*, but a *tsaddik*.

Though Ari did not believe in Yeshua, he prayed with these men. Why should he not? His best friend Baruch prayed here. The men of this synagogue accepted him, though they knew he came from a far country, knew that he was not fully a man of Jerusalem, not a follower of The Way of Yeshua. If they would have him, why should he not have them? A man needed a community, even if he could live only at its edges.

His life was shards anyway, and one paradox more or less would make no difference.

Silence fell over the congregation of men. Ari raised his *tallit* — his prayer shawl — over his head and let its softness enfold him. Such customs were foolishness, of course, but they were a harmless foolishness. And the ritual had a way of centering his mind on the prayers to come next.

Ari closed his eyes and waited. Thick silence fell, heavy with the presence of HaShem. Brother Shmuel the prophet began chanting, his deep and powerful voice a river that would carry them to the throne of the Blessed One. The others quickly joined in. Ari did also.

"*Baruch, Attah Adonai, Eloheinu, v'Elohei avoteinu ...*" Blessed are you, Lord our God and God of our fathers ...

Ari had suffered through this very prayer many times as a boy. Now, as a man, he loved it, though it made no sense that a man of reason should love a foolish ritual. Perhaps it was simply in his blood to love it.

It was the best part of any day, and Ari could easily see why his fathers for a hundred generations had endured torture and death for the sake of such prayers.

A pink dawn was breaking over the city of God when the prayers ended. Ari felt wonderful. Then he remembered the matter of the *dinars*, and coldness settled over his heart. They had food for today's *Shabbat* meals, but that was all. After today, they would go hungry — and Hana was six months pregnant. How could Baruch be so calm in the face of that?

Ari folded his *tallit* and was putting it into the folds of his belt when he heard a deep, pleasant voice.

"Brother Baruch, please, you will pray for me."

Ari turned to see Shmuel the prophet standing before Baruch. Shmuel stood only a few centimeters shorter than Ari. In this city of poorly nourished men, that made him practically a giant. A young man in his early twenties, Shmuel was a *Nazir*, which meant he never drank alcohol and he had not cut his hair for a very long time. Thick black dreadlocks hung to his waist. Rivka considered him weird, hyper-religious, but the men of the synagogue held him in high honor and called him a prophet. Ari did not know what to think of Shmuel, but he did not believe he was a prophet. Shmuel held out his left hand to Baruch. The smallest finger was bent inward at a right angle at the second joint.

Ari sighed. Yet again. Shmuel had been born with his finger defective, and Baruch had prayed for him twice a week since Ari came to the city. To no effect. Another prayer would be *meshugah*.

Baruch beamed at Shmuel. "Of course, Brother Shmuel. Brother Ari, you will lay hands on him with me, please."

Ari did his best to smile pleasantly. It was foolishness, but he would do it. He placed both hands on Brother Shmuel's shoulders. Baruch took Shmuel's hand in both of his. Other men gathered around, laying hands on Shmuel, waiting for Baruch.

Ari had seen this so often, he could have done it himself. First Baruch asked the Spirit to rest on them. Then he waited for some minutes. Ari felt nothing, other than a sense of quiet. Baruch wore a look of deep concentration, as though listening to a voice many miles away. The other men prayed this or that. They meant well, but Ari had never seen any of their prayers have any effect.

Whereas Baruch . . .

Baruch could really heal, sometimes. Often, Ari knew, there might be a psychological explanation. The placebo effect. And yet, occasionally, something real happened. Something beyond reason. Last summer, Baruch had saved Ari's life when he should have died of a hornet sting. Since then, Ari had been stung twice, with no reaction. Baruch had healed him permanently of a fatal allergy. That was why Ari believed in HaShem, why he consented to all this craziness. It was logic to believe, even if he did not understand.

Baruch finally stirred from his reverie. He touched Shmuel's finger and commanded it to be straight, in the name of Yeshua.

Nothing happened.

Ari was not surprised. He had seen Baruch pray for Shmuel many times. Nothing ever happened to Shmuel.

Baruch continued praying for some time. A feeling of warmth filled Ari. This too was common. He did not understand it, but he thought there was some natural explanation.

Finally, the prayer ended. Ari took his hands off Shmuel.

Baruch kissed Shmuel on both cheeks. "Go in peace, my friend, and trust in HaShem." He turned to Ari. "The Spirit was strong today. Did you feel it?"

"No." Ari had never felt the Spirit. But Baruch did, and perhaps that was why Baruch could heal and Ari could not.

"Perhaps tomorrow, Brother Shmuel." Baruch took Ari's arm and guided him toward the door.

When they were out in the street, Ari asked, "Why do you continue to pray for Brother Shmuel? You know nothing will happen."

Baruch gave him an enigmatic smile. "Rabban Yeshua commanded us to pray. Therefore, I pray. There is a secret room in Brother Shmuel's heart, and this I cannot enter. Not yet."

"A room?" Ari studied Baruch. "What is in this room?"

"On the day Brother Shmuel chooses to unlock it, then I will know, and then his finger will be a simple matter." Baruch drew in a deep breath and gazed up at the clean, cloudless *Shabbat* sky. "Now you will explain to me about the electron again. You are much disturbed by this electron, and I do not understand why it should be a hard matter."

Ari could not help smiling. It was their private tradition that they walked in silence to the morning prayers, but they returned home afterward discussing physics. Baruch loved to hear of the majesty of HaShem's creation, and he never took offense when Ari told him something that contradicted the Torah. He seemed to think that contradictions were merely HaShem's invitation to a deeper understanding.

"The problem is this," Ari began, and they stepped into a universe of ideas far from the city of God.

Rivka

Rivka peered through the window slits into the early-morning light. The men would be home soon and then . . . she wasn't sure what would happen next. Hana had just told her upstairs that Baruch had given the dagger-men all the money in the house — every single *dinar*. Rivka shivered in the December cold and snuggled her cloak around her shoulders.

Hana came downstairs, yawning fiercely, and looking like a million *dinars*. As usual.

Rivka still felt like a king-sized fool for being taken by the dagger-men. "Hana, what are we going to do?"

Hana shrugged, her eyes distant. "All is in the hands of HaShem." She studied Rivka's face. "You are well, Sister Rivka?"

"I ... didn't sleep well last night. Are you well?"

Hana slumped onto a wooden stool at the one-legged stone table. "The shade of the wicked man troubled my dreams again."

Rivka sighed. There wasn't any such thing as a shade, but she couldn't tell Hana that. Hana was always talking about spirits. It was a little weird, but Rivka was used to it. "Have you asked Baruch to pray about these ... nightmares?"

"They are not nightmares." Hana put on her obstinate look. "It was the shade of the wicked man."

Rivka didn't want to argue. The wicked man. Damien West. Ari's former colleague. A large, grinning blond man with a cherubic face, the man responsible for bringing her here. A man who would have killed the apostle Paul, along with Rivka, Ari, Hana, Baruch. Yes, he had been a wicked man, but ... now he was a very dead man. And dead people didn't go around clanking chains. Or whatever.

Rivka put her arm around Hana. "Ask Baruch to pray for you and this ... shade thing will go away."

"Yes, of course," Hana said in a wooden tone.

Voices. Rivka turned to look at the door. It swung open.

"... so they discovered that an electron can be both here and not here at the same time," Ari said. "It is a strange idea, yes?"

"Not so strange," Baruch said. "Brother Ari, this electron of yours is much like the Spirit. The Spirit is here, and yet not here, do you agree? And this is a mystery, but it is not a mystery. I do not see why you consider this electron so strange."

Hana harrumphed loudly. "I think certain men are both here and not here, would you agree, Sister Rivka?"

Ari and Baruch looked up, startled. As usual, they must have walked home on autopilot, their bodies navigating the cramped streets of Jerusalem while their minds wandered in a strange universe of ideas. Ari had nobody in all the city to talk physics with, except Baruch. But Baruch was enough.

Rivka felt grateful once again that Ari had such a friend. "And how were the morning prayers?"

"Most wonderful," Baruch said. "The Spirit came while we prayed the *Amidah*, and I knew that all will be well."

Which was just a little naive, but Rivka didn't want to say so. "What did the men say when you told them about the dagger-men?"

"We will not tell them of this matter," Baruch said.

Rivka wanted to ask why not, but Ari gave a little shake of his head.

Baruch sat at the table. "We have food for *Shabbat* and we will take delight in *Shabbat*. Come! Let us give thanks and eat!"

Rivka opened the small pantry and brought out their morning meal. Barley bread. Goat's cheese. Pickled cucumbers. Soured milk — like yogurt, only not quite. Water, mixed half and half with beer. Everybody here drank their water mixed with either wine or beer. The alcohol killed whatever bacteria infested the water. It was a good system, really, though it probably would have shocked the daylights out of Rivka's best friend back home in Berkeley, a Baptist.

They all washed hands and sat down on stools around the tiny table. Baruch raised his eyes to heaven and gave thanks to HaShem. "Blessed are you, Lord, God of our fathers, King of the Universe, who brings forth bread from the earth." It was identical to the prayer Rivka had learned in her Messianic Jewish synagogue in San Diego, two thousand years in the future. Despite the culture shock coming here, some things hadn't changed a bit.

While they ate, they talked of the future. Hana's baby. Baruch's Torah scrolls. Ari's prospects for finding work. Rivka barely listened. Was she the only one of them worried about what they were going to eat tomorrow? It was fine to talk about how HaShem would take care of them, but realistically, what were they going to do?

But Baruch was not going to let dirty reality mess up his *Shabbat*. Neither would Hana. And Ari, as usual, just went along. He was easy to get along with, but . . . infuriatingly passive. This whole situation was just frustrating, and the sooner Ari found work so they could move into their own house, the better.

After some time, Rivka realized that the others were looking at her. Waiting. Of course. The blessing after meals. She had spaced out again. "I'm sorry."

Baruch raised his eyes to heaven and prayed the blessing again.

After the meal, Hana and Rivka put the food away. Baruch and Ari went outside to look at the weather. Ari poked his head inside. "It will be a fine *Shabbat*."

Rivka and Hana kissed fingers to the *mezuzah* on the way out and they locked the house. Baruch took Ari's arm and started toward the synagogue. "Now, Brother Ari, you still have not explained to me why this electron bothers you so much . . ."

The two women fell in step a few paces behind the men. Something inside Rivka squeezed into a hard, tight knot. Always behind the men. In Jerusalem, in this century, in this culture, a woman never walked beside her husband. You walked behind him. You covered every strand of your hair. If you were upper class, or a virgin, or very pious, you wore a veil over your face. Rivka felt thankful she was none of those, so she escaped the veil, but there was no way in the world to get out of covering her hair.

And a man did not talk to his wife — not in public, only in private. Nor would he talk to any other woman ever, not in public and not in private, unless he must. This world of Jerusalem was two separate worlds. There was a man's world — the house of prayer, the marketplace of ideas, the fellowship of Torah. And there was a woman's world — the house of chatter, the marketplace of fruits and vegetables, the fellowship of women and children. Parallel universes.

It was driving Rivka nuts. Thanks be to HaShem that Ari and Baruch bent the rules a little. The four of them lived in one house together — much too cramped for two pairs of newlyweds. Until Ari found work, they would be living like this, all sleeping on the floor in one room of a very small house, living on the wages of one poorly paid scribe. Within that house, Baruch did his utmost to treat "Sister Rivka" as a human being. Not merely a woman, but a real person. He understood that she and Ari came from a different land, a different time, with different customs. On the street, though, he followed the customs of Jerusalem. Ari did the same.

It hurt. A lot. Rivka knew the rules. Understood why they had to do it. And yet it made her angry. Furious. She was trying to get over it. Trying desperately hard.

Failing miserably.

Whereas Hana was happy as a kitten in her new life. When Rivka had met her, Hana was working the streets in what preachers called The World's Oldest Profession. Rivka hated stupid euphemisms. In blunt speech, Hana was a *zonah* — a whore. Had been a *zonah*, anyway. No longer, thanks to Rivka and Ari and Baruch.

Now, Hana was a respectable married woman. *Pregnant*, even, and thrilled to death over it. She was the wife of Baruch, a Torah scribe, a good and honorable man who followed The Way of Rabban Yeshua. She lived in the upper city now, far from her former haunts in the filthy Ophel district south of the Temple Mount. Few here knew Hana's past. Men in this part of the city didn't leer at her in the street. Women didn't spit at her feet. Children didn't shriek horrible names at her from the safety of their doorways. Here, barely half a mile from her former life, Hana had dignity. Blessed be HaShem.

They turned left onto the street of their synagogue. Ari led the way, pushing forward through the narrow street, crowded as always. Rivka felt claustrophobic. This street — an alley, really — was barely wide enough to drive a Volkswagen. A narrow stone gutter on each side stank with the detritus of the city. Rotting vegetables. Dead rats. Human waste.

There was no sidewalk. The doors opened directly onto the dirt street. To go into a house, you stepped over the open gutter, and heaven help you if you missed your step.

The whole city was like this. Unsanitary. Disgusting. Gross.

Home.

Rivka was getting used to it. So far, she hadn't died, or even caught any kind of weird disease. She didn't trust the drinking water, but oddly enough, that wasn't an issue, thanks to the beer.

If anything was going to kill her, it was the culture shock. She had been raised in a Messianic Jewish home. She had known before she came here that the Jerusalem church was an ultraconservative Jewish community. Even so, she was astonished. Half the followers of Yeshua here were *Pharisees*. Nice people, but just ... awfully Orthodox. And some of them seemed incredibly ignorant about what Yeshua had actually taught. Of course the New Testament wasn't written yet, and all the apostles were long gone to foreign lands, but still. Rivka wished The Way was just a little more ... Christian.

"Brother Baruch! Brother Ari!" A familiar voice from up the street shouted a greeting to the men. Ari and Baruch waved both hands overhead. Hana shrieked with delight and hurried forward, throwing her arms around ...

A man. Not just any man. The kindest, strangest, holiest man in the city — Yaakov the *tsaddik*.

Yaakov wrapped his arms around Hana and gave her a full body hug, the kind an American daddy might give his young daughter. Definitely not the kind a sixty-something Jewish man here in ancient Jerusalem would give a young married woman on the street.

Yaakov kissed Hana on both cheeks. Then he stepped back and admired her bulging belly, his eyes shining with pride. He put both hands on Hana's unborn child and raised his eyes to heaven. "Blessed are you, King of the Universe, Maker of Heaven and Earth, who brings forth life and hope out of death and despair." He leaned forward and whispered something in Hana's ear. Hana hugged him.

And then Yaakov turned to Rivka. Opened his arms to her. She jumped forward and hugged him tight. It was so *good* to hug a man in public, to be touched, to be loved, to be treated like a . . . person. Rivka felt the anger melting out of her heart.

Yaakov's strong hands patted Rivka gently on the back. He leaned down and whispered into her ear. "I have a word for you from Brother Shmuel the prophet. You shall not be afraid of the terror by night, nor the arrow that flies in the daylight. If a thousand fall at your side, or ten thousand at your right hand, the evil one will not touch you."

Tears welled up in Rivka's eyes. "Thank you, *Abba*."

Yaakov kissed both her cheeks. "Fear no evil, my daughter, though you are a stranger in a strange land. You were brought here for a purpose, and you must obey your calling."

"What calling?" Rivka asked.

Yaakov gave her an enigmatic smile. "That is for you to find. But do not turn from your task, be it ever so small, if the Spirit leads you." He released her and stepped back.

Rivka's mind began racing. What could Yaakov possibly mean by that?

Yaakov turned to Ari. "Come, my son, Aryeh, you young lion. Let me kiss you. And I have a word also for you from Brother Shmuel."

Rivka felt a glow of warmth encircling her. Yaakov was a special man. A holy man. A *tsaddik*. The history books had got him wrong. Completely. Even his name, they got wrong. "James the Just," they called him. Or "James the Righteous."

Which was like calling a certain famous physicist "Einstein the Patent Examiner."

According to a fragment recorded by Hegesippus, James was some kind of an ascetic, a self-flagellating martyr, the kind who spent all his time in a hair shirt, praying on bleeding knees.

Dead wrong. James — Yaakov in Hebrew — was a *tsaddik*, which was about as far away from a fourth-century desert ascetic as you could possibly get. It was worth the humiliation and the stench of this wretched city to see a real, live, breathing, honest-to-God *tsaddik*. A *tsaddik* who didn't care if you were peasant or king, bond or free, man or woman, because when he looked at you, all he saw was a child of HaShem. When Rivka looked at Yaakov, she saw Yeshua. If the rest of the men in Jerusalem could have been like Yaakov, the city would have been bearable.

"*Shalom* to you, Baruch, my son." Yaakov kissed Baruch on both cheeks. "You will rejoice in *Shabbat* in peace and the fullness of joy, be glad and celebrate." He stepped back and raised his hands in blessing over the four of them. "Now may HaShem bless you children and watch over you, may his face shine upon you and be merciful to you, in the name of Yeshua the *Mashiach*. Amen!"

Yaakov waved to someone coming up the street. "Brother Yehudah! I have a word for you from Brother Shmuel the prophet!" He hurried away, beaming.

Rivka noticed a tall young man standing quietly near the synagogue. Long black hair hung to his waist. Brother Shmuel the prophet. When he saw Rivka looking at him, his face reddened and he turned away.

Rivka smiled. Yaakov the *tsaddik* and Shmuel the slightly wacky prophet. Extreme extrovert and extreme introvert. She loved them both.

"Blessed be HaShem," Baruch said. "The Spirit is here. Do you feel it, Brother Ari?"

Ari looked dazed.

Hana's face beamed. "The *tsaddik* told us we will celebrate today."

Rivka shifted on her feet, wishing it were that simple.

The four of them went into the synagogue. Baruch reached inside his tattered old belt and pulled out his *tallit*. A coin clattered onto the stone floor. All four of them stared at it. A silver *dinar!* It was a day's wage for a working man, enough to buy food for all of them for three days. Baruch shook his head and laughed. "Yaakov!"

"Blessed be HaShem!" Hana said.

Rivka felt a pulse of joy in her heart. That was just like Yaakov, to slip someone a little money in secret. And just like Shmuel to know where it was needed.

Baruch turned to Ari. "The *dinar* is like the electron, yes? First it is not here. Then it is here."

Ari mumbled something. His eyes glittered, vague and unfocused. Distant. Infinitely sad.

THREE

Ari

The next afternoon, obeying the "word" Yaakov had given him, Ari slipped off quietly and attended the afternoon sacrifices in the Temple alone. Not exactly alone. Ten thousand other worshipers packed into the open-air Court of Women. But . . . yes, alone. Ari had been alone all his life.

After the service, Ari let himself be carried along with the crowd leaving the inner Temple. Yaakov the *tsaddik* was a strange man, and the message he had whispered into Ari's ear yesterday still tingled in Ari's mind. *After the sacrifices, hurry to the Royal Portico. Do not turn to the right or the left. Whatever your hand finds to do, do it with all your might.*

That was all. If Ari did not know Yaakov, he would dismiss the whole thing as craziness.

Everything Yaakov said was both crazy and brilliant. Like quantum mechanics. That was foolishness too. Nobody would believe it if you explained it to them. The average man on the street in America thought physicists had some logical explanation for the universe. But they did not. They had quantum mechanics. And if the average man understood quantum mechanics, he would lose all faith in science. It took a physicist, a crazy person, to believe in physics and keep his faith in the universe.

And Yaakov was just the same. A crazy man, to hug women in the street, to kiss their cheeks, to speak to them as if they were men. But nobody accused Yaakov of impure thoughts, because that would be twice crazy. Any fool could see Yaakov was a holy man. Such men lived by their own rules.

Therefore, Ari trusted Yaakov. They were both crazy men. They understood each other.

Ari saw a cluster of men gathering under Solomon's Portico. In the middle, a short man with a thin wisp of a beard and piercing eyes sat down to teach. Rabban Yohanan ben Zakkai.

Actually, not yet. Someday he would be known by the title "Rabban." *Our Teacher. Our Master.* Someday, when he was dead, all *Yisrael* would value this great man who had walked among them. But for now he was simply Rabbi Yohanan, one of many sages teaching Torah to a few students. This man would save the Jews from desolation — after the destruction that was coming.

As a schoolboy, growing up in Haifa, Ari had learned about this man, Rabban Yohanan. The Talmud called him Mighty Hammer. Tall Pillar. Physically, the words did not match the reality of the tiny rabbi. But in the world of the heart, the mind, the spirit — yes.

Around Rabbi Yohanan, half a dozen young men knelt to listen. Pious men, they all wore *tefillin* strapped to their foreheads and left arms, small leather boxes containing certain Torah passages inscribed on parchment. Signs of HaShem's presence. *Tefillin* were more craziness. Ari wore them during the morning prayers, but they were a foolish custom. Baruch wore them all day, every day, except *Shabbat* and holy days, which were already signs. For Baruch and men like him, *tefillin* were precious, but for Ari, they were more shards of his fragmented life, signifying nothing. And yet he loved them also. Like the electron, Ari could be both one thing and another. It no longer bothered him that he was both believer and skeptic.

Ari stopped to watch the school of Rabbi Yohanan, as he often did. Here was wisdom, esoteric and profound. He did not understand their discussions on Torah. Did not even wish to understand. It was all complex yet elegant, specialized yet general, abstract yet concrete. Far too much for a physicist who only wished —

Ari shook his head. How long had he been standing here? A minute? Two? Five? He tore himself away from the circle and continued walking south along the eastern edge of the outer courts of the great Temple Mount.

He only wished for work. Not alms from a holy man. Work. To take alms was dishonor. What was so hard about finding work? He was a physicist. In the United States, he could have found a hundred jobs. In the State of Israel, also many jobs. But he had left all to come to this city of God — for a girl. For Rivka. He got the girl, but he also got ... unemployment. In this city and this century, nobody needed a physicist.

Ari was not needed, and that hurt. He understood the deep structure of the universe and the atom, knew the workings of solid and liquid and gas and plasma, could conjure the magic of electricity and magnetism and light. If nobody needed *that*, he could understand. People here could not be expected to make use of his mind.

But why not his body? Ari was strong. Taller than anyone in this city, where the average man stood only a few centimeters taller than Rivka. He could dig, or carry stone, or do any of a thousand other menial tasks. Theoretically, he could even work in the Temple — he was a *cohen*, a man of priestly family. That was obvious from his family name, Kazan.

He had gone once to ask for work at the Temple. Any work.

"Your name is Ari?" A shake of the head. "A strange name. And you are a priest?"

"Yes."

"Very well, Ari the Priest. Where are the records of your family?"

"They are lost. I come from a far country."

"Not so well, Ari the Foreigner. Without records, you are not a priest."

"I can work hard. I can dig or carry or whatever is required."

Another shake of the head. "We have many born in Jerusalem who need such work, and not enough for them. Perhaps you should return to your far country?"

He was a foreigner in a land of high unemployment. And he was *issah* — a priest of uncertain lineage, one without records.

Unemployable.

He could not work as a scribe, like Baruch. His handwriting was too poor. He could not set up in trade. He had no money, no credit. He was a refugee in his own city, with no job, no hope, no dignity, living on the charity of his friend Brother Baruch. And now taking alms from a man who had nothing, Yaakov the *tsaddik*.

He would have done anything to find work, but there was nothing he could do. And the hopelessness of it all was crushing him. Rivka would not understand. And Brother Baruch could not help —

A scream slit open the lazy afternoon. The sound came from under the Royal Portico. For no reason and every reason, Ari began running. *Do not turn to the right or left.* Something deep in his heart told him that he had made a terrible mistake.

Under the portico, a cluster of men stood in a circle. Ari rushed to see. A man lay on the ground, his leg crushed under a large flat block of stone — many hundreds of kilograms. Several men strained to lift one end of it. The man on the ground lay silent — already in shock.

Ari pushed forward and grabbed a corner of the stone.

"Try again!" shouted an older man in priest's garb.

Together, they all heaved on the stone. Slowly, slowly, the end lifted a few centimeters. Another man wedged a large rock under it and they all released their load.

Ari straightened up slowly, his back aching with the effort.

The man next to him pounded his shoulders. "Good work, Tall One!"

Others pulled out the injured man. Blood pulsed from the stump of his right leg. Ari whipped off his cloth belt and pushed forward. He knelt beside the man and made a tourniquet around his upper leg. "Get me a stick!"

Somebody handed him a short length of wood. Ari looped the belt around it and turned the stick until the blood flow slackened. He hoped this was the right thing to do, but nobody else seemed to know anything. If it was wrong, it was wrong.

The priest in charge stepped in. "Very good. Are you a physician?"

Ari shook his head. "It was only common sense."

"Uncommon sense, it seems to me."

"The physicians are coming!" someone shouted.

Three white-garbed men in priestly linen raced up. One of them spread out a thick sheet of some kind of sturdy material. They expertly lifted the man onto the sheet. Ari wondered how often they did this kind of thing.

A minute later, the three physician-priests had co-opted half a dozen men to carry off the hurt man. Ari stayed behind. "What happened?" he asked, to nobody in particular.

"An accident," said the priest in charge, a gray-bearded man, thickly built, with authority in his eyes. He wore no *tefillin*, though most of the workmen did. "We were replacing one of the paving stones and the crane tipped sideways."

Ari studied the fallen crane. It was an A-frame-type device, very simple. Stay-ropes were attached to the top, allowing it to lean forward at a slight angle without toppling. A block and tackle hung from the peak of the A. The legs of the A pivoted in notches at the base, allowing for limited tilt forward and backward. But something had failed. It should be an exercise of ten minutes to figure out why.

"It was the will of HaShem," said a short man with a scarred nose.

"No, it was a bad design." Ari knew at once that this was exactly the wrong thing to say, but he had said it without thinking.

The old priest in charge scowled at Ari, his face darkening to purple. "It tipped to the side without warning. Nobody could have prevented it."

Anger boiled inside Ari at such stupidity. Did these people think things happened for no reason? Then they would use the same design tomorrow and next week and next year. Nine times out of ten, it would probably work. But the tenth, it would fail and they would not know why, because they had not the least idea of physics.

Physics.

Ari swallowed. *You are meddling, Ari Kazan. Nobody will listen to you, a foreigner from a far country with no record of your family.* "I could have prevented it."

His quiet words fell like bricks on the hard pavement.

"Nobody can prevent the will of HaShem," said the man with the scarred nose.

"It is not the will of HaShem to crush a man's legs. It is stupidity." Ari knew this was craziness. He had no hope of winning such an argument. But he had nothing to lose either. Blind fury clawed at his heart. *Foolishness* had caused a man to be crippled for life. That man would never work again. Never walk. He would be forced to beg. Forced to live on charity, as Ari now did. Because another man was stupid. That was wrong. That was evil.

The gray-bearded priest in charge stepped forward and jabbed a finger at Ari's face. "I suppose you know how to do better? What is your name called?"

"My name is called Ari Kazan, and yes, I know how to do better. What is your name?"

The priest looked surprised that anybody should not know his name.

Somebody said, "He is called Hanan ben Hanan, and he is *sagan.*"

The name meant nothing to Ari, but he knew that the *sagan* was the second in command of the Temple. This man Hanan ben Hanan was in line for the high priesthood. Ari looked around the circle of men. Hostility hardened in their eyes.

Hanan ben Hanan glowered at him. "And how does a man with the name of a beast know better than a priest of the living God?"

Hanan's arrogance aroused rage in Ari's heart. He stood up to his full height and stared down at Hanan. "Because I too am a priest of the living God. I come from a far country, and I have studied the secrets which are not permitted for an ordinary man to know. I know the secrets of the creation of the universe, and of the sun and the moon and the stars in the heavens. And if you permit me, I will reveal the secrets of the crane to you, so that no such accident will happen again."

Around the circle, a murmur of excitement ran. "A man who knows the secrets of HaShem!" "Perhaps he is a magician from Babylon, or out of Egypt." "What sort of name is that for a man — Ari?"

Hanan ben Hanan studied him with narrowed eyes. "Very well, Ari called Kazan, magician from a far country. Show us these … *secrets.*" He said the final word with a sneer that said plainly he did not believe Ari knew any secrets.

A shiver ran through Ari. He required time to redesign the crane. It was wrong — that was obvious. But finding the solution would take some thought. Ari shook his head. "I require one day to prepare the secret."

Something like triumph flickered in Hanan's eyes. Clearly, he thought Ari was lying, trying to save face. "Tomorrow at this hour, Ari called Kazan will show us the *secrets* of the crane. If this man Kazan is telling the truth, then it will be well. If he is lying, then it will not be so well."

Ari held Hanan's eyes without flinching. "Tomorrow." He turned his back and began examining the crane. His heart hammered inside his chest.

Because the truth was … he knew not the first thing about engineering a crane.

Excellent thinking, Ari Kazan. You have twenty-four hours to become an expert.

Hanan ben Hanan

Hanan ben Hanan watched in disbelief as the tall arrogant man turned his back on him. He had not dismissed Kazan, and yet he turned his back. It was an intentional challenge to Hanan's honor. A statement that he, Kazan, was of higher rank than Hanan, the *sagan.*

What sort of name was that for a man — Ari? And Kazan — what did that mean? It sounded Babylonish.

No matter. Kazan was a fraud, a liar, a wandering magician of some sort. Such men could not be trusted. It was men such as this who led the people astray, promising miracles from the heavens, a sign from the Great King of the Universe, victory over the Romans, a *mashiach* to end all troubles. Lies! Rage slicked Hanan's hands with sweat. He would not permit such men to poison the hearts of the people.

Such men did not love the Temple. Because of such men, the Romans might come and destroy the Temple of the living God. Such men were evil.

Hanan loved the Temple of the living God. The Temple was in his blood. His father had served as High Priest, and his four older brothers also, and his sister's husband. They were the caretakers, the true sons of the Temple. The others — the Pharisees, the false prophets, the messianics — they were wolves. They did not love the Temple, and therefore the Temple must be protected from them.

And that was Hanan's job. That was why he had been appointed *sagan*, the captain of the Temple guards. His guards loved the Temple. They would die for the Temple — as Hanan would, because the Temple meant more to him than life.

Tomorrow, Kazan would attempt his foolish magic spells. He would perform his incantations and they would fail and then Hanan would have grounds to arrest him. One could not permit magicians to stir up the people before a feast. Such men were evil, dangerous. It was best to deal with them quickly.

The matter of the failed crane was more difficult. Problems like this fascinated Hanan. The Temple required the solution to all sorts of building problems. Lifting paving stones. Maintaining a flow of water through the aqueducts. Constructing gates of sufficient size for the festival foot traffic. Of such things, the Torah had little to say. And the solutions of the fathers were no longer adequate. Hanan was now old, already more than fifty years, and in his long life Jerusalem had nearly doubled in population. The Temple, expanded by King Herod a hundred years ago, was again too small.

So Hanan had taken it on himself to innovate. The others of chief priestly family were too cautious. They were conservatives for whom the old was good enough. It was not good enough for Hanan ben Hanan, head of the great and powerful House of Hanan. He would solve the many problems that threatened the peace of the Temple of the Great King.

But this mystery of the crane had so far proven too hard. The paving stones in this part of the court were broader than normal. For some reason, this caused the ropes to break sometimes, even though they were easily strong enough to support the weight. Hanan knew instinctively that the solution was to make the crane taller. This new crane was the tallest he had yet constructed, and now it had failed. A man's leg was crushed and that was tragic, but it was not the fault of Hanan. Such things happened from time to time. It was necessary in order to do the holy work of perfecting the Temple of the living God.

Tomorrow or next week or next month, Hanan would solve the mystery of the crane. And he would do it without the magic incantations of wicked men such as Kazan.

FOUR

Rivka

Do not turn from your calling, be it ever so small. What had Yaakov meant by that? Rivka paced through the quiet street in the northern district of Jerusalem on her daily afternoon walk alone. This was a sparsely populated district, the New City — built outside the walls of the original city. The New City had walls, but they were incomplete and would be difficult to defend in the coming war.

A dozen years from now, Rome would breach these walls and destroy the city. Rivka shuddered. People *paid* fortunetellers to tell the future? It was torture to know the evil coming — to know, and be unable to prevent it.

Or so Ari said — that she could not prevent it. According to him, the best they could do would be to run before the fury of the coming storm. Before the troubles came, they would fade into the countryside, cross over to Transjordan, and live out their lives in peace.

And abandon our people.

Rivka knew what it was to be abandoned. No. She could not do that.

And yet, what difference could she and Ari make? One woman and one man against the stream of history? It was absurd. Crazy. Ari wouldn't put up with such foolishness. He had told her that a hundred times already.

Fine then. She would have to do it —

A small boy raced out of a house and barreled into Rivka. She staggered backwards, grabbing the boy to keep him from falling in the dirt.

He struggled in her grasp. "Let me go!"

"Little boy, aren't you going to say you're sorry first?" Then Rivka saw the tear tracks in his grimy face.

"My *Imma* said not to stop for anything! Now let me go!"

Rivka tightened her grip. "What's wrong? Is your mother in trouble?"

"I have to find the midwife and then fetch *Abba*. *Imma* said to run very fast."

"Can I help your mother?"

He squinted up at her. "Are you a midwife? *Imma* fell down this afternoon, and the baby is coming untimely, and she needs the midwife right now!"

Rivka didn't know a thing about midwifing, but she could at least make the woman comfortable. "I can stay with your mother while you find the midwife."

The boy led her into the house. Four young children sat on the flagstoned floor, playing with small carved balls of wood and ivory. Ivory toys! These people had a bit of money. A moan filtered through a doorway.

The boy pointed. "She's back there in the birthing room."

Rivka strode forward. "Go find the midwife. I'll take care of your *imma*." She heard the door slam behind her as she walked through a large room with no furniture except a one-legged stone table. A dining room? Receiving room?

The next room had to be the kitchen, judging by the cooking fireplace and the stone table covered with ceramic pots. Then another large room, with plaster walls, frescoed with geometric designs. Several rooms opened from this one. Another moan. Rivka followed her ears to the birthing room. It had a low wooden bed on one side. Empty.

"Blessed be HaShem, you've come!" A woman wearing a large, billowy tunic of excellent linen squatted in the corner of the room, clutching the hand of a very frightened-looking girl of about ten. *Squatting?* Why wasn't she lying in the —

Pain slashed across the woman's face. "Help me!"

Rivka rushed to kneel beside the woman. Her knee knocked against something hard. "Ouch!"

"Be careful of the birthstool, sister. I am so thankful you have come. I was afraid little Yoni would not find you in time. Sarah here does not know what to do."

"I'm not a midwife," Rivka said.

"You are a woman. That is what — " The woman caught her breath and gripped Rivka's left hand. "Another . . . birthpang," she said through clenched teeth. For a long minute, she said nothing. The girl Sarah's eyes widened in terror.

"Is this your mother, Sarah?" Rivka said.

Sarah shook her head. "I live here and work for my keep."

A servant then. Maybe an orphan, or maybe her family was too poor to keep her. Slowly, the woman's grip on Rivka eased. Her hair hung limp in her face. Rivka tied it behind her head. "My name is called Rivka."

"My name is called Yael."

"I'll stay with you until the midwife comes. Tell me what to do."

Yael's face tightened with determination. "The baby will be here before the midwife. The birthpangs are fast now."

"How many babies have you had?"

"Six."

And four of them were out in the front room. With Yoni, that made five. Rivka knelt beside her again. "And you lost one? I'm so sorry."

"Only one." Pride showed in Yael's face.

Rivka wondered what the infant mortality numbers were here. High, she guessed. Not to mention that a lot of women died in childbirth. She shivered. Those risks were part of this world she had chosen, and it was scary, but . . . even scarier was the horror coming to this city. In less than a decade, Jerusalem would be at war. Rabban Yeshua was right — in such times, it was better not to have children.

She had discussed the matter with Ari and they had reached a hard decision. They would try not to have children. At least not until Ari found work and they could move somewhere safer, out of the coming war zone. Babies were adorable and Rivka wanted one — someday. She had to fight back tears sometimes, seeing Hana's swelling belly, knowing that she had to put off motherhood, maybe forever. And the decision was hard on Ari, too, because —

"Oh! Another birthpang coming." Yael began squeezing the life out of Rivka's hand again. She closed her eyes and moaned softly. The sinews stood out in her neck, and her carotid artery throbbed. Rivka took a discreet look at her watch, which she kept hidden well up her arm inside the long sleeve of her tunic. 3:48 p.m. She'd better start timing the contractions. If only she knew what the times meant.

Yael opened her eyes again, and her iron grip relaxed. "It will be soon now, Sister Rivka. When a baby comes early, it comes fast."

"Early?"

"A month early, at least."

"Oh, my!" Rivka felt her breath squeezing out of her. "That's . . . not good."

Yael's eyes glistened. "The one HaShem took was born early."

The girl Sarah began whimpering softly. Rivka fought panic. Sarah was *not* helping. "Sarah, do you have anything to wash the baby in?"

Sarah shook her head. "With what would I wash the baby?"

"The midwife would bring salt," Yael said.

"Salt?" Rivka repeated, feeling stupid. *Oh, as an antiseptic.* She had read something about that somewhere. Probably in Jeremias's book. No, on second thought —

"Oh!" Yael's voice tightened, and then she was gripping so hard Rivka thought her hands would pop. Finally, the contraction began easing. Rivka checked the time again. Less than two minutes apart.

"Do you have salt?" Rivka said. "And . . . a knife, and some very thick thread?"

Sarah nodded. "We have salt — "

"Not enough," Yael said. "The midwife is to bring some."

Panic bubbled in Rivka's chest. What if the midwife didn't get here in time? "If you don't have salt, we'll have to use something else."

Sarah stared up at her stupidly. "It is the custom to use salt," Yael said. "The midwife — "

"Beer," Rivka said. "Sarah, do you have beer in the house?"

"Of course." Sarah jumped to her feet. "Shall I fetch some?"

"A pitcher full, and a small basin to wash the baby in. And a towel."

"You must find a cracked basin," Yael said. Pain washed across her face. "Ah! Ah! Ah!" A long contraction followed, during which she crushed Rivka's hand in hers. Sweat stood out on her forehead.

"Why cracked?" Rivka asked.

Yael gave her a strange look. "It will be unclean afterward."

"Of course," Rivka said. *I knew that.* Pottery was susceptible to ritual uncleanness — and a newborn baby was definitely unclean. The basin could not be purified, so they would throw it away afterward.

Sarah hurried into the room with a basin and pitcher, a linen cloth draped over her shoulder.

"Don't forget the knife and thread," Rivka said.

Sarah dumped everything on the bed and disappeared.

"*Oh!*" Yael said. The sound of liquid gushing onto the floor followed. Rivka felt her knees turn wet. She looked at the clear fluid seeping into her tunic. Thank God it wasn't bloody, but she would need to wash it tonight.

Yael's grip was a vise now, mashing Rivka's hand. The contraction went on and on. Finally it eased. "My waters have broken. The time is short."

"I have the knife and thread!" Sarah returned, waving a large kitchen knife.

Ten anguished minutes passed, and still no midwife. Sweat drenched Yael's face. "It is time," she grunted through clenched teeth.

Rivka knelt in front of her and pulled up the linen garment that shrouded Yael, wishing she had a clue what to do. "Sarah, hold this up."

The girl grabbed it and stood there, mute with fear.

The seat of the birthstool was shaped like a horizontal U, with the open end forward to give a midwife access. The stool supported Yael's weight, allowing her to squat for more leverage.

A dark mass bulged out of Yael's birth canal. Rivka reached up and felt it — the soft bloody head of the baby. "I'm ready."

Yael gripped the handles on either side of the birthstool and gave a low moan. The air in the room turned electric with the crushing strength of her push. The whole head emerged, slightly misshapen, with soggy black hair. Rivka hoped that was normal. She waited, but nothing happened. "Push again when you can, Yael. We're almost there."

Another tremendously powerful push and then ... the *whole* body emerged in one long sweeping movement. So fast! Rivka caught the wet, slimy baby as it emerged.

Now what? Her mind spun furiously. A pulsing bluish cord still connected mother and child. Rivka realized she was weeping. Tears of joy. And terror. "It's out," she said. "I've got the baby in my hands."

The baby felt very small, very light. A thin oily film covered its body, as if somebody had smeared butter all over it. Rivka waited, her mind numb. Should she cut the cord? Or let the placenta come out? "Yael, what am I ... what should I do now?"

Yael grunted, sounding exhausted. "You may ... cut the cord. The afterbirth will come out ... in its own time."

Rivka turned the baby over. "How wonderful! A boy. Sarah bring the knife."

Yael's sweaty face glowed with a holy pride. "Blessed be ... HaShem."

Rivka held the cord while Sarah sawed through it, whimpering.

"Sarah, you stay with Yael and help her." Rivka carried the baby to the table and laid it on a fresh linen towel. The child was perfect. She began wiping off the tiny body. The heart beat rapidly under her fingers. Something flickered in her mind. Something not quite right.

The child's heart missed a beat.

A rush of panic shot through Rivka. This was wrong. She leaned down and peered into the baby's face. Of course! The baby was supposed to be breathing. You were supposed to spank it or something. She turned him over and gave his skinny buttocks a tentative swat.

Nothing happened. Panic made Rivka's mind feel fuzzy. She swatted the baby again. "Come on, breathe!"

Still nothing. Rivka was hyperventilating now, her insides turning to jelly. If anything happened to this baby . . . She turned him over. His face had gone red, his mouth gaping feebly. A dark mass inside — what was that?

Rivka cautiously put a fingertip inside the mouth, then pulled it out. Something dark and squishy stuck to her fingers. Whatever it was, it blocked the boy's breathing.

She reached in again and scooped out a small chunk. The boy's face had gone blue. Frantic, Rivka checked his heartbeat. Rapid, shallow, erratic.

She dug into the boy's mouth again and pulled out another glob. And another. Another. "Please, God, help me, I don't know what I'm doing! Help!" She turned the tiny body over, pushed gently on the back, hoping to squeeze whatever it was out. Tears streamed down her face, and she couldn't see any longer, couldn't breathe, couldn't think.

Seconds passed. Minutes. Rivka's heart slammed against her chest as she worked desperately to clear an air passage. *Please, God.* The baby was not moving now. Rivka's fingers seemed huge in the child's mouth, and she could *not* make them do what she wanted.

After a quarter of an hour, she slumped to her knees, bitterness burning her eyes. The child's face had gone dark and silent, its heartbeat was still. She had lost, and she wanted to die. Would have died, if that would save this child.

"What have you done?" A voice in the doorway, harsh, angry.

Rivka turned, her eyes blurry. A very short old woman stood there, fury in her eyes. "What have you done?"

Rivka had seen this woman once, six months ago, and made a fool of herself. "I . . . there was nobody to help."

The woman strode to the table and peered at the child. "He swallowed his own waste before he was born. You should have sucked it out of his mouth first, before anything else."

"Sucked it . . . out?" Rivka stared at her.

"Yes, with a hollow reed, and then spit it on the floor. Do not look at me like that, fool. If you will meddle in the business of midwives, you should be prepared."

"I . . . didn't know."

"That much is evident." The old woman spun on her heel and stepped to the bed. "Little Yael, I am so sorry."

Yael's eyes flickered open. "Midwife Marta! I . . . must have fallen asleep. I want to hold my baby."

Midwife Marta knelt beside her. "I am very sorry. I came as soon as little Yoni found me, but it was too late. And this fool attending you did not know what to do."

Rivka staggered toward home in a daze. She had done her best, and it was not good enough. A doctor could have saved that baby. Or a nurse. Or a first-century midwife. But Rivka hadn't known how to help. Because of her ignorance, the baby was dead.

My people are destroyed for lack of knowledge.

Rivka began walking faster, heartsick, furious with herself. Angry at God. It wasn't fair. Wasn't the baby's fault. It was just . . . bad luck to be born while Midwife Marta was busy elsewhere, with nobody but stupid Rivka there. Bad luck.

Rivka strode faster, charging forward into the twilight. Ari and Baruch and Hana would be worried about her. She'd been gone for hours. For what? To botch a delivery? Stupid! She'd blown it.

Okay, chill, Rivka. You did your best. Now how about a little perspective? You made a mistake. One baby died. It's not like you bombed Auschwitz.

Okay, fine. People would tell her it was just a small thing. In a city of a hundred thousand souls, what was one baby? Infinitesimal, right?

Dead wrong. Rivka had been born in 1974, the oldest child of two parents, the first grandchild of four grandparents. Which meant there were eight great-grandparents, sixteen great-greats, thirty-two in the generation before that. Two thousand years made a hundred generations. Give or take. So the number of her ancestors now living was two times two times two . . . a hundred times. Way more than the number of people alive now. Therefore, practically every Jew of the first century was her ancestor in a bazillion different branches. Take away any one of them, and she would . . . not be.

Of course, she *did* exist, but that wasn't the point. Every person now living would have an impact on the far future. *Every one.* Every Jew of the twentieth century depended crucially on these simple, provincial folk. Albert Einstein. Chaim Potok. Jonas Salk. Woody Allen. Everybody in this city was special.

Do not turn from your calling, be it ever so small.

Rivka turned the last corner, saw Ari pacing outside the house, shouted. "Ari!"

He turned. Relief washed across his face. Rivka ran to meet him. He crushed her in a fierce hug. "Rivka, we have been very worried. Where have you—"

"Not now, Ari, please. Just . . . hold me." *And please don't think I'm foolish, but I'm going to become a midwife.*

FIVE

Ari

Ari lay on his thin bedroll, too tense to sleep. He had stayed up till midnight, doodling on a pad of paper, trying to figure out what had gone wrong with the crane. A simple static problem. The crane operated at essentially zero velocity. To an excellent approximation, at each point the sum of all forces had to be zero.

So much was easy. But how much did the stones weigh? How much force could the beams bear under compression? At what tension would the ropes break? What about the joints? The pulleys?

Without such information, a man could not design a crane. One must know the constraints. In physics classes, it was permitted to assume infinitely strong and massless parts. In the real world, no.

Rivka's body spasmed. She muttered something in her sleep. Ari wrapped an arm around her. She cried out, fought him.

"Rivka!" Ari shook her.

"Augghh!" Rivka shuddered. "Ari, is that you?"

Ari stroked her hair gently. "What happened?"

"A nightmare. Those horrible bandits. I'm sorry I woke you."

"I was awake still. Doing physics."

"Have you figured out what went wrong with the crane?"

Ari shrugged. "It tipped sideways, this is all I know. There must be a reason, some instability, and yet I do not see it."

Her eyes gleamed in the darkness. "What's different about this crane?"

"I do not understand. It is a crane."

"And yet usually it works. Yesterday it failed. Why? What did they do differently yesterday?"

"I . . ." Ari's heart skipped. "Rivkaleh, I did not ask if something was different. It appeared to me that this was a common occurrence."

"Ask somebody."

"I am not certain whom to ask. The old priest Hanan took a dislike to me."

Rivka turned to look at him, her eyes wide. "Who?"

"I told you about him already, yes? He is *sagan*. His name is called Hanan."

Her breath caught, and Ari felt her body tighten again. "You didn't tell me his name. Hanan who, Ari? Who's his father?"

"Hanan ben Hanan." His heart lurched. "Do you know this man?"

"Ari, whatever you do tomorrow, you'd better kiss up to Hanan ben Hanan."

"What does this mean, to kiss up to someone?"

"Ari, this guy is dangerous. In English his name is Annas."

"This name means nothing to me."

"It would if you had read the New Testament. His father killed Yeshua."

Ari sighed. He did not wish to make another argument on this matter. "With respect, the Romans killed Jesus."

"You're right and you're wrong. The Romans did it, sure, but the sources are very clear that a few Jews were involved too. A few Sadducees on the Sanhedrin, and we know their names. Annas — Hanan — was the one pushing hardest. His son-in-law Caiaphas was high priest the year Yeshua was killed, but the trial was held in the palace of Hanan. The man you met yesterday is his youngest son."

"Rivka, it seems hardly fair to judge a man by the actions of his father."

"Haven't you ever read Josephus?" Rivka sounded impatient.

Ari frowned. "I know of this Josephus. A traitor, a Roman collaborator."

"He was also the best source we've got for the next fifteen years of Jewish history. He has nothing good to say about Hanan ben Hanan." Rivka's breathing rasped, hoarse and uneven in the silent room. "Hanan is dangerous. He . . ." Her voice choked off.

Ari's pulse pounded in his neck and his lungs burned. "Tell me, Rivkaleh."

Rivka took a long slow breath. "He . . . is going to kill Yaakov the *tsaddik*."

Ari felt like she had punched him in the stomach. "No. Please say this is a lie. There is no reason to kill a man such as Yaakov the *tsaddik*. When is this to happen?"

"The dates are a little fuzzy. Most historians put it in the summer of A.D. 62, give or take a year."

"That is very soon — less than five years from now."

"Give or take a year."

Ari swore softly in Arabic.

Rivka clutched at his arm. "Kiss up to Hanan ben Hanan tomorrow, okay? Whatever you do, don't make him your enemy."

Ari kissed Rivka's ear and enfolded her in his arms. "Sleep well, Rivkaleh."

She snuggled up to him. "I love you, Ari."

Minutes later, her soft and even breathing told Ari that she was asleep again. He lay alone with his thoughts for a long time. He still was not sure what it meant to kiss up to someone, but one thing was certain.

Ari Kazan would never kiss up to an evil man, no matter how dangerous he was.

Ari hurried through the outer court of the Temple toward the construction site with Rivka three paces behind him. He hated so humiliating her, but this was the way of Jerusalem. He could not afford to fail today. He must learn what had changed in the design of the crane. That was the key to yesterday's accident.

When he arrived, the site was buzzing with activity. The crane lay where it had fallen. Dozens of men were busy breaking up some of the old cracked paving stones and hauling out the old pieces.

Rivka remained behind in the shadow of the portico. Ari strode up to a knot of half a dozen men. "*Shalom*, my friends. I should like to ask a question about the crane which failed."

The men looked up at him. An uneasy silence shrouded them. The leader turned his back on Ari. One by one, the others did the same.

"Just a question!" Ari said. "What has changed in the design of the crane?" He walked around to stand in front of them. "I must know —"

The men turned their backs on him again.

Ari shrugged and went to another cluster of workmen. "*Shalom*, my friends —"

The men turned their backs on him.

What mischief was this? Ari walked to the fallen crane. He could see no obvious reason for the failure. But yesterday it had tipped. Why not the day before?

He could see no answers here. Ari turned and strode back toward Rivka. She said nothing as he walked past her. He wished he could speak openly with her, but he dared not risk it in public. These people ignored him to his face, but they would surely be watching him now. He must do nothing to alienate them further.

Ari strolled aimlessly north in the shade of Solomon's Portico. Despair slit through him. He had lost. Hanan ben Hanan would win.

After walking perhaps a hundred meters, he stopped near the small school of Rabbi Yohanan ben Zakkai. He stared at them dully. Nothing mattered now. It was craziness to battle Hanan ben Hanan. With more profit, he might study Torah with these gentle fools. Whether he understood them or not made no difference. These earnest, crazy, single-minded men of Torah would preserve his people for a hundred generations. Without them, Jews would lose their identity in the storm to come.

Rabbi Yohanan's method of teaching was simple, yet profound. First, he repeated a saying of one of the sages several times. The students repeated it after him in unison. Then Yohanan would expound on it. Then he would invite one of his students to expound on it further. Ari had seen this many times. The students never satisfied their master. Rabbi Yohanan pursued them mercilessly with questions until they could not answer. It was a good system. The master refused to accept limits.

Somebody tapped Ari on the shoulder. He turned and saw . . . Rivka! His pulse leaped. How dare she touch him in public? What would people think?

Furious, Ari stepped away from the school of Rabbi Yohanan, out of the shelter of the portico and into the thin winter sun. Rivka followed him.

"What are you doing?" Ari hissed. "You must not — "

Rivka shook her head. "Ari, I don't have time for the male chauvinist thing right now. I just spotted somebody who might be able to help you."

Ari wished that just once Rivka would learn to behave as a proper woman of this century. His throat tightened. "Yes? I am listening."

Rivka pointed toward the far side of the crowd of students around Rabbi Yohanan. "See that short little man with the big head and the wild black hair?"

"I see him." Ari pushed her hand down. "Please do not point. People are looking at us."

"His name is Gamaliel, and I know him."

Ari gaped at her. "You have spoken with this man? How — "

"He's the nephew of Saul of Tarsus. I helped him rescue his uncle last summer."

Ari narrowed his eyes. "You are certain it is him?"

"Ari, you know I never forget a face. It's him and he'll help you. He'll do anything Rabbi Yohanan asks."

This was foolishness. Ari peered over his shoulder at the old rabbi. "Rabbi Yohanan does not know me from the prophet Eliyahu."

Rivka smiled. "He's an old friend of mine and he owes me a favor. When his little class breaks up, take me with you and go speak to him. I guarantee he'll do anything you ask."

Ari stood far back in the deep shadow of the porticoes watching Gamaliel talking to the young priests at the construction site. Gamaliel pointed to the crane and asked another question. The priests nodded and walked along the crane, pointing at two different points in the construction. Gamaliel was a short man, even by Jerusalem standards, more than thirty centimeters shorter than Ari, but powerfully built. His head and hands were large, his arms thickly muscled, and he wore a cheerful grin that made Ari feel welcome. He wore *tefillin* on his forehead and left arm. A pious man.

After a quarter of an hour of discussion, Gamaliel thanked the priests and strode briskly north along the portico past Ari. Ari waited a few seconds, then followed him.

Five hundred meters later, at the far northern end of the court, Gamaliel stopped and waited for Ari. "You have an enemy." Gamaliel's face tightened. "Hanan ben Hanan has let out word that none of the workmen may talk to you."

"I do not fear Hanan ben Hanan."

"You should fear him."

"He is endangering his workers," Ari said. "He knows just enough of cranes to make a hazard. What did the men tell you?"

Gamaliel explained in a few sentences.

Ari took a pen and sheet of paper from his belt and sketched an A-frame. "Hanan made the new crane taller but not broader, like so, yes?"

Gamaliel touched Ari's paper in wonder. "What . . . is this?"

"It is papyrus from a far country, the land of my birth." Ari held up his Uni-ball pen. "This is a reed pen from my country." By good luck, he had come through the wormhole with his backpack, which had two full pads of paper, some Uni-ball pens, and his calculator.

Gamaliel's eyes glowed. "I would like to visit your wonderful country, my friend."

"It is a remarkable place, but not all men love Torah there. You would find much to dislike."

"Not all men love Torah here in Jerusalem. I am not concerned with such men."

Ari smiled. He liked this earnest young man. "My friend, we will speak another time of my far country. First, the matter of the crane. Why was the crane made taller?"

"Because in this part of the pavement, the stones are wider than is usual. The men say that the crane can only lean over a certain distance without falling over. Since the stones are wider, the crane must be taller to accommodate the extra distance. In addition, there is an extra pair of pulleys in the tackle."

Ari's heart leaped. "How many pulleys are usual?"

"Three. Two above, one below. Now there are five — three above and two below. The men say this allows the device to lift more weight. I do not understand —"

"It gives a greater mechanical advantage," Ari said. "The rope must now be pulled farther in order to lift the stone the same distance, but it requires less force."

Gamaliel raised his eyebrows. "You are learned in these matters?"

"I have been given to know the deep secrets of the universe." Ari sketched the crane as viewed from the front. The rope ran up and down between the pulleys several times, then angled down to wind around the horizontal bar in the A-frame — an axis that could be turned by a capstan, giving still more mechanical advantage. As the capstan turned, the rope wound around the axis, spiraling from right to left —

Ari stopped drawing. Yes! That was the solution. The new crane required more rope to lift the same distance, because of the extra pulleys. Therefore, the rope wound farther to the left. And the crane was taller but not wider. When the rope wound too far to the left, the forces became unstable. With any small perturbation, the crane would tip to the left. Ari smiled and put the paper in his belt.

"You are happy?" Gamaliel said.

"It is solved. Can you come with me this afternoon when I confront Hanan? His designs are dangerous."

Gamaliel's face tightened. "You are asking much. Hanan ben Hanan is not a man to trifle with."

"I promise to be careful."

"It is still much. I must think on this." Gamaliel studied Ari for a moment.

Ari met his gaze without blinking.

Gamaliel narrowed his eyes. "Are you looking for *Mashiach* to come?"

The question caught Ari like a slap. For most of his life, the only people he knew who looked for *Mashiach* were the *Haredim*, like his stepfather, who had made his life a misery. Here in old Jerusalem, many looked for *Mashiach* — a hero to destroy Rome.

Sadly, there would be no such messianic figure. The Romans would come instead, and all this city would burn. This city Ari loved above all other cities on earth. He blinked twice, feeling his throat squeeze his breath.

"I see that you do," Gamaliel said. "I also look for *Mashiach*. When he comes, he will destroy the dragon and purify the Temple of the wicked priests and — "

"Wicked priests? Who are the wicked priests?"

Gamaliel looked around cautiously. "Men such as Hanan ben Hanan and the high priest Hananyah ben Nadavayah. HaShem will deal harshly with them in the Day of the Lord."

"You are correct," Ari said. "The wicked priests will be destroyed."

Gamaliel's eyes gleamed. "You know this for a certainty?"

Ari nodded.

"Did your woman tell you this? Rabbi Yohanan says she is a *ro'ah*."

"Yes, she is a seer woman. HaShem has given her to know the future for many hundred years."

Gamaliel blinked. "That is a terrifying thing."

Ari capped his pen. "My friend, all knowledge is terrifying, but ignorance is worse. It is an evil thing to see power in the hand of an ignorant man. Men of knowledge are on the side of *Mashiach*. HaShem has given me knowledge of the deep secrets of cranes, and with this I must battle Hanan. I will ask you one more time — will you help me? Or will you stand aside and wait?"

Gamaliel's forehead gleamed with a sheen of sweat, and his eyes shone bright like a polished sword. "You are named well, Ari the lion. I . . . I will stand with you against the wicked priests . . ."

Ari breathed deeply. Most excellent. He had an ally.

"... when *Mashiach* comes. But today? My friend, you ask much. The time is not yet for me to stand openly against Hanan ben Hanan. You come from a far country, so perhaps you know nothing of this man. Hear my warning. Do not become an enemy of Hanan ben Hanan. He is a tiger, the son of a tiger. The House of Hanan has an evil name."

Cold fear washed over Ari's scalp. He staggered back half a step. How could he face Hanan alone? But how could he not? Yaakov's words of yesterday ran through his mind. *Whatever your hand finds to do, do it with all your might.*

Ari shook off his disappointment. "I thank you for the help you have given me. HaShem will reward you for it." He turned and headed for the western exit. There remained some computations to work through, and he required privacy for that.

"Ari the Kazan!" Gamaliel shouted after him. "You will do nothing to make this man your enemy, correct?"

Ari kept walking.

Yes.

No.

I do not know. May HaShem be with me.

SIX

Hanan ben Hanan

Hanan walked down the steps of the inner Temple and past the partition that marked the boundary of the *goyim*. The afternoon sacrifices were completed. For another day, the needs of the living God had been met.

And for once, Hanan did not care. The wild black beard and piercing eyes of Kazan filled all his mind. Reports told that Kazan had come asking questions this morning. The men had not answered, of course. But clearly Kazan intended to answer Hanan's challenge. Kazan knew something, or thought he did. He would bring some magic today. Some surprise.

Hanan would bring a bigger surprise — three dozen surprises. Some time ago, he had recruited a cadre of zealous young men, loyal to the Temple. All were priests, and their leader was the son of the high priest, a wild young horse named Eleazar, a giant of a man who could break Kazan with his little finger.

Kazan would come and be broken. Hanan had looked in Kazan's eyes yesterday and seen fire. Fire and ice. Kazan feared nobody. He would learn to fear Hanan ben Hanan.

Hanan strode the length of the southern court of the Temple in the shade of Solomon's Portico. Every dozen paces sat another self-proclaimed sage. Teachers of Torah, so-called. In truth, they were frauds — in their own way as dangerous as Kazan. True teachers of Torah would teach Torah only. But these men, these Pharisees, taught an esoteric wisdom far from Torah. If it were possible, Hanan would throw them out of the Temple. But the people would not stand for it, and even Hanan could not control the many ten thousand common folk. So he tolerated the Pharisees, so long as they did not teach revolt against Rome. He did not have to tolerate a magician like Kazan.

When he reached the fallen crane, Hanan saw Kazan standing in the center of a silent circle of priests. He had come alone, which meant he did not know his danger. Hanan stepped through the circle of men and walked around in front of Kazan.

Kazan looked at him. And smiled.

Something cold slid down Hanan's neck. Had Kazan prepared some devastating magic? No — that was not possible. There was no magic under the sun. No magic, no angels, no elemental spirits of the universe, no prophets, no visions, no resurrection, no World to Come. All were lies. Only Torah was truth, the plain word of Moshe, the one true prophet.

Hanan studied his enemy for a moment. "So, Kazan. You have returned. Will you now reveal to us the *secrets* of the crane?"

Kazan reached inside his cloth belt and withdrew something. It was impossibly thin — some substance Hanan had never seen before — and cut with perfect precision in the shape of a rectangle. Hanan stepped forward, his eyes locked on the thing in Kazan's hand.

Kazan held it high, letting it flutter in the afternoon breeze. It crackled in a way that papyrus did not. "I have brought a magic papyrus with the secrets of the crane which have been revealed to me by HaShem." Kazan held the papyrus in front of Hanan's face. Dozens of light blue lines had been scribed on its surface, perfectly straight and finer than any reed pen could draw.

Hanan gaped. His heart fluttered. He reached for the papyrus with nerveless hands. Was it possible that Kazan had . . . real magic?

Kazan waved the magic papyrus aloft at the circle of priests. "Have any of you seen papyrus of this fine quality? I come from a far country where such papyrus is common. A *dinar* will buy many sheets, and children make toys with it. In my country, we have cranes a hundred times the size of this poor construction."

Hanan felt sweat running down his sides. Kazan knew something. Knew many things. Many secrets. With such knowledge, what could he not do? He was more dangerous than any of the pious frauds — the sages, the prophets, the messianic pretenders.

Kazan was *real*. The enemy of all who loved the Temple.

Kazan began speaking. He pointed out the weak points in the crane — at the joints, the pulleys. He spoke of the poor design which required a stay rope to keep the crane from falling over, and why such a design was inherently flawed. He spoke of strange and ethereal matters — *mechanical advantage, force, torque, static and dynamic instability, compressional and tensile strength*. Hanan did not know what any of these words meant, but he saw that Kazan knew their meaning.

Kazan had access to some secret knowledge, an inner fund of magical wisdom that gave him power. Hanan hated him for it.

At last, Kazan finished speaking.

Hanan waited. Now Kazan would show the magic. Now he would repair the crane. Would show them all the meaning of his secret words.

But Kazan did no such thing. He merely stood there, smiling at Hanan.

A terrible and wonderful thought whispered in Hanan's mind. Quickly, it grew into a certainty. Kazan had no skill to back up his words.

Hanan stepped forward and snatched the papyrus from Kazan's hands. He crumpled it. The papyrus made a noise surprisingly loud and unpleasant. "Show us the meaning of the words." Hanan threw the ball of crushed papyrus to the ground. "Rebuild the crane. Now."

The first hint of uncertainty crossed Kazan's angular bearded face. He hesitated.

"Show us the magic of the crane." Hanan took a step forward, jutting his chin at this ... fraud, this magician. "Any liar can talk about his magic. Words are not deeds. Show us your magic."

Kazan cleared his throat. "I ... have explained the matter to you. Order your workmen to build the machine as I said, and you will find — "

"No." Hanan felt the joy of the hunter. "You, Kazan. *You* show us. Now."

The circle of excited faces around them grew taut. The faces of wolves, eager for blood sport. Hanan would give them sport.

"Can you not perform the magic?" Hanan said. "Is it perhaps because the magic is mere talk? Words without substance?"

Kazan's forehead gleamed, and he licked his lips. "The words carry their own intrinsic truth. You will provide the workmen and — "

Hanan shook his head. He snapped his fingers and gestured toward the edge of the circle. A towering young man with a black beard and the arms of a giant stepped through the circle. Eleazar ben Hananyah — a man zealous for the Temple. From all around the ring, other young men appeared, their faces grim. They surrounded Hanan and Kazan in a tight noose.

Hanan smiled. "Kazan, you are found guilty of teaching magic in the jurisdiction of the Temple, contrary to the Torah of the living God."

Kazan's jaw fell open and his eyes opened wide so that the whites gleamed large in his sweating face. The giant Eleazar stepped up behind him and seized both arms.

Hanan balled his left hand into a fist and smacked it into his open palm. "Eleazar, you will take this false magician to the Hinnom Valley and beat him." Hanan turned and walked away.

A hiss of excitement raced around the circle. Hanan strode through the circle of priests. The abject terror on their faces told him he had won a great victory.

The rage of the living God burned in his heart.

Rivka

Rivka pounded on the thick wooden door of the large house. The last time she had come to this house, six months ago, she had made a royal fool of herself. Luckily, Marta had forgotten.

No answer.

Rivka knocked again. She never took no answer for an answer.

The door jerked open. Midwife Marta peered out. "You! What do you want with me? Did you not cause enough trouble yesterday?"

"I came to apologize," Rivka said. "I did the best I could, but I didn't know what to do for the little one. If you'd been there, the child would have lived."

The old woman scowled at her. "So what do you want with me? I cannot bring the child back from the dead."

"I want you to teach me to be a midwife."

Marta shook her head. "A fool like you? I would be twice a fool to try to teach you anything." She began closing the door.

Rivka stuck her foot in the doorway. It was time to gamble. "I know somebody who is the nephew of Renegade Saul."

Marta yanked the door open, her eyes wide, scanning the street. "What do you know? Tell me!" She stepped backward. "But inside, not out here."

Rivka followed her in and waited while the old woman shut the door and led the way into the kitchen. She pointed to a wooden stool at a round one-legged stone table. "Sit."

Rivka sat.

Marta sat down across from her and scowled. "Speak."

"I know a man, Saul, who comes from Tarsus," Rivka said. Which was a stretch. She had met Saul for about five minutes last summer. But she had read every word the man had ever written. In *koine* Greek. She knew Saul.

"So?"

Rivka leaned forward. "Renegade Saul is in prison in Caesarea. In eighteen months, he will speak to King Agrippa and the governor. From there, he will be sent to Rome to speak before Caesar. He will die in Rome."

Marta leaned back and folded her arms across her chest. "Only HaShem knows the future. Your tale is idle."

"You will remember my tale and when it comes to pass, you will know that I have been given to know the future. If you need evidence now, you may speak to Rabbi Yohanan ben Zakkai, who teaches a young man named Gamaliel, the nephew of Renegade Saul, who lives in this house. Rabbi Yohanan will vouch for the truth of what I say."

Marta's eyes narrowed. "Have I seen you before yesterday?"

Yes, but since you don't remember, I'm not going to remind you. Rivka didn't blink. "I have told you these things so you will know you have misjudged me."

The old midwife shook her head, looking doubtful. "You have told me things you cannot prove. What do you want?"

"I want . . ." Rivka hesitated. "I want you to teach me to be a midwife."

Marta's face showed nothing. "Do you think I am a fool?"

Rivka sighed. This was crazy, to come to this brusque old woman. She could find another midwife, one who wouldn't find fault with everything she did. And yet . . . something told her that Midwife Marta should teach her. Was it HaShem telling her? Or was she riding off on another whacked-out hobbyhorse? "Please?" Rivka said. "I am begging you."

Marta stood up and made a shooing motion with her hands. "The answer is no. Now go."

Ari

Fear burned in Ari's veins as Hanan ben Hanan walked away. His arms ached under the tight grip of the huge priest named Eleazar. Eleazar was nearly as tall as Ari, but outweighed him by a good fifty kilos, all muscle. Ari had not seen such a large man since coming to this century. Eleazar wore enormous *tefillin*, proportionate to his body. That was comforting. If he was a murderer, at least he was a religious one.

Ari pondered his options. Perhaps he could talk his way out of this. "My friends, please, I wish to say something — "

"You will move, Kazan," said Eleazar's deep voice behind him. "The time for talk is past."

Ari moved. Eleazar pushed him roughly through the circle of workmen. Ari looked wildly around. What had he done? He was only trying to help! Why could Hanan not see that?

Many young priests closed in on all sides, their faces closed, their eyes dark. Ari tried to think. These thugs would take him out and beat him. And he had no escape. No wonder Gamaliel had refused to stand with him. Nobody could stand against Hanan ben Hanan.

In a tight silent knot, they marched toward the nearest exit, a hundred meters away. Many hundred people turned to stare at Ari, but nobody tried to stop them. At the exit, they plunged into the darkness of a long stairway that led down through the belly of the Temple Mount to the Huldah Gates on the south side. The stony tunnel smelled of mildew and wet rock. Far too soon, they reached the level below and emerged into daylight. Ari was breathing so fast, his head felt light.

You brought this on yourself, Kazan. You could have said nothing. Could have stayed away from Hanan ben Hanan. Could have let him save face. But you had to tell the truth, the whole truth. If you survive, perhaps you will learn tact.

But how could he have kept silent? Ari shook his head. Because of Hanan's ignorance, a man had lost the use of his legs. Who could hold silent in the face of such injustice?

The men stopped on a long platform that ran the length of the southern edge of the Temple Mount — three hundred meters of teeming humanity, eager worshipers heading into or out of the Temple. Many hundred strangers. None of them knew or cared that Ari Kazan was about to be beaten. Steps led down to a crowded public plaza below. The worst part of Jerusalem stretched out south before them, the Ophel district, the original city of David.

The iron grip released on Ari's arms. Eleazar stepped around in front of Ari wearing a mysterious smile. "Men, where shall we take him?"

"To my house," said a familiar voice.

Ari's head whipped around.

Gamaliel gave him an enormous grin. "You are a brave man, Ari the Kazan."

Eleazar took Ari's hand in his massive fist and they clasped hands halfway up the wrist, holding the grasp for several seconds before releasing. It was both like and unlike the handshake Ari had known in the modern world. "Ari the Kazan, my name is called Eleazar ben Hananyah, son of the high priest." A broad smile creased his face. "You have a powerful enemy and a most persuasive friend."

Ari gaped at him.

The priests closed in on Ari, laughing, smiling, pounding his shoulders, all talking at once. "Well said, Ari the Kazan!" "You put the fear of HaShem into ben Hanan today!" "I could smell the sweat of his fear!"

Ari wiped his forehead. "Perhaps you smelled me instead."

Eleazar bellowed with laughter. "You were a true lion, Ari the Kazan. Nobody ever stood up to Hanan ben Hanan as you did. Such courage must be rewarded." He turned to the men around him. "An hour from now, you will report to ben Hanan that the magician Kazan has been beaten twice as hard as he deserved."

Laughter greeted this. The group of men broke up in all directions. Soon only four of them were left — Ari, Gamaliel, Eleazar, and a slim young priest of medium height with bright, intelligent eyes and polished *tofillin* that looked very expensive. The priest put out his hand. "My name is called Yoseph ben Mattityahu."

Ari clasped hands with him. "My name is called Ari the Kazan." He looked at the three men, perplexed. "I do not understand. Why have you disobeyed Hanan? Do you not fear he will learn what you have done?"

Eleazar shrugged his massive shoulders. "What have we done? Nothing!"

"But . . . he ordered you to beat me."

Eleazar turned to the priest Yoseph. "Explain the law to him, Brother Yoseph."

Yoseph's eyes gleamed. "It is not permitted to beat a man on the Temple Mount. Therefore, Hanan ordered us to beat you elsewhere. But regrettably, Hanan ben Hanan is *sagan* only within the Temple Mount, and his jurisdiction ended when we came through those gates. Likewise, his authority over us as Temple guards extends only to the boundaries of the Temple. Therefore, his order to us, though given inside the Temple, has only the force of a *suggestion* when once we have left its bounds." Yoseph shook his head and winked. It was clear that he enjoyed bending words to his own will. "Hanan ben Hanan made an unwise suggestion, and we have chosen to ignore it. You have something we need, Ari the Kazan."

Ari wondered what he could possibly have that these men needed.

"You will come to my house," Gamaliel said. "We must talk about a matter of importance, but not here."

Ari wondered if he had a choice.

Gamaliel led the way down the steps and turned right onto the crowded market street at the base of the western wall of the Temple Mount. Two thousand years from now, Jews would gather here to pray at the *kotel*, the Western Wall. Now it was just a market.

Ari cleared his throat. "You will be punished when Hanan ben Hanan finds out what you have done."

"What can ben Hanan do to me?" Eleazar said in a light voice. "He answers to my father the high priest. Besides, flouting his honor raises my own. Just as your honor was raised today, Ari the Kazan. By this evening, all Jerusalem will know there is a man who dared stand up to ben Hanan. Your honor will be high in Jerusalem."

"I did not do it for honor."

"Then why?" Brother Eleazar sounded genuinely surprised.

"Because ... it is wrong to allow a fool such as Hanan ben Hanan to create dangerous machines. A man was hurt yesterday. I could have prevented it."

An intense silence followed. Ari turned to see all three men staring at him with open mouths.

They maneuvered up the crowded market street. By local standards, it was a broad avenue, at least four or five meters wide. On each side, small shops clustered. Olive oil merchants stood cheek by jowl with linen merchants, sellers of handcrafts in wood and ivory and tin, sandal makers, ceramics merchants selling unglazed red pots with abstract designs. The odor of roasting goat meat assaulted Ari's nostrils. Salted fish. Goat's cheese. Spiced vegetables not too different from the *kim chi* that a Korean friend at MIT had once coaxed into Ari's mouth. And everywhere, people. Women in head scarves. Children racing through the crowd shrieking. Torah students. Old men. Everywhere, the smell of stale sweat and garlic and wool.

These were Ari's people and this was his city and he felt perfectly at home and perfectly a stranger, both at the same time. Like the electron.

When the four men reached the Fortress Antonia, they took a left turn onto the broad avenue leading diagonally across the city toward the northwest gate. The street was crowded, but less so than the market street behind them.

Ahead, a noise caught Ari's attention. People moved aside, left and right. Eleazar reacted quickly. "Out of the street! Soldiers ahead!" He pulled Ari to the right.

Ari looked stupidly up the street. Romans? So?

The street emptied swiftly as people scrambled out of the way. A troop of Roman soldiers marched up the avenue toward them, their javelins poking fists at the heavens. Their arrogance appalled Ari. The servility with which the Jews moved aside appalled him more.

Ari heard a woman scream. He turned and saw a small girl wander into the center of the avenue, oblivious to the oncoming soldiers. Shocked, Ari could not think what to do. Before he could move, Gamaliel sprinted toward the child. The soldiers made no change in their pace. Ari held his breath. *Please, HaShem . . .*

Gamaliel reached the girl, scooped her up, and leaped out of the way. The Romans tramped by, rank on rank, five to a row, looking to neither side. As if the Jews were worms — worth less than a glance.

Quickly, they passed. Ari glowered after the soldiers, feeling rage wash through him. When they were gone, Gamaliel rejoined his companions. Ari looked at him with admiration. "That was well done, Gamaliel."

Gamaliel flashed a broad smile. "HaShem gave me speed."

They came to a branch street and turned right, walking rapidly now. This was the New City, and the streets here were broader than in the older part of Jerusalem, the houses more spacious. It was the residential district for a growing middle class — merchants and builders and men who dealt in wholesale of barley and olive oil and grapes.

Shortly, they stopped at a house. Gamaliel took out an iron key, inserted it, turned a quarter turn, and pulled. An iron latching mechanism clicked on the other side of the door. Gamaliel pushed the door inward and reversed the operation to withdraw his key.

Rivka stood before them, gaping.

SEVEN

Rivka

Rivka stared at the four men in front of her, astonished. "Ari! What are you doing here?"

Ari looked astounded that she had spoken to him in public.

Rivka bristled. She was sick to death of being treated like a . . . woman. Like a child.

Ari's face tightened, and then he gestured to the men. "Rivkaleh, these are friends of mine. You have met Gamaliel already. And these are his friends, Eleazar and Yoseph, who are now also friends of mine. My friends, this is my woman Rivka. She is a seer of exceptional intelligence, and we come from a far country where it is the custom to speak to women. Please, you will honor this custom if you honor me."

Rivka smiled at the three men, looking each of them directly in the eye as if she had every right in the world to speak to men.

Gamaliel's face reddened. He looked at her for an instant, then averted his gaze. "I greet you, seer woman, friend of Rabbi Yohanan."

The giant, Eleazar, flicked his eyes over her with an interest that Rivka found . . . uncomfortable. "*Shalom*, Rivka the Kazan."

The young priest, Yoseph, looked right past her, refusing to make eye contact at all, and muttered something unintelligible. Shuddering, Rivka recognized him. Last summer he had told Ari to take her home and beat her well. Rivka wondered if he remembered. Probably not.

Ari's face had burnished to the color of a brick. Rivka felt like an idiot. She could pretend all she wanted that she was the equal of these men, but if they didn't get it, she only made herself look foolish. She was blowing this badly. Every man in the city played the game of honor, a game with vastly complex rules. Even after a lot of coaching, she and Ari still understood only the rudiments. In America, people's worth was measured by their money. But this society measured personal worth in units of honor, an elusive quantity that changed by small increments from moment to moment.

And the simple fact was that only a man could have honor. A woman did not have honor any more than she had a beard, and pretending could not change that.

"Ari the Kazan, we must talk," said Eleazar. His quick glance toward Rivka made his meaning clear. *Dismiss your woman so that we can get on with it.*

Ari did not look ready to dismiss her.

Shame cut through Rivka. "Ari, perhaps I should be going home now. I came to visit Gamaliel's grandmother and —"

"*Savta!*" Gamaliel shouted. "*Savta,* have you been speaking with the woman of Ari the Kazan?"

Another rule, Rivka guessed. A man could speak to his grandmother in public. Ridiculous — a grandmother but not a wife.

Midwife Marta appeared, a scowl on her face. "I —"

"Rabbi Yohanan says she is a seer woman," Gamaliel said. "You will make her feel at home while I speak with Ari the Kazan."

Marta's eyes widened, and a toothless smile creased her face. "A seer woman? Rabbi Yohanan says so?" She took Rivka's arm. "Come with me, child. Why did you not say so?" Gently she guided Rivka into the kitchen.

Rivka wanted to call her a liar, a fraud, a hypocrite. But of course she could not. One look at Marta's face told Rivka that the old woman was perfectly sincere. Just like *that*, because Gamaliel told her, Marta believed Rivka was a seer woman. This was a crazy, stupid, ridiculous world and anyone who —

"So. Rivkaleh." Marta led her to the same table where they had sat earlier. "A seer woman! That is wonderful! When do you wish to begin learning the arts of the midwife?"

If Rivka wasn't so happy, she would have shrieked.

Ari

Ari followed Gamaliel and the other two men into a sparsely furnished sitting room. It had two flat couches made of wood — something rare enough in this city that Ari had never seen even one. Gamaliel must be quite well off.

Eleazar sat on one couch and motioned to Ari to sit on the other. Gamaliel and Yoseph remained standing, one on either side of their leader. A matter of honor.

Eleazar studied Ari. "You are a priest, Ari the Kazan?"

Ari nodded. "I was born in a far country and my fathers in a yet farther country. The name Kazan in that country means *cohen*. But I lack written documents."

Eleazar shook his head. "So you are *issah*. It is a shame."

Ari felt bitterness in his throat. *Issah*. A priestly family of uncertain lineage. Usually, it referred to families in which a woman had been captured by enemy men in wartime. Her sons thereafter could not be proved to be legitimate sons of a priest — even those born years later. Ari felt no shame to be *issah*. The shame was in a foolish system which classified men so.

"We are three men of one *havurah* — one fellowship," Eleazar said. "We are called the Sons of Righteous Priests, and we look for *Mashiach*. Are you also looking for *Mashiach*?"

Ari shook his head. He must be honest. Of course there would be no *Mashiach*. But his people would suffer for the next twenty centuries because of a man called by that title. "I will not look for *Mashiach* until I see his face."

A broad grin split Gamaliel's face. Ari had never known anyone so cheerful and easy to please. Eleazar nodded and smiled, his thick black beard bobbing up and down. Even the quiet priest Yoseph seemed delighted. Ari wondered what he had said.

"Very well, Ari the Kazan," Eleazar said. "And when *Mashiach* comes, he will need an army, yes? And men? Machines of war?"

Ari felt cold wash over him, bathing him with ghostly fingers.

"Yes?" Gamaliel said. "You agree when *Mashiach* comes, he will need these things?"

"Yes." The Americans had a saying about pigs and wings, but Ari could not remember it.

Eleazar's eyes brightened and he smiled at both Gamaliel and Yoseph as if Ari had made a huge concession. "Ari the Kazan, you are learned in the secrets of the universe. It is as clear as the wart on the nose of ben Hanan. But you are unskilled in the construction of machines. You must learn this skill. *Mashiach* is coming, and when you see him with your eyes, it will be too late to learn the skills you will need. You will learn the secrets of the catapult and the siege tower and all other weapons of war. When *Mashiach* comes, you will join us."

Ari did not know what to say. *Boys, dreaming of war, please find a clue, as the Americans say.*

"Yes?" Gamaliel said. "When *Mashiach* comes, you will join us?"

Ari smiled. There would be no *Mashiach*, but how could he explain that? "Yes," he said. "If *Mashiach* comes, I will join you." The safest promise imaginable.

Eleazar leaned forward and his eyes burned with a hidden fire. "Ari the Kazan, we will make sure you have what you need to learn the construction of machines. We have men in our *havurah* with skills in working metal, but they do not know the secrets of the universe. You will teach them these secrets and they will instruct you in the working of bronze and iron. Yes?"

Ari felt an odd constriction in his throat. They would teach him skills? Give him a chance at honest employment? And all he had to do was teach them physics?

And they will take what they learn into the Temple, despite the protests of fools such as Hanan. They will make the world a better place.

"Yes," Ari said in a strangled voice.

Eleazar stood up and his face shone. "*Mashiach* is coming, Ari the Kazan. You will be ready for him." Not a request but a command.

Gamaliel and Yoseph smiled and exchanged triumphant glances.

Apparently this extremely weird interview was now over. Ari stood up too, wondering if he had won or lost.

On the way home, Ari allowed Rivka to walk beside him. He was tired of this Jerusalem foolishness, and anyway he had much to tell her. He explained to Rivka about his confrontation with Hanan ben Hanan.

"I lost," he concluded. "I explained all about the theory of the crane, and Hanan did not understand any of it, so he ordered me to be beaten."

Rivka clutched his arm. "You were so brave."

"I was *meshugah*. Had I known he would order me beaten, I . . ." Ari wondered what he would have done. He sighed. "I am not sure what I would have done. But ben Hanan is a fool and — "

"Ari, don't say things like that!"

Ari looked down at her, amused. "What should I not say?"

"You called him ben Hanan. That is highly discourteous. You knew that, didn't you?"

"No. How do you know?"

"I read something about it in the Talmud once. Didn't you ever read any Talmud?"

"No." Ari scowled. "Talmud is foolishness. Eleazar and Gamaliel called him ben Hanan, therefore I also. Why is this considered rude?"

"I don't know, but it is. He lost face in their eyes when you stood up to him."

"But he won. And therefore, I lost."

"Maybe, but you gained honor. Big time."

"I do not understand."

"Honor has nothing to do with winning and losing. Remember Saddam Hussein in 1991?"

Ari scowled. "He missed me with his SCUDs."

"He lost the Persian Gulf War, would you agree?"

"Of course. Your President Bush should have finished him at once."

"Hussein lost. Bush won. So whose honor went up in the Arab world?"

Ari thought about that for a moment. "Hussein's. He spit in the eye of the American president and lived another day."

"That gained him a lot of honor in Arab eyes. It's the same here, Ari. Standing up to somebody gains you points — even if you lose. Everybody is afraid of Hanan. You aren't. You faced him down as if he was nobody. That's why Gamaliel and Eleazar and Yoseph respect you. And that's why they called him ben Hanan in your presence — because you had dishonored him."

"I was foolish."

"You're not kidding. That was the craziest thing you could have done. And if you do it again, you'll sleep in the street for a week." Rivka tightened her grip on his arm and smiled. "But I wish I had seen it. I'm so proud of you. And . . . thank you for honoring me today before your friends. You don't need to do it again."

"You are welcome, Rivkaleh. People are now staring at us because I allow you to walk beside me. Should I put you again to the back of the bus?"

Rivka laughed. "Deal with it, Ari the Kazan."

"You are a most complicated and infuriating woman, Rivkaleh."

She tickled his ribs. "Then I'm exactly what you deserve."

EIGHT

Rivka

The next two months passed in a blur for Rivka. She worked with Midwife Marta every day, learning to be a midwife.

Ari found work for a week with a man in Gamaliel's *havurah*, a bronze worker who worked for a building contractor in the New City. After that week, the contractor was so impressed with Ari's solution to a difficult problem that he paid Ari a bonus of fifty *dinars* and hired him as an engineering consultant, rather than a day laborer.

Ari gave half the money to Baruch and used the rest to rent a house two streets over. It was a large, two-story home, and Rivka felt thrilled to have a place of her own. For the first time since they had been married, she and Ari had some . . . privacy.

Hana's belly grew bigger as her time approached. Baruch's face shone with expectation of the coming child. It would be a son, he told everyone. He had prayed to HaShem for a son. Therefore, a son.

Rivka spent most of her free time with Hana, who seemed increasingly tense. Which was only to be expected, of course. Rivka knew already that a first child would be no picnic, and furthermore, Baruch was being unreasonable about the son thing. It would just serve him right if he got a girl, wouldn't it?

Hanan ben Hanan

Hanan stared at the elevated water tank in the Court of Priests. The workmen had built it to twice the height of a man and now they were sealing it up with pitch. What foolishness was this? He had been gone to oversee his farms in the coastlands for several weeks during the coldest part of the winter. In his absence, some fool had begun a complex and difficult project. And Hanan did not see how it could possibly work.

Hanan strode up to a workman. "Who ordered this?"

Fear hooded the man's eyes. "I do not know who ordered it." He pointed to a short, thin man with a gray beard. "Yosi hired me."

Yosi was a building contractor who built many houses in the New City and oversaw much of the construction and repairs in the Temple. Hanan snapped his fingers. Yosi came at once, smiling. "It is clever, do you agree? The water will flow down through many pipes to the lavers at which the priests wash their hands and feet. Your priests will no longer need to carry water."

"How do you intend to fill it, fool? The water will not lift itself into the tank."

Yosi smiled. "That is the clever part. I have designed a new type of pump which requires little effort. Two men can fill the tank in a short time, enough for a whole day of—"

"*You* designed it?" Hanan scowled. Yosi was skilled in managing workers, but he had no knowledge of pumps or other machines. Hanan found the matter of the pump fascinating, but such devices required more effort than they saved. The Temple required vast amounts of water, and a pump would be most useful if it could be made to work. But Hanan knew it could not. Better to order the common priests to carry water.

Yosi nodded happily. "I have the design here." He pulled out a thin sheet of—

Hanan snatched the papyrus from Yosi's hand. "Kazan! You received this from the hand of Kazan!"

"He is a talented architect," Yosi said. "He solved a difficult problem for me in the design of a house. I saved four hundred *dinars* in labor costs, and paid him fifty. An excellent bargain, do you agree?"

"You will not employ him anymore."

Yosi blinked twice. "He is much in demand from the other builders. If I do not employ him, others will."

"You will not employ him anymore."

"Of course," Yosi said without conviction.

Hanan saw that Yosi would continue to hire Kazan. He would not even bother to hide it. Hanan tugged at a corner of his beard, furious. Kazan was causing him to lose honor.

"The pump is very ingenious," Yosi said. "It turns a screw inside a cylinder set on a slant to elevate the water."

Hanan wanted to tell Yosi to say no more on the matter of the pump. But he also wanted to know how the pump worked. "How is it turned?"

Yosi showed him the diagram. Kazan had designed two vertical tread-wheels, one on each side of the sloping screw. Men walked inside the treadwheels, causing them to turn.

Hanan shook his head. "This is not new. I have seen many such tread-wheels. But they have a horizontal axle. The screw rises along a diagonal. How do the treadwheels connect to the screw?"

"Kazan calls the device a gear train." Yosi pointed to a strange-looking diagram. "This horizontal axle turns this gear, which meshes with another at an angle, which turns the screw."

"At an angle?" Hanan knew this could not possibly work. "This is fool-ishness."

"Kazan says they build many such gear trains in his country."

Hanan stared at the finely inked lines on the magical papyrus. The design surprised him. He had seen gears before, using wooden pins for teeth, but such devices broke easily. These teeth were thicker, differently oriented, and they meshed much more smoothly. This was either great fool-ishness, or . . . extraordinarily clever. "How are the gears to be constructed?"

"I have employed a skilled bronze worker. Ari the Kazan says the gears must be made of bronze."

Hanan shook his head. "It is impossible. Such a device cannot func-tion. The gears will not turn when mated together. You will cancel the con-tract."

"But it is completed, except for sealing the water tank and assembling the gear train."

"You will cancel it, or else the Temple will find other builders."

Yosi shook his head. "The other builders would also hire Ari the Kazan and then I would have lost him, to no gain. Therefore I will not cancel the contract. I will allow no man to say that Yosi the Builder does not complete what he has contracted. Also, I wish to see if the gear train will work."

Hanan glared at him. *You wish to learn the secrets of the gear train at the expense of the Temple treasury.* "I will cancel the remainder of the contract. You will not be paid another *dinar* for this work."

Yosi smiled. "Then I will finish the project at my own expense. I have already received three parts of the money from the Temple treasury, so I lose only my own profit. If the gear train works . . ." He shrugged eloquently.

Then Kazan will have made you the owner of something new in the world. Hanan turned on his heel and stalked away. This magician Kazan had stolen the hearts and hands of his contractors. It was time to find out more about him — where he lived, what manner of man he was.

And whether he had a family.

Rivka

Rivka wasn't feeling right this morning, and she had a scary hunch why.

Midwife Marta strode briskly beside her. "Please, you will keep up, Rivkaleh. The woman's waters have broken and her husband is frantic. Of course, a husband is always frantic, but still I am concerned."

Rivka smiled and tried to walk faster. Marta was always concerned. The woman in question was seventeen years old, and therefore a bit old for her first pregnancy. She had been married three years, and only gotten pregnant now? She must be less fertile than most. Therefore the husband was concerned. Likewise Marta.

A queasiness deep inside forced Rivka to stop. She leaned against the wall of a beautifully constructed stone house and closed her eyes. *Think about something pleasant.*

Marta stopped and came back. "Rivkaleh, are you well?"

Rivka opened her eyes slowly. "*Savta*, I'm . . . late." Rivka felt a rush of fear. Ari was going to be furious when he found out. She had been desperately hoping for the last three weeks that she was wrong, but there was no denying what she was feeling now.

"Ari the Kazan will be much honored. He must have been very concerned."

Rivka didn't want to even think about telling Ari. They had *agreed* not to get pregnant. She squeezed her eyes shut against the tears. This ought to be the most exciting thing in the world. Now panic crushed in on her whenever she thought about what a horrible world this would be for a baby.

Marta shook her head and muttered something.

"I'm sorry?" Rivka said.

"I meant no offense, child, but . . . you must be almost twenty already."

"Close," Rivka said. Women aged rapidly here. Marta would faint if she knew Rivka was twenty-six, and that it was common to be unmarried at that age in her far country.

Marta clucked her tongue. "I feared you were barren. I have been praying much to HaShem for you."

"Thank you, *Savta.*" Rivka took a deep breath. If Marta knew what was coming in the next decade, she might pray for all women to be barren. "I think I can walk. We must hurry."

"We will not hurry." Marta set an easy pace. "You will be the mother of many sons in *Yisrael.*"

When they reached the house, the husband was pacing outside in the street, wringing his hands and frowning. Rivka had never met him, but she knew from his wife that his name was Mattityahu, that he was a Torah student of Rabbi Tsaduq, that his trade was leather-crafts, and that he had inherited many *dinars* when his father died. Rivka sized him up quickly. A nervous young man in his early twenties, with a crooked nose, nervous eyes, the standard-issue untrimmed black beard, and already a bald alley under his *tefillin.*

Mattityahu rushed up to them. "My woman is having many pains already. Why have you not hurried?"

"Take us to the birthing room," Marta said in the brusque tone she reserved for flighty husbands who would faint if they knew how much blood was about to spill.

Mattityahu led them to the back of the house into a small room. Marta went in and knelt down beside the bed. "Miryam, how are you feeling?"

Miryam turned to her, eyes wide and fearful. "Blessed be HaShem, you have come. My waters have broken."

Marta snapped her fingers. "Mattityahu, you may go. Rivkaleh, you will examine her."

Rivka poured water over her hands and scrubbed them in vinegar. Not the best disinfectant, but she hadn't seen an infection yet in her patients, and that was not usual. She knelt and reached up underneath the linen tunic. Two months ago when Rivka began her training, Marta would not have dreamed of letting her perform a pelvic examination. Now, she insisted on it. Rivka's small hands were less intrusive than Marta's thick mitts. Rivka probed inside Miryam's birth canal. "She is dilated almost three fingers."

Marta patted Miryam's forehead. "Rest, child. Your waters broke early, and you still have some hours."

A rush of . . . something seemed to fill up the inside of Rivka's head. She gasped and bent over.

"Rivkaleh?" Marta sounded both tender and businesslike. "Are you feeling nauseous?"

Rivka nodded. She closed her eyes and tried to think of home.

Marta's footsteps retreated out of the room. Rivka heard her shouting something at the husband of the house. The queasiness in her stomach grew and grew. Footsteps again. "Child, use this basin if you need it." A cracked flat vessel of red clay appeared in front of Rivka.

She wobbled to her feet and clutched it. "Thank you, *Savta*. But I don't think I —" Rivka spent the next five minutes proving herself wrong.

Marta handed her a stone cup of beer. "Rinse out your mouth with this. And perhaps a breath of fresh air outside."

Rivka swished and spit. "How is Miryam?"

"Go outside. Breathe some air. I will call when I need you."

The husband gave her an anxious look when she went out, but Rivka shook her head. "Your woman has still some hours."

Your woman. Now I'm thinking like them. The language had one word, *ishah*, for both wife and woman. Until now, Rivka had always kept them separate in her mind. But the lines were blurring. Memories of San Diego were dimming. Walking in public without a horrible head-covering over her long silky black hair. Talking to guys and being treated like an equal — mostly. Wearing T-shirts and cutoffs at Horton Plaza. Bikinis on the beach at La Jolla Shores. It was another universe.

Rivka pushed outside. *Just don't think about it, girl. You are not part of that world anymore. You can't go back to the future. The only future you have is the one you're entering second by second.*

She took a cautious breath of fresh air. It was chilly today. Chilly and bright. The street was quiet. A woman walking with a shopping basket. A few children playing chase in the street. An oxcart hauling wood to the wood-market. A man loitering against a wall a few houses down. A beautiful —

Rivka felt a rush of fear. *A man loitering against a wall?* Not normal. Suspicious, she began walking toward him.

The man pushed off from the wall and strode away from her.

But not before Rivka got a good look at his face. She had seen this man before. Two days ago, while walking with Marta. And possibly last week, though she hadn't got a clear look then. Rivka never, ever forgot a face. This man had an ordinary face, one like a thousand others. Yet she knew perfectly well that she could pick him out of that thousand.

This man was following her. Why?

She had been stalked before. A romance in Berkeley that went sour. She had been forced to go to the cops then, get a restraining order, the works. She had even applied for a permit to carry a gun, had forced herself to take a course in firearms, even though she hated the things. Then her father offered her the money to go work on an archaeological dig for the summer in Israel. Which was how she got here.

Now it was happening again. Only this time, she was carrying a passenger.

Rivka put her hands on her hips and glared up the street at the retreating man. *You better run, buddy. You better be scared. Nobody messes with Rivka Meyers Kazan when she's got a baby on board.*

NINE

Ari

Ari pushed his way up the crowded market street with half the Sons of Righteous Priests behind him. Today he felt nervous. And proud. They had worked hard on the gear train, but it was something new, and therefore it required testing. Today, it looked like the whole city would be watching this final test.

The teeth of the gears meshed smoothly in the shop of Levi the bronze worker. But would they mesh well when installed? The Temple had cancelled the contract, shorting Yosi the Builder. If the device failed, Yosi would be angry and Ari would lose honor.

Lose honor. He was concerned now with honor?

Gamaliel slipped up alongside Ari in the noisy crowd. "Ari the Kazan, you should know something."

Ari peered down at his friend. "What should I know?"

"Hanan ben Hanan has been asking questions about you."

"What sort of questions?"

Gamaliel looked all around them, his eyes alert. "Questions. His men are following you and your woman. This is all that I know. I heard it from a friend. You will be careful, please."

"Thank you, my friend."

They turned east and walked up the steps at the southern edge of the Temple Mount. Ari looked back. Levi the bronze worker grunted under his load — one of the five gears in the gear train. Eleazar carried one in each massive arm. Two other Sons of Righteous Priests carried one gear apiece. Ari would have carried one, but the men would not allow it. Ari the Kazan, entrusted by HaShem with the secrets of the gear train, must do no menial work. Whereas the men who did work in his service gained honor by serving him. The whole system was twice crazy. He should put an end to it. But he might as easily turn off the sun.

Earlier today, the men had performed the ritual washing for entry onto the Temple Mount. They bypassed the public baths and went in through the twin Huldah Gates — the first level of purity of the Temple. Up a couple of hundred steps and out into the clean winter sunshine. Fear gnawed at Ari. He could not afford to fail.

They continued toward a waist-high barrier wall. A sign on the gate informed them in Aramaic, Greek, and Latin of the death that would face any Gentile who entered. Ari could not read the Greek and Latin, but Rivka could. This was the second level of purity.

They ascended a series of steps to the gates of the inner Temple and walked into the Court of Women, the third level of purity. It was now nearly noon, midway between morning and afternoon sacrifices. A good time for installing the gears, when few worshipers clogged the courts. They turned left and walked across the vast court to the semicircular steps — fifteen broad stairs where the Levite musicians sang during the hour of sacrifice. During the worship hour, a man could feel an awe descend on him, surround him, wash him. Ari had experienced it many times. He did not feel it now. Dread wrapped its cold fist around his heart.

They walked up the steps and through the gleaming Corinthian bronze gates into the fourth level of purity. This was the Court of *Yisrael*, where any Jewish man could come if he brought a sacrifice. It was forbidden to women. Ari had been here twice for consultations on the pump. Then he had felt this same strange sense of quiet or solitude or . . . peacefulness.

The men around him had grown quiet, reverent. Ari hesitated. They now stood facing west before the great altar. Behind it towered the golden facade of the Temple itself, on the same site where someday a mosque with a golden roof would stand. Ari knew only one word to describe this place.

Kadosh.

Holy.

Separated from the world of men and chatter. This was the Temple of the living God, and whether you believed HaShem was a manlike being with head and hands and heart, or whether you considered him the primordial First Cause, you could not miss that something of substance — something *heavy* — dwelled here.

Today, Ari felt a holy terror. He had heard rumors that Hanan ben Hanan would find a way to stop this project. Would crush Kazan. Destroy his honor. Ari fought the urge to turn and run. Craziness, to fight Hanan on his own turf.

Eleazar nudged him. "Ari the Kazan, we must install the device."

"Of course." Ari kicked off his sandals — one did not wear shoes beyond this point — and ascended yet a few more steps into the fifth level of purity, the Court of Priests. Only priests were admitted here, but any priest could enter, even an *issah* priest like Ari. He walked past the altar to the pump.

Ari pushed aside his fears. If he had miscalculated, Hanan would win. So be it. He could not turn back now. He would use the mind HaShem had given him and he would fight Hanan.

Before him lay a tank the size of one of those small swimming pools so common in America. An aqueduct fed the tank with a steady stream. A line of sweating priests waited at the pool, dipping bronze buckets and carrying them to a dozen destinations.

The pump looked much like a huge screw inside a giant drinking straw. The straw was set at an angle, rising from the lower tank to the upper. Turning the screw drew water up the trough. It was ingenious, and of course not Ari's invention. The Greeks had been building these for centuries.

The central problem, unsolved by the Greeks, was efficient energy transfer. The axis of the screw pointed upward at an angle of thirty degrees. How to transfer the energy of the treadwheel into rotational motion at such an inconvenient angle? Of course this required gears. But the problem had resisted the cleverest Greeks for centuries because their gears were of inferior design — pins attached to wheels, and set parallel to the axle. Such gears could transmit rotational energy through a right angle, but not one of thirty degrees.

Any modern child would know to thicken the pins and shape them into true teeth and point them radially outward. But this was three innovations at once, a difficult step. The Greeks had not yet solved the problem.

But Ari had, with the help of Levi the bronze worker. He felt no compunction at introducing this new technology to the world. Nothing he could do would change the stream of history. He was a part of history now, and anything he did now was something that had already happened long ago and had made the past what it was. The universe was just as consistent with or without a timelike self-intersecting loop. It chose still a single trajectory through phase space.

Ari turned to Levi the bronze worker. "You will install the first gear, please."

Levi took off the secondary axle, which ran parallel to the water screw. He slid gears onto each end of the axle and locked them into place using iron pins. The device now looked like a barbell. Several men lifted it into place beneath the water screw on bronze sleeve bearings.

Levi grabbed the teeth of the lower gear and gave it a spin. The axle rotated smoothly on its bearings. Levi climbed up to the upper water tank. Brother Eleazar handed him another gear. Levi fitted it onto the primary axis of the water screw and slid it down so that its teeth meshed with the upper gear on the secondary axis. He made some small adjustments, then nodded.

Ari grabbed the lower gear and rotated it. Now both the secondary and primary axles turned. A shout went up from all the men. The device transmitted power from the secondary to the primary!

Ari said nothing. These two axles were parallel. Of course the gears would mesh correctly and drive the system. The difficult part lay ahead.

Levi climbed down and fitted one of the remaining gears onto a horizontal axle. Several men helped him fit this to a vertical treadwheel. The wheel was about twice the height of a man — large enough for even Ari to walk inside it like a hamster, turning it to drive the system. The men worked for the fourth part of an hour to align the teeth of the treadwheel gear with the teeth of the lower gear on the secondary axis. This was a delicate task. The two gears must mesh precisely to transmit energy through the proper angle.

When they finished, Levi and his men installed the last gear on an identical treadwheel on the opposite side of the pump. Two men would power the system.

An enormous crowd of priests had gathered around. Hanan ben Hanan stood to one side, his face twitching with anticipation.

Ari pointed to Brother Eleazar. "You and I will test the device." He stepped into the first treadwheel. Brother Eleazar stepped into the second.

Ari's heart pumped madly. This must not fail.

"Walk!" he called to Brother Eleazar. Both men stepped forward, and the great wheels began to move, creaking ponderously. Step. Step. Step. The gears groaned, and Ari saw ripples in the lower tank as the pump began drawing water upward. Ari's treadwheel turned, turned, turned. A quarter turn. Half turn. Three —

The wheel slammed to a halt, throwing Ari forward onto the floor of the treadwheel. A collective hiss ran around the circle of priests.

His face burning, Ari stood up and stepped off the wheel.

Levi the bronze worker appeared next to him. "Ari the Kazan, what is wrong?"

Ari pointed to the gear train. "The gears are binding."

"That is impossible. I made them perfectly." Levi wore a defensive look.

"Of course." Ari smiled at Levi. "Yet still the gears are too tight. The device will not turn. We must make an adjustment."

Levi's eyebrows bunched up. "What sort of adjustment?"

Ari pointed to the teeth of the gears. "We must pull the gears apart and file down the teeth where they are binding."

Levi shook his head. "A bronze file will not file bronze gears."

Ari shrugged. "I told you to bring an iron file."

Low murmurs ran around the circle. A strange look of panic crossed Levi's face.

Ari felt cold sweat on his back. "This is a small request, yes? Did you not bring a file?"

Brother Eleazar appeared at Ari's elbow. "We must discuss this privately, Ari the Kazan." His face looked tight, controlled.

Ari looked at the big man. "Is something wrong?"

"We will discuss this privately."

Ari's stomach knotted. What was so hard about this? "We need only to file the teeth a bit here and there. It is a small adjustment, to make the gears mesh."

Hanan ben Hanan stepped forward. He had said nothing until now, but his face told Ari the entire story.

Hanan was smiling.

Rivka

As evening fell, Rivka stumbled toward home, her heart raw with grief. She and Midwife Marta had tried everything they knew, but Miryam's baby had been born dead. Cold shadows darkened the street. Rivka yanked her cloak tighter around her shoulders and tramped along on wooden feet. This was February in the western calendar, and her toes had felt frozen for months.

If it hadn't been so late, Rivka would have stopped by to see Hana, who was due in a couple of weeks. But today, no. Rivka had to talk to Ari. Was terrified to talk to Ari. What was he going to say when he found out she was pregnant?

Two streets farther on, she turned left. The narrow street followed the natural curve of the hill. Rivka found the door unlocked. Ari must be home. She stepped into their main downstairs room, which functioned as living room and study. A dark cold interior greeted her. "Ari?" Her voice quavered.

No answer.

She closed the door and peered into the next room, the kitchen. Nobody. No fire. She climbed the stone stairway to the second floor and pushed open the door into their bedroom. Ari sat on a squat wooden stool, elbows on knees, hands over his face. A little light filtered through the vertical windowslits above his head.

"Ari?" Rivka rushed to him, needing a hug. "Ari?"

He looked toward her, his eyes vacant, hollow.

She put her arms around him. "Ari, what's wrong?"

A long silence, then a deep sigh. "He hates us, Rivka. For no reason."

"Hanan ben Hanan?"

Ari sighed. "I can understand, perhaps, why he hates me. He fears me, fears my technology. But you — this I do not understand."

Rivka's heart lurched. "Hanan knows . . . about me?"

"Gamaliel warned me today. Hanan has hired men to follow you."

"I saw a man loitering in the street today. What does Hanan want?"

"I do not know." Ari wrapped his strong arms around her. "Perhaps he wishes to destroy us."

Rivka felt tears bubbling up from some deep well in her soul. She put her face in Ari's chest and cried. Told him about her horrible day. How she'd seen that man in the street. How she'd scared him off. Then spent the day doing her utmost to help birth a dead baby. She wept until she was good and cried out. Exhausted. She wanted to tell him about her pregnancy, but . . . she just couldn't. Not yet.

Rivka wiped her eyes on the sleeve of his tunic. "Ari, this is too much. I can't stand it anymore. I want to go back to the future where we belong."

Ari stroked her hair. "The only future we have is here. Tomorrow. The next day. The far future you speak of is our past, and we have no return."

Rivka snuffled and looked up into his face. Did she dare tell him? His tight jaw and closed expression frightened her. Something must have gone terribly wrong today. "Ari, I'm sorry. I forgot to ask how your day went."

Pain crossed his face. "It was disaster. The gears meshed excellently in the shop. There remained only the test in place under load. I would have performed the test alone, quietly, but we needed men to carry the gears. We went to the Temple with always more friends following us, all of them confident of our success. Many dozen priests came to watch. And ben Hanan stood there smiling."

Ari closed his eyes. A single tear formed at the corner of each of his eyes. "Rivka, the fit was too perfect. When we began turning the treadwheel, the gears began binding. They had not enough play between them. This was by design. I thought to trim them as needed. It is easier to remove metal than to add it. But Levi did not bring a file with him. I had told him to bring an iron file to trim the bronze gears. He knew this was foolish, but out of respect for my honor, he did not wish to affront me by telling me so. So he did nothing."

Rivka put her hands on his. "I don't understand."

"Iron tools are not allowed on the Temple Mount."

Rivka gasped. "You're kidding."

"It is an old tradition — one I knew nothing about. They say the altar was built in the time of King Shlomo without benefit of iron tools. And to this day, none are permitted."

Which was crazy, but there was something in the books about that, wasn't there? Rivka closed her eyes. Concentrated. The image of a page slowly formed in her mind. Tractate Middot 3:4 of the Mishnah. She read the words out loud. "'Iron is created to shorten the days of a man, but the altar is created to lengthen the days of a man. It is not judged fitting to wave that which shortens over that which lengthens.'" She opened her eyes.

Ari nodded. "I have never heard this thing until now."

"And you're telling me they apply this principle to the whole Temple Mount today, a thousand years later? That's . . . incredible." Rivka wished, just once, that all those books she had read in graduate school actually gave all the information she needed. It was frustrating, working with only one percent of the facts. People called her the seer woman — thought she knew the future. And yet she felt so painfully ignorant.

Ari gripped Rivka's hands. "It is *meshugah*. Hanan was delighted. He told us no iron tools can be brought to the house of the living God. Nor could we remove the gears to take them home. They are now a permanent part of the Temple, and he will not permit that they should be removed."

Rivka felt a cold lump in her belly. "But . . . they don't work."

"That is his purpose." Ari shook his head. "He could work with me if he wished, but he prefers to oppose me, to dishonor me. He will not allow me to repair the device there. Nor will he permit its removal."

"Catch–22."

"Hanan hates me for no reason except that he hates me." Defeat washed across Ari's face. "Rivka, I am alone against this man. All my friends, Gamaliel and Eleazar and Yoseph and the rest — they will aid me in private, but none of them dares to stand openly against Hanan ben Hanan, *sagan* of the Temple. He will be the next high priest and they fear him."

"Ari, he won't be the next high priest. Ishmael will be. Ishmael ben Phiabi. After him, Joseph Kabi. Then Hanan."

Ari looked at her doubtfully. "Perhaps your books are in error. It is said everywhere that Hanan will be next. That is the purpose of the office of *sagan*. It is preparation for the high priesthood."

Rivka studied Ari's face. Her secret was burning now, scorching her insides. She had to tell him. She didn't dare tell him.

Ari put his head in his hands. "I am dishonored today. Hanan ben Hanan has destroyed me, and he gloated in his victory, and nobody will hire me ever again. We are lost. You and I will go back to living on charity. I am one man alone against Hanan, and he hates me. He hates a monster named Kazan. And now he hates you, though he knows nothing of you, only because you are Kazan's woman."

Kazan's woman. Rivka flinched as if Ari had slapped her. She wanted to shriek at him. *I'm your wife, not your woman!* But that made no sense. Wife ... woman — they were the same word. Ari had said nothing wrong. The language gave him no choice.

But something had happened to her ears, her mind. She no longer heard *wife*, she heard *woman*. She had been here too long, immersed in this wretched culture. Her culture. Her people. Her city. Jerusalem the Golden, city of God. Oppressor of women. And now she was pregnant. Her eyes flooded.

Ari reached out to her. "Rivkaleh, I am sorry. Because of me, Hanan hates you. I should never have crossed him. Please do not be afraid. Whatever he does, I will never let him harm you."

Rivka shook her head. She had to tell him now, before her courage failed. "Ari, I'm not afraid for me. But ... I didn't tell you yet." Her voice caught. Tears burned down her cheeks. Tears of weariness. Joy. Rage. Frustration.

"Ari, I'm . . . pregnant." She held her breath, waiting for the explosion. "I'm sorry. I know it's a horrible time to — "

"No." He put a finger to her lips. "You will not apologize."

Ari laughed out loud, a deep, bold, defiant laugh, then leaned over and kissed her softly. He wrapped her in his arms, crushing her gently in his love. "Blessed be HaShem, Rivkaleh. Today is of all days, most perfect."

Hanan ben Hanan

Late that night, Hanan took a visitor in the receiving room of his palace. They sat on backless stone benches, leaning against the plastered wall. The man was named Yoni, a priest, a son of the Sadducees, a man who loved the Temple. His father had sat on the Sanhedrin thirty years ago and helped Hanan's father send a certain false *mashiach* to his cross.

Yoni leaned toward Hanan. "They belong to that sect called *HaDerech*."

Hanan nodded. *The Way*. Kazan was a follower of the man Yeshua, falsely called *mashiach*. This sect did not love the Temple, and some of them had called for its overthrow. They were fools, charlatans, messianics. Hanan would deal with them when his day came.

Yoni continued. "Kazan's woman is a midwife and has a reputation as a seer woman. It is said that she reads the future as easily as a man reads a scroll."

Hanan tugged at the corner of his beard. The woman was a fraud, of course. All seers were liars. He stood up and put a hand on Yoni's shoulder. "My friend, I thank you. This is useful information, but perhaps no longer needed. I have destroyed Kazan today. Nobody will hire him anymore, forever."

Yoni stood also. "If you require more information, I am here — send me."

Hanan nodded and saw Yoni to the door. He stood in his courtyard staring up at the cold black sky, filled with the shining heavenly hosts which fools and magicians like Kazan worshiped — an abomination to the living God.

Sooner or later, Kazan would return to Egypt or Babylon or whichever far country he came from, and another threat to the Temple would be removed.

TEN

Ari

Pounding at the door downstairs woke Ari the next morning. He looked at his watch. 5:12 A.M. Much too early to go with Brother Baruch to the morning prayers. Rivka lay huddled beside him, her long black hair tangled about her face.

More pounding.

Ari reached for his tunic and tugged it over his head and down inside the thick scratchy wool blankets. Rivka muttered in her sleep and snuggled close to him, clutching his arm.

"Rivkaleh." Ari worked her fingers loose. "We have a visitor."

The pounding downstairs continued.

Ari rolled out of bed and flung on his cloak. The house was freezing. He jammed his feet into his camel-leather sandals and wished for summer. At the door, he shouted, "Who is it?"

"Brother Ari, bring Sister Rivka!" Baruch's voice. "Hana says it is her time."

"We will come quickly, Brother Baruch."

Six hours later, Ari sat in the downstairs room of Baruch's house, wondering why they had hurried. Upstairs, Rivka and Midwife Marta were attending to Hana. Of course, all men were banished from the birthing room. Baruch paced back and forth, a human metronome. Sunlight filtered in through the window slits high up in the wall. Ari wished he could speed the process. This waiting was unbearable, and Baruch's pacing would drive them both insane.

Ari stood up and took Baruch's arm. "My friend, I have a problem I would like to discuss with you."

Baruch shot a nervous look upstairs.

Ari shook his head. "They will call us when the time comes." He led the way outside. They sat down on a bench facing the sun, letting it warm their faces. Ari told Baruch all about the disaster with the pump. Baruch nodded dully at first, but soon the story caught his attention.

"You should not have made Hanan ben Hanan your enemy," Baruch said. "This man is dangerous. His father killed Rabban Yeshua, and he is a man of violence like his father. When he becomes high priest—"

"Rivka says he will not," Ari said. "Not soon, anyway. She says a man named Ishmael will be the next high priest."

"Ishmael ben Phiabi?"

"Yes."

Baruch shook his head. "It is not possible. Ishmael was never *sagan*. Everyone knows Hanan ben Hanan will be the next high priest. Perhaps Sister Rivka meant Ishmael ben Phiabi's grandfather. He was high priest long ago."

"I am . . . not sure," Ari said. "Rivka seemed certain."

"Sister Rivka tells a dark tale of the future," Baruch said. "She frightens me, Brother Ari. Such a tale of dread cannot be true."

Ari shivered. Rivka had told Baruch almost nothing—only hints that an evil time approached.

"Do you believe her?" Baruch said.

Ari did not wish to answer this question. To answer was to face the reality that he could not escape the coming horror. He had chosen to live in this city, in this time. For Rivka's sake. Had it all been a mistake? Evil stalked this city, waiting to pounce. The terrible unfairness of it crushed him. He had discussed this with Rivka once. The Problem of Evil. If HaShem was all-powerful and all-good, then why did he allow evil? An all-powerful being who allowed evil could not be all-good. An all-good being who could not prevent evil was not all-powerful. Ari preferred to think HaShem was good. Therefore, HaShem was not all-powerful. A disturbing thought.

Rivka believed that HaShem was both all-good and all-powerful—so good that he created people, so powerful that he gave them free will. And that made evil possible. If men could not choose evil, then they were not free. Therefore, the existence of evil was proof of HaShem's great power to create those who could choose to oppose him.

But it still seemed terribly wrong. What of those who suffered because of the evil others chose? Had they no rights? Did the rights of the wicked to choose evil outweigh the rights of the innocent to be let alone? Ari believed in a personal God, but he preferred that his belief make sense. He believed in quantum mechanics, which did not make sense, but one such belief was enough.

Baruch was now pacing in the street. "Brother Baruch, why does HaShem allow evil?"

A contempl ative silence. Baruch ran his fingers through his beard. "Why does HaShem allow darkness?" A typical Baruch answer.

Ari grappled with that. Darkness was not like evil. Darkness was the absence of light. A man could eliminate darkness by turning on a light. A man could not so eliminate evil. Darkness was a matter of physics. Evil was a matter of . . . what? Spirit?

Ari resisted such words. What was spirit? He found it difficult enough to believe in HaShem. His evidence consisted of one fact — that he was alive when he should have been dead. A hornet sting which should have killed him had not — because of a prayer by Brother Baruch. Furthermore, his allergy to hornet stings was now . . . gone. He had been healed, and more than healed. A miracle on a most personal level.

One could not have a personal miracle without a personal miracle-maker. Therefore, the reasonable man must believe in a personal God. In HaShem.

Still Ari felt troubled. Belief in a personal God was one thing. Belief in personal evil was another. Yet all the evils he found objectionable were personal. Some considered earthquakes evil — but earthquakes were merely a tectonic mechanism for renewing the carbon cycle, maintaining life on earth. The occasional seismic hiccup was a small price to pay for the gift of life, renewed over billions of years. Other natural disasters were similar. Hurricanes, tornadoes, floods. True, they destroyed life, but on a local scale, and without malice.

But men were different. Men like Hitler, Stalin, Mao. Such men were evil by intent, without bounds on their malice. Hitler would have destroyed all Jews. These men had chosen evil and the only restraints on them were . . . other men. HaShem did not restrain them. Good men did. Some, like those who tried to assassinate Hitler, died for their efforts.

Ari shivered. He did not wish to oppose evil in that way. He only wished . . . what? A little justice? A small reduction in evil? Did ultimate evil require ultimate sacrifice? Why? If so, there was a deep imbalance in the universe.

"You are quiet, Brother Ari." Baruch sat beside him again.

Ari sighed. "I think too much. It is good to have you as a friend. Nothing unbalances you."

From overhead, a sharp cry split the morning stillness.

Ari and Baruch bolted to their feet.

Rivka

It won't be long, Hana." Rivka washed her hands again in vinegar, then wiped them on a blood-streaked towel. For a first-time mother, Hana was fast. And stoic. No screams, no cursing her husband. Just a businesslike determination to get through each contraction, to work with her body to bring this baby to light. Hana squatted on the birthstool now, breathing hard from the last birthpang.

Rivka knelt in front of her. "Let me check you one more time." She eased her hand inside and —

Contact. The baby's head was only an inch or two from daylight. The last inch was generally the hardest, and the quickest.

"Another few contractions." Rivka felt light-headed, queasy, exhausted.

Hana grunted, and Rivka knew that another contraction had begun. Hana gripped her hands. Midwife Marta felt Hana's belly. "You will not push on this one, Hana, my child. Not yet."

The contraction went on and on and on. Finally Hana's face slackened, her death-grip on Rivka's hands eased.

Rivka stood up quickly and stretched her cramped thigh muscles. She felt a stirring in her own belly. She grabbed her vomit bowl and quietly heaved a few times. Her stomach was empty, but her body didn't seem to care. This was an inconvenience, nothing more. She had seen women who spent the whole nine months with morning sickness, women who *lost* weight during their pregnancies. Her mother had spent four months in bed with preterm labor before Rivka's younger brother was born. Next to that, a little morning sickness was nothing.

"Be ready, Rivkaleh," said Marta. She squatted behind Hana, kneading her back. "Only a few more, child, and you will hold your son. Only a few —"

"Aughhh!" Hana gave a sharp cry. "Another!" Her face was a mask of pain. Joy. Exhaustion. Hope. Fear.

Rivka hurried to kneel before her again. The muscles of Hana's belly quivered, knotted. A bulge beneath.

"It's crowning!" Rivka held her breath. If anything would go wrong, it would happen soon. *Please, God. Let it be healthy. And if it's a son, Baruch would be so —*

Something emerged. Round. Bloody. Hairy.

Blond.

Rivka could not breathe for a few seconds. *Blond?* That was not possible. Both Hana and Baruch had black hair.

The pale head squeezed slowly out.

"Rivkaleh, what do you see?" Marta said.

"The head." Rivka put out her hands, cupping the head underneath. "Face down. It's . . . perfect." It was not perfect and she knew it.

By the time the contraction ended, the entire head was out and Rivka's heart was quivering like jelly. *Please, God. No. Anything but this.*

"You will push on the next one, my child," Marta said. "Once more and all will be well."

Rivka bit her lip to keep from crying. All would not be well. Nothing would be well for Hana, ever again.

Hana

The last hours had been joy for Hana. She had heard women speak in whispers of the pain and joy and fear of childbirth.

The pain was very great, but against that was joy. It was joy to suffer for the sake of her son. She knew it would be a son. A son for her man, her husband, her blessed Baruch. He was a good man, a kind man, a loving man. She did not deserve such a man. She would bear any pain, any sorrow for such a man, would give him many sons. This pain was nothing, nothing to the joy of giving her man a son.

The joy was very great, but against that was fear. Fear on account of the wicked man from Rivka's far country. The wicked man had done an evil thing to her, once. Hana had prayed much to HaShem about this matter, but . . . still she felt much fear. The shade of the wicked man had haunted her dreams for many months.

The fear was very great, but Hana clung to joy. All was in the hands of HaShem.

"You will push on the next one, my child. Once more and all will be well." Midwife Marta was kind also. A true mother in *Yisrael*. Hana closed her eyes and gripped the sides of the birthstool, frightened by the strange look on Sister Rivka's face. She waited.

The next birthpang came soon. Hana pushed. The pain engulfed her, rolling over her like a wave of the sea. She could not breathe, could not think. Could only feel the joy, sudden and sharp as a scream.

And then it eased and she knew the child was born. Her son. It must be a son. Tears blurred her eyes. The great pain was over, and it had been a small thing next to the joy that welled in her heart. Blessed be HaShem. Baruch would have a son.

Blinded by her own sweat, Hana heard every move. The wet sound of Rivka's practiced hands holding the child. The rush of Marta's breath in her ear, murmuring something. The shrill cry of the child. It was joy to hear such a cry.

"A boy," Rivka said. "You have a son, Hana."

Baruch has a son. He will be so happy. Hana wanted to stand, to dance, to exult in the deep ache in her body.

"Child, hold," Marta said. "There is still the afterbirth, and then you must rest."

Still unseeing, panting from her great work, Hana waited. Finally, her belly knotted again. She let her body push for her. She had pushed once — that was enough. Rivka had told her that her body would do the work if she allowed it. Hana waited out the birthpang.

"The boy is breathing easily," Rivka said. "His heart beats strongly. He is . . . beautiful."

Hana felt her body go limp. Her suffering was over and it had been such a small thing next to the joy of bearing a son. If she had strength, she would leap and dance for joy.

"Rest, child." Marta wrapped her arms around Hana and massaged her belly with strong, sure strokes. "You are a mother in *Yisrael*." She kissed Hana on the neck. "Rejoice and be glad."

Hana remained on the birthstool until she had caught her breath. A great weariness engulfed her. She felt her body sag. Her eyes were slits against the bright daylight. Joy rolled through her, but fear rose up like a storm. "I want . . . to see my son."

"You must rest a little." Marta grasped Hana at the elbows. "Rivka, help me."

Hana heard Rivka bend down. Together, the three of them stood. A great ache stabbed at Hana, but it was nothing to what she had endured. They moved to the bed. Hana floated downward into the softness. Cold. So very cold. Shivering seized her. Dear Sister Rivka lay in the bed beside her, warming her with her body. Marta covered both of them with blankets and wiped Hana's face with a damp cloth.

Hana shivered and for a time, she knew nothing.

Warmth. A deep ache. Joy. Thirst. Desire for her son. Fear.

Hana opened her eyes. She heard Sister Rivka talking with Marta in hushed whispers. Hana reached for the stone cup of water near her head. Her hands could not grasp it. The cup fell over.

Rivka turned. "Hana, don't strain yourself. I'll get you some water. And . . . your son is hungry."

Marta filled the cup with water from a pitcher and brought it to Hana, her ancient wrinkled face gumming a smile. "Drink it all, child. You must drink much water today."

The cold water chilled Hana, but she drank the whole cup. "I want my son. I want to feed my son."

A pounding at the door.

"Your husband knows he has a son," Marta said.

Hana covered her hair. Rivka brought the child, swaddled in a long swath of linen so that only his face showed. She put the tiny bundle in Hana's arms. Inside her body, he had seemed huge, a giant. Now, he was nothing. Like a jug of water, no more. His wrinkled, red face screwed up into a wail. Marta went to the wooden door and opened it. "You may now see your son."

Baruch strode directly to Hana. "Blessed be HaShem."

Hana knew only that there was no joy and no fear greater than this — to give her man a son.

Baruch knelt beside Hana, laughing, weeping. "Our son." He loosened the swaddling.

"Not yet," Rivka said. "Baruch, I think — "

But Baruch, like every man, must see for himself the evidence that he had a son. He folded back the edge of the linen. The covering fell away from the baby's head.

Hana felt all joy rush out of her heart.

Shock widened Baruch's eyes. His mouth twisted in a knot of sudden fury. He spun and stalked out of the room. His footsteps thudded on the stairway. Downstairs, the door slammed.

Grief took Hana like a flood.

Baruch

A roaring sound filled Baruch's ears as he staggered down the street. Evil! This was a great evil!

Rage pounded in his heart. The wicked man had done this. The man who fought like a devil. The man with a name like a *daemon*. The man with yellow hair who came from a far country.

The wicked man was dead. The man who had come to destroy the order of the universe, to overturn the will of HaShem. He was dead, and yet now he lived again. The child Hana had carried was his seed.

The wicked man had stabbed a knife into the belly of the world. Where was justice? Where was mercy? Where was ... the wrath of HaShem against such unrighteousness?

The wicked man had tied a knot in the deep order of the universe, and who could untie it? He had wounded Baruch, and who could heal the scar? No wisdom ran deep enough, no mercy wide enough, to cleanse this evil. Only wrath remained—the wrath of HaShem. A holy wrath against evil.

Baruch reached the Essene Gate and stormed through, down the steep hill toward the Hinnom Valley. A sharp wind blew, whistling in his ears, freezing his heart.

Rage like a river filled his soul.

Rivka

Rivka wrapped up the baby and held it to her chest, rocking it gently. "Shhhh, sweet baby. Don't cry."

Soon, he was asleep. Ari stood in the doorway, his eyes wide. Hana lay still, weeping softly. Midwife Marta scowled while she mopped up the blood on the floor.

Rivka handed Ari the baby.

Panic pooled in his eyes.

"Just ... hold him. Rock him." Rivka went to sit on the bed. "Hana." Sniffles.

"Hana. What happened?"

Hana wiped her face and rubbed her nose on a blanket. "The wicked man came . . . looking for you one night. With the thing that throws fire."

"The gun." Rivka remembered her terror of Damien. "He came to kill me."

"Yes. He was . . . angry when he found you were not there. He kicked me . . . He told me to find you. Then . . . he laughed and closed the door and . . . did a wicked thing to me."

Weeping.

"Hana, I'm so sorry." Rivka's heart felt jagged and raw. Hana had suffered for her and she had never even known. No wonder Hana had nightmares about Damien.

"Then he took me into the street. I knew he wanted only to find you. Then he would have killed us both."

"And that's why you knew you had to run? Oh, Hana." Rivka leaned over and hugged her.

"I should have chewed a few leaves from the herbs in my house," Hana said. "Then I would not have . . ." Hana's voice broke.

Rivka looked at the tiny bundle in Ari's arms. So Hana kept some sort of abortifacient herbs in her home? That explained how she had worked as a *zonah* and not gotten pregnant.

"Many things happened in the next few days," Hana said. "Always, I forgot to return for my herbs."

Because of me. And Ari. And Baruch. Rivka patted Hana's shoulder. "Hanaleh. You did not sin. The wicked man sinned. Against you. Against Baruch. Against HaShem."

Hana snuffled. "I should have told Baruch."

"Then he would not have —" Rivka covered her mouth, horrified at the thought. No. Baruch was a good man. He had not known what Damien did, but he knew Hana had been a *zonah* and he had married her anyway. Because he loved her. Because HaShem had done a great thing in his heart. And because he too had sinned. Baruch would still have married her.

Rivka stood up and went to Ari. "Go find Brother Baruch." She took the baby and peered into its tiny inscrutable face. "Talk some sense into him, okay? Tell him this is going to happen to a lot of women after the war that's coming. So many women that the rabbis will change the rules so a Jew is defined to be one born of a Jewish mother."

Ari gaped at her. She saw in his eyes a horror that something like this might happen to her someday. That maybe he wouldn't survive to protect her.

"Ari, I knew what this century was like when I chose to stay here. So did you. Now go find Baruch and talk to him. He'll listen to you."

Ari nodded dumbly and went out.

Rivka went and sat on the bed and wept. She had lied to Ari. She hadn't thought at all about anything like this when she decided to stay. A horror was coming to her land. To her people. To her.

Rivka wept, because the worst thing in the world was to be a prophet, to know the height and depth of the desolation to come, and to be powerless to prevent it. For the first time in her life, she understood why Moses didn't want to be a prophet. Why Daniel lost all strength for days after seeing the far future. Why Jeremiah was always crying his eyes out. Because the only thing worse than not knowing the future was . . . knowing the future.

Ari

Ari walked the streets in a blind panic. What if he found Baruch? Then what would he say? He had no skill in talking of such matters. If it were a matter of Hilbert spaces, fiber bundles, complex linear operators, then yes, he had some skill. But matters of the heart, no.

He was a dunce and an ignoramus and it was *meshugah* for a fool like him to meddle in this matter.

He hurried along the street asking people he knew. Had anyone seen Baruch passing by? Yes, several had — going toward the Essene Gate. Ari walked, his heart cold with horror.

Baruch's honor had been stolen. His woman was violated, and the evidence showed plainly in his child. He could divorce her, of course, but . . . Baruch would never do that. He loved Hana. Besides, it had not been her fault. The fault lay with a man beyond the reach of vengeance. Damien had done this evil. He had dishonored Baruch, and nothing could restore his honor.

Ari walked. At the Essene Gate, he looked down into the Hinnom Valley. No sign of Baruch. Perhaps he had gone some other way. Ari looked back to the crowded city.

No, Baruch would wish to be alone. He would go out here, because it led to the desolation of the Hinnom Valley.

Ari walked down the steep path from the Essene Gate. The gate was named so because Essenes took the path to a place outside the city where they defecated in the fields, obeying the Torah commandment not to foul the camp. They carried small trowels in their belts for the purpose of digging holes to obey this holy calling.

People did many such absurd things to obey HaShem. They refrained from eating pork. They rested on *Shabbat*. They killed animals and offered the fat to HaShem. Who could understand such things? Was HaShem pleased with this behavior? Ari's stepfather would not turn on an electric light on *Shabbat*, nor eat meat within six hours of eating milk. To honor HaShem.

Ari shook his head. Honor was *meshugah*. He turned a corner and saw the burning-pits. People brought their garbage here and threw it into pits. There were always fires burning in this valley, always the stench of rotting food, of refuse. Half-wild pariah dogs raced among the pits, scavenging. It amused him that in another place and time, dogs would be considered *pets*. Here they were feral beasts, reviled, hated, mangy, pitiful, disgusting. To call a man a dog was the greatest insult you could make.

Ari rounded a bend in the road. A pile of ash stood mounded near a burning-pit. At its foot sat Baruch, throwing ashes over his hair, his clothes. Tears streaked his face.

Ari slowed as he approached his friend. This was *meshugah*. An empty gesture, signifying nothing. It meant something only because Baruch thought it meant something. Just as kosher and *Shabbat* and sacrifice meant something to those who thought they meant something.

But *Shabbat* was part of this city, part of this people. Likewise kosher. Likewise the blood of bulls and goats.

Likewise honor.

Ari slowed as he approached Baruch. He took off his sandals. Knelt beside his friend. Took a handful of ashes.

And poured them over his head, letting the bitter taste of Baruch's dishonor fill his soul.

ELEVEN

Ari

A week passed and Baruch remained hostile on the matter of the boy. On the eighth day, a dark and wet winter morning, Ari nervously decided to break their tradition of silence on the way to the morning prayers. They would be holding a circumcision ceremony that afternoon, and a name was required. Baruch refused to name the boy after himself.

Ari locked the door of his house and turned to Baruch. "My friend, have you decided what to name the boy?"

Baruch shook his head and slogged through a puddle.

Ari stepped over it. "What about Shmuel? It is an excellent name. Brother Shmuel the prophet would be much pleased."

Baruch said nothing.

"What about Yonatan? Gift of HaShem? You could call him Yoni for short. Or Yaakov. You could name him after the *tsaddik*."

Stony silence.

"Or Dov! It is a common name in my country. My own cousin —"

"It is not done in Jerusalem, to name a child Dov."

"So start a tradition. In my country, we name boys often for animals. Ari the lion. Zev the wolf. Dov the bear." *Caleb the dog.* Ari held his breath. He would not suggest Caleb.

"It is not done here."

Ari felt frustration welling up. Baruch must come out of his ill mood. Today was a day of rejoicing. For the boy's sake, he had to shake off this evil spirit.

Evil spirit? Ari wondered what was happening to him. Since when did he believe in evil spirits? Slowly, slowly, he was becoming a man of this time. It was not a matter of intellectual capitulation. It was a matter of . . . adopting the language. One must use the prevailing words of the place.

They reached the synagogue of The Way of Rabban Yeshua and went in. Ari took out his *tefillin* and strapped them to his forehead and left arm.

He draped himself in his *tallit* and closed his eyes, waiting for Brother Shmuel the prophet to begin the prayers. Then he remembered that Shmuel had gone to the desert two days ago, the better to hear from HaShem. Ari did not know when he would return. Another man raised up his voice to pray, but it was not the same as Shmuel. Ari felt dislocated. The ritual had been changed, and it would take time to come to a new equilibrium.

Just so with Baruch. He too needed only time, and he would find the balance he had lost.

Only time.

Hana

As the hour approached for the circumcision, Hana held her son tight to her chest and prayed to HaShem that Baruch would not do something terrible. She had suffered much in the last week. Baruch also had suffered. He was a good man. She did not deserve such a good man, and yet he loved her and treated her with respect and tenderness. She must give him many sons.

Baruch did not blame her in this matter. He had once fought the wicked man and found him to have the strength of ten. No woman could be expected to fight off such a man. Hana had done no wrong, and Baruch still loved her.

But he did not love this child, this seed of the wicked man. He had not said so, but Hana knew it, as surely as she knew when a cloud hid the sun, whether she looked with her eyes or not. One could not mistake the heat of the sun or its lack. Just so, one could not mistake the heat of a man's love or its lack.

Baruch did not love his son, and yet he must name the boy. And Hana felt a great fear. Baruch was a good man, but he had a will forged of iron. He would do whatever he would do. She could not stop loving Baruch, but she could not stop loving her son either. If she must choose one or the other, she would choose . . .

Both.

Ari the Kazan might smile at that, might say that she should study a matter he called *logic*. Hana had no confidence in logic. In matters of the heart, she had nothing to learn from Ari the Kazan.

A knock at the door. Hana turned but made no move.

Baruch went to answer. Outside stood Ari the Kazan with Sister Rivka. Baruch kissed Ari and greeted Rivka with affection. Behind them waited Yaakov the *tsaddik*. Hana felt her heart surge with joy. No better man lived in Jerusalem than Yaakov, except perhaps Baruch. Yaakov was the brother of Rabban Yeshua, and some said that to see Yaakov was to see Yeshua. Others said that Yaakov was but a pale shadow of Rabban Yeshua. Hana did not care. She could see and touch Yaakov. She could not see or touch the Rabban. Therefore, she loved Yaakov, and hoped for the return of the Rabban.

Yaakov crossed the room quickly, and his eyes warmed Hana's heart. "The child." He reached out with eager hands. Hana gave him her bundle. Yaakov drew back the swaddling that covered the boy's head. His eyes gleamed with delight. "Such a beautiful child. Blessed are you, Hana, my daughter." He kissed the boy's head, then turned to Baruch. "Baruch, my son, you are a man favored by HaShem."

Baruch lowered his eyes. "Thank you, my father." He did not look like a man favored by HaShem.

Yaakov looked around the room and his face shone with joy. "If we are all gathered, we may begin. Rivka, my daughter, you will be the child's *sandakit*, yes?"

"Yes, my father." Rivka took the boy.

Hana felt happy. A boy could have no better godmother than Rivka.

Rivka kissed the child's head and said the traditional words to begin the ceremony. "*Baruch haba b'shem Adonai.*" Blessed is he who comes in the name of the Lord.

Hana and the others repeated these words.

A silver cup filled with sweet wine sat on the stone table. Rivka dipped her finger in the cup and placed a drop in the boy's mouth. He sucked on it, not knowing the pain that would soon follow. Rivka handed him next to Ari the Kazan, the *sandak*. He was a good man, and he loved Baruch and Rivka. Therefore, Hana loved him, though she found him a man of hard words.

Ari the Kazan took the child and placed him with loving care in the empty chair by the table, the chair of Eliyahu the prophet. He said a blessing over the boy and then sang a song from his far country about Eliyahu the prophet. Ari the Kazan had no skill in singing, but what matter? A baby knew nothing of music. The child's wide solemn eyes studied Ari the

Kazan. Hana wished he would smile, but Rivka had told her it was not usual for an infant to do so.

When Ari the Kazan finished his song, he lifted the child and carried him to Baruch. Baruch also did not smile, and this was not usual.

Hana found that she could not breathe.

Ari the Kazan raised the child. "What name has been chosen for the son of Baruch?"

Baruch had said nothing since the others arrived. His eyes looked with sorrow on the boy, and Hana felt her heart pierced. Better that the evil man should have killed her than that Baruch should know such sorrow.

"His name . . ." Baruch's voice sounded strangled. "His name shall be called . . . Dov."

Hana did not know what to say. Such a name — who had ever heard of such a name?

Rivka laughed out loud. "Ari, he is named after your cousin!"

Yaakov the *tsaddik* beamed. "A wonderful name! Dov ben Baruch."

But Baruch had said nothing about whose son Dov might be.

Ari the Kazan took the child and placed him on the table. As *sandak*, it would be his duty to hold the child during the cutting. He unwrapped the swaddling.

Yaakov the *tsaddik* stepped up beside him. He took from his belt a flint knife and examined its edge in the light from the window slits above. "Blessed are you, Lord our God, King of the universe, who has made us holy in your commandments, and given us the commandment of circumcision." His hands moved quickly, swift, sure strokes.

A burning ring of blood. Hana gasped.

Dov ben Baruch, son of the covenant, screamed.

Baruch

Days passed, and then weeks, and Baruch's heart was wood within him. He did not understand why HaShem did not put love for the boy into his heart. If Baruch could have made love grow, he would have done so, whatever the cost. Hana pled with him. Brother Ari gave him logic. Sister Rivka said little, but her eyes showed her anger.

All of them were right, of course. He could not reject a defenseless child, set him loose in the world as a fatherless *mamzer*. This was the son of his woman, his beloved Hana.

But it was not his son, and he could not love what he could not love.

The first month of Dov's life came to completion, and now came the day of Dov's redemption, the ceremony of *pidyon ha'ben*. Redemption of the firstborn son. A simple thing, commemorating the redemption of Yisrael by HaShem from Egypt. *We were slaves in Egypt, and HaShem bought us back, slaying the firstborn of Egypt and sparing ours.*

The ceremony required a righteous priest. Baruch had chosen Brother Ari. Baruch and Hana walked carefully down the hill toward the Temple with Brother Ari and Sister Rivka. And the boy.

Baruch knew his duty before HaShem. He felt for the lump tied up in his belt. Five silver *shekels* of the Temple. The redemption price for his son. The son of the wicked man. A reminder forever of the wound to Baruch's honor. He had failed to protect his woman.

They crossed the bridge to the western side of the Temple Mount. The outer courts buzzed with the voices of many thousand men.

Brother Ari led the way, his steps eager. Today, he would have the chief honor in the ceremony. Even an *issah* priest could receive the redemption money for *pidyon ha'ben*. He could not offer the sacrifice, but that was a minor thing. He would accept the redemption money with gladness. Brother Ari and Sister Rivka loved the boy, and it burned Baruch's heart that he himself did not. Rabban Yeshua had commanded him to love, but Baruch could not find it in himself to obey. Hana's face glowed with love for her son. Her son, not his.

They passed through the barrier into the second level of purity, then slowly ascended the steps and came into the Court of Women.

It was noon, a good time for a private ceremony in the large court. Torah did not specify where the ceremony must occur. Ari led the way to a quiet corner where they could look up through the gleaming bronze gates and see the splendor of the altar of the living God. They could not see the pump Ari had built, the monument to his dishonor.

The others waited now for Baruch. He took the boy carefully from Hana and looked into his sleeping face. He did not hate the boy. The father, yes, but not the boy. He hated the father with an everlasting hate, with the very wrath of HaShem, with the holy rage of a man dishonored. If the father still walked beneath the sun, Baruch would have pursued him to the farthest corner of the earth and avenged his dishonor. But the father had gone down to Sheol, and no man had power over those who wandered in that dark land. Baruch had only rage. Only rage.

He turned to Ari and began the ceremony. "This is the firstborn son of his mother, and HaShem has commanded us to redeem him, as it is written in the Torah." He then handed the boy to Ari the righteous priest.

Baruch knew the Torah passage by heart. He had learned it long ago, in preparation for his son. "When HaShem brings you into the land of the Canaanite as he swore to you and your fathers, then you must give every firstborn male animal to HaShem. You will redeem every firstborn donkey with a lamb, or else you will break its neck, and every firstborn son, you will redeem. And when your son shall ask, you will tell him that with a mighty hand HaShem brought us out of Egypt, out of the house of slavery. And when Pharaoh opposed him, HaShem killed every firstborn son and animal in the land of Egypt. Therefore, I sacrifice every firstborn animal and redeem every firstborn son."

Ari smiled. "And now do you choose to give me your son for service to HaShem, or do you choose to redeem him?"

It was a ritual question of course, requiring a ritual answer. Nobody ever left a son to the Temple. Not since the time of Shmuel the prophet, many hundred years ago, had a man left his son to HaShem.

Baruch reached into his belt. Pulled out the linen cloth. Unbound the five shining silver *shekels*. Looked at the son of his woman. *What do you choose, Baruch?*

His heart clawed at his throat.

Hana's eyes gleamed with sudden fear.

Baruch closed his eyes, because he knew he must not act merely from love of Hana nor from a sense of duty. To do so would be to lie. To redeem this child was to accept him as his own son forever, to declare him Dov ben Baruch.

Baruch wavered, his soul balanced on the point of a knife.

Rage whispered through him. Hana's shining eyes tore at his heart.

He waited, hoping to hear the voice of HaShem. But HaShem held silent and Baruch's heart remained cold. Baruch opened his eyes, knowing that he had only one choice.

He wrapped the *shekels* in the cloth and put them back in his belt.

Hana gasped.

Ari said, "Brother Baruch . . ."

Sister Rivka made a furious clucking sound. "Ari, stop him!"

Baruch turned around and walked away. Despair filled his heart. This thing HaShem asked was too much. He was only a man. If he could not love the boy as his own, he would not redeem him.

HaShem had no right to ask him to redeem a child he could not love.

Rivka

Months passed. Despite Hanan ben Hanan's victory in the Temple, Ari's career skyrocketed — to his own amazement. Yes, Hanan had beaten Kazan in the matter of the pump, but he had not destroyed him. Everyone knew that Ari the Kazan was a man who did not fear the mighty House of Hanan. Furthermore, Hanan had won on a technicality. By losing, Ari the Kazan gained much honor.

Soon every builder in the city came to Ari with requests for the solutions to difficult problems. Ari had more work than he could handle, more money than he could possibly want. He funneled the excess to Yaakov the *tsaddik*, who took delight in distributing alms to the neediest.

Rivka's reputation soared also. Partly because she was the woman of Ari the Kazan. Partly because she had become an excellent midwife who rarely lost a child or a woman. And partly because Midwife Marta told her vast personal network that Rivka the Kazan was a seer woman, given by HaShem to know the future.

When Rivka went to the market, women stopped their gossip to watch her walk by. Men nudged each other and whispered behind their hands. Sometimes a bold child would approach her and shyly ask Rivka to tell his or her fortune.

All of which drove Rivka nuts. What had she ever predicted? Nothing! But when she pointed this out, she saw only knowing smiles. The seer woman was modest, yes. A fitting thing in a woman.

Baruch continued to refuse to touch his son Dov, would not even look at the boy. Of course he had not abandoned Dov to the Temple. But neither would he pay the five shekels for the boy's redemption. Dov was in limbo. When Ari or Rivka tried to discuss it with Baruch, he retreated into icy silence. Hana came to Rivka often in tears over the matter. Rosh HaShanah came in with the blast of the *shofar*. Then the Ten Days of Awe, ending on Yom Kippur.

The next afternoon, Rivka went out shopping with Hana. Now past eight months pregnant, she felt like a moose, so they walked slowly. By the time they returned home, Rivka realized she was in labor. Preterm labor. Three weeks early, which meant the baby would be small but probably healthy.

The delivery took barely twelve hours. It was the sort of labor men called "an easy birth." No woman would ever say anything so foolish. The whole time, Hana hovered over Rivka, singing softly, swabbing her forehead with cool water, and encouraging her. Midwife Marta sat on the floor, a rock of calm. Rivka waited while her body labored through the night.

Now you may push, child." Marta said.

From a zone beyond all pain, Rivka pushed. It was the hardest thing she had done in her life. Hana caught the baby. Rivka waited, afraid to breathe.

"You have a beautiful little girl," Marta said.

"She is . . . wonderful!" Hana cried. "Rivkaleh, you are a mother in *Yisrael* now!"

Rivka closed her eyes and smiled. *Rachel. I'll name her for my cousin Rachel.* Exhaustion settled in around her, and for some time, the world went muzzy and indistinct. She vaguely knew that Hana cut the cord and washed baby Rachel, that she expelled the placenta, that Marta helped her back into her bed. She had seen all this many times, but . . . experiencing it was a very different game.

"Child, your husband wishes to see the baby."

Rivka let her eyes flutter open. Marta stood above her, rubbing her back, grimacing.

Hana went to the door with the baby. "Shall I call the men?"

Marta emitted a disapproving cluck. "Rivkaleh, you must cover your hair." She gathered Rivka's filthy hair into a sweaty knot, binding it inside a scarf. "Yes, Hana child, but for a very short time. Rivkaleh must feed the—"

Hana pulled open the door and called down the stairs. "Ari the Kazan! Come and see your daughter!"

Footsteps thudded up the stone steps. Hana stepped back, laughing. Ari burst into the room, his face shining. Hana gently put Rachel into his arms. A look of wonder spread across Ari's face. Rivka felt her heart leaping inside her body. She wanted to laugh, cry, shout, sing, dance.

Ari picked a path across the room with exaggerated care, looking scared to death. "Rivkaleh." His voice broke.

Rivka was so tired she could hardly think. She put her hand out. It flopped loose at the side of the bed. Ari knelt down and smothered her hand with his. He kissed Rachel's tiny, perfect, rosebud face. "Rivkaleh . . . thank you."

Rivka felt peace singing through her soul like a chorus of angels. The labor had been horrible. Terrifying. Gut-wrenching.

Wonderful.

To know this joy, to give her man a child, yes, it had been worth it.

From a great distance away, Rivka heard the sound of Hana staggering down the stairs.

Weeping softly.

PART TWO

SEER WOMAN

Spring, a.d. 59

Woe unto me from the House of Boetus!
Woe unto me from their lances!
Woe unto me from the House of Hanan!
Woe unto me from their whisperings!
Woe unto me from the House of Qathros!
Woe unto me from their reed pens!
Woe unto me from the House of Ishmael ben Phiabi!
Woe unto me from their fists!
For they are high priests
And their sons are treasurers
And their sons-in-law are overseers
And their servants beat the people with clubs!

— Lament of *Abba* Saul,
Babylonian Talmud, *Pesachim*, 57a

TWELVE

Rivka

When I give him another son, then he will love the first also," Hana said, stubbornness etched across her pinched face.

"Of course." Rivka closed her eyes and leaned back in her chair. As far as she knew, there were only two rocking chairs in the world, and she owned both of them. Rivka didn't know what Ari had paid for them, except that he ordered them specially from the best wood craftsman in Jerusalem, and the sum was outrageous. And worth it.

It was a fine spring day two weeks before *Pesach*. Rivka and Hana sat in the two rocking chairs, holding their babies, talking. As always before one of the feasts, the air felt heavy with dread. In the streets, there was talk of discontent with Rome, of trouble between Jew and Gentile in Caesarea, of bad blood between the feisty Galileans and the irritable Samaritans.

Rivka desperately wanted to get out, to find out what was going to happen next. Fat chance of that. Between mothering Rachel, midwifing difficult pregnancies across the city, and commiserating with Hana, Rivka had no time for politics.

This thing with Baruch had gone on way too long. He still refused to touch the boy, barely looked at him. Baruch admitted he was wrong, but claimed he could not love what he could not love. All of that would change, Hana insisted, when she could give Baruch a second son. Then love would awaken in his heart, and surely some of that love would spill over onto her firstborn son.

That was Hana's plan, anyway. Apparently, Baruch was cooperating fully, whether he knew her motives or not. Rivka thought it was only a matter of time. Hana was fertile and Baruch eager, and that was pretty much a guarantee of success, wasn't it?

Rivka smiled over her precious Rachel, a small baby with black hair, deep chocolate brown eyes, and a smile that could melt steel. Dov had grown into the fattest baby Rivka had ever seen. Not obese fat. Big-boned fat. He had inherited Damien's thick build and Hana's gorgeous good looks. His blond-at-birth hair had darkened a shade to a light brown. He had laughing eyes the color of champagne and a quick smile. A lady-killer under construction, as Rivka's father would have said.

The door downstairs slammed. Footsteps pounded up the stairs. Ari burst into the sitting room, his face twisted with rage. "There has been a massacre in Caesarea."

Rivka gasped. Rachel opened her eyes and started crying. Dov belched magnificently. Hana began rocking faster.

Rivka leaned forward, shushing Rachel gently. "Tell me what happened."

Ari paced the length of the room, clutching at his beard. "I heard it in the market square near Herod's Palace. A merchant convoy just arrived with the news. Three days ago, there was a riot in Caesarea. Apparently many *goyim* live there."

"You knew that, didn't you?" Rivka rocked Rachel gently. "Caesarea was a Gentile settlement before King Herod made it his capital. They called it Strato's Tower. It's probably got more Syrians living there than Jews."

Ari's eyes narrowed. "How was I to know that? You are the one having the photographic memory."

Rivka leaned back, stung. "Eidetic memory. But—"

"And with your eidetic memory, I suppose you knew there was to be a riot but conveniently forgot to tell me?" His tone was harsh, sarcastic.

Rivka wondered what she had done wrong. "Ari, please. I know only a little of what's going to happen, and the dates are fuzzy. Josephus says there were some riots in Caesarea about this time. At one point, the Jews got the upper hand on the Gentiles, and Governor Felix sent in the army to cool things down. A bunch of Jews got killed. That's all I—"

Ari slapped his open palm against the wall. "A *bunch*? You call them a *bunch* when over a hundred of our brothers were murdered?"

It hit Rivka's heart like a hammer. Josephus hadn't said how many. Only that the episode got Governor Felix in a lot of trouble. "A ... hundred?" Her voice came out in a squeak.

"Yes, a hundred." Anguish shone in Ari's eyes. "Murdered by the man appointed to keep order."

Tears ran down Rivka's cheeks onto Rachel's face. She hadn't known. Hadn't seen it coming. Josephus was so ... brief. A paragraph or two. Rivka brushed madly at her eyes. "Thank God Felix won't be in office much longer. Nero's going to kick him out."

"When?" Ari knelt in front of Rivka's chair, his face eager. "What else is to happen?"

Rivka wondered what had happened to her dispassionate physicist. Did he think he could change the events to come? Hadn't he lectured her on the impossibility of all that? She mentally opened her copy of Josephus. "I'm afraid there isn't much in the books. This is the spring of the year 59. Felix is going to make the two sides send delegations to Nero. The Jews will lose, but Nero will replace Felix with Governor Festus."

"That is all? Nothing more for this year?" Ari clutched the arms of Rivka's chair.

"Not in Josephus." Rivka switched to the New Testament. "The new Governor Festus will hold a trial for Renegade Saul this July in Caesarea. Oh, and Tacitus says Nero's going to murder his mother in March. Maybe that's happened already. Are we in March or April? Anyway, Rome is going to wig out, especially after the eclipse — they'll think it's a sign."

"Eclipse? What eclipse?"

"The eclipse of the sun. Let me think. I've got a date for it — April 30 in the Roman calendar. I don't know when that'll be in the Jewish calendar."

"The end of the month Nisan," Ari said. "Two weeks after *Pesach*. A month from now."

Rivka shrugged. "I'll take your word for it."

"It is certain, if your April 30 is accurate. A total eclipse?"

Rivka concentrated. *Ninety-one percent.* That was the number she remembered. That was a total eclipse, or so close you couldn't tell the difference. "Yes, it was total."

Hana had been following this exchange with a bewildered look. "What is this word — *eclipse?*"

"When the sun goes dark for a time," Rivka said.

"And you know this will happen after *Pesach?*" Fear lit up Hana's eyes.

"Hana, there's nothing to be afraid of. The moon passes in front of the sun for a few minutes. Darkness covers the earth. The birds go to bed and the . . . cows come home. Then it's all over."

"I have heard of this thing," Hana said. "Once in Babylon this happened, and the people fled to the temple of an idol to call on his name. Many ten thousand were trampled."

Rivka narrowed her eyes. That must be an exaggeration. Tens of thousands? No way. She'd never read of any such thing in Babylon. What did Hana know about Babylon? For her, it was a distant land of fable and legend, a galaxy far, far away.

Ari began pacing again. "Rivka, you know for certain that there will be a total eclipse on April 30?"

Rivka nodded. She never forgot a date. And the eclipse had been widely seen. There had been reports in both Rome and Armenia. One source said it was also visible in Jerusalem.

Ari leaned against the wall and twisted a strand of his beard between his fingers. "Does your Josephus mention any panic here in Jerusalem on account of an eclipse?"

Rivka shook her head. "He doesn't even mention the eclipse. If there was a panic, I'm sure he would have. That's just the kind of thing he'd report in every lurid detail. He's living here now—you may very well see him every day without even knowing it. He'd be about twenty."

Ari's face relaxed. "Blessed be HaShem. For a moment, I feared there would be trouble."

Hana's eyes were very bright. "Rivka, if this thing is to happen to the sun, you must warn the people."

Rivka looked down at her daughter. Rachel slept at peace, secure and content. Because Rivka kept watch over her. Rivka had an obligation to watch over her child. Was she likewise obligated to her city? If so, how far did that obligation go? She wasn't a prophet, whatever people thought. She didn't have a pipeline to God. All she had was a few books locked away in her brain—a few pitiful snatches of fact, easily misinterpreted.

But an eclipse. That was pretty close to a slam dunk, wasn't it? Astronomy was astronomy, and you could compute the position of the moon to the inch, right? Somebody could. Somebody had. That eclipse was coming on April 30, around three in the afternoon. Ready or not.

Rivka began rocking, feeling a surge of excitement in her veins. "Ari, maybe there's a reason nobody was killed."

His eyes narrowed to slits. "What reason?"

"Maybe the same reason Saul of Tarsus is still alive." Rivka gave him her biggest smile. "Because dear little Rivka Meyers came prancing through a wormhole and changed something."

"Rivka, you changed nothing. All that you did merely ensured that it would happen as you had read in your books."

"Exactly!" Rivka leaned forward. "Don't you think — "

"Rivka." Ari gave her an exasperated look. "You can change nothing."

Rivka stood up and laid Rachel in her cradle. She turned and put her hands on her hips. "Ari, you're going to have to decide what you want. A hundred people are dead in Caesarea, and I did nothing to prevent it, because I didn't know. And you yelled at me — "

"You could have done nothing." Ari came and put his arms around her. "Rivka, I am sorry for shouting — "

"But for this eclipse, I know everything. I know the event. I know the date. I even know the time. The books say around 3:00 P.M."

Ari studied her, his eyes skeptical. "What do you wish to do?"

Rivka tried to think. What could she do, anyway? "Warn people. Just . . . let them know what's going to happen. So they won't be afraid when the lights go out."

Hana rocked quietly. "All will believe the seer woman, Ari the Kazan. The people believe your woman. If she says this thing will happen, they will trust in her word."

Still Ari looked uncertain.

Rivka clutched his arm. "Please, Ari. What harm can it do?"

Ari's eyes turned inward, distant. "None, of course. You will change nothing, and we know that no harm came of the eclipse."

Rivka put her arms around him and kneaded the small of his back. "So . . . I can warn the people?"

Ari gave a deep sigh. "Yes, but it is foolishness. You may do as you will, but nothing will come of it."

Berenike

After her midday meal, Queen Berenike retired to her chambers, pleading a headache. She had no headache, but she desperately needed to be rid of her stupid servant girls. She could not get rid of Shlomi, her principal servant — even during a midday nap, propriety required that she have at least one servant attending her.

But that was fine, because her plan required Shlomi.

Shlomi was Jewish and unmarried and the servant of the queen, and therefore she wore a costume that covered her thoroughly — a loose-fitting tunic of fine bleached wool, a cloak of thick goat's hair to keep out the late spring chill, and a veil that gave no hint of her face or her hair. Most important, Shlomi was the exact same size as Berenike.

That was the only way in which Shlomi resembled her. Shlomi was fifteen years old and still unmarried. Berenike was on the wrong side of thirty and had been widowed twice. Shlomi had a plain and simple face and dull wits. Berenike was beautiful — she could pass for a woman ten years younger — and she had the razor mind of her papa, Marcus Julias Agrippa, also called Herod, formerly the Great King of Judea, Samaria, Perea, and parts of the Golan, and for the past fifteen years, dead. While he lived, Papa had been the best player in the world at the only game that counted.

Power.

The game Berenike loved more than life. It was simply ... *delicious* to exercise naked power. If only she were a man! Then the world would see what a player she was. Or if only her brother Agrippa had a decent level of ambition. He was king of a small and insignificant territory to the north. Not the Great King of Judea. Not yet. Agrippa was happy — actually happy — living like a swine, eating, drinking, keeping company with empty-headed women. Agrippa had little interest in the great game, other than to keep the status quo.

Whereas Berenike loved the game, adored it, lived to win, hated to lose. If she were a man, she would already be ruler of the world. Therefore, HaShem had made her a woman — strictly to make it a fair fight for all the others.

If she were to win the great game, Berenike needed another husband. Her first had died untimely in his youth. Her second — crusty old Uncle Herod — had died a couple of years later than Berenike would have liked, leaving her with two sons, a modest fortune, and no throne. People still called her Queen Berenike, recognizing her status as the widow of a king, but it was an empty title without lands and subjects. And without power. She must marry again, as soon as possible, but her prospects grew dimmer each year, and Agrippa was doing nothing to find a suitable match for her.

Berenike had now lived ten years without a husband, and that was extremely inconvenient, because this morning she had admitted to herself that she was pregnant.

Pregnant! Ridiculous! And her a mistress of every herb, flower, root, bark, and stem known to the civilized world. An expert in poison, she took a small dose of arsenic daily to build her tolerance. In her chambers she had a chest full of potions against pregnancy. Silphium, from northern Africa. Rue. Leukoinos. Pennyroyal.

Any of these should have prevented this unfortunate occurrence. But they had not. Now she needed an herb not found in her chest, and she must have it today. One must act quickly in such matters. She must buy the herb, and she must do it in secret. One word of this pregnancy, and all would be lost. *All.* A woman could survive many evil chances in the great game, but not scandal.

At the door of her chambers Berenike turned to her servants and put on an appropriate pained scowl. "I shall sleep for three hours. I require Shlomi to attend me. The rest of you are free to do as you will, only do not create a noise!"

The servants bowed and backed away with terror in their eyes. The fools would not disturb her even if the palace burned.

Shlomi opened the door and Berenike swept through into her chambers. She marched to her window and pulled back the ivory shutters. The Temple Mount spread out before her at a distance of little more than a furlong. The outer courts swarmed with many ten thousand of her people. Foolish people, yes, but her people. They loved her, their beautiful, wise, and learned Queen Berenike. None of them would guess that she could possibly be pregnant by her own brother. They must never know.

Today, she could not risk being seen. Her veil would not hide her identity if she went out surrounded by palace bodyguards. Berenike turned to Shlomi. "Take off your clothes."

Shlomi gasped. She was a modest little fool, and had perhaps never undressed in front of anybody.

Berenike had never dressed herself in her life, and therefore felt no shame in being seen naked. And furthermore, she had no time to waste. She snapped her fingers. "Quickly, quickly. I need your clothes. You may wear something of mine while I go out."

"Out?" Shlomi gaped at her. "Where are we going?"

"*I* am going out. *You* are not. Help me take off this *tunica*." Berenike turned and waited. Shlomi's hands undraped the long white *tunica* from her shoulders. Berenike turned. "Now quickly, I need your clothes. I have a medical problem which requires immediate attention. This morning I felt a burning pain when I passed water. I require an herb from the market, and it must be of the finest quality."

"But . . . it is not fitting for you to go out alone." Shlomi's black eyes showed disbelief.

Berenike let anger creep into her voice. "I will be the judge of what is fitting. Now off! Off! I need your clothes. I will *not* have the whole palace gossiping on my medical condition. And they will — count on it! If I took one of those wretched German bodyguards, he would find out why, and then tongues would be wagging everywhere. Now you will take off your clothes or I will sell you to an Arab!"

Shlomi's face blanched. She removed her veil, then her hair scarf, then her cloak. Timidly, she pulled her body-length tunic up over her head.

"Quickly!" Berenike said. "Dress me and then find something in my closet to cover up with."

Shlomi dressed her, then scurried to the closet. Berenike inspected herself in a large polished brass mirror. It was the best quality, but even so the reflection showed only a dim and distorted image. She had never seen her own face. What a tragedy that others could admire her beauty but she could not. Berenike peered through the veil at her image. The woman in the mirror looked like Shlomi, but could she trust the mirror? The illusion must be perfect, or she would be out of the game forever.

Shlomi returned in the cheapest garment Berenike owned, a sleeping tunic of fine linen with silk ruffles. Berenike turned in a circle. "Do I look like a slave girl?"

Shlomi nodded, her eyes wide.

"Very well, then. Expect me back in an hour. If anyone asks for me, you will inform them that I am overcome with weariness, that I am *not* to be disturbed, even if *Mashiach* himself has the rudeness to appear while I am indisposed."

Berenike took a few *dinars* from the coin purse on her dresser and strode to the door. She turned to give one last glare at Shlomi. "Is that clear?"

Shlomi's mouth hung open, and fear haunted her eyes.

"Is something wrong? Quickly! I need haste."

"Mistress, you are . . . dressed as a slave girl, but . . . you walk as a queen."

Berenike's heart skipped. Of course. That was foolish of her. A slave girl did not carry herself with her head held high and her shoulders back. A slave girl behaved . . . how? She must find the persona of a slave, or she would lose this round of the game. Berenike closed her eyes and called to memory the night Papa died.

Papa had been a man, a real man. A liar, a scoundrel, a gambler, a rogue, a player. In short, a Herod, and the best man who ever lived. The family spent years moving from city to city around the empire, with Papa always one step ahead of angry creditors, always charming new ones with tales of the rewards for his friends on the day he came into his kingdom. Papa could spin stories out of nothing, a warm, funny man, with the charm of a puppy dog, the luck of a fox, and the dazzling beautiful looks of all the Herod men.

Born rich, Papa squandered his inheritance young. When his money ran short, he borrowed and wasted the fortunes of his friends. When his friends ran short, he took charity from his family. When his family ran short, he found honest work as an influence peddler, from which he advanced to fraud, and finally to treason against Caesar. For no good reason at all, he wound up in prison. And from prison, of course, he became the Great King. Papa had the luck of the fox.

As King Marcus Julias Herod Agrippa, Papa built, taxed, entertained, taxed, squandered, taxed, and generally feasted on the very guts of his kingdom with all the cunning he had acquired over a long life of gluttony. Though he had the ill fate to be born and sliced a Jew, he lived the life of a Roman aristocrat.

Despite all this, his Jewish subjects loved him and his Gentile subjects hated him, which only showed that nine parts of the world were fools. Perhaps all ten parts, excepting those few of the family Herod.

Then one day at the age of fifty-four, Papa's luck finally ran short. He took ill suddenly and made a horrible and dramatic exit from the great game. It had to be arsenic — all the symptoms pointed to it — but nothing was ever proved.

The night he died, Papa's enemies stormed the palace in Caesarea. Berenike was sixteen and between husbands, so she was living with the family. A mob of evil men surrounded the palace, waving clubs, throwing stones, brandishing torches. The family servants and palace guard fought them off, but it was a near thing. If they had broken through . . .

Berenike caught her breath and imagined the scene.

If they had broken through, Berenike and her sisters would have been hauled out in the street, stripped naked, abused by wicked men for sport, and auctioned off as slaves. She would have been bought by some leering, horrible *goy* who would take her home and subject her to a life of endless misery until she wept for mercy and begged HaShem for death and—

Shlomi gasped and fell on her knees at Berenike's feet, clutching her. Berenike looked down at her, annoyed. "Whatever *is* the matter?"

Shlomi's eyes glistened. "You . . . changed, mistress. You turned yourself into a . . . slave. It was horrible! Please, never do that again! I was so . . . frightened."

Excellent, then. She had found the persona she needed. And it would be well to remember that if anyone learned of her pregnancy, this very persona might be her fate.

"Stand back." Berenike put on the heart of a wretched slave girl and opened the door and walked up the hallway and down the broad stairway and past the leering German guards at the palace door and through the courtyard and out of the gates . . . into a world she had never seen before — the world of a servant, alone in the vile streets.

Her heart leaped for joy within her. This would be such *fun!*

THIRTEEN

Hana

Hana woke at Dov's first cry. The night was still young. Baruch lay beside her, asleep, unmoved. He was a good man, a kind man. He treated her with tenderness, gentleness. If only he could love Dov, then she would be happy. Yes, then she would be happy.

Hana rolled over and pulled Dov to herself. His fat, eager mouth tickled her, and then . . . then, yes, her milk began. She felt the strong tug of his tender lips. It was a good feeling. This child of her body needed her, wanted her, loved her. He was a good child, and her heart felt full with the joy of him. His fine, pale hair smelled of milk and baby sweat and love. Someday, Dov would grow to be a tall man, a strong man, a follower of Rabban Yeshua. A man like his father.

A man like me. The voice whispered from a dark corner of her mind.

Hana flinched. The shade of the wicked man had come back.

He will be a man like me.

Hana clutched at her son. No, she would not allow him to be like the wicked man. Dov would become like his father, Baruch. A good man, a —

I am his father. Baruch has rejected him, and I will have my son.

No. Hana squeezed Dov tighter to herself. He stopped suckling and cried out. Hana felt the slow dribble of milk slide down her breast. She stroked Dov's head softly. "Peace, little bear. Peace."

Dov found her again and began suckling with greedy joy.

I will have my son and I will have you.

Hot tears formed in Hana's eyes. No. She would never allow the shade of the wicked man to possess her. Rabban Yeshua would not allow it. The wicked man had done evil to her once, but from that had come a good thing. Dov was a good child, and the wicked man could not touch him. Never, ever, ever.

You filthy woman. You are nothing but a zonah.

Hana blinked against the tears, but many rolled down her cheeks. She was not a *zonah*. She was a righteous woman, a follower of the Rabban, a daughter of HaShem. The wicked man spoke lies, and she must not listen. He knew that the way to her heart was through rage. She would not give in to this rage pressing in on her. Never again. She must go to Yaakov the *tsaddik*, and he would pray the words of peace and silence the wicked man's voice forever. HaShem would listen to the prayer of the Righteous One, Yaakov, brother of the Rabban.

Long after Dov slept, Hana lay awake, guarding her heart.

Baruch lay sleeping.

Berenike

At midnight, Berenike stood at her stone table grinding oleander flowers with a stone spoon in a stone bowl to make a pessary. Stone, always stone, in this city addicted to ritual purity. According to the rabbis, stone was not susceptible to any kind of impurity. But the rabbis would not approve of what she was making.

Berenike added water to the crushed flowers a little at a time until the mixture became a wet paste. When it was ready, she put it all on a little square of linen, drew the corners together, and bound it up with fine silk thread. She stared at it for a moment, wondering if the poison would be too strong.

Berenike flinched. She did not know how strong it should be because she did not know how far this pregnancy had advanced. Perhaps because of her daily arsenic dosage, her monthly *niddah* uncleanness came at irregular intervals, sometimes two or three months apart. She had become sure of her pregnancy only this morning in the bath. Pressing very hard on her belly, she had felt a tiny lump in her womb. In a few weeks it would be large enough for Shlomi to see. Weeks after that, all would see.

Therefore, Berenike must act without hesitation. She regretted giving in to Agrippa's advances, but regrets now were useless. If she did nothing, her sin would be discovered. But before that, before the scandal could ruin the family's honor, Agrippa would have her discreetly killed. He was enough of a Herod to kill his own sister — the proof was that he was enough of a Herod to seduce her. She had been a fool to give in.

Now, Berenike had no choice. Yes, it was a sin to poison the child of her own womb, but if she did nothing she would die and the child also. If she wished to live, the child must die. That was a decision any Herod could make instantly.

But she must be careful. The poison would cause her heart to race faster and faster. At the right time, she must pull the pessary out by the thread. If she waited too long, she would be forced to take another poison to slow down her heart. That would be dangerous — two poisons in her body, fighting each other. She must risk it for the sake of the game.

Berenike checked the knot again, tugging the thread to be sure. If it broke, she would have no way to remove the pessary and she would die. The knot held secure. She tiptoed back into her sleeping chamber. Tonight was the new moon, and only starlight filtered in through the windows. Shlomi lay asleep in a small bed, dead to the world. Shlomi always slept deeply — one reason Berenike kept her as principal servant.

Berenike sat quietly on her bed. It was knee-high, constructed of ivory, and outrageously expensive. She pulled her legs inside the blankets and lay back, feeling her heart beating madly. The pessary clutched in her right hand felt damp. Already, its poison was leaking out. She must use it now.

If HaShem did not approve of how she played the game, he should not have made her a woman.

Baruch

Baruch awoke before dawn, as always. He rolled over to admire Hana. HaShem was good, very good. Not one man in ten thousand had a woman so beautiful. Brother Ari had Sister Rivka, a good woman in some ways, but Baruch did not understand what Brother Ari saw in her. HaShem did not intend that a woman should be too intelligent, nor too bold, nor too opinionated. She was all three, and yet Brother Ari loved her anyway. A fine man, but lacking sense.

Hana lay with her arm around the boy. She loved the boy and that was natural. He was her own flesh. Baruch hooked his arm over Hana, reaching for the boy.

He felt the boy's hot breath on his fingers. Slowly, slowly, he lowered one finger toward the fat cheek. Closer. Closer.

Contact.

Baruch jerked back his hand, his finger burning like fire. Always the same, every morning. Like fire.

Why, HaShem? I do not hate this boy, but neither do I love him. Why does his very touch scorch me?

But the heavens held silent. It had been so since the birth of the boy. HaShem had closed Baruch's ears and he could no longer hear the Spirit. The evil man had wounded him, cutting him off from the woman of his heart and the voice of the Spirit.

Baruch closed his eyes against the pain that drove a spear through his heart. Brother Ari had been right and he had been wrong on that day when the boy was born. There *was* evil in this world — evil incomprehensible — and one could not answer it with any wisdom known to man. If evil had a reason, it would no longer be evil, but merely the natural course of things, like Brother Ari's electron. This electron was ordained by HaShem and therefore it was good. Evil was not ordained by HaShem. One day, all evil would face the wrath of HaShem, when Yeshua the *Mashiach* returned to heal the hurts of the world. Let it come, the wrath of HaShem. Let it come quickly.

Baruch felt a deep sigh shudder through him. Soon dawn would arrive. Before then, he must go with Brother Ari to the morning prayers. He kissed Hana's ear and then rolled out of bed, shivering in the chill.

He dressed quickly in his four-cornered tunic and *tzitzit*, put on his *tefillin* and cloak and sandals, took his *tallit*, and went out into the street. Brother Ari met him on the way and they continued on toward the synagogue in their customary silence. Baruch could not bear to walk in silence this morning. "Brother Ari, you will explain to me again the theorem of this man Gödel."

Brother Ari gave him a questioning look.

Baruch pressed on. "It is a hard matter, this theorem. I do not think your Gödel was a happy man."

Brother Ari tugged at his beard. "Perhaps an example this time. Let me think." They walked in silence for a few paces, then Brother Ari said, "True or false: 'Brother Baruch cannot prove this statement true.'"

Baruch stared at him. What sort of foolishness was this? "Of course I cannot prove such a thing true. How would I prove it true?"

"Then you have just proved it true, yes?"

Baruch thought for a moment. "Yes, I suppose that I have." A little shock ran through him. "But ... the sentence says that I *cannot* prove it true!" He laughed out loud. "Brother Ari, you are making a joke on me! The sentence is not true!"

Brother Ari gave a crafty smile. "So you have proved it false?"

"Yes." Baruch hesitated. "But ... if the sentence is false, then it is naturally impossible that I could prove it true. As it says. And therefore ... it must be true! But if it is true, then how can I have proved it, since it asserts that I cannot?"

Brother Ari laughed out loud. "You see the paradox? You can prove it neither true nor false. Your logic cannot solve this puzzle."

Baruch shook his head. "It is a trick, then. A trick of logic. Brother Ari, you are overmuch concerned with this logic. Not all things must be either true or false."

"No, you are wrong." Brother Ari gave a deep sigh. "You have not yet understood the depths of the matter. Logic has failed *you* in this matter, but it has not failed *me* — because I easily prove it true. You can never prove the statement true. Therefore, it is true. I prove this with no effort, and you understand my proof completely, and yet even with this knowledge, you yourself *still* cannot prove the statement true or false. And a like condition holds for me and for any man or machine or system of thought or mathematical theory. That is the crux of Gödel's Theorem."

Baruch grappled with that for the rest of the walk to the synagogue. Yes, it was all very simple. No, he did not understand it. And yet he did. The thing was very disturbing after all. There was a knot in this thing called logic. For each man, a separate knot. Brother Ari could solve Baruch's knot, but not his own. And likewise, Baruch could solve Brother Ari's, but not his own. Did HaShem also have a knot too hard to solve? No, that was not possible.

They arrived just behind Yaakov the *tsaddik* and slipped into place. The hot smell of men filled the room. Baruch put on his *tallit* and closed his eyes and waited.

All was silence for a time. Someone began praying aloud. Others joined in. "*Baruch, Attah Adonai, Eloheinu, v'Elohei avoteinu ...*" Blessed are you, Lord our God and God of our fathers ...

Baruch loved the words, the cadence of the *Amidah*, the standing prayer. He had prayed it every day since he became a man and he would pray it until he died. As every day, he waited, but the Spirit did not fall on him today. It had not fallen yesterday, nor the week before, nor the month before. Not since the birth of the boy.

When the prayers ended, Baruch remained standing with his eyes shut, wishing for a touch, just one touch of HaShem. He heard men talking, then an awkward silence.

"Brother Baruch." Ari put a hand on his elbow. "There is a man here with a boil on his neck."

Baruch opened his eyes. Of course, there would be someone. Every day, someone.

The man was a stranger, a neighbor of Brother Yosi. A small knot of men had gathered around him. Baruch stepped forward and the others made room for him.

"My name is called Baruch."

"My name is called Yohanan."

Baruch examined the large boil on Yohanan's neck. It had already begun to fester, its livid red center swollen with pus. Baruch put his hand on the sore. Other men put their hands on top of his. Brother Ari put his hand on the man's shoulder. Yaakov the *tsaddik* came up behind Baruch.

From habit, Baruch waited. The Spirit should come now and tell him what to pray and then he would pray it and the man would be healed. That was the way HaShem had ordained it.

But he was deaf to the Spirit. Because of the boy. Baruch sighed. What had once been easy had become the most difficult thing in the world.

Men around him began praying quietly. One prayed against an evil spirit. Another against a curse. A third begged HaShem to remove his hand of affliction. All of these were wrong—they would not work on this kind of illness. Baruch did not know how he knew this, but he knew. He waited, helpless.

Nothing happened.

Yaakov the *tsaddik* began whispering something. Baruch strained to listen. Yaakov was a righteous man, the holiest man in the city, but he had no gift of healing. "I command you to be healed in the name of Yeshua the *Mashiach*."

Nothing happened.

And yet Baruch knew Yaakov had heard true. A man knows when he knows. Baruch cleared his throat. "I command you to be healed in the name of Yeshua the *Mashiach*."

A shock pulsed through them all, as sudden and sharp as a blow to the nerve at a man's elbow. The men lifted their hands, their faces lighting up with surprise and fear and delight. When all hands had been removed, Baruch also lifted his hand.

The boil looked as red and angry as before.

"By this time tomorrow, it will be healed," Baruch said. He knew it was true, but he did not know how he knew.

The man, Yohanan, looked skeptical. Brother Yosi took his arm. "We will go. The Spirit was here — did you feel it?"

The other men nodded. "Yes, the Spirit was here. You will certainly be healed."

Baruch turned to Brother Ari. "Did you feel the Spirit?"

Brother Ari gave him an enigmatic smile. "Did you?"

A deep well of sadness opened in Baruch's heart. "No."

Ari

On the way home, Ari asked Baruch the same question he had asked last evening. "Will the eclipse cause a panic?"

"I do not know. I have never seen an eclipse."

"But what do you think?"

"I think . . ." Baruch hesitated. "Please do not be offended, Brother Ari, but I think a few moments of darkness is little to fear. Women may be afraid, but not a man."

"That is because you have never seen an eclipse."

"Have you seen one?"

Ari smiled. "No, but I have heard reports. It is a solemn moment. Darkness sweeps across the land like a flood. When the moon fully covers the sun, one may safely look at the sun, and it appears as a deep hole in the sky, from which tongues of flame shoot out."

Baruch shuddered. "Then the people will panic when they see it. Sister Rivka is certain of this eclipse?"

"She read about it in a book. It was seen as far as Rome, and the people there saw it as a portent of evil — as vengeance of the gods on account of Caesar murdering his mother."

"I have not heard that Caesar murdered his mother."

Ari flinched at Baruch's skeptical tone. "You think Rivka is lying?"

"Brother Ari, you must understand. I love Sister Rivka. I believe that you and she come from a far country, from a far time. I believe she speaks true. But she is a woman, and a man does not base his actions on the word of a woman."

Ari frowned. "The people hold her to be a seer woman. They will believe her."

"Brother Ari, you are not listening. Yes, the people will believe her. No, they will not follow her advice. It is not honorable to follow a woman."

Honor. Foolish honor. Ari spun on his friend. "Baruch, that is *meshugah*. A man is no better—"

"Please!" Baruch's voice shook with impatience. "I am not interested in what you will tell me about the customs in your far country. This is Jerusalem. The customs here are the customs here. You yourself show little interest in the words of your woman. How should you expect others?"

Ari stared at him. "I believe her. But I do not know what is the right thing to do. This meddling—"

"You are certain of this eclipse?" Baruch studied him with intense eyes. "You know with certainty it will come on the next new moon?"

"With all my heart."

"Then it will cause a panic unless you warn the people."

"I will permit Rivka to warn—"

"No, not Sister Rivka. You. Brother Ari, if you have a weakness, it is that you fear to act. HaShem has given you great gifts, but you wish always to stand aside and think more. You fear to make a mistake, so you do nothing. If you say nothing, if you merely allow Sister Rivka to speak, then the people will say that Ari the Kazan does not believe his woman. Therefore, why should they?"

"What should I do?"

"If you believe your woman, then act as if her words are true. But do not do nothing. To do nothing is to shout that your woman is a fool and a liar."

Ari thought about that for a long time. Finally he cleared his throat. "Perhaps you are correct, Brother Baruch."

Baruch smiled.

"But on another point, you are wrong." Ari stopped. This might make Baruch very angry, but . . . he had to say it. "You are much mistaken if you think the word of a woman is nothing."

"I . . ." Baruch's face hardened. "Brother Ari, I have never heard a woman say anything that I did not know."

Ari nodded. "Very well, my friend. We can remedy that. Come with me."

Rivka

Rivka paced back and forth, patting Rachel's back. "Come on, sweetheart, burp for Mama. You can do it."

Downstairs, the door opened. "Rivkaleh!"

Two pairs of feet on the stairway. Rivka realized her hair wasn't covered.

Ari burst through the doorway. "Rivka, Baruch and I would like —"

"Ari, my hair!"

Baruch came in behind Ari, took one look at Rivka, and backed out.

Rivka handed Ari the baby. "Here, burp Rachel."

Ari put Rachel on his shoulder and began patting her, his big hands thump-thump-thumping on her back.

Rivka grabbed a head-covering and expertly coiled her hair into it. *Good grief, this is too natural. I've become one of them.* "Brother Baruch, you may come in now!"

Baruch came in, his face burning. "Sister Rivka, please forgive me."

"Of course, and you will forgive me also, Brother Baruch."

Ari was pacing now. "Rivka, I have been thinking on the matter of the eclipse."

Rivka sat down in her rocking chair. "It's okay, Ari, I realized this morning that it's not going to be much use. Nobody's going to listen to me. They call me the seer woman, but what have I ever foreseen? I'm a big fraud. When I tell them the sun will disappear, who's going to believe me?"

"They will believe you, because I will vouch for your word," Ari said.

"Really?" Rivka's heart did a double back-flip. "You'd . . . do that for me?"

Ari shrugged. "You should thank Brother Baruch."

Rivka gave Baruch a big smile, then caught herself and looked back at Ari. "Please thank Brother Baruch for me."

Ari continued patting Rachel's back. "Now, perhaps you will do a small favor for Brother Baruch."

"Of course. Just name it." Rivka wondered what was going on.

Ari pointed to the tall stone writing table. "Brother Baruch, there is papyrus and a reed pen. Make ink and write."

Baruch went to the table and took a reed pen. He sharpened it with a knife, then took a small cube of dried ink and mixed it with water into a gummy paste. At last, he was ready.

Rachel burped. Ari let out a little yelp. A fair amount of Rachel's breakfast oozed down his back. Rivka hurried for a rag to wipe up the mess. When she finished, Ari handed the baby back to her. "Please, you will tell Brother Baruch what you know."

"I will . . . what?" Rivka sat down in her rocking chair and stared at him.

Ari began pacing. "You have a reputation as a seer woman. Based on what? On the word of Midwife Marta, based on the word of Gamaliel, based on the word of Rabbi Yohanan ben Zakkai, based on nothing."

"It was something," Rivka said.

"Very little," Ari said. "Rivka, you are effectively a prophet, yes?"

"No."

"You have been given to know the future. That is the function of a prophet."

"Ari, you've got it way wrong. A prophet is not a fore-teller, he's a forth-teller. The prophet speaks forth for HaShem. Once in a while, a prophet makes a prediction, but that's not the point. If a prophet fore-tells, it's in order to warn against a wrong action, or to persuade in favor of a right action. Yes, I know the future, but no, I don't speak for HaShem. I'm not a prophet and I don't want to be one."

"And perhaps that is what qualifies you to be one," Ari said. "Moshe did not wish to be a prophet. Nor Isaiah, nor Jeremiah. HaShem called them to be prophets. If he calls you, where is your right to refuse?"

Rivka stared at him. Ari had come a long way in two years. But he was still off-base. "Ari, you aren't getting it. HaShem hasn't called me to be a prophet. He's allowed me to know a few things that are going to happen."

"Then please, you will tell Brother Baruch some of those things."

"Why?" Rivka began rocking in her chair.

Ari tugged at his beard. "Because . . . it will serve as objective validation. There will come a day when men ask for proof that HaShem has given you to know the future. They will ask for more than the word of a woman. Then Brother Baruch will vouch for you. It may save many lives on such a day, to have a man who will swear that you speak true."

"Sister Rivka?" Baruch looked directly at her, blushing fiercely, and held her gaze. "Please. I ask you as a . . . friend."

Rivka felt her pulse racing. A man who looked a woman in the eye, who spoke directly to her, who admitted to having her for a friend. Ari wasn't the only person who'd come a long way. Rivka peered down at Rachel's sleeping face. *And I also have come a long way. A wife. A mother in* Yisrael. *But a prophet? That's the last thing I want to be. Sticks and stones will break your bones, even if you're a prophet.*

Especially if you're a prophet.

But I'm not a prophet. Just a plain old garden-variety seer woman.

Rivka knew she was probably going to regret this, but . . . what else could she do?

She focused on Rachel and began rocking. "Let's begin with the high priests, then we'll do the governors. The high priest is now Hananyah ben Nadavayah. After him will come Ishmael ben Phiabi, then Yoseph Kabi, then Hanan ben Hanan, who will rule for only three months . . ."

Hanan, who will kill a great man — Yaakov the tsaddik *— and go unpunished.* Unshed tears burned in Rivka's heart.

Baruch's pen moved furiously as he scratched down the names. Ari paced back and forth, a tense smile on his face. Rivka rocked in her chair, her eyes on the face of her beloved Rachel, fore-telling the future of her people.

Fore-telling, but not forth-telling. She was not going to let anyone call her a prophet. Not now. Not ever.

FOURTEEN

Rivka

Rivka woke with a start. Her watch told her it was past 3:00 A.M. The little battery was fading. Someday soon, it would die, and another link to her past life would die with it. She heard pounding at the door downstairs.

"Rivkaleh, are you awake?" Ari's whisper felt hot on her ear.

She yawned. "I am now. I guess somebody needs a midwife. I'd better get dressed. Can you go tell whoever it is that I'll be right out?"

Ari sighed and got up. Rivka pulled her clothes into the warmth of her bed and began dressing beneath the blankets. What had possessed her to become a midwife? Somebody should have explained to her that, two nights in every week, some stranger would come knocking on her door and she could not tell him to take two aspirin and call her in the morning. She had to go now. She ought to retire, that's what she ought to do. It was nuts being a midwife with a baby in the house.

Ari stumped up the stairs and into the bedroom. "There is a man outside who says he requires the assistance of the seer woman."

Rivka pushed back the covers and pulled on her cloak. She tried to ignore the pang of annoyance. "*Requires?* Who is he that he thinks he can order people around? Some chief priest?"

Ari shrugged. "He is clean-shaven like a Roman."

Rivka slipped on her sandals. "Let's go talk to him."

They went down and out into the street. A man of medium height, cloaked and hooded, stood in the shadows. He carried a sword, but neither torch nor oil lamp. "I require that you will come with me at once."

Rivka stared at him. "Excuse me? Who are you and why are you giving me orders? Where are we going?"

"A young servant girl in my house has suffered a miscarriage two days ago and now has a fever. We fear she may die."

Compassion swept through Rivka. The girl no doubt had an infection — maybe some kind of toxic shock. She would probably die, whatever Rivka tried. "Where is your house?"

The man's face tightened. "You will come at once. Alone."

Rivka narrowed her eyes. This was getting weird. "Listen, I don't know who you think you are, but I don't go anywhere in the middle of the night without my husband."

"He may come with us as far as the gate."

Rivka put her hands on her hips. "*What* gate?"

"There is no time. You must come now. Both of you."

Rivka stepped back into the house. "Wait. I need my things."

"I require — "

Rivka turned and hurried upstairs. Good grief, this had to be some rich, spoiled aristojerk who thought he could just order people around. He had probably waited too long, and now when the girl died, he would blame the midwife. It was almost certainly a lost cause, but she had to go because . . . she had to go. If she had a chance to save the girl, she had to try.

Upstairs, Rivka bundled up Rachel and grabbed her soft leather bag holding the tools of the midwife. She hurried back down and outside. Ari put a sword in his belt and locked the house.

Rivka handed Rachel to Ari and they set off through the streets of the upper city. They headed north first, then turned east on the deserted avenue that led downhill toward the Temple Mount. A few aristocrats lived over here, mostly the very oldest families. But this made no sense. Those families were of the highest repute, Sadducees, old blood. Blood so blue it was purple. Men of those families didn't shave like Romans.

They hurried past the palace of the high priest, a horrible man named Hananyah ben Nadavayah. Everybody hated him, even the other Sadducees. Past another mansion — one Rivka had seen excavated when she visited Jerusalem in the twentieth century. A left turn and . . .

The man stopped and turned to Ari. "You will be quite safe here, seer woman. You will not take the child in."

Rivka felt all the breath vacuumed right out of her lungs. The Hasmonean Palace — built two centuries earlier by the Maccabees. The palace of King Herod Agrippa. She had never dreamed she would enter this palace.

Ari laid a hand on her arm. "Be well, Rivkaleh. I can take Rachel to nurse with Hana until you are done."

Rivka stood on tiptoes and kissed his bearded cheek. "Bring Brother Baruch here to this gate," she whispered in English. "Right away."

"The king requires that you hurry," said the hooded man.

"All right, all *right!*" Rivka kissed Rachel, then turned away. "Show me the girl."

The man led the way to the great iron-barred gates. He said something and a stout wooden door next to the gate swung in. Rivka followed him through. A large blond man stood there, and for an instant Rivka's mind conjured up an image of Damien West. But no — it was one of those infamous German bodyguards the king employed. Germans were supposed to be big, stupid, and loyal. Well, she could vouch for *big*. This guy could have played on the San Francisco Forty-niners. And the vacant look in his eyes told her that *stupid* was probably accurate too.

They continued through a small courtyard to the palace itself, past a pair of Germans, up some stairs, and into the palace. The receiving room had an incredible floor of marble, inlaid with a mosaic pattern. They strode across it to a vast staircase, also marble. Up the stairs and a left turn and a long hall. A right turn at the corner and down to the end of yet another hall.

As they walked, Rivka let her mind wander. A servant was sick — possibly one of the servants of Queen Berenike. Would she get a chance to meet the queen tonight? Wouldn't *that* be something? She had never seen the queen, but she had seen a picture back home of a bust in the National Museum in Rome. A statue of Queen Berenike — one of the few artistic representations of any person in the Bible. The queen had perfect high cheeks and a classic straight nose and pensive eyes. The woman was drop-dead supermodel gorgeous. For sure, this was going to be an interesting night.

At the doorway, the man paused. "The girl's name is Shlomzion," he said. "She is a favorite of the queen, and you must not let her die."

Rivka shot him a look. *Like there's a lot I can do now.* "Show me the girl."

He pushed open the door. The room was a sumptuous sleeping chamber. Silk hangings on the walls. An enormous bed with an ivory frame and satin blankets. *Ivory!* The girl lay in the bed, her thick black sweaty hair strewn over her face. A thin linen sheet shrouded her slim young body. A servant girl knelt beside the bed, tears on her cheeks, holding the dying girl's hand.

Rivka knelt on the other side and put one hand to the patient's chest, the other on her forehead. Shallow, rapid heartbeat. High fever. A foul smell. "How long has she been sick?"

"Three days," said the servant girl.

A day longer than the man said. Bad news. Rivka probed at the girl's belly with strong fingers. By pressing . . . there, she could feel the uterus. It was hot and swollen. A miscarriage, the man claimed. Or maybe a botched abortion? In the last year, she had seen a number of those. She pressed again, harder, and felt something that might be a tiny fetus. The girl moaned and her hands fluttered weakly, pushing at Rivka's. She was unconscious, horribly infected, probably near death. Without a miracle, there was not much hope. A damp rag lay beside her head next to a bowl of water.

Rivka put the rag in the water, wrung it out, and smoothed aside the woman's hair —

She jerked back, terrified. *Please, God, no!*

High cheekbones. An aristocratic, razor-straight nose. A face of marble beauty. Rivka tried to get her breath back, to act normal.

This was no servant girl. This was Queen Berenike. The man had lied.

Rivka spun to look up at the man who had brought her. He had thrown back his hood. Even in the flickering light of a dozen oil lamps, the family connection sprang out, sharp and clear. No wonder he had such an imperious manner. He could only be Berenike's brother, King Herod Agrippa. She had read all about the Herod family. The Herod men were passionate, cruel, ambitious, greedy, clever. Ruthless.

Agrippa's eyes gleamed, hard and sharp as Damascus steel. "Something is wrong?"

Rivka did her best to recover. "N—nothing." She put the cool rag on the queen's face and wiped away the sweat. When she wrung out the rag in the water, it felt warm. She tried to set it aside, fumbled, dropped it. Her breath was coming in little gasps now, and her head felt light. According to Josephus and Juvenal, Agrippa had an affair with his sister Berenike. She heard a step and looked up at Agrippa again.

In an instant she saw that he knew that she knew. And she read the cold look that flickered in his eyes before the shutters closed on the windows of his soul. Rivka's heart began thumping. *I'm expendable.* Now his secret was out — and he would kill her with no more thought than men gave to a cockroach.

She had to act. Right away, before Agrippa got any ideas. *Oh, God, help me — I can't do this.*

I have to do this.

Rivka stood up and snapped her fingers in Agrippa's face, then spoke to him in her best Latin, which the servant girl would not understand. "You lied to me! The queen is in mortal danger. Why did you delay?"

Agrippa's mouth gaped open. Clearly, nobody *ever* talked to him like this.

Rivka pressed her advantage. "Her life dangles by a thread, but I can save her. You will do a task for me, and you will do it *now* or she will die. You must personally fetch a large bowl of vinegar and a small jug of olive oil, along with some clean linen towels."

"But —"

"Go!" Rivka said. "Or else kill me now. But I swear before God that your sister will die if you raise a hand against me." She crossed her arms across her madly pumping heart and stepped back, putting on her sternest scowl. "The seer woman has spoken."

Agrippa hesitated for a long second, then hurried to the door and went out.

Rivka dared to breathe. She had bought herself a little time. Now Agrippa would wait until he saw whether the queen lived or died.

But it looked bad, really bad. Massive internal infection — without antibiotics, that was going to be fatal. The best she could do would be to clean out the queen's uterus and then pray for a miracle. Right, pray for a miracle — and she couldn't cure a headache if her life depended on it.

The crazy thing was, she knew it was going to work. Knew it as surely as the eclipse that was coming at the next new moon. The history books said Berenike would live — for a number of years after this. Which gave Rivka the confidence to act outrageous, to spit in the king's eye if she had to. It was the only way to save the queen. But how was she going to save her own life too? Agrippa came from a family that made the Godfather look like Mr. Rogers.

Sweating, Rivka knelt beside Berenike's servant girl and took her hand. "My name is called Rivka."

"My name is called Shlomi."

Rivka nodded. *Shlomi. Short for Shlomzion. The peace of Zion.*

"Shlomi, my friend, I can save the life of your mistress, but I need your help, please."

Shlomi's eyes widened. Nobody ever said *please* to her, you could bet on that. Especially nobody who talked to Agrippa like an angry nursemaid. Shlomi clutched Rivka's hand. "Tell me what I can do."

"I will need some papyrus, a reed pen, and some ink very quickly, please."

Shlomi hurried away. Rivka pulled back the fine linen sheet covering the queen's body. Berenike had one of those genetically perfect bodies that any woman in her right mind would kill for. And any man would too. She covered the queen with the sheet, trembling.

Shlomi returned with the writing materials.

Rivka tore the papyrus sheet in half and laid both pieces on the marble table next to the bed. She prepared the ink and scratched out a message in English.

Ari: Queen Berenike was pregnant with King Agrippa's child and had a miscarriage. I am in danger and held captive. Don't try to rescue me — that will only make things worse. If I don't return by noon, you are to spread this story throughout Jerusalem. Love, Rivka.

She waited for the ink to dry, then folded the papyrus and handed it to Shlomi. "Please, my friend, if you love your mistress, do exactly as I say. Go outside the palace through the front gate and wait there until two men arrive. One of them is called Baruch. Tell him Rivka the seer woman needs him. You will bring him here. He is a righteous scribe, and HaShem hears his prayers. He will save the queen's life, I promise you. The other man is very tall, and his name is called Ari the Kazan. You will not allow him to come into the palace. Give him this papyrus and then return quickly, before he reads it."

Shlomi repeated the instructions back exactly as Rivka had given them.

Rivka nodded. "Yes, correct. Go with the peace of HaShem. You must bring the man Baruch here quickly, or else the queen will die."

Shlomi hurried to the door and went out. Rivka returned to the table and wrote on the other half of the papyrus in Greek.

Rivka the seer woman, to Marcus Julias Agrippa, greetings. You think to do me harm, but you are a fool. By secret arts, I have sent a written message outside your gates. If I do not walk out of your palace alive by noon, your secret will be known throughout the city and you will never rule this city as king. If you spare my life, I swear by the name of the living God that I will hold your secret in confidence. Choose with wisdom.

The door swung open. Agrippa entered, carrying a bowl and a jug. Linen towels were slung over his shoulder, and his eyes burned with pure malice.

Rivka's pulse ratcheted up. Oh good. A humble servant-leader type *and* a good loser. She cleared the writing materials off the table and pointed. "Put them there."

Agrippa set them down. "Where is the servant?"

"She went to pass water." Rivka handed him the letter and waited for the explosion.

Agrippa mouthed the words silently as his eyes raced over the lines she had written. His eyes narrowed with suspicion and he held out the letter. "*You* wrote this? *You* can write Greek?"

Now was not the time for modesty. Rivka snatched the letter and read it aloud to him, then translated it into Latin. "I come from a far country, and yet I know more of you than your fellow men. I know with certainty that the queen was pregnant by you. I can save her life and your honor, but I ask for my own life in exchange. Now how do you choose?"

"You drive a crafty bargain."

"I know you will choose well." Rivka washed her hands in the vinegar, then dried them off. She laid her midwife's bag on the bed, draped the towel over her left shoulder, dipped the fingers of her right hand in the olive oil, and knelt beside the queen. "If you have a weak stomach, you should wait outside, King Agrippa."

"What do you intend?"

"What it is called here, I do not know." Rivka reached under the linen sheet. "In my country, I believe it is called a D&C."

Within twenty minutes, Rivka finished her task and covered up the barely breathing body of the queen. As she had thought, there had been a dead fetus inside, driving the infection. Rivka had cleaned things out as best she could. Now it was in the hands of HaShem and a wounded healer named Baruch.

One thing was absolutely clear. This was not a miscarriage. Berenike must have aborted the child. Which meant she was desperate, because an abortion was risky. That desperation meant that Rivka had read Agrippa correctly — he would not dare risk the hint of a scandal. Not his own. Not his sister's. If people knew the child was his, even the Romans would be scandalized, and Agrippa's political life would be over. *If that happens, you'll never work in this empire again, buddy. So you just treat little Rivka Meyers Kazan like a porcelain jar, got it?*

If he didn't get it, she was in big, big trouble.

The door creaked open behind her. Rivka turned and saw Shlomi come in with Baruch. Agrippa followed, and his decision was written all over his face.

She was going to live.

Baruch

Baruch hurried into the room. "Sister Rivka!"

Sister Rivka's red eyes told him she had lost much sleep. She pointed to the still form of a young woman on a bed. "Brother Baruch, here is the servant girl. You must pray to HaShem and heal her."

Baruch felt his ears turning hot. The girl was young and quite beautiful and she wore no hair covering. "Sister Rivka, you will cover the girl's hair please." He turned away from this temptation and waited.

Rivka said, "You may look now. Please hurry. She is near death."

Baruch knelt beside her, but stopped. It was not fitting to lay hands on a young woman. "Where is her husband? He must lay hands on her and then I will put mine on his."

Rivka shook her head. "The girl has no husband. It is a tragedy." She put her hands on the girl's forehead. "Brother Baruch, you will put your hands on mine and pray to HaShem, please."

Baruch's heart lurched. He could not do this thing — to dishonor his own friend Brother Ari by touching his woman.

Rivka gave a sigh and pointed to the man who had followed him into the room. "Sir, you will lay your hands on the servant girl."

The man grunted something, but he knelt beside Baruch and put his hands on the girl's forehead. He smelled of perfume, and his face was shaved like a Roman's, and he was willing to touch a woman. Would it be fitting to touch such a man?

"Please pray," Sister Rivka said.

Baruch sighed and laid his hands on the man's. Panic surged through his heart. He could not hear the Spirit, and so he would not know how to pray, and the girl would die.

Sister Rivka raised her eyebrows. "You may begin."

"I . . ." Baruch's voice felt strangled. "I do not know what to pray."

A long moment of shock hung in the air. The perfumed man tried to draw back his hands, but Baruch refused him.

"Pray this," Sister Rivka said. "Command the evil bacteria to die in the name of Yeshua the *Mashiach*."

"What are *bacteria*?"

"Just *do* it, Brother Baruch."

He sighed. "Very well."

Berenike

Berenike lay floating in a hot sea, wishing for death. She had been here forever. There had never been a time when she was not here. All was evil, heat, stench, vapor, death. All was —

Coolness splashed her face. It spread downward, refreshing her chest, her belly, her arms, her legs. Her body shuddered in an ecstasy of . . . life. She opened her eyes. Four hands lifted off her head. Faces swam into view. Her brother. A bearded man with burning eyes. Shlomi. And an intelligent-looking woman.

Thirst. Had she never drunk water in all her life? "Water." Berenike struggled to whisper the word.

Three of the faces showed astonishment. The bearded man looked . . . sad.

Shlomi bustled forward with a stone cup of water. Dear, sweet, innocent, foolish Shlomi. Berenike drank deeply. She saw the bearded man turn away, blushing. So he was one of *them*. One of the too-pious-to-look-at-a-woman ones. What was he doing in her bedroom? What were any of them doing here, other than Shlomi?

Memory returned. The disguise. The trip to the herb market. The pessary. The cramping. The fever. What did they know about that?

Agrippa shepherded the bearded man and the intelligent woman away. Berenike heard voices at the door. Shlomi patted her face. Berenike closed her eyes. She wanted to rest. To sleep. To sing and shout. She had been to the valley of death, and come back.

The sound of a door. Footsteps.

"The righteous man will wait in the courtyard," Agrippa said in Latin. "You will join him shortly, seer woman."

The seer woman? Berenike opened her eyes again. This was the famous seer woman?

The seer woman stepped back into view. "You have until noon to let me go."

"It is just dawn," Agrippa said. "You have earned your freedom and you shall have it."

"Then let me go." The seer woman's voice sounded harsh, demanding.

"First, you will tell us our futures."

"I do not tell fortunes, and you are very rude."

Berenike felt a smile curling across her face. This seer woman had a gift for plain speaking, but if she did not learn caution, Agrippa would teach it to her.

Agrippa laughed out loud. Berenike knew this as a warning signal. A laugh meant that he wished to put his listener at ease — before the knife thrust. "Seer woman, you have defeated me. Still, I ask a favor. Is there anything you can tell me of my future? Ask what you will, and I will give it, if it is in my power."

The seer woman looked at Agrippa, her eyes calculating, hard as obsidian. Finally she nodded. "It is not given me to know all, but what I know, I will tell. I will name my price first, and then if you agree, I will tell you what is to come in the next five years."

"You bargain with me?" Agrippa's tone was light, mocking.

"I do not bargain when I hold the advantage," said the seer woman. "You will say yes or no, but I will not bargain."

The hiss of Agrippa's breath told Berenike that the seer woman had scored a point. He narrowed his eyes. "Name your price."

"You must swear a solemn oath never to name Hanan ben Hanan to be high priest."

Agrippa laughed again, and Berenike heard real mirth in this laugh. It was a foolish request, and of course he would not grant it. He had already taken a substantial gift from Hanan in exchange for a promise of the high priesthood at the next opportunity.

"Agreed," Agrippa said.

Berenike felt every muscle in her body tighten. Agrippa played a dangerous game, lying to the seer woman. If he could play, Berenike could also. With knowledge of the future, she could not lose in the great game of power. She would be as HaShem, knowing all. She must have this knowledge, and to get it, she would lie, cheat, do anything. Any Herod worthy of the name would do the same.

Berenike turned her head to look at the seer woman. "I also wish to know what lies ahead. And I will give you whatever you ask. Name your price."

The seer woman told her.

Berenike found the terms insulting. "You seek much."

"And you seek a husband."

Berenike frowned. "Tell me something not known to every street-corner child."

"I know of a king willing to be circumcised to marry you. Is his name worth my price?"

A *husband?* Berenike's heart beat like a drum. With a royal husband, she could play the great game and . . . win. And she could escape from her lecherous brother.

A smile curved Berenike's lips. "Yes, you will tell me what you know."

The seer woman spoke for the fourth part of an hour. When she finished, Berenike simply nodded. Agrippa was pacing, his face tight. "Have you told all you know?"

The seer woman nodded. "Have I earned my price?"

Agrippa stopped his pacing. "You have."

Berenike drank more water. "Yes, you may go."

The seer woman bowed slightly and backed toward the door. "I will depend on both of you to fulfill your promises."

FIFTEEN

Ari

As it turned out, Baruch was wrong. Even with Ari's backing, nobody paid any attention to Rivka's prediction of the coming eclipse. The word of Ari the Kazan went far if you were building a pump or a crane or a wall. But what could Ari the Kazan know of events in the heavenly realms? The heavens were not the earth. After many arguments, Ari realized that nobody understood that earthly physics applied to the heavenly bodies. Isaac Newton would prove this someday in the far future, but that was no help now. Ari could not prove there would be an eclipse.

Frustration gnawed at Ari's heart. The science was trivial, and he could have done the computations with a reed pen and papyrus and a pocket calculator, but he lacked data, lacked the instruments to acquire the data, lacked the technology to build the instruments.

He could not prove things he knew to be true. He must appeal to authority. Two thousand years in the future, men would prove these things. His situation was identical to that of his ultra-orthodox stepfather, who had likewise appealed to a far-off authority for the many customs he followed.

At the end of this month, the sun would eclipse. Ari knew it, yet he could not prove it, and he had so far convinced nobody. He had only the word of his woman, and that was not proof. If there was a panic on the appointed day, then people would believe his woman, but it would be too late for those dead.

Pesach came, bringing with it a river of discontent. The massacre in Caesarea had gone unavenged, and the streets bristled with rage. Daggermen murdered a nephew of Hanan ben Hanan in the Temple courts during the worship hour and slipped away in the panic. A self-proclaimed "prophet" created a stir on the fourth day of the feast. On the fifth day, he was not seen in the city, and rumors swirled of a midnight arrest. Roman soldiers patrolled the roofs of the porticoes surrounding the Temple courts, a brutal reminder that Rome was overlord to Jerusalem. At such a time, who cared what a woman had to say, even a seer woman?

When the eight-day feast ended, the city emptied of its visitors, but anger lay like a fog on the streets. Ari decided there was nothing more to be done in the matter of the eclipse. He had warned the people, and as expected, nothing had come of it. The streams of history would bring what they would bring, and no amount of precognition could change that. If there would be a panic, then there would be a panic.

The day after the feast, Ari walked with his friend Gamaliel up the slopes of Mount Scopus toward a threshing floor. It was a dazzling spring day, and the bright bowl of the sky filled Ari's heart with peace. To the east, an endless series of rounded hills dropped like steps toward the Jordan River, thirty kilometers away.

Gamaliel pointed toward the top of the hill they were climbing. "We are late. They have already begun."

Ari squinted. He could see a huge pile of barley — the tithes that had been paid for the upkeep of Temple priests. In truth, the tithes could never keep all the priests of Jerusalem from starvation, but they were all that many of the poorer priests had. A priest himself, Gamaliel did not need tithes, but Ari knew many who did. Ari hoped to design a machine that could thresh the barley faster and with less waste. Gamaliel was fascinated that such machines existed in Ari's far country.

When they reached the top of the hill, Ari saw a dozen priests spreading the barley in thin layers on the hard floor of stone. The sun shone warm on the backs of the men. It was a fine day to work outdoors.

Gamaliel spent an hour showing Ari each phase of the threshing procedure. After spreading the barley on a natural limestone floor, they dragged a heavy threshing sledge over it several times to break the grain out of the barley heads. Then they scooped it all into winnowing baskets and tossed it in the air, letting the stiff springtime breeze blow away the chaff. Ari saw that most of the effort was wasted. A machine powered by one man could accomplish far more than several men working by hand.

Ari knew there were threshing machines in his far country. He had never seen one, so he must invent one, keeping within the manufacturability constraints. It was one thing to design a machine. Quite another to design one that the craftsmen of Jerusalem could actually build with bronze and iron and wood.

He closed his eyes and enjoyed the simple delight of sun and wind on his face. It was a different sort of life here. Very little wealth, but much joy. The morning prayers brought him more contentment than he would ever have guessed. The rhythms of the week, the month, the year. Life here was good. Even for a stranger from a far country who did not believe in foolish superstitions. A man whose life was shards.

Perhaps half an hour passed in which Ari did nothing. That was enough of a break for one day. There was a problem to solve, and his head felt clear now, ready to work. He tried to visualize what must happen to a single head of barley in order to thresh it. The sledge was ridiculously inefficient for this task. In fact —

"No! Go away!"

Ari turned to look. Several priests had gathered at one end of the threshing floor. He went to investigate. A number of hard-faced strangers had come up the hill with a caravan of mules. One of them was talking to Gamaliel while the others waited, smirking. The strangers outnumbered the priests, and they carried clubs. The priests fingered their wooden pitching forks. Ari picked one off the threshing floor.

"You will leave now!" Gamaliel said to the leader of the strangers. "The tithes are for the priests of the living God."

The leader sneered at him, then turned to his men. "The short one says we must leave. Very well. We shall leave." He whirled around and swung his club at Gamaliel.

Gamaliel ducked under it and slugged the stranger in the gut. The man staggered back. The priests behind Gamaliel surged forward, swinging their weapons. Ari charged after them and cracked one of the strangers across the back. The man dropped his club. Ari dove for it and came up swinging. He hit a man in the belly. The man screamed and fell to the ground.

All around him, men shrieked. Gamaliel and one of the strangers wrestled in the dirt at Ari's feet.

Ari swung his club back for another blow. Someone grabbed it from behind and yanked. Ari spun around. One of the thugs held the other end of his club. Ari pulled, but the other man would not let go. Ari yanked again. The other man released it. Ari staggered back, twisted around.

He saw a club swinging toward his head. He threw up his left hand to block it.

Pain shattered his arm.

Ari lost his grip on the club. His arm was on fire. No, it was numb. Somebody slugged him in the kidneys. He toppled forward, watched the ground wobble toward him, the world spin out of control, the bright sunlight stipple to gray. The ground pulled him into a stony embrace. A club smashed against his leg. He covered his head with his good arm, felt a kick to his ribs.

Then darkness.

When Ari came to, the sun hung low in the sky and his head throbbed without mercy. One of the priests bent over him.

Ari tried to speak, but dust coated his tongue and his lips felt thick.

"Wine!" said the priest. "Bring Ari the Kazan some wine."

A wineskin appeared in Ari's face. Grateful, he guzzled a mouthful. It stung his mouth and burned his throat. "Thank you." He blinked several times, trying to focus. "Where are the men?"

"Gone." Gamaliel's voice, somewhere behind him. "They stole the barley."

Ari could not believe that. It made no sense. "Why?" He struggled to sit up. Pain stabbed through his left arm.

"Your arm is broken, Ari the Kazan," said a priest.

"Help me sit up." Ari put up his right hand.

Several hands helped him up. Most of the muscles in his body screamed. Ari gasped. He had never imagined how much pain one body could feel. "Why?" he said again.

"They were Hananyah's men," Gamaliel said. "I have seen them at his house."

Hananyah? Ari turned to look at Gamaliel. "The high priest Hananyah ben Nadavayah?"

Gamaliel nodded. "The father of Brother Eleazar. The men said his farms in the Sharon Valley had a poor harvest, and he wished for compensation."

Rage flooded into Ari's heart, rushed through his veins. "But . . . he cannot do that!" His head felt stuffed with cotton and he could not seem to find his balance.

"The high priest does as he wishes," one of the priests said.

Ari leaned forward and forced himself to his feet. His right knee wobbled beneath him. Gamaliel caught his arm and steadied him. Slowly Ari straightened his battered body. "Who appoints the high priest? The San-hedrin? We must complain to the Sanhedrin."

Gamaliel shook his head. "You do not understand. King Agrippa appoints the high priest. He will not listen to us."

Ari felt a slow smile slide across his face. "He will listen when he learns how loud Ari the Kazan can shout."

Rivka

Rivka sat at her stone kitchen table tightening the splint on Ari's left arm. "I hope I set that right. I'm not very good with broken bones." She turned to Gamaliel. "Gamaliel, are you in much pain?"

Gamaliel shook his head. "Ari, you will please tell your woman that I am fine."

Rivka did her best not to laugh. The tight set of Gamaliel's mouth told her he was lying. Fine, then. If he wanted to be Mr. Macho, afraid to let a woman help him, unwilling to even talk to a woman, then let him live with his pain.

"The other priests believe there is nothing to be done," Ari said.

"I wonder . . ." Rivka tried to concentrate. "Hananyah is going to be deposed sometime soon. Maybe this year, maybe next. Josephus is really fuzzy. But there's a doublet about this episode."

"Doublet?"

Rivka felt nausea rising inside her. Why hadn't she seen this coming? "Ari, I'm so sorry, but . . . I knew about this. It's in two places in Josephus."

"And you did not warn me?" There was deep hurt in Ari's voice.

"Ari, I didn't know it was coming so soon. Josephus puts it later. Of course, that may just be a thematic ordering, rather than chronological — "

"Rivka, do you *care* that ten men are injured?" Ari's eyes shone with black fury. "Perhaps you are concerned with *thematic* ordering, but I have a broken bone and one of our friends lost an eye. This is not an intellectual exercise."

Rivka felt like he had slapped her. Didn't he get it? "Listen, Mr. Important the Kazan, I'm doing the best I can. If you'd just let me finish, I'm telling you there aren't any dates in Josephus. Hardly any. This incident with Hananyah stealing the tithes is well known, but nobody in the world could tell you what year it happened. Now I know, but it's too late. You keep going on about how I'm supposed to know everything, but look at you!

You're in the same boat without your instruments, aren't you? You have the same problem I — "

"Rivka, peace." Ari put up his hand. "I . . . apologize."

She sighed. "I'm sorry too. It's just . . . you've got to understand. All I know is a little and it's very confusing. It's a jigsaw puzzle, with most of the pieces lost. I have to make this an intellectual exercise, or I'd go crazy. If I knew every broken bone and broken heart that was coming, I'd just . . . die."

He patted her hand. "Rivkaleh, I was wrong to put that burden on you. Now let us think what to do. You said Hananyah is to be deposed."

She rested her hand on his. "Agrippa will name Ishmael ben Phiabi as the new high priest."

Gamaliel shook his head. "Ari the Kazan, please explain to your woman that the *sagan* of the Temple will be the next high priest. Hanan ben Hanan."

Rivka stamped her foot, furious that Gamaliel was talking past her, as if she were a child. "No! Ishmael is to be the next high priest. I know this with certainty."

Gamaliel merely smiled at Ari. "Ishmael is a man of slow wits and he was never *sagan*. It is not possible that he should be high priest."

Ari's eyes narrowed to slits. "My woman says that Ishmael will be high priest next. She says also the sun will fail to give his full light on the day of the next new moon. I believe HaShem has given her to know these things. I propose a test. We must form a delegation to King Agrippa and demand a new high priest. Then we will see whether my woman is a true prophet of HaShem."

Rivka's throat tightened. Ari was playing a risky game here. One mistake and she'd lose whatever credibility she had.

"It is too late to seek an audience with the king today." Gamaliel drained the last of the beer in his stone cup. "But I will speak to Rabbi Yohanan and the priests."

"Tomorrow, then," Ari said. "We will give Agrippa a taste of democracy."

"What is this thing *democracy?*" Gamaliel said.

Ari smiled. "It is the most dangerous weapon in the world. You will like it."

Rivka shivered. The problem with weapons was that they were just as powerful in the hands of a bad person as a good.

"You will show me this democracy," Gamaliel said. "And you will show it to Brother Eleazar and the brothers of my *havurah*. Tomorrow." He went to the door and opened it. "Be well, Ari the Kazan."

"*Shalom*, Brother Gamaliel," Rivka said, wishing just once he would speak to her.

The door clicked softly shut.

SIXTEEN

Hanan ben Hanan

The streets were already buzzing with early-morning foot traffic when Hanan stepped out of his palace. Four bodyguards surrounded him. He never went out on the street without bodyguards, not since his brother Yonatan had been murdered a few years ago by the dagger-men.

Things would be especially dangerous after that foolish move the high priest Hananyah had made yesterday, and with the feast hardly over. At this time of year, the people's passions always ran high. The fool! Stealing tithes from men who had nothing — what sort of craziness was that? Many indigent priests lived in Jerusalem. They served a few weeks per year in the Temple, but their pay would not keep them from starvation. They depended on the agricultural tithes.

And the drought in the Sharon Valley this past winter meant the tithes were less. Hanan himself had felt the pinch. The barley harvest on his farms had been hurt, but that was the nature of farming. Some years, the second rain failed and there followed a poor harvest. It was of little consequence to him personally. He would not go hungry, and prices would rise because there would be a food shortage.

But . . . stealing tithes! A high priest could not do that! The Temple depended on the labor of many ten thousand priests. To steal from them meant to destroy the goodwill of those who offered sacrifices to the living God. If they refused to labor in the Temple, then the sacrifices would fail. Hananyah had not stolen merely from a few indigent priests. He had stolen from the Temple. A high priest who did not love the Temple did not deserve to be high priest. Hanan intended to lodge a protest with the king and see what came of it.

King Agrippa was scum and Hanan hated him. Agrippa's father had been a swindler and a cheat, a man who came of Edomite stock only four generations back. Agrippa shaved his face and wore a toga — he was a Roman citizen, and did not understand that this was a disgrace. In public, his sister had the sense to dress conservatively, but inside her palace she dressed like a Roman society woman. In blunt words, like a prostitute.

As he approached the palace gate, Hanan slowed. The public square was very crowded. In just such a rabble, the dagger-men loved to hide, waiting for a chief priest to happen by. *Pesach* was the most dangerous time of year.

But he had no choice. If he wished to speak to Agrippa, he must go this way. Hanan spoke to his bodyguards. "Gather close and force a way."

His men squeezed in around him and they pressed forward. He heard the murmurs of the common folk, the whispering of his name. Felt their anger. Smelled their sweat. Tasted their . . . rage. It took some time to push through to the gate of Agrippa's palace. The iron gates were shut, and that was not usual at this hour. Many hundred men pressed against the gates, shouting at the palace. Noise pummeled Hanan's ears. He and his men pushed through to the stout wooden door beside the gate. The shutter hung open and one of Agrippa's palace guards stood just inside, looking out with frightened eyes.

Hanan put his mouth to the shutter and shouted, "Hanan ben Hanan, *sagan* of the Temple, to see King Agrippa!"

The guard flinched and stepped back. He shouted something in the ear of a messenger boy. The boy ran toward the palace.

Hanan waited. This was good. The people were angry. Agrippa was a weak king who worried about what the people thought. A strong leader would not care for the opinions of street rabble. By now Agrippa must know that he had to depose Hananyah.

The messenger boy came running back across the empty courtyard. He shouted something to the guard. The guard turned to Hanan. "You may come inside, but your bodyguards will stay outside."

Hanan nodded. That was not usual, but he did not fear Agrippa. He heard the grinding sound of a bolt sliding back. The door thrust inward. Hanan slipped inside. The door slammed shut behind him and the guard threw the bolt.

Hanan strode across the courtyard toward the palace. He had come here before and he always felt soiled afterward. He would not touch Agrippa, of course. And he would immerse in his ritual bath when he returned home.

He ascended several broad, shallow steps and walked inside the open doors of the palace. Two large men with yellow hair and blue eyes stood inside, one on each side. Germans. Agrippa kept just such unnatural men for his palace guard. Hanan felt ill in his belly. He walked to the center of the receiving room and waited.

Presently, Agrippa's chief of staff arrived. He was a young Syrian who shaved his face like a Roman and wore perfume like a Greek. "The king will see you now." He spoke Greek, a language Hanan had learned from his Egyptian Jewish nursemaid before he was old enough to know that it was a language fit only for dogs.

Hanan followed him through a door and down a short corridor into the Hall of the Hasmoneans. Here, the Hasmonean kings, sons of the Maccabees, had ruled two centuries and more ago. A few drops of their rich Hasmonean blood flowed in Agrippa's veins, but he was not worthy of his ancestors. Agrippa was a Herod, worthy only to be spit on.

The king sat on the Hasmonean throne. A secretary knelt on the marble floor beside him, holding a writing board on his thighs, his reed pen ready. Two bodyguards stood in the background.

"Hanan ben Hanan to see the king," said Agrippa's chief of staff.

"A pleasure to see you again." A smile played at Agrippa's lips. "No doubt your duties have prevented you from coming to see me as frequently as you would like."

Hanan tipped his head forward the smallest fraction, the nearest thing to a bow he would make to this . . . cockroach. "Your majesty will have heard of the disgraceful conduct of Hananyah ben Nadavayah yesterday."

Agrippa's eyebrows raised. "I understand he was officiating in the Temple."

Hanan put his hands behind his back where Agrippa would not see his clenched fists. "Hananyah's men beat a number of the lower priests and stole their tithes."

"And you have come to see justice done. How noble."

Hanan nodded. What was the king playing at? He had received a handsome gift from Hanan at the last New Year. Was it not enough? They had discussed this matter before, and they had reached a clear agreement. If Agrippa —

"Berenike?" The king turned his head. "Where is Berenike? Andreas, fetch my sister."

The chief of staff turned and went out. Hanan waited, his heart thumping. Something had gone wrong, very wrong.

Footsteps. Hanan turned to see the chief of staff returning with . . . that woman. Hanan shuddered. She wore a sleek silk tunic of a deep rich blue.

Her hair was uncovered, braided atop her head like a crown. She wore no veil, and her eyes looked unnaturally large and liquid. She smiled at Hanan and met his gaze directly, like a common *zonah*. Hanan's heart quivered, and he fixed his eyes on the ground. Vile woman!

"Berenike, our friend Hanan ben Hanan is quite distressed at the performance of the high priest yesterday," Agrippa said. "I think it would be most fitting if he were to help us choose the replacement. Have you brought the list of names the seer woman gave you?"

Seer woman? Hanan's head jerked up. He stared at Agrippa.

The rattle of papyrus.

Hanan turned to look at Berenike. She unrolled a sheet of papyrus and gave it to him, her hand coming so close to his arm that her warmth scorched him.

He read the names. His own was not on the list.

"Choose one of those names," Agrippa said. "We are most interested to hear your opinion."

This must be an evil joke. Hanan looked at the king, then at . . . that woman.

Laughter danced in her eyes. "Pick any name."

They were making sport of him. If he refused their foolish game, he would lose all chance of ever becoming high priest. But if he accepted, he must name an interloper, someone to displace himself. Sweat ran down Hanan's sides. He scanned the list again. Who would make the worst high priest? A name leaped out at him.

Ishmael ben Phiabi. The man's grandfather had been a high priest many years ago. His father had a low intellect and had never been considered worthy of the office. Ishmael had the dull wits of his father.

Hanan smiled. If Agrippa wished to make a fool of him, he would return the favor.

"Ishmael." He handed the papyrus back to Berenike. "You will find him a worthy successor to Hananyah ben Nadavayah." Hanan made his best imitation of a bow and backed out of the room.

Berenike

Flickering gray spots danced before Berenike's eyes. Ishmael! She had written the names of eight men on the papyrus, and Hanan had chosen the one — the very one — whom the seer woman said would be next. HaShem was making sport of her again. Did she dare cross him . . . again?

"Give me the list." Agrippa reached an arm toward her.

Berenike handed him the papyrus, her fingers shaking.

Agrippa ran his finger down the list, then stared off into space. "You wrote down eight names, and still Hanan chose . . . Ishmael."

"It means nothing." Berenike's pounding heart told her this was a lie.

"I could name another and the seer woman would be proved wrong," Agrippa said. "I could choose Hanan."

"If you wish to violate a solemn oath, you could choose him." Berenike shook her head, frightened. "And the seer woman could . . ." She dared not think what the seer woman could do. The seer woman had promised to keep their secret safe, but would she hold to her promise if Agrippa violated his? They were sold to the seer woman.

The papyrus fell out of Agrippa's hand.

"Ishmael," Berenike said.

Agrippa nodded to his secretary. "Take a letter."

Ari

This democracy is a wonderful thing!" Gamaliel shouted into Ari's ear, his voice almost drowned by the din of the mob he had organized.

Ari was not so sure. The anger of the crowd terrified him.

"Tell the king again!" The young giant Brother Eleazar shouted to the mob from his perch on a small stage they had made of bricks.

"Away with Hananyah!" shouted the crowd. "Away with Hananyah!"

Which was ironic, because Hananyah was Brother Eleazar's own father. From what Ari understood, they did not get along well. Had not for ten years, ever since Eleazar broke with family tradition and left the Sadducee party.

Worry gnawed at Ari's heart. Brother Eleazar was a born demagogue. *What have I created?*

"Here comes the king!" somebody shouted.

Ari turned to look. The crowd surged forward, pressing him up against the iron bars of the palace gate.

A shadow emerged from the palace. No, it was not the king. Hanan ben Hanan stormed down the palace steps and into the courtyard. His face had gone purple with rage, and he strode across the court without looking at the crowd.

"Woe unto me from the House of Hanan!" Brother Eleazar's great voice boomed across the court.

"Woe!" shouted the crowd.

Ari's stomach knotted. This was not democracy. This was foolishness. Aristocrat-baiting. It would lead to—

Hanan made eye contact with Ari and stopped in midstride. His face twisted and his eyes narrowed to slits. Ari tried to push away from the gate, but he was pinned by the crowd.

"Woe!" Brother Eleazar shouted again.

"Woe!" the crowd echoed, to general laughter.

Hanan came toward Ari. A vein throbbed in his neck.

"Woe!" the crowd roared. "Woe unto me from the House of Hanan!"

Hanan stopped in front of Ari.

Ari tried to breathe, but his chest had become iron. *If Hanan has a dagger, I am a dead man.* Behind him, the mob pressed tighter, jamming Ari's face up against the bars of the gate.

Hanan spit in Ari's face.

"Woe!" screamed many hundred voices. "Woe!"

Rivka

Rachel had fallen asleep nursing. Her fat little tummy rose and fell, rose and fell. Rivka leaned back in her rocking chair, smiling. If she could freeze this moment forever, she would be happy. A beautiful spring morning. A contented sleeping child. A few moments of peace.

A perfect day.

Downstairs, the door banged open. Footsteps raced up the stairs. Ari dashed into the room. "Ishmael!" he shouted.

Rachel woke up wailing.

"Ari, please!" Rivka rocked Rachel. "Shhh, shhh, sweetie! Back to sleep, Racheleh. Back to sleep."

Slowly, Rachel quieted. Ari paced back and forth. "Rivka—"

"Just *wait.*" Rivka continued rocking Rachel. "I've almost got her asleep." She stood up slowly and walked to the cradle, bouncing Rachel gently in her arms. "Now sleep, sweetheart. Just sleep for an hour, okay?" She nestled Rachel into her cradle and kissed her pink forehead. The smell of baby filled her nostrils.

She turned to Ari and pointed downstairs. They tiptoed out.

Ari's face was shining. "Rivka, I am sorry I woke Rachel, but . . . Ishmael ben Phiabi has just been named high priest!"

Rivka raised an eyebrow. "Well, of course. Didn't I tell you he would? I just didn't know when."

Ari put his good arm around her. "Rivkaleh, I never doubted you. But the others did."

Rivka's body stiffened. "Others? What others?" She tilted her head to look up at Ari.

Joy lit his face. "All the others. Baruch. Gamaliel. Eleazar. Yoseph. All the Sons of Righteous Priests. I told them Agrippa would choose Ishmael — that you predicted it, that it was a certainty. And now they have seen and they believe!"

Irritation twisted a knot in Rivka's belly. She had *known* Ishmael would be next. But these men still had to test her word — just because she was a woman. It was so . . . silly. If she was a man wearing some leather prophet-suit, they'd come flocking and eat up whatever she said. But a woman? A woman had to actually be right.

"You do not see it?" Ari looked gleeful. "Now they will believe your prediction about the eclipse! Rivkaleh, this is the breakthrough we needed! Now all will believe the words of the seer woman. It is the will of HaShem, I think. Yes, the very will of HaShem." He bent over and kissed her.

"Ari, please — don't go telling everyone I predicted Ishmael. I don't feel right about it. People are going to come asking me to tell their fortunes." *And I've already given in once.* "Promise me you won't go telling the whole world about my prediction."

Ari gave a guilty shrug. "It is perhaps too late for that."

Rivka felt a sudden rush of queasiness. "What *are* you talking about?"

"There are many hundred men who were with me at the palace of Agrippa this morning. All of them are now telling the whole city that Rivka the seer woman predicts that the sun will turn to darkness on the day of the new moon."

"That's only seven days from now."

Ari nodded. "The whole city will know by this time tomorrow."

SEVENTEEN

Rivka

On the morning of the eclipse, it rained. Only a little, but rain after *Pesach* was not usual in Jerusalem. People muttered and stared at the heavens and bought extra food at the market. After midday, the skies cleared and tension began mounting in the city. Many people went to the Temple to await the eclipse predicted by the seer woman.

Rivka refused to go. Despite Ari's confidence that there would be no panic, last-minute doubts gripped her. Was it possible that *because* of her prediction, people would panic? She fed Rachel at noon and put her to bed for an afternoon nap and went up on the roof to await the spectacle in the heavens.

Thanks to Ari, the whole city knew the eclipse was coming and what it meant. It was not a dragon eating the sun, nor Satan battling HaShem in the heavens. It was just the moon moving in front of the sun. True, you wouldn't see the moon until the sunlight was completely blocked out. Then it would be safe to look up, and you would see that a round object obscured the sun. The moon. All very simple and scientific.

Rivka was trembling.

Her fears did not make sense, of course. Ari's logic was foolproof. Today was the last day of the lunar month. The eclipse had to come today. Ari didn't know the exact time of what he called the "syzygy," but Rivka was pretty sure it would come around three in the afternoon. She waited, her eyes fixed on the circle of light cast by a pinhole camera Ari had built out of papyrus.

The sun beat down on her.

Around 1:30, she went back inside to get a drink of beer. When she returned, she saw that the circle of sunlight in the camera had a small bite missing from it — like one of those Apple Macintosh logos. All of a sudden, sweat stood out on her arms. The eclipse had begun. Minutes passed, and the bite in the circle of light grew larger. Larger.

Ari

The Sons of Righteous Priests cheered when Ari's pinhole camera showed a small slice missing from the sun's light. "It is beginning!" Brother Eleazar roared.

They had gathered in the very center of the Court of Women in the Temple. The place surged with humanity — tens of thousands, Ari estimated. Only those few nearest the camera could see the circle of light, but that would soon change. When totality arrived, all the world would see.

At Eleazar's shout, many in the crowd looked up nervously at the sun — something Ari had warned them not to do. Until totality, the sun remained dangerous to look at. Even with ninety-nine percent of its disk obscured, the ultraviolet radiation could blind you.

Ari felt calm, confident now. Thanks be to HaShem, with the help of his woman, he and his friends had prevented a panic — just as history said they must. He scanned the crowd for signs of disorder. North, east, south — all was calm. A tense calm, but no signs of fear. Like the last moments before the fireworks began on the Americans' Fourth of July.

Ari turned to the west, toward the altar and the sanctuary. Hundreds of priests packed the Court of Priests and the steps leading down from the Nicanor Gate. The afternoon sacrifices were due to begin in a bit more than an hour. By then, the eclipse would be ended. It would be good to worship HaShem today. Though he had never seen a total eclipse, he had heard that the event inspired extraordinary feelings of awe. Perhaps today he would feel the Spirit?

"It is two parts gone!" Eleazar shouted. "The moment is approaching!"

Ari looked back at the image on the stone pavement. Two-thirds of the sun was missing, and yet still the difference in daylight was very little. That would change very soon now.

"There he is!" A grin broadened Gamaliel's voice. "Our friend has come out of hiding to see the prediction of Ari the Kazan come true."

Ari turned once more toward the Temple. Hanan ben Hanan stood on the uppermost steps, just inside the Nicanor Gate. Even at this distance — at least fifty meters — Ari read the hatred on his face. He shrugged. Hanan had chosen to make him an enemy, had scoffed at this "eclipse of Kazan," had darkly warned against the sorcery of Kazan. After today, it would not matter. Nobody would ever listen to Hanan ben Hanan's scoffing again.

"It is nine parts gone!" Eleazar bellowed.

An expectant hush settled over the people.

Ari looked at the camera again. Yes, nine-tenths of the disk had vanished. He risked a glance up at the sun. Its radiance scorched his eyes. As he should have known. The sunlight seemed hardly lessened from an hour ago. The darkness would come in a flood in the last few seconds before totality, the vast shadows racing across the landscape at terrifying speed. If they were lucky, totality would last six or seven minutes and then—

"Ari the Kazan, what is happening?" Gamaliel asked.

Ari looked again at the disk on the camera. It had not shrunk at all in the last couple of minutes, and that seemed odd. "Just wait a little. The darkness will surely come."

Eleazar cupped his hands to his mouth. "Ari the Kazan says that the darkness will surely come in just a few moments! The mouth of HaShem has spoken it through the seer woman! Be ready!"

They waited. A lethargic breeze pushed the hot stifling air around the crowded court.

Ari wiped the sweat off his forehead. Was it his imagination, or—

The quiet mutter of voices ran around the circle of men who could see the pinhole camera. Ari blinked twice. No. This was not possible.

"Ari the Kazan." Gamaliel cleared his throat. "The sun is now only four parts gone."

Ari did not know what to say, but his eyes told him that Gamaliel was correct. Only four-fifths of the sun was now obscured. "Just . . . wait," he said.

"Ari the Kazan says to wait!" Eleazar bellowed to the throng. "Wait just a little longer for the sun to be darkened!"

Fear like a flame heated Ari's belly. As the minutes ticked by, the circle of light grew to half the disk, then to two-thirds. The sound of whispering assaulted his ears on all sides.

When the sun's disk had restored itself to nine-tenths of its original size, Ari admitted the truth to himself. He looked up at Brother Eleazar. "It is . . . not going to happen." Something blurred Ari's vision. "Please tell the people not to panic, but there will be no more eclipse today."

"Tomorrow?" Gamaliel said.

"No." Ari turned and closed his eyes, feeling the full horror of what he had done. Better to have done nothing than this disaster. "Not tomorrow. Not ever. There will be no eclipse, except what we have seen."

Which was precious little. Those few men near the pinhole camera had seen what Ari saw. They knew he had been right — mostly.

And the many ten thousand who had waited in dread for the great sign in the heavens? They had seen nothing. The sun had dimmed a small amount — as if a bit of cloud had covered it. But for them, there had been no eclipse.

For those tens of thousands, Kazan and the seer woman were false prophets.

Baruch

Baruch's heart burned within him as they walked home. Brother Ari walked as a blind man, staggering in the full light of day. Baruch guided him by the arm. "Courage, Brother Ari."

A rotten egg sailed from an unseen hand above them on a rooftop, splattering their feet. "*Navi shakar, Kazan!*" False prophet.

Baruch quickened his pace. "I saw the circle of light! Nine parts of the sun disappeared, whatever the people may think."

"I am a fool, Brother Baruch. I should not have meddled. We knew there was to be no panic. We should have let things take their course."

"It was an honest mistake." Baruch tried to sound convincing, but he felt no conviction. Had not Sister Rivka assured them that the eclipse would come? In what else might she have erred?

When they reached Brother Ari's home, Baruch helped unlock the door and they escaped inside.

Sister Rivka stood waiting for them, her face shocked and pale. "Ari!" She threw her arms around Brother Ari. "I . . . Ari, please don't be angry with me! The book said nine parts of the sun would vanish. I thought that would be almost the same as a total eclipse."

Baruch turned his head, unable to look on the dishonor of his friend. He knew what it was to be dishonored through no fault of his own.

"Ari!" Rivka began weeping. "Can you forgive me?"

Baruch wondered that a woman could ask such a foolish question. Had she no understanding of honor? Did she know nothing of what she had done? Ari's honor was destroyed, smashed beyond redemption.

A false prophet could never hope to recover his honor, not while he walked under the sun.

EIGHTEEN

Berenike

Berenike was nursing her newborn daughter when Agrippa came for her. "Give it to me now." Agrippa reached for the child.

Berenike gripped her baby tight and twisted away from him. "No! Go away! She is mine!"

Agrippa snapped his fingers toward the door and two huge Germans barged into her quarters. She screamed and clutched her daughter. "No! Stay away from me, you filth! She is mine!"

Each man took hold of one of her arms. Agrippa seized the child.

Berenike screamed in rage. "No!" She kicked at him with both feet, spitting, biting, screaming. He would not take her daughter! He would not!

The Germans tore at her arms.

Slowly, slowly, her fingers lost their grip. Agrippa pried at the child. "Give it to me! It is a scandal and a disgrace, you shameless woman!"

The baby wailed. Berenike lost her grip. Agrippa staggered backward, holding her daughter, her precious daughter. He shook loose the swaddling, grabbed the baby by the feet, and laughed as he swung it around hard in a great arc. As the child's head smashed against the cruel stone table, Berenike screamed.

She woke up crying.

"Mistress!" Shlomi's soft, gentle hands comforted her.

Berenike's heart raced madly in her chest. She felt with both hands for her child, but . . . it was gone. The dream was a lie. Agrippa had not killed her baby. She had.

"Mistress!"

Berenike clutched at Shlomi's hands and let the tears roll. It had been five weeks since she killed her child. She felt sure in her heart it was a daughter. A girl who could have been a comfort to her. Not like her noisy, mocking, ill-mannered sons, whom she had sent to Rome to "finish their education" because she could no longer tolerate them in her house. For the sake of Agrippa's foolish honor, she had killed her own daughter and nearly died herself. Now HaShem tormented her with evil dreams, a punishment for her sin.

Shlomi dried Berenike's face with a silk cloth. "Peace, mistress. Peace."

Berenike sighed. Would she ever have peace? She was losing her mind, her soul. Becoming weak. Soft. Unworthy to be a Herod.

And she did not care. Perhaps it was not such a wonderful thing to be a Herod, if to do so meant to kill her own daughter. For the first time in her life, Berenike knew guilt. Shame. She squeezed Shlomi's hands. "In the morning, you will send for the seer woman."

"Yes, mistress. I will be glad of seeing her again. Hold my hand and sleep."

Berenike closed her eyes and clutched Shlomi's hand. She lay awake until dawn.

Rivka

Rivka sat quietly in Berenike's chamber, rocking baby Rachel in her arms, admiring the exquisite tapestries on the wall, letting Berenike talk. And talk. The woman had everything — wealth, beauty, brains. Everything except peace of mind. Everything except a friend.

Rivka knew she could not be the friend Berenike needed. Their worlds were too different. She could listen to Berenike, empathize, talk about repentance and forgiveness. But Berenike wasn't listening. She wasn't ready to get forgiveness yet. Berenike had a long, long way to go before she'd be ready for that. She had been trying to be a man for so long, she needed to just talk to a woman. An equal woman. And it was already clear after an hour's talk that she did not consider Rivka her equal. Berenike desperately needed a friend, someone who could be a sister to her —

Rivka's heart skipped a beat. Well, of course! Some things were so obvious you couldn't see them until they punched you in the nose.

Berenike leaned forward. "What did you see, seer woman?"

"See?" Rivka felt her cheeks warming. Good grief, Berenike thought she was having a vision or something crazy like that. "I saw nothing."

"You did." Berenike stared at Rachel with hungry eyes. "Tell me."

Rivka sighed. It must be nice to be a queen, able to order the little people around. "You need to visit your sisters. Have a long talk with them."

Berenike frowned and leaned back. "I have only one sister."

That was ridiculous. Rivka drummed her fingers on the marble table-top. "You have two sisters, Mariamme and Drusilla."

"Mariamme is in Rome. I have nothing to say to . . . that other one."

"Drusilla will be going back to Rome soon. You may never see her again."

"Good." Berenike took a sip of wine. "How do you know she is going back to Rome?"

"Because her husband is about to be recalled by Caesar."

"Husband?" Disgust washed across Berenike's face. "She left her husband six years ago."

Rivka knew only a little of this — a paragraph from Josephus. "I understood she got a divorce and married Governor Felix."

"She left her husband, the little *zonah*. He never gave her a divorce."

Rivka leaned forward. *That* wasn't in Josephus or the New Testament. "You're telling me her marriage to Felix is invalid?"

"You should know that if you are a true seer woman."

Well, I'm not. All I know is what I read in the newspapers. I don't have a pipeline to God. Rivka tried again. "I know that Governor Felix will be replaced this summer. He and Drusilla will be leaving for Rome soon after that. You must visit her. Talk to her."

Berenike scowled and threw a small brass mirror across the room. "I would sooner kiss a cobra."

Rivka said nothing — just looked at her.

Berenike's eyes hardened. "You will stop looking at me in such a way! I will not visit her!" Her cheeks pinked. "I refuse to talk to you anymore. You will leave at once!"

Rachel woke up and began screaming.

Good grief, I really punched her buttons, didn't I? Rivka stood up, shushing Rachel. "I'm sorry if I offended —"

"I do not wish to see you again. Now I know that the rumors are true."

Rivka turned to stare at her. "What rumors?"

Berenike smiled. "If you do not know, then you are no true seer woman, and the rumors are proved true."

"What rumors?"

"You will leave at once or I will call for the Germans."

Rivka backed toward the door, wondering how she was going to stay on her feet when her head felt like somebody had spun her around for half an hour on one of those crazy rides at the fair.

An hour later in the New City, Rivka rapped on a wooden door. Midwife Marta had to be home. She just had to be. Hana had refused to speak about the rumors when Rivka asked. All of her friends had dodged the question. But Marta would not dodge. You could always trust an old woman to tell the truth.

No answer.

Rivka gently rocked Rachel in her arms. The tiny face dissolved into a blur. Rivka turned and stumbled blindly toward home. She collided with somebody.

"Oh! Child, is it you?" Marta's voice, very old and tired.

Rivka couldn't see a thing. "*Savta?*"

"Come inside, out of the sun, child. The little one should be at home."

Marta opened her house and slumped inside. "It was a difficult birth today. I should have sent for you, but . . . that was not possible."

Not possible? Rivka realized that it had been a whole week since any of the midwives in the city sent for her on a hard case. Not since . . . before the eclipse.

"Child, let me look at Racheleh!" Marta led Rivka into the sitting room and guided her to a seat on one of the wooden couches. "She looks more like you each day. Such a delight. Would you like a drink? Some beer?"

"Beer would be fine." Rivka could just hear what her mother would say about drinking beer while she was nursing Rachel. But what was she supposed to do? The alcohol might pass through to Rachel, but was that worse than drinking tainted water and maybe getting diarrhea or some weird intestinal bug?

Marta hurried to bring her a stone cup filled with the local ale. "Child, how have you been? Gamaliel told me about . . . what happened in the Temple."

Rivka looked her straight in the eye. "*Savta*, is there something I should know? About what people are saying about me?"

"It is only an idle rumor, child. Tell me about that little terror, that Dov. What has he broken lately?"

"*Savta*, I need to know." Rivka clutched her arm. "What is the rumor?"

"Nobody believes it. Foolishness, that is what I call it."

Rivka wanted to shriek. "*What* is foolishness? If nobody believes it, why won't you tell me?"

Marta took Rachel and rocked her gently, pacing back and forth in front of Rivka. "There is a rumor — a very foolish rumor — that you have a familiar."

Rivka gasped. "A . . . what?" Understanding came in a rush. A familiar spirit. There were two kinds of false prophets. One claimed to hear from God when he had heard nothing. The other claimed to hear from God when in fact he heard from a lying spirit.

"They are calling you . . . the witch woman."

Cold sweat leaped out on Rivka's face. They thought she was . . . some kind of a witch. Like the woman of Ein Dor whom King Saul visited. A medium.

Which was crazy. *Do I look like something out of Harry Potter?*

But of course, nobody was claiming she was a black-caped, cauldron-stirring, spell-casting, broomstick-riding *witch*. That was so . . . medieval — so Eurocentric. A witch in this culture meant something different — a medium, a spiritist, a consulter of the dead, a diviner of the future.

Rivka put her face in her hands. She had to stop this lying story. She had a lot to give to this city. As a midwife and as a seer woman. But how could she help if everybody thought she was a witch woman? Hanan ben Hanan had to be behind this lie. Just wait till she got her hands on him. She'd —

"Child, nobody believes these rumors." Marta handed Rachel back. "Pay no attention to — "

The outside door opened. "*Savta!* I am home!" Gamaliel's voice. Footsteps in the kitchen. "*Savta*, did — " The sharp intake of breath.

Rivka turned to look at Gamaliel. His face had turned a pale shade of green. She walked toward him. He backed away. He was one of Ari's best friends and he was scared to death of her.

Frustration welled up inside Rivka's heart. "I'm not a witch woman!" *Oh great, the lady doth protest too much.*

Gamaliel held up his hands, palms outward, and looked to his grandmother. "*Savta* — "

"Gamaliel, you silly goose!" Marta advanced on him, her finger jabbing holes in the air. "Are you also listening to this foolishness? Does Rabbi Yohanan think she is a witch woman? Does he?"

Gamaliel pursed his lips. "Rabbi Yohanan . . . does not know what to think."

Rivka felt like somebody had stuffed her head with cotton. If even Rabbi Yohanan had doubts . . .

"Shame, shame!" Marta wagged her head. "What would your father say? Or your mother?"

"Or your uncle Saul," Rivka said. She clapped her hand over her mouth. What an idiot thing to say.

"Or your uncle Saul — what would he say?" Marta tapped her finger on Gamaliel's chest.

Gamaliel's face turned hard, cold.

Rivka decided to tackle this thing head on. What did she have to lose? She strode up beside Marta and jutted her chin at Gamaliel. "Go ask your uncle!" she said in a quiet voice. "Your uncle Saul gave me a blessing once. Ask him about it. Ask him if I'm a witch woman. But you'd better hurry. He's still in prison in Caesarea, but he'll be sailing for Rome at the end of the summer and you'll never see him again."

Suspicion narrowed Gamaliel's eyes. He scowled at Marta. "Has HaShem told her what my uncle will be doing next fall — as he told her about the sun?"

Rivka swallowed hard. There was no way to back out of this swamp. She would either have to drive through, or sink into quicksand. "HaShem has given me to know much about your uncle. This summer, the governor will ask him to speak before King Agrippa and Queen Berenike and — "

"The *governor?*" Gamaliel gave a harsh laugh. "*Savta*, she speaks foolishness. The king and queen hate Governor Felix, on account of his stealing their sister from her lawful husband. This woman has not heard from — "

Rivka stamped her foot. "No, no, not Governor Felix. He will soon be deposed. Caesar will send a man named Festus to replace him."

Marta put a hand on Rivka's arm. "Child, you are overwrought. You will upset Racheleh. Please — "

But Rivka was not going to be timid here. "No, *Savta*, I know what I'm talking about." She pointed at Gamaliel. "Two months from now, you will hear that Governor Festus has arrived in Jerusalem, and then you will know that I have heard from HaShem. Then I ask you, take me and Ari the Kazan to Caesarea to meet your uncle Saul."

Gamaliel shook his head. "*Savta*, this is foolishness. I have never heard of this Festus, and therefore I will not — "

"I said, *when* you hear," Rivka said. "In two months, when you hear that Festus has arrived here in Jerusalem, then you will take us, please."

"I—"

"Please!"

Marta cackled. "What do you fear, Gamaliel? If there is no Festus, then she asks for nothing. But if this Festus comes here . . . will that not be proof that Rivkaleh has heard from HaShem?"

Gamaliel's eyes danced with uncertainty. Finally, he nodded. "Yes. I do not see how such a thing could happen, but yes."

Hana

Hana paced in front of her door, her heart pounding almost as loudly as the rapping on her front door. She did not wish to face Sister Rivka in her hour of shame.

"Hana!" Rivka shouted again from outside. "I know you're home. You will let me in, or I will beat the door down!"

Hana could not think what to do.

"Hana!" More pounding. Little Rachel began wailing outside.

That was too much. Hana unlatched the door.

Rivka stood in the street, tears leaking down her face, blindly rocking Rachel.

Hana threw her arms around her. "It is a lying tale."

Rivka looked at her through bleared eyes. "Why didn't you tell me?"

Hana saw people staring at them in the street. "You will come inside, please. The sun is hot."

Rivka came in and Hana shut the door on the horrible stares. They were fools to believe Rivka was a witch woman, but they were also her neighbors. When Hana had lived as a *zonah*, the worst part of her life was the neighbor women who spit at her feet in the street.

Rivka quieted Rachel. Hana brought two wooden stools and they sat.

Rivka smeared the sleeve of her tunic across her eyes. "They say I have a familiar."

Hana patted her arm. "You will pay no attention and this lying tale will die."

"Hana, this is going to ruin everything!" Rivka's eyes glowed with anger. "Nobody is sending to me for help in midwifing. And . . . I have things to tell this city. A terrible time is coming soon. I have to warn the people!"

"Only wait a little," Hana said. "Then they will forget."

"I don't have time to wait! This is important! If I don't warn people, nobody will!"

Hana reached down and touched Rachel's tiny, delicate nose. "All is in the hands of HaShem."

"Well . . . of course." Rivka sighed deeply. "I guess I believe that, but . . . I also think HaShem sent me here for a reason. You know — for such a time as this. Like Queen Esther. I don't have time for some stupid rumor. Who has familiar spirits these days, anyway?"

Hana felt her jaw drop open. "But . . . Rivkaleh, have you forgotten? When you first met me, I had a familiar."

"You . . . what?" Rivka gave her a disbelieving smile.

"You will not look at me like a child, please." Hana folded her arms across her chest. "I told you about the truth-tellers."

"Yes, but . . . I thought that was all a figure of speech." Rivka's eyes sank to the table. "I thought maybe you were just making things up, or . . . hearing voices."

Hana did not know how such an intelligent woman could be so ignorant. "But of course I *was* hearing voices. The truth-tellers. I had a spirit of rage and a spirit of lust and a spirit of fear. And a familiar — she warned me of danger many times."

Rivka's eyes widened. "Hana, that's dangerous! A familiar spirit — if you really had one — was there to lie to you, to lead you into deception."

Hana could not look at Rivka's eyes. "You will not be angry on me, please, but . . . the truth-tellers made me lie to you once."

Rivka put her hand on Hana's arm. "When?"

"On the day we met, you asked me the name of the high priest. I said it was Ishmael ben Phiabi. My familiar told me to say this name, and so I said it, though I knew it was a lie."

"Why?"

Hana shrugged. "I do not know. One does not ask a familiar why. Baruch made her go away, her and all the others."

"You don't hear them anymore?" Rivka sounded frightened.

"No." Hana took Rachel's tiny hand in hers and studied the fingers intently.

"Hana, you do, don't you?"

Hana closed her eyes. "Only sometimes. The shade of the wicked man."

"Damien."

"Yes. I wake sometimes in the night and hear his voice. He torments me, but he has no hold."

"Hold? What do you mean, no hold?"

Hana curled her fingers into a fist and raked them lightly over Rivka's arm. "You see? Here, I have no hold." She opened her hand and gripped Rivka's arm. "Here, I have a hold. Just so with the spirits. They have a hold, or they have no hold. The wicked man has no hold on me."

"But . . ." Rivka shook her head. "How do they get a hold?"

"Through sin, of course." Hana wondered sometimes that Rivka was such a child. "If rage is found in you, then a spirit of rage will find a hold. If lust, then a spirit of lust." Hana stood up and went to the window. She looked out at the shining blue sky, so pure, so clean. It was like the sky, to live free of the spirits. She lowered her eyes to the white stones of the city. These stones were not pure, not free. "There is a spirit of rage on this city."

Rivka said nothing.

Hana came back and sat at the table. "You do not have a familiar, Rivkaleh. Any fool can see that."

"But . . . it isn't fair," Rivka said. "When Ari the Kazan makes a mistake, he loses a little honor. When I make a mistake, they turn me into a witch woman."

Hana studied her intently. "Rivkaleh, please! Do not give rage a place in your heart. You are angry at these lying tales. Yes, it is unfair, but that is the way of the world. You do well to be angry, but if you cross over to rage, you will not do well."

"But . . . how long do I need to put up with these lies?" Rivka's eyes glittered. "I have things I need to do. Soon!"

Hana patted her cheek. "All is in the hands of HaShem."

NINETEEN

Hanan ben Hanan

As expected, Ishmael ben Phiabi turned out to be a terrible high priest. Hanan felt pleased. Soon Agrippa would come to his senses. Spring passed into summer while Hanan waited. The feast of *Shavuot* came and went and nothing happened. Then shocking news came from Caesarea that Judea had a new governor. A man named Festus.

On the hottest day of the summer, Hanan and three dozen other priests of good family stood sweating in the reception room of the palace of Ishmael ben Phiabi. Ishmael was a tall man with a thick gray beard and vacant eyes. He knew that the other aristocrats considered him stupid, and he knew that Hanan had recommended him for the high priesthood. He therefore treated Hanan as his closest friend and ally and kept him as his *sagan*. He inclined his head to Hanan. "Have you heard much of this man Festus?"

Hanan shook his head. "You will allow me to ask him about the matter of the *apikoros?*"

"Of course," Ishmael said. "Your father would wish it so."

That stung, though Ishmael no doubt thought it a compliment. Hanan's father was the man responsible for Renegade Saul becoming an *apikoros*. He had sent Saul to Damascus to put a stop to the foolishness that had sprung up there. Who could have predicted how badly that would turn out? Now Saul was an *apikoros* — a renegade. A messianic, a purveyor of lies, an apostate. A man who did not love the Temple. Saul had spent the past three decades spreading his filth throughout the empire. Teaching Jews to despise the Temple, the Torah, the customs of the fathers. If he continued so, Jews in the diaspora would no longer support the Temple and its services to the living God. Saul had even tried to bring his fanaticism back to Jerusalem, when it had long been crushed here.

For the good of the Temple, such a man must be sacrificed. The *apikoros* had to die.

Trumpets rang outside the palace. Every man in the reception room stood just a little straighter, a little taller. Presently, Ishmael's steward bustled in. "Governor Festus to greet Ishmael ben Phiabi and the elders."

The elders moved to the edges of the room, forming a semicircle. Ishmael stepped to the center. "You will show the governor in."

Hanan tensed. Would this governor be an incompetent like Felix? One who despised Jews and crushed the people of the land to enrich his own purse? Hanan had heard whispers of revolt among the young men. Rumors of *Mashiach*, who would destroy the dragon and purify the Temple.

Fools! Young men did not know the fruits of war — disease, death, destruction. Young men hoped for glory in battle, believing that courage alone would bring victory. Young men thought themselves immortal, invincible. They did not know that a brave man also can die, a holy city can be taken, and the Temple of the living God burned with fire.

It had happened once, many hundred years ago, and it could happen again. A man who loved the Temple must do anything in his power to prevent it. The messianics, in their mad rush to glory, would end by destroying the Temple. To stop them, the righteous man, the man who loved the Temple, must be prepared to do anything. To lie. To cheat.

To kill.

Hanan stepped into the center of the room, taking his place slightly behind Ishmael at his right hand. Ishmael had no Greek, so he had asked Hanan to translate.

A tribune entered the room, and behind him, the new governor from Rome. Festus was a military man of medium height with hard eyes and a sallow complexion. The tribune saluted Roman fashion, his right arm extending out in front of him. "Porcius Festus, governor of Judea!" he said in Greek.

Hanan translated this into Aramaic. Ishmael stepped forward and clasped hands with the new governor. Hanan moved smoothly forward alongside him and said in Greek, "Ishmael, son of Phiabi, high priest, greets you."

The governor and the high priest studied each other for a moment, neither blinking, neither speaking. Finally Ishmael stepped back and nodded to Hanan. Hanan stepped forward and extended his hand. "I am called Hanan, son of Hanan, and I am captain of the Temple, second in the Temple hierarchy."

Governor Festus grasped him firmly at the wrist with both hands. He had a moist, meaty, sturdy grip. A soldiering man, with a head crowned by a few gray wisps. Hanan guessed he must be nearly sixty, an old man, not one who could be easily fooled or brow-beaten. A man of reason.

Excellent. The way to his heart on the matter of the *apikoros* would be through reason. Simple facts, plain words.

Hanan stepped back and the next man came forward to greet the governor. "Yeshua the son of Gamaliel," Hanan said. Yeshua was his protégé, the most intelligent man in the room, learned in Torah. Even the self-appointed sages of the Pharisees respected Yeshua ben Gamaliel. He clasped hands with governor Festus and spoke to him in fluent Greek.

The other chief priests followed Yeshua. Hanan introduced each of them in turn, translating for those who had no Greek. "Yoseph, also called Kabi, the son of Shimon." "Yeshua the son of Dannai." "My nephew, Mattityahu, the son of Theophilus." "Hananyah, the son of Nadavayah, until recently the high priest."

Governor Festus greeted each elder politely, but with few words. Finally, the line of men ended.

"And where is King Agrippa?" Festus asked Hanan. "I had hoped to meet him. I knew his father in Rome many years ago. A most delightful man."

Delightful? Hanan worked to keep his face impassive. That was not a word he would associate with Agrippa Senior. "The king has gone to his palace in Banias for the summer."

"Send word that I wish to see him in Caesarea." Festus gave a half smile. "There are some points on which I would like to ask his advice."

"I will send a messenger in the morning," Hanan said. "In the meantime, the elders would like to know more about you — your record of service to Caesar and your philosophy of governing."

Festus nodded. "I would be more interested to hear your own concerns, but I will say a few words about myself first. You will translate?"

"Certainly." Hanan escorted the governor to the center of the room and took a position next to him. Yes, this would turn out most excellently. The governor had come to listen. He would hear all that his ears could hold.

The priests took seats on the stone benches set against the walls at the perimeter of the room. Festus looked around the room, waiting for quiet.

"My friends, I come of an equestrian family in Rome and have spent my career in military service," Festus began. He quickly reviewed his accomplishments in Spain, in Germany, and most recently in Syria. On retiring to Rome, he had come to the attention of Caesar Nero through a family friend named Seneca, who had tutored Caesar when he was a boy.

"And so, though I am grown gray in the service of Rome, Caesar has sent me here to replace Governor Felix on account of his mishandling of the unfortunate riots in Caesarea. I stand before you at your service." Festus bowed his head a fraction. "Now I would learn from you. Judea is a small but complex province, and my predecessors have failed to maintain peace here. I will do my utmost to improve the situation."

A moment of stunned silence followed. Nobody had expected much from a governor of Rome. Hanan allowed himself to hope that disaster could be averted.

The former high priest Hananyah ben Nadavayah stood up. "The situation in Caesarea is dangerous. Jews there are condemned to a second-class citizenship, which is unacceptable. The *goyim* beat them, destroy their market stalls, and provoke them without mercy. We demand justice."

Hanan translated this to Greek, but he did not demand justice. He politely requested it.

Governor Festus nodded gravely. "I will meet with the principal citizens of Caesarea when I return there. I have been told that this story has two sides, and I will hear both. My mandate is to bring peace, and my long experience tells me that peace follows from justice. Therefore, I will pursue justice. For both sides."

Hanan repeated this in Aramaic. Heads nodded around the room. They had not expected more. Most had expected much less. Festus was clearly cut from a different cloth than Felix. But that was only to be expected. Festus came of a family of aristocrats, whereas Felix was scum, born a slave, a man who bought his freedom and then thought he was as good as other men born free. A man who did not hesitate to seduce a woman of the house of Herod from her lawful husband. A man who robbed the country to ruin.

Next, Yoseph Kabi stood and presented a complaint about the banditry in the countryside. Felix had done nothing to stop the outlaws, and his policies increased the banditry by taxing the land beyond what it could bear, driving the poorest from their farms. Now it was no longer safe to travel on the roads because of the bandits, who robbed and killed without mercy. Jerusalem was unsafe during the festivals, when dagger-men came in from the countryside and hid in the crowds.

Festus promised to deal with the matter justly. He had no intent to enrich himself beyond the normal amount that any governor would take, and therefore he would set the taxation at an equitable level. He would execute justice for the province and bring the bandits to trial swiftly.

Justice. Hanan liked the sound of this man. Festus was committed to justice.

"Very good, then. What more?" Festus said.

Hanan cleared his throat. "Excellency, there is a matter of justice which Governor Felix left unresolved. Two years ago, we arrested a man in the courts of our Temple."

All around the room, the chief priests sat up straighter, leaned forward, turned their heads to hear better. Not all of them looked eager for Hanan to continue, but he cared nothing for them. Such men were soft, unwilling to do a hard thing, though necessity demanded it.

"This man, a Jew of Roman citizenship, whose name is called Paulos in Greek, had taken a Gentile with him into the inner courts of the Temple — a violation of our laws. Caesar has given us the right to execute the death penalty against such a man. However, the tribune of the Fortress Antonia took this criminal from us with great violence and sent him to Felix for trial. As you have heard, Felix cared nothing for justice, and left the man to rot in prison while expecting a bribe. Now we ask that you do us this favor as a token of your goodwill — to send this man Paulos back to Jerusalem to be tried according to our laws."

Governor Festus narrowed his eyes and scanned the room. "You wish me to return only this one man to Jerusalem? This is the only favor you ask?"

That was good. The governor saw this request as a small thing. "Yes, Excellency. Only Paulos. We wish to try him according to our own laws, as Caesar allows us."

"But . . ." Confusion and doubt spread across the governor's face. "What of the other man?"

Hanan struggled to keep his face neutral. "We ask only for Paulos."

"Yes, I understand." The governor did not look like a man who understood. "But what became of the man you arrested with Paulos? The Gentile he took into your Temple?"

Hanan coughed, stalling for time. There was no Gentile arrested with Paulos, but he could not possibly say so. If he admitted this, his case would collapse. But if he pursued the lie further, Festus would continue asking for more evidence. He seemed a man who deliberated fully. "Excellency, Caesar has sent you here to perform justice. This is a matter of our own religious law, and we ask — as a favor — that you give this man into our hands."

"You said he has Roman citizenship?" Festus said. "Such a man has rights under Roman law. I will not give him into your hands until I have given him a hearing myself. It is a matter of simple justice."

"He has violated our laws — "

"I will speak to him myself," Festus said, and his voice took on the hardness of steel. "I am returning to Caesarea when I complete my business here. If you have any charges against Paulos, you may send a delegation to the hearing."

"But — "

Governor Festus crossed his arms. "Are there any other matters you wish to raise?"

Hanan bit back his fury. It would do no good to argue. He had failed this time. He would not fail in Caesarea. He would say the words needed to bring Paulos back to Jerusalem.

On the way, there would be a most unfortunate attack by bandits, and one fewer messianic would be left to trouble the world.

Ari

Ari did not know what to expect on this trip to Caesarea. Certainly, it would do Rivka good to break free from Jerusalem for a few days. Whispers about the "witch woman" followed her wherever she went in the city. She had now gone two whole months without assisting in a delivery. Therefore she enjoyed more sleep, but . . . it hurt her deeply. She had not yet recovered from the disaster of the eclipse.

Whereas Ari's reputation had suffered little harm. For a few days after the eclipse, he had seen little business. Then the builders of the city, knowing a good thing when they lacked it, descended on him again with new problems to be solved. Ari the Kazan had high honor in the city of God, while Rivka was feared and distrusted.

My life has broken into yet more shards.

Ari looked back to where the few women in the merchant caravan walked. Rivka walked alone. The other women treated her as a non-person. Ari wished he could walk with her, but for a man to walk together with his woman — that would make a scandal. The merchants would not allow them to walk with the caravan, sharing in the benefits of the hired guards. And that would be too dangerous. Ari had done much craziness in his life, but even he was not such a fool to walk alone with Rivka and Gamaliel to Caesarea, when the hill-country teemed with bandits.

Nor would Gamaliel have agreed to such craziness. It had taken much persuasion, even when Rivka's prediction came true, to get Gamaliel to agree to this journey. It was a three-day walk, about a hundred kilometers, in the heat of the summer. All so that Rivka could take a message to Renegade Saul. A woman instructing a man. Foolishness.

Ari would not have come, except that Rivka promised to show him a great sight. Gamaliel's uncle, Renegade Saul. The man Ari had loathed all his life, the man who would turn these harmless followers of Rabban Yeshua into a Gentile church that would ruin the world. Rivka promised that Ari would see the real Saul, a man different than Ari had heard of. A man who might repair the shards of Ari's life.

It was a chance, and Ari knew it would not come again. So he came. But he did not think Renegade Saul could teach him anything he cared to hear.

They were walking up the coastal highway today. To their left, the Great Sea glittered in the sunlight. Along their right, the farmland of the Sharon Valley. Wheat fields. Cattle ranches. Far to the east loomed the brown hill-country of Samaria north of Jerusalem. Renegade Jews lived there, Samaritans, with their own customs, their own temple, their own Torah. Mortal enemies of Jews. All this enmity between Jew and Jew was foolishness.

Ari noticed that Gamaliel was now studying him. "Yes?" he said, amused. "You have a question?"

"When we met, I asked if you were looking for *Mashiach*," Gamaliel said. "And I said no."

"But now? Already, you see the birthpangs. Are you now looking for *Mashiach*?"

"Birthpangs?" Ari squinted down at his short friend. "What birthpangs?"

Gamaliel rubbed his hands together, as if he had been waiting many months to discuss this. "Before the coming of *Mashiach*, there will be great troubles. Many in *Yisrael* will turn to HaShem, and he will shake the heavens and the earth. The stars will fall, and the earth will tremble. Wicked men will turn to evil — robbery, oppression, immorality, and a falling away from Torah. These are the birthpangs of *Mashiach*. They will last for seven years, and then *Mashiach* will come."

This was different than what Ari had heard from either Rivka or his step-father. It was still craziness, but a new kind of craziness. "And you believe that these birthpangs have begun already?"

"Of course," Gamaliel said. "Are we not walking in an armed company for fear of robbers? Are we not oppressed by Rome? Has there ever been such immorality, such trampling of the Torah?" He shook his head. "I do not think we can bear yet seven more years of such birthpangs."

Seven years. Ari did a quick calculation, and realized that . . . in seven years, the Jewish revolt would begin. In the summer of the year 66. At the instigation of Gamaliel's friend, Brother Eleazar.

Gamaliel's face broadened into a grin. "I see that you understand. The birthpangs have begun. The powers of the air will fight a great war in the heavens. Men will fight a corresponding war on earth, *Mashiach* ben Yoseph against Armilus the wicked king of Rome, who — "

"Who is this *Mashiach* ben Yoseph?" Ari said. "*Mashiach* is to be the son of David."

"But there are to be two *Mashiachs*," Gamaliel said. "Everyone knows there will be two. Eliyahu the prophet will come first, announcing *Mashiach* ben Yoseph. He is the Servant spoken of in Isaiah, and he will suffer much for the sins of the people. He will arise from Galilee and battle the wicked King Armilus in Jerusalem, where he will be slain."

"Slain?" Ari looked at him suspiciously. "I have not heard *Mashiach* would be slain."

Gamaliel shrugged. "You are not looking for him. We who are looking for him know that *Mashiach* ben Yoseph will be slain, and then HaShem will raise him to life by the hand of *Mashiach* ben David."

Ari could think of nothing to say to this. These tales of *Mashiach* were not those he had learned as a boy. They were shards, broken bits of legend, signifying nothing.

Gamaliel's eyes glowed with zeal. "The birthpangs are upon us, Ari the Kazan. Be ready for the coming of *Mashiach*."

TWENTY

Rivka

Renegade Saul was the ugliest man Rivka had ever seen. He sat at a wooden table in a cell of the barracks in Caesarea, chained to a bored-looking Roman soldier. Mostly bald, Saul had the deeply weathered skin that Rivka had seen on street people back home in San Diego. The left side of his forehead was actually dented. And his left eye socket was empty.

Rivka followed Gamaliel and Ari into the cell, which smelled of mold and sweaty feet. Saul stood at once, a brilliant smile lighting up his face. Rivka held her breath. She had wanted this meeting partly for herself — she'd been dreaming for the past two years of seeing Saul again. But she wanted it even more for Ari. Wanted him to see that Saul wasn't the big bad wolf. Wanted him to know how Jewish Saul was. Wanted him to . . . know Yeshua.

"Gamaliel!" Saul said. "My heart was glad when I heard you had come!" He threw his arms around his nephew and kissed him on both cheeks.

Rivka hadn't remembered how *short* Saul was. She guessed he stood no taller than she did, an inch or two over five feet. Which was how he got his Greek name — Paulos. *Little*.

"Uncle, I have brought a friend." Gamaliel turned to Ari. "Please meet Ari the Kazan, who comes from a far country. He is a *cohen*, and his woman accompanies us. Ari is given to know the deep secrets of the universe."

Rivka pursed her lips. What was this? She didn't even rate an introduction?

Saul studied them both gravely. "Blessed be HaShem." He nodded to Rivka. "I have seen you before, yes?"

Rivka felt her breath taken away. "Yes," she said faintly.

"And what is your name called, my daughter?"

"Rivka." A whisper. Where had her courage gone?

"A delight to meet you again, my child."

Warmth burst over Rivka's heart like sunlight.

Saul pointed to backless wooden benches around the table. "Sit, my children."

They all sat.

Some small talk followed. Saul wanted to know how their trip had gone. Gamaliel said it went well, and asked if Saul was getting enough to eat. Saul said it was difficult, because the Romans were none too particular about buying his food from Jewish markets. Nor could he get a *minyan* of ten men for the prayers. He said his morning prayers alone, usually, but he would be glad if they could pray the *Amidah* together. Gamaliel said that they would. Then he asked about the hearing Saul would be having soon.

Saul raised a pair of battered eyebrows. "Hearing? What hearing?"

Gamaliel shot a look at Rivka, then muttered something about a mistake.

Saul fixed his one good eye on Rivka. "Do you know something I do not, my daughter?"

Rivka felt herself blushing fiercely. "There is to be a hearing before Governor Festus soon."

Saul frowned. "I have heard nothing about a hearing." He looked up at the soldier behind him and fired a question at him in rapid street Greek. The soldier answered in the same language, which meant he was probably a Syrian auxiliary. A Roman would have spoken Latin.

Saul tugged at his wispy gray beard. "He tells me there is to be a hearing in two days. How is it that you know of this and I do not?"

Gamaliel pointed to Ari.

Ari said, "My woman is given by HaShem to see some of what shall be."

Saul turned his penetrating gaze on her. "Do you have a word from HaShem for me?"

Rivka had been waiting for this for months, and now her tongue felt like wood. "You will be taken before the governor and his *consilium* to answer charges brought by chief priests from Jerusalem. They wish you to go to Jerusalem to stand trial in the matter of the incident in the Temple two years ago."

Saul nodded pensively. "Another opportunity to go to Jerusalem." He smiled. "This is good. I failed last time. I will not fail again."

Rivka gawked at him. *Good?* No, this was not good. "My father, with respect, you must not go to Jerusalem."

Saul shook his head. "This I have heard many times before I came to Judea. I came, and it turned out well. I was given to speak before the Sanhedrin. This is the work of HaShem."

Rivka felt like she was strangling. "My father, if you go to Jerusalem ... men from the chief priests will kill you on the road, and you will never speak before Caesar in Rome."

Saul's one good eye probed her. "Do you mean that HaShem will make a way at last for me to speak before Caesar?"

Rivka stared at him. *Of course.* Didn't he know that? Panic gripped her heart. What should she tell and what should she not tell? Was she meddling again, like the eclipse thing? Or was she ... just a tool in the hand of HaShem to make happen what would happen?

Saul leaned closer. "My daughter, you will tell me what HaShem has shown you, please."

So Rivka told him. The chief priests would try to convince Festus to yield Saul to their jurisdiction. Festus would make a counter proposal, retaining jurisdiction, but changing the venue to Jerusalem. The chief priests would agree to this.

Saul tugged at his beard. "Very strange. I have never heard of such a thing, that a Roman governor would judge a trial in concert with the Sanhedrin. It is not done this way."

"When you see it, you will know it was foreknown by HaShem." Rivka leaned forward. "If you wish to see Rome, you must appeal to Caesar."

Saul's eye widened. "An extreme measure. Will Caesar set me free?"

Rivka said nothing. Nobody knew the answer to that question. Some said Saul preached to Nero, then was freed and ultimately went to Spain. But most thought he was executed in Rome, without ever being freed. And yet he would make an impact there, one which could not be calculated. "My father, I am not given to know all ends, but if you go to Rome, you will testify before Caesar. Please ... think on it."

"Bless you, my daughter, I will pray on it." Saul put a gnarled hand on hers and closed his eye. "I have a word from HaShem for you also." Silence for a moment. "You will walk a hard road, and a dangerous, and a lonely, but you must persevere to the end, whether it is long or short, and you must not run faster than HaShem will lead you."

Tingling, Rivka committed the words to memory.

"Now we will pray the *Amidah* together, yes?" Saul looked at each of them in turn.

Rivka realized with a thrill that he meant to include . . . her! Tears welled in her heart.

Ari

That afternoon, Ari stood alone with Rivka on the beach at Caesarea, squinting out at the sea. The coastline here was a straight line, with no natural harbor. A U-shaped concrete breakwater extended out a hundred meters into the sea, forming a manmade harbor. Ari found it astounding that already a hundred years ago, King Herod's engineers had known how to make concrete that could be poured underwater.

"What do you think of Saul, now that you've met him?" Rivka said.

Ari did not want to think about Renegade Saul. "He is different than I expected." An understatement. After praying the *Amidah*, they had all eaten together. Saul spoke much — of the life of Yeshua, of his death, of his appearance to Saul on the Damascus road. Of the work in Asia and Greece, of Jews and *goyim* receiving Saul's doctrine of a suffering *mashiach* who returned from the dead and ascended to HaShem. Of opposition from those who wished to make Jews of the *goyim* or *goyim* of the Jews. Saul was a passionate man, and he could not hide his scorn for his opponents, nor his love for *Torah*, nor his desire for both Greek and Jew to live at peace under the rule of *Mashiach* ben David.

"Is he the horrible man you read about in the history books?"

"Rivka, nothing is as I read in the history books. Come, let us walk." Ari took Rivka's arm and guided her north along the waterline. "Your own Christian historians were also wrong about him, yes?"

"Yes and no." Rivka put her hand in Ari's. "The book of Acts consistently shows him acting Jewish. It even quotes him calling himself a Pharisee — "

"Then why does nobody take this seriously? I was led to believe that he was a man who renounced Judaism, ate pork, spat on *Shabbat*, and urged Jews to abandon circumcision."

"Ari, that's what Christianity meant for Jews in Europe for sixteen or seventeen centuries. You came to Jesus, you dumped Moses — that was the rule. Getting baptized meant getting uncircumcised. But it wasn't like that before Constantine. And it isn't that way now. You know that's true in our synagogue in Jerusalem. I'm telling you, it's like that everywhere. Saul never dumped Moses, and he doesn't teach other Jews to. He's in trouble for not making *goyim* get circumcised and keep kosher."

"And you knew this? Before you came to this century?"

"I think I tried to explain it to you that night in the café."

"You threw water in my face. A most unusual debating tactic."

"You deserved it."

Ari sighed. Yes, he had deserved it. But the shock of that water was nothing to the shock of meeting Renegade Saul today.

The man was a Jew. A Jew as orthodox as Ari's arrogant stepfather. Saul had a thick gray beard and wore the ritual fringes — the *tzitzit* — that marked the orthodox in Israel, in America, in every unenlightened shtetl in Russia for a thousand years. Saul put on *tefillin* and a *tallit* when he prayed. If you dressed him in black and put him on the streets of Meah Shearim in modern Jerusalem, nobody would look twice at him.

Saul is a Jew, and I am not.

That stung. Ari had grown up hearing of this man who created a *goy* religion, Christianity, a syncretistic mix of Jewish messianic prophecies and Persian avatar myths and Hellenistic dualism. A man who renounced the customs of the fathers.

In fact, Saul had not. But Ari had. His own father, his real father, was a secular Israeli who despised ultra-orthodox foolishness. After he died on army reserve duty, Ari's mother married a man of the Lubavitcher sect. Ari was nine years old, and much too old to believe in God. Pork tasted good, and *Shabbat* was no different from any other day. The customs of the fathers were quaint traditions, something you put on for a *Pesach* Seder or your wedding, and took off again the next day, because they signified precisely nothing. Or so he had thought.

Saul is a Jew and I am not.

It was some consolation that this real Saul — the orthodox Jew — who violated everything Ari knew, also violated everything the Christians knew. If they could see him now, they would refuse to believe the evidence of their eyes. The proof for that was evident. According to Rivka, the Christian New Testament spoke plainly of these things, and yet nobody believed it. The real Saul had never taken off Judaism, he had merely put on Jesus. The Saul of the history books was a sham, a concoction created by people who did not know the facts.

Just as I am.

Ari stopped walking. He had lived in this place and this time for two years, all the while living the customs and praying the prayers and being a fraud. He was not a Jew and never had been one. Not in the sense these people would recognize. He was a secular Jew, a cultural Jew, a . . . phony Jew.

He believed in HaShem, yes, but he did not follow the customs from his heart. He was the man he had always thought Saul was — a false Jew. And Saul was something different — a Pharisee, a Jew, a follower of Rabban Yeshua.

"Ari . . . what are you thinking?"

Please, not now.

Rivka was looking up at him, her eyes eager. "What did you think of what Saul said about . . . Yeshua?"

Ari's heart began racing, and something hot boiled up inside his stomach. *Jesus.* Yes, he had thought about That Man. Many times. The name enraged him. Not the man — only the name. There had been a real man named Yeshua. Ari had been sure of that for two years now. A good man. A *Rabban* to his people. A prophet. A *tsaddik.* Believed by many to be *Mashiach.*

But believing a thing did not make it true. Ari knew something that none of these people knew. Rabban Yeshua, good as he must have been, was not going to come back and be the *Mashiach* ben David. A suffering *Mashiach,* yes, perhaps, this dying *Mashiach* ben Yoseph that Gamaliel had spoken of. But Rabban Yeshua would not return as the *Mashiach* that all Jews everywhere looked for, to reign in power. It was an unfortunate fact, but no, he would not. Twenty centuries would come and go, and his people would sorely need a *Mashiach* many times. Yet he would not come.

A rational man must conclude that Yeshua was not *Mashiach* ben David. Rather than saving his people, he would be their doom. Under the sign of his cross, millions of Jews would be murdered by the sword or the stake. Murdered by good, honest, Bible-believing, sincere, Jew-hating Christians. Christians who deeply believed that the whole Jewish nation had killed Christ, had taken corporate guilt for his death. Christians who knew beyond all doubt that Jews mixed the blood of Christian children in their *Pesach matzah* dough.

For Baruch, for Saul, for Yaakov the *tsaddik,* none of this had happened. They could innocently believe in Yeshua the *Mashiach* and Ari found no fault in that belief. It was mistaken, but it was sincere and honest.

Yet for him, he could not. Never, ever, ever. To believe in Jesus, after the six millions of the Holocaust, the uncounted millions of the pogroms, the Inquisition, the Crusades?

No, never.

Ari sat down in the sand. "Sit with me, Rivka."

She knelt beside him, snuggling up to him, her bright and shining eyes locked on him.

Ari held her tight, felt her heart thumping against him. "Rivkaleh, I must tell you something."

Rivka

And that is why I cannot follow Jesus," Ari said. "Not now. Not ever. But after speaking with Saul, I see plainly that I must make a decision. And this is my decision — I will follow Moshe. Today, I am a Jew. Not to make a joke of it, but today I am born again. Do you understand?"

Rivka tried to catch her breath.

Yes.

No.

I don't know. She could not find words to tell Ari of the deep ache in her heart. And the deep joy. He had come so far. She wanted so badly for him to come the rest of the way. To be like her. To know Yeshua.

And it wasn't going to happen. Not today anyway. Maybe not ever. Ari was rejecting Jesus in the same way Baruch had rejected Dov — not on account of anything he had done, but on account of what someone else had done. Couldn't he see how wrong that was?

Rivka's eyes blurred, and her chest ached, and her whole body burned with a longing she could not express. She threw her arms around Ari and kissed him. "No, I don't understand. I'm trying to. I want to. I don't. But even if I never understand you and you never understand me, I still love you. I'll love you forever, Ari the Kazan."

And I'm going to pull you the rest of the way into Yeshua's kingdom, even if it kills me.

TWENTY-ONE

Hanan ben Hanan

A week and a half after meeting Governor Festus, Hanan arrived in Caesarea to deal with the matter of the *apikoros*. He brought six chief priests from Jerusalem, sound men of Sadducee families. Because the hearing would be in Greek, Ishmael ben Phiabi had declined to come. Hanan would make the case against Renegade Saul.

Hanan hated this wretched city, Caesarea. The hot, humid weather. The streets swarming with *goyim* — Syrians, Greeks, Romans, Arabians, Egyptians, Cretans, and a dozen other nationalities. And Jews of the most vile sort, men who did daily business with *goyim* and were not particular about taking a ritual bath afterward. These Jews cared more for their stalls of merchandise or their tradecraft than they did for the customs. These Jews did not love the Temple.

Hanan turned to his companions and raised his hands for silence. "Men, we are about to enter the palace known as the Praetorium. It was built by King Herod many years ago. I warn you that there are statues in this palace, so you will guard your eyes. Remember the commandments of the living God whom we serve."

The men all nodded.

Hanan strode down the path and into the Praetorium. He had come here once before. Herod had built it on a small spit of land that projected into the water. The palace, surrounded on three sides by the sea, made him feel ill in the stomach.

They entered the courtyard and marched past the pool — yes, there was a huge pool in the middle of the palace — and past the vile statues surrounding the pool. Herod had been a false Jew, an *apikoros*, a man who obeyed the commandments if he chose and ignored them if he chose. A man like Renegade Saul. Herod had rebuilt the Temple, an act of public piety that hid the fact that he did not love the Temple except as a place to glorify himself by pretending to glorify the living God. Just so, Renegade

Saul pretended piety, the better to ingratiate himself with true Jews who loved the Temple.

At the west end of the palace, they reached the hearing room, looking out to sea. Renegade Saul sat quietly between two Roman soldiers, his legs chained together, each arm chained to a soldier. He looked confident of success in today's hearing. He would not be so confident if he knew Hanan's strategy.

The plan was very simple. Hanan did not have to produce any witnesses. He had only to confuse Festus, to keep insisting that this was a religious trial, one in which Festus had no competence. One that must be tried before the full Sanhedrin in Jerusalem. He would hammer this point until Festus released Renegade Saul into his custody.

On the way home, bandits would attack them and tragically kill their prisoner.

Hanan waited. After some time, the local magistrates entered. One of them stepped to the podium. "All rise for the governor." Everyone stood.

Governor Festus strode in and took a seat. The magistrate said, "You may be seated."

A secretary entered and spread papyrus on a tall wooden writing table. He mixed ink and water and sharpened his reed pen, then nodded to the governor.

"Who will present the case against the prisoner?" Festus said.

Hanan rose. "Excellency, I will state the case."

"Proceed."

Hanan stepped forward into the open space before the governor. "Excellency, our religion is a legal religion, one approved by the Roman Senate. Caesar has granted us the right to rule ourselves according to our own ancient laws, so long as they do not conflict with those of Rome."

Hanan looked at Saul. The prisoner was sitting straight in his chair, his right eye fixed on Hanan, his left eye . . . closed.

"According to our ancient law, no Gentile may come within the purified section of the Temple courts. We have erected a barrier wall there, with signs in Aramaic, Latin, and Greek, warning that no Gentile may enter, on pain of death. If a Jew brings a Gentile within the wall, both suffer the penalty."

Hanan waited while the secretary finished taking notes on what he had said so far.

"Now this man Paulos, who is also called Saul in our language, is notorious throughout the empire. He has caused disturbances in Antioch, in Asia, and in Greece. This is well known, and does not require witnesses.

"Excellency, the cause of the disturbances is quite clear. This Paulos teaches Jews throughout the empire to forsake our legal religion, the customs of our fathers, and to follow an unknown religion, one not approved by Caesar, an illegal religion. And he urges Gentiles to do likewise — including Roman citizens.

"This man arrived in Jerusalem more than two years ago and caused a disturbance there. He attempted to bring a Gentile into the inner court of the Temple — "

"Attempted?" Festus said. "You say he attempted to bring in a Gentile?"

"Yes, we have witnesses who will attest to this in Jerusalem."

Festus scowled at Hanan. "You told me some days ago that he actually *took* a Gentile into your sacred area."

Hanan held up an open palm. "Perhaps I misspoke. Some time has passed since the incident in question. But we know for certain that he attempted to bring in this Gentile, and a riot resulted in the inner courts. We have many witnesses in Jerusalem — "

"Why did you not bring your witnesses here?"

Hanan felt sweat slide down his arms. "The purpose of this hearing was to explain the charges against the prisoner, which are of a religious nature. These are not matters of Roman law. They deal with Jewish law, and should be tried in Jerusalem before a Jewish court. This man has violated our laws — "

"But you said only moments ago that Paulos advocates an illegal religion, one not approved by the Senate. Surely, this is a matter for a Roman court?"

"Excellency, perhaps some charges might be brought against him in a Roman court, but the specific charges which we bring are those of Jewish law, and they are extremely serious. The penalty for taking Gentiles into the forbidden court is death. If your Excellency wishes to prosecute charges more serious than these — "

"Paulos, how do you respond to these charges?" Festus pointed a thick finger at the prisoner. "Hanan, you may be seated."

Hanan sat. Paulos stood with his guards and stepped forward to face the governor. Hanan held his breath. Renegade Saul was a crafty trickster.

"Governor Festus, the charges made by Hanan son of Hanan are vague and insulting to the intelligence of this court. He claims that I have caused disturbances throughout the empire — "

"This is a matter of common knowledge," Festus said. "You have a reputation, Paulos. Do you deny causing riots in Phillipi, and in Ephesus, and in Corinth?"

"Excellency, I have faced magistrates in each of these cities and been acquitted each time," Paulos said. "I have caused riots in the same sense that a deer causes arrows to fly at it." He raised his left eyelid with his finger. "You will observe that I am missing an eye. This happened in Lystra, when I was stoned at the instigation of evil men. It is a matter of public record that I have each time been found innocent. So Hanan the son of Hanan has no grounds for bringing charges against me here for *those* disturbances."

Festus narrowed his eyes. "What of the other charges? Do you advocate an illegal religion, contrary to the laws of Caesar?"

"I am a Jew, as you see," Paulos said. "I belong to the sect of Jews called The Way. We are followers of a man named Yesous, who is called in our language Yeshua, a righteous Jew who broke no laws."

"I have heard of this fool Yesous," Festus said. "I have not heard whether his followers teach a legal or an illegal religion. But we digress. What of the specific charge that you attempted to take a Gentile into the forbidden courts of your Temple?"

Paulos shook his head. "You will notice that the charge is *not* specific, Excellency. First they told you I *actually* took him in. At my hearing with Governor Felix two years ago, I pointed out that no such Gentile was arrested, and none was ever executed. Why not? Because there was no Gentile! Now, they tell you that I *attempted* to bring him in. If so, where is he? Next they will tell you that I *intended* to bring him in, as if they can read the thoughts of a man's heart. This is nonsense. They have no witnesses, no Gentile, no evidence, no case. They hate me only because I follow a different sect from theirs, teaching the resurrection of Yesous. But I am a Jew, just as they are. I pray the same prayers to the same God, the One God of Israel. My religion is as legal as theirs, because it is the same religion. We are merely different sects of the Jewish religion."

Festus turned to Hanan. "How do you wish to respond to that?"

Hanan wiped his wet palms on his tunic and stood up. "Excellency, we do have a case, and witnesses, and evidence. But our witnesses are in

Jerusalem, as I have already said, and the case should be tried there. Paulos has just admitted that our differences are matters of interpretation of our laws. Therefore, we respectfully request that you release him to us for trial by our own judges according to our own law." He sat down again.

Festus pointed to Paulos. "And your response?"

Paulos shook his head. "The judges in Jerusalem are the men bringing charges against me — men such as Hanan ben Hanan. They are biased, and to stand trial before them is to be tried beforehand."

Festus sat in quiet thought for some time. "Here is a reasonable compromise. Paulos will face trial in Jerusalem, but I will personally act as judge."

Hanan jumped to his feet, putting on a mask of indignation to cover the joy in his heart. "Excellency, this is a Jewish matter — "

Festus cut him off with a wave of the hand. "It is a reasonable compromise. If Paulos accepts it, surely you can?"

Hanan waited a suitable period, as if giving the matter thought. He need only get Paulos out on the open road, unprotected except by a few soldiers. "Very well. We agree."

Festus turned to the prisoner. "Paulos, are you willing?"

"Excellency," Paulos said. "I stand in Caesar's court, the proper venue for this trial. I have done no wrong, nor violated any of our Jewish laws, though if I had, I admit that I would deserve death. But there is no basis for these lying charges against me, and I will not be handed over to them." He cleared his throat. "*Ad Caesarem provoco!*"

Festus jerked his head back, and his mouth dropped open. He turned to the magistrates behind him and they all began whispering in excited voices.

Hanan turned to his assistants. "Who speaks Latin? What did Renegade Saul say?"

The youngest chief priest pursed his lips, his face taut with fury. "He . . . appeals the case to Caesar."

Hanan stared at him. "But . . . how can Festus grant such a request? It is absurd."

The young priest wiped sweat off his forehead. "The governor has to grant the request. Renegade Saul is a citizen of Rome. It is a point of stupidity in Roman law that a citizen may interrupt legal proceedings at any time to appeal to Caesar."

Hanan turned back to look at the prisoner. Why had Saul appealed to Caesar? He must know the dangers of a long sea voyage, the capriciousness of Caesar. Why refuse a trial before Festus — an eminently reasonable and unbiased man?

Renegade Saul was studying him, a knowing smile curving up the corners of his mouth. A terrible thought struck Hanan. But no, it was not possible.

Nobody could have warned Renegade Saul. Nobody.

TWENTY-TWO

Berenike

The midmorning heat of Caesarea oppressed Berenike, a damp blanket smothering her breath. It had been long since she visited this city, because her sister Drusilla had lived here. The wretched little *zonah*, who thought she must automatically be the most beautiful of the sisters, only because she was youngest. Despicable, the way people fawned over Drusilla. All because she consorted with Governor Felix — that was the only reason. Now that Felix was recalled to Rome in disgrace, Drusilla would learn what people really thought of her.

Berenike and Agrippa sat in separate chairs, each carried by four sweating Germans. A humid morning breeze blew in off the ocean, making the heat all the more horrid. She should have stayed in Banias.

Except that Agrippa needed her. He would never admit it, but she understood the subtleties of politics better than he did. She knew the game and he did not. If he ever hoped to become the Great King of Judea, he would need recommendations to Caesar from the governor and the chief priests. He needed her help, her quick analyses of the personalities. And today, that meant doing a small favor for the new governor. Festus had held a hearing a few days ago for a certain prisoner, and required help in determining the charges against him. Now the governor requested Agrippa's help, and of course he had agreed. That would put the governor in his debt.

Berenike's heart leaped. What fun! She had heard about this man Paulos. He was intelligent, educated, pious — and quite possibly insane. For the next hour, she would have a marvelous opportunity to match wits with Paulos and Festus, manipulating one against the other for her advantage, while each tried to do the same with her. All three were players of great skill. This was the game as it was meant to be played, and she loved it.

When they arrived at the Praetorium the Germans lowered the chairs. Berenike stepped out and took a moment to admire the palace. It was a thing of beauty, something only a Herod could have imagined.

Her great-grandfather had built the palace to occupy an entire small peninsula jutting into the Great Sea, creating the illusion that the palace itself floated on the ocean. On the left side was a pier from which you could step directly into a boat. The palace had a courtyard with a great pool and sculptures worthy of any Roman temple. Gorgeous! Splendid! A palace worthy of a Herod.

Governor Festus came out to greet them. "Grace to you, King Agrippa," he said in Greek. His eyes took in Berenike with manly appreciation. "And this must be your lovely sister. I have heard rumors, but truthfully, words do not do her beauty justice."

Berenike smiled. Here in Caesarea, she dressed as a Roman woman — with hair braided in a crown on her head, and without one of those horrible veils that covered up her beauty. Her fine silk *tunica* showed off her magnificent body, rather than hiding it like those terrible sacks women wore in Jerusalem. How excellent to meet a man who appreciated such things! She inclined her head a fraction to the governor. "Grace and peace to you, Governor Festus."

Festus led the way into the Praetorium and all the way back to the auditorium. Berenike had not come here in more than six years, and the view stole her breath. The sea, blue as lapis, surrounded them on three sides. To the north lay the harbor built by her great-grandfather — the largest manmade harbor in the empire, and surely the most beautiful. To the south, a beach of white sand stretched beyond the reach of her eye. If Agrippa added Judea to his territories, he and she would live in this palace, a dwelling place fit for the gods.

Agrippa had to get Judea. She had to help him.

If that meant she must lie, or cheat, or steal, or commit murder — she would do so, as any Herod would. Anyone who balked at such things was not fit for the throne.

After a short wait, Roman soldiers arrived with the prisoner. Berenike had heard much of this man. Tales told that he was ugly, but the tales were understated. A deep scar dented his forehead, next to his *tefillin*. He was nearly bald, with a dark weather-beaten face and an untrimmed gray beard. And ...

His eye! His left eye socket was empty. Oh! How delightfully revolting! Berenike fanned herself with her ivory fan.

A number of dignitaries came in and sat down in the audience. Most of them were local aristocrats, but half a dozen were chief priests from Jerusalem. Berenike felt their cold stares on her unveiled face, saw their hot, furtive glances stolen at her silk-sheathed body. How wonderful! They disapproved! Surely these fools must know that in Caesarea, a queen dressed in the Roman style? Did they think every city was like Jerusalem? Berenike turned her eyes wide and innocent and looked directly at Hanan ben Hanan. His face colored, and he averted his gaze. Good, let him suffer. If she could catch the prisoner's eyes, she would try to fluster him also. He was said to be very pious. Such a man would be embarrassed to look on her.

Governor Festus began speaking in stiff Greek — the usual peacockery about how delighted he was that they had all come. Berenike concentrated her attention on the man Paulos. His eyes were both closed and his ugly, brutalized face looked ... serene. Berenike smiled. She would see how long that lasted. What man could withstand the heat of her eyes?

"... since it seems ridiculous to me that I should send a prisoner on to Caesar without also including the charges against him," Governor Festus said.

Agrippa leaned forward. "Paulos, you may speak on your own behalf."

Paulos opened his right eye and stood up, clanking his chains as he moved toward the center of the room, trailed by his chain-mates, two bored-looking soldiers.

"King Agrippa, I am delighted to stand before you today to discuss the charges brought against me by a few of our countrymen." Paulos bowed his head respectfully, then turned to Berenike.

She widened her eyes, scorching him with a seductive gaze that Gentile men found irresistible, and Jewish men found humiliating.

Paulos gave her a brotherly smile, and his one eye met both of hers squarely, as if he and she were old friends. "And what a pleasure to meet the queen, also. I have prayed much on behalf of your ... health recently, and I trust you are well again."

A shudder ran through her. He had prayed that she was well ... *again?* Why? What did he know? Who had told him of her secret illness? She managed a smile and then dropped her gaze. "Thank you. I have been ... quite well." Her heart pulsed against the unbearably thin fabric of her *tunica.* Surely, everyone must see it thumping?

"I know that both the king and the queen are knowledgeable in the many points of our Jewish law," Paulos said. "I thank you in advance for

your patience while I discuss the controversy that has pursued me throughout the empire."

Berenike tried to relax, to will her face to stop blushing. Of course, it was
foolishness to think Paulos could know anything of her recent . . . problems.
It was politeness, nothing more.

"As every Jew of Jerusalem knows, I belong to the sect of the Pharisees,
and have lived my life in strict obedience to the customs of the fathers."

Berenike narrowed her eyes. This was not what she had heard. Rumors
told that he had abandoned the commandments and taught other Jews to
do likewise. Was he a liar? Were his *tefillin* for show?

"And as a Pharisee, I believe in the mighty hope of the resurrection of
the dead. It is not for any criminal action that I am on trial today, but for
this hope alone that I stand accused before you. The question is simply
this — why should it be considered too hard for God to raise a man from the
dead?" Fire flashed in his eye and he turned to look at Berenike, probing
her, peering into her heart. "What is death to the living God?"

An image branded Berenike's vision. Agrippa seizing the legs of her
newborn daughter, swinging her in a high arc, dashing her brains against
a stone table. Revulsion welled up inside her. She struggled to breathe,
trembling, afraid she might vomit. She could not look away from this man,
though he seared her. He had only one eye, but . . . it was the eye of a seer.
Paulos was playing foul in this game. He had come to the table with knowledge of things hidden.

Paulos continued talking, but Berenike's mind raced far ahead, pursued
by this man's burning eye. What did he know? And what . . . would he reveal
to this court?

Paulos said that he had met this resurrected man Yesous when he jour-
neyed to Damascus to slay the innocent. His one live eye burned her flesh
as he spoke of it. She fought to turn from that gaze and could not. Behind
his eye, she looked into his mind and saw that . . . he knew. Yes, he knew
what she had done.

Berenike felt faint. She knew what it was to slay the innocent. To save
her own life, she had killed her child. None knew her secret except Agrippa
and . . . the seer woman. Was it possible that Paulos had heard this thing
from her? No, the seer woman had sworn an oath to protect her secret.

But HaShem also knew what she had done. HaShem saw all, and he would
not forgive. HaShem would not excuse the powerful who killed the weak.

Paulos said that he had gone to both Jews and Gentiles, preaching repentance and the forgiveness of sins, lest they be punished for their wicked deeds.

Wicked deeds. Berenike's heart fluttered in her chest. Paulos was mocking her, reading her thoughts and laying bare her secrets in a code that only she understood. He knew. He knew what she had done, and now he toyed with her, enjoying her torment, watching her squirm while he prepared a fatal thrust of truth that would leave her skewered, gasping before all, naked in her sin, ruined. Paulos was crucifying her with his words.

Paulos said that he taught that this Yesous was *Mashiach*, that the prophets taught he must suffer and die, and rise again — the first of all who would rise from the dead, from the greatest warrior to the smallest infant.

Infant. Berenike felt her sin like a weight in her chest, burning like fire, freezing like a cold breath from the grave. The single eye of Paulos held her pinned now, tortured, screaming, weeping, begging, dying. Cold sweat sheathed her body, and the pounding of her heart must surely fill the room. She wanted to scream, to cry out for mercy, to —

"Paulos, you have gone mad," Governor Festus said. "You have spent too much time with your books, and you have lost your mind!"

Silence.

Berenike tried to breathe, to think, to feel something in her numb heart.

Paulos shook his head. "Excellency, I have lost nothing more than an eye — my mind is fully intact. You may ask the king and queen of the truth of these matters. It is not as if Yesous lived and died and rose again in some dark corner. King Agrippa, you believe the prophets, do you not? And you, Queen Berenike, you know that in ancient times, seers were given to know the secret things of our God?"

Berenike nodded, clamping her eyes tight against the tears that threatened to burst out of her. The seer woman, yes, she knew many secrets which only HaShem could have taught her. Yes, the prophets of old —

Agrippa laughed out loud. "Paulos, you amuse me! You should have been an actor. Do you think in such a short time, you can persuade me to play the role of one of those Khristianoi?"

Berenike shuddered and then relaxed. Somehow, Agrippa's laughter had broken the spell. What foolishness had come over her? It was some trick of his voice, of his madman's eye.

Paulos laughed too, a deep rich musical laugh. "King Agrippa, I do not care whether it takes a short time or long, but I pray that you and your lovely sister and all who have heard me today should become just like I am. Except for my chains, of course!"

"Enough of this nonsense." Agrippa took Berenike's arm and stood. Berenike stared up at him, feeling as limp and helpless as a clump of seaweed floating in the ocean. He looked down at her, and his eyes plainly told her that she was an idiot. She tugged at his arm and fought her way to her feet. Her head seemed to float far above her body and all the world swayed gently.

Agrippa scowled. "Paulos, you can keep your chains and your nonsense. Governor, we must be going. This fool does not deserve death, and he is no danger to anyone. If he had not appealed to Caesar, I would tell you to set him free. Maybe you could put him in the amphitheater and earn some money—if anyone would pay to hear him jabber."

They left the room in a flurry of laughter from the audience. Berenike wobbled along beside her brother, clutching his arm. Paulos was a horrible man. That probing, hideous eye of his! He had no right to look at her like that, to speak to her of sin, of repentance, of punishment. No right at all.

Rivka

He'll be fine, Gamaliel." Rivka gripped Ari's hand and watched the entrance to the Praetorium, where Saul was having a hearing before the king and queen. "He's going to Rome, and there's nothing King Agrippa can do to prevent it."

Sweat covered Gamaliel's forehead. He stood silently, eyes glued to the palace.

Ari said nothing.

Voices. Movement inside the palace.

Several Germans appeared. Behind them came King Agrippa. Queen Berenike stumbled along beside him, clutching his arm with trembling fingers, her eyes slits of fear, her face a white mask. Governor Festus came next, speaking in Greek and laughing like a jackal. They passed by without a glance at Rivka and Ari and Gamaliel.

More soldiers. Saul stepped out, blinking in the bright sunlight.

"Uncle Saul!" Gamaliel stepped into the road to greet his uncle.

Saul and his escorts stopped. "Blessed be HaShem! All is well, Gamaliel." Saul turned his good eye at Rivka. "My daughter, I thank you once again for sharing with me what HaShem has given you to see."

The soldiers clanked Saul's chains.

He shrugged. "Gamaliel. My friends. Please come visit once more before you return to Jerusalem."

The three stepped out of the road and watched Saul march toward his prison, his step as light as if he were going to a wedding.

Ari hissed and squeezed Rivka's arm. "Rivka . . ."

She turned to look at him, then froze. Hanan ben Hanan strode out of the Praetorium, his face on fire, taut with fury. As he passed Rivka, he spit at her feet.

Rage seared her flesh. "Hey!" Rivka shouted in English. "You . . . jerk!" She lunged after him.

"Rivka!" Ari held her back.

Rivka shook her fist at Hanan's back. "Creep! Who do you think you are? Come back here, Hanan, and I'll — "

"Rivka, silence!" Ari shook her hard. "Do not make things worse. He knows."

She spun to look at him. "Knows *what?*"

Ari's face was pale and sweaty. "He knows . . . that you have been meddling in his business."

"Who cares? I'm no longer afraid of him."

Gamaliel shook his head, and ghostly white framed his eyes. "Your woman is not wise, Ari the Kazan. Only a fool does not fear Hanan ben Hanan."

TWENTY-THREE

Rivka

On the road back to Jerusalem, Rivka walked alone, filled with longing to be home, to get Rachel back from Hana's care. She had done what she came to do — she had saved Saul. But she still had to save Ari. Silence shrouded her. The other women in the merchant caravan all knew she was the famous witch woman, and they would have nothing to do with her.

The countryside changed slowly over the next two days as they went south along the fertile green coastal plain, then turned inland and up into the hill-country of Judea. The road wound along the contours of the land, passing through small villages. The landscape changed to brown, rocky hills, steep canyons. Avraham had walked this country. David. The Maccabees. Yeshua. The land lay dense with memories.

As they entered the long steep grade leading up to the pass of Bet-Horon, Rivka tensed. Seven years from now, Jewish rebels would destroy the rearguard of the Twelfth Legion here, one of the great victories of the war. This pass had seen many ambushes throughout history. Had she not warned Saul, he might well have —

A shout echoed up ahead. Three men at the head of the caravan ran forward. Rivka hurried toward Ari. If there was trouble, she wanted to be with him, fitting or not fitting. More men went running up the road. Rivka saw Gamaliel among them.

Rivka reached Ari and clutched his arm. She craned her neck, trying to see. Slowly the caravan came up to the knot of men clustered around something beside the road. The buzz of flies filled Rivka with anxiety. A pair of woman's legs, bare.

Rivka felt dizziness slide a fist inside her head.

Ari put his arm around her. "Rivkaleh, do not look, please."

Gamaliel broke away from the crowd and hurried back to Ari and Rivka. Tears stood large and round in his eyes. "Bandits. Perhaps a day ago."

A huge lump formed in Rivka's throat.

Ari held her tight. "How many dead?"

Gamaliel's face had gone pale as the white belly of a fish. "A father, a mother, two children. And one unborn child. The bandits made wicked sport of the children and . . . ripped open the mother's belly." He turned away and vomited on the ground.

Rivka struggled for breath.

Two men nearby were whispering: "It is the birthpangs of *Mashiach*."

"Yet twelve miles to Jerusalem. We must hurry. We can do nothing for these dead."

Gamaliel looked back at the bodies on the ground, then turned to face Rivka. "I . . . thank you for what you have done for my uncle. Whatever others may say, I believe you are a true seer woman." His face reddened and he stared at the ground.

Rivka smiled. Gamaliel had spoken directly to her.

Hanan ben Hanan

When Hanan arrived back in Jerusalem, he immersed in his *mikveh* and waited until evening. After sundown, he went to report to the high priest on the disaster in Caesarea.

He remained fuming in Ishmael's reception room for the fourth part of an hour. Why this delay? That fool Ishmael should be waiting on him, and not —

"Yes, Hanan ben Hanan, what is it?" Ishmael bustled in, impatience scrawled across his face.

"We . . . failed," Hanan said. "Governor Festus ordered the *apikoros* to come to Jerusalem to stand trial."

"And . . . ?" Ishmael narrowed his eyes. "How is this a failure? That was what you promised would happen."

"The *apikoros* knew about it!" Hanan smashed his left fist into his right. "He was warned — and he appealed to Caesar."

"What does this mean, to appeal to Caesar?"

"It is his right as a Roman citizen to interrupt the proceedings and appeal the case to be continued in Caesar's court."

"But . . . that means a long journey by sea," Ishmael said. "Why would Renegade Saul request such foolishness?"

"Kazan warned him. Kazan and his wretched woman."

Ishmael folded his arms across his chest and narrowed his eyes to slits. "You are concerned overmuch with Kazan and his woman."

"I saw them talking with the *apikoros*," Hanan said. "And also with his nephew, that young Temple guard Gamaliel ben Levi. I am certain they told the *apikoros* to appeal to Caesar."

"You are telling me they discovered your plans?" Ishmael's face darkened.

"Yes, somehow."

"To whom did you tell these plans before you left?"

"The young men who were to attack the *apikoros* on the way back. I chose reliable men."

"One of them is not reliable." Ishmael paced back and forth. "I knew this was foolishness. You are obsessed with the matter of the *apikoros*."

"The messianics are arousing the hatred of the people — against Rome and against us. There is talk in the streets of the birthpangs of *Mashiach*. We must quash the messianics with a heavy fist."

Ishmael's face hardened. "Again? You know nothing, fool. Your father tried that, and made a hero of that man Yeshua. Then he thought to smash those who remained, and only scattered them throughout Judea and to Syria. Then he turned Saul into an *apikoros*. Enough! Your house makes things worse with your fists."

"If you had a house worthy of the name, you would —"

Ishmael turned his back. "You are dismissed, ben Hanan."

"I refuse to leave."

"I mean you are dismissed from your office. I will appoint a new *sagan*, one who is not intent on enflaming the people."

"And if I tell the king of your part in the plan we made?"

Ishmael turned and gave him a thin smile. "Then you will never be high priest, ben Hanan. If you throw me over that cliff, I will pull you with me."

"What office will I be given instead of *sagan*?"

Ishmael spread his hands. "Woe is me, but all the offices have been filled with worthy young men. Perhaps when the next high priest comes to office, he will find something for you — if you have learned more sense by then. I wish to hear no more of your provoking the messianics."

"I will do as I will —"

"You will obey me or you will lose what remains of your good name."

Hanan spun and stalked to the door. Fury flooded his heart, and his hands tingled with rage. He strode down the steps and joined his body-guards in the palace courtyard.

Ishmael was a fool. Therefore, he would not last long as high priest. Next time, surely Agrippa would come to his senses and choose a man who knew to keep order. There must be no foolish talk in the streets of the birth-pangs of *Mashiach*. That way lay trouble with Rome.

Soon enough, I will be high priest.

Then let Kazan and his woman — and every messianic who dared cross the House of Hanan — look to their own safety.

Ari

Within a week of Hanan ben Hanan's replacement, the new *sagan*, a man named Yoseph Kabi of the House of Qathros, hired Ari to complete the work on the pump. Ari and Levi the bronze worker made careful markings on the gears, took them to Levi's workshop, and filed the teeth with an iron file. One day later, the Sons of Righteous Priests gathered in the Temple to watch the final installation.

Ari stood in the first treadwheel and signaled to Brother Eleazar. "Walk!" Both began walking the treadwheels. A quarter turn. Half turn. Three-quarters. One full revolution. Another.

The priests around the pump shouted a great shout. A cheering throng of men hauled Ari out of his treadwheel, shouting congratulations, pound-ing him on the back, dancing around the altar. Ari felt a great joy. His dis-honor was turned to honor. HaShem had changed his fortunes, and for this he felt grateful.

Afterwards, the men went to a beer-shop to celebrate. "What next for you, Ari the Kazan?" Brother Eleazar tipped back his huge head and drained a stone cup of beer.

Ari smiled. "King Agrippa's steward has offered me many *dinars* to design a new dining room for his palace."

Eleazar's black eyes glowed. "I spit on Agrippa and all the House of Herod."

Ari shrugged. "The money he spends will hire many men, and that will aid the city."

Eleazar did not look interested. Ari knew it was useless to teach eco-nomics to him. As well teach physics to a bear.

Gamaliel's friend Brother Yoseph brought more beer. As he handed Ari a cup, Yoseph said in a quiet voice, "Ari the Kazan, I heard something in my father's house today."

Yoseph, like Eleazar, came of an aristocratic family and occasionally heard useful gossip. Ari knew him to have a sober mind and good judgment. "Yes, what did you hear?"

Yoseph looked both ways, then leaned close to Ari. "Hanan ben Hanan is angry at you."

Ari gave a wry smile. "I had some inkling of this already."

Yoseph took a sip of his ale. "He has sworn vengeance on Kazan."

"I am not afraid of ben Hanan." Which was a lie, but Ari could not think what else to say. "He is only a man, after all, and not even King Armilus of Rome."

Eyebrows went up around the circle. Smiles. Laughter. Ari saw that he had scored a point.

A look passed between Eleazar and Gamaliel. Eleazar took a long swallow from his ale. "Speaking of Armilus, Ari the Kazan, have you given thought to the matter of *Mashiach?* We have given you much aid. When *Mashiach* comes, he will need war machines for his army. You must come to our aid before then. It is not enough that you will join him only when he appears."

Ari hesitated. This was foolishness, but . . . what could he tell them? They could not see the far future. "I will . . . think on the matter."

Eleazar studied him intently. "Do not think too long, Ari the Kazan. The birthpangs have begun. Soon all creation will writhe in the wrath of HaShem before the great and terrible Day of the Lord."

PART THREE

BIRTHPANGS

Summer, a.d. 60

Take care that no one deceives you. Many will come using my name and saying, "I am he," and they will deceive many. When you hear of wars and rumors of wars, do not be alarmed, this is something that must happen, but the end will not be yet. For nation will fight against nation, and kingdom against kingdom. There will be earthquakes here and there; there will be famines. This is the beginning of birthpangs.

—Rabban Yeshua,
Mark 13:5–8, Jerusalem Bible

TWENTY-FOUR

Hana

Hana woke up weeping. Little Dov lay beside her. She must not wake him, no, she must not. Behind her, Baruch snored. Soon he would wake and go to pray and then he would spend the day copying Torah scrolls. He was a good man, a kind man, a lonely man. He much desired a son of his own. Prayed to HaShem for a son of his own.

But she was barren. In the night, she had woken and found that again this month, she was not pregnant. Tears washed her cheeks. She had done what she could, and yet HaShem had not heard her cry. She was barren, like that other Hana, the mother of the prophet Shmuel, who went to the tabernacle and cried to HaShem. Then the priest Eli prayed for her and she bore a son for her husband.

Dov woke with a start and kicked his legs. Hana soothed him with her hand. "Shhhh, little bear."

He turned toward her. She heard the sounds of his hunger and she felt glad. Next year he would be three, and then she would wean him. Then perhaps HaShem would take away her barrenness and she would rejoice. If HaShem gave her a son, she would call his name Shmuel, after the prophet, the righteous man. Hana pulled Dov to her. He seized her breast with his fat hands and began suckling.

Hana stroked his fine hair and sighed. It was joy to be a mother in *Yisrael*, yes, joy. She would pray to HaShem and he would grant the desire of her heart.

He is mine, fool. Mine, and I shall have him.

Hana shuddered. She had not heard the voice of the wicked man in many months. Yaakov the *tsaddik* had prayed for her, and the voice had gone. He was a good man, Yaakov, a very good man, and he loved Baruch and little Dov. She must go to him and he would make the wicked man's voice go away again. And he would pray to HaShem for her son who would be born. Yaakov was a righteous man, and HaShem would grant his prayer, and she would name her son Shmuel. A good name.

He is mine.

Hana squeezed her fists so that her nails dug into her hands. The wicked man would not win, no, never! He had done a wicked thing once, but he had no power anymore forever. Yaakov the *tsaddik* would pray to HaShem in the name of Rabban Yeshua, and the evil man must go. He would never touch Dov. HaShem would protect Dov from the —

Laughter. High and far away, riding the wings of the night, the wicked man laughed. *Fool. HaShem cannot protect him. HaShem did not protect you, and he did not protect Dov. Neither will he protect Shmuel. That one too is mine!*

Hana moaned. Dov stirred in his sleep, then released her and began screaming. Baruch stirred behind her. She felt his strong hand on her shoulder. "Hanaleh?"

She cuddled Dov to her. "Do not touch me. I am unclean again."

Baruch pulled back his hand. Hana wanted to cry out that she was sorry, that next month it would be different, that she would bear him a son, that she would call his name Shmuel. But her mouth could not make the words. Dov found her again and suckled noisily.

Baruch said nothing, and his silence cut Hana like a knife. At last, when a little pink light shone in at the window, he stood up and began dressing.

Dov stopping nursing and pointed his fat hand at Baruch. "*Abba!*" He laughed out loud and stood up. "*Abba!*" He ran to Baruch and threw his arms around him. "*Abba, up!*"

Baruch's face became wood. Hana's heart felt cold. If only Baruch would pick him up, then love would grow in his heart. A man could not hold the son of his woman in his arms and not feel love.

But Baruch stood as still as stone. "Hanaleh."

A pain stabbed at her chest. "Yes, Baruch." She sat up and tugged on Dov's little arms. "Come, little bear. Come to *Imma. Imma* loves you. *Abba* loves you. Now he must go and pray to HaShem."

Dov turned and smiled at her, such a smile that it would break a man's heart. "*Abba!*" He snuggled into her arms and laughed out loud. "*Abba!*"

Baruch took his *tallit* and went out.

Hana wanted to weep, but she had no more tears.

Baruch

Baruch strode toward his synagogue, feeling ice in his heart and fire on his leg where the boy had touched him. The wicked man had scorched him with fire, with hot iron, with pain beyond pain. Why did HaShem allow this thing? Fierce anger filled Baruch's heart at the evil done by the wicked man. He would pray to HaShem to unleash his holy wrath against the wicked man, even in Sheol. And he would pray again that he might . . . somehow grow to love the boy, as Rabban Yeshua commanded.

If Baruch could raise up love in his heart, he would have raised it up. A thousand times, he would have raised it up. But it was not possible. It would be a lie against all nature, and Baruch would never lie. He reached the door of Ari the Kazan and raised his hand to knock.

The door opened. Brother Ari stumbled out, his eyes hollow and tired.

They walked in silence to the synagogue. When they arrived, the brothers of The Way had already begun the morning prayers. Baruch closed his eyes and tried to enter into the *Amidah*, but his mind would not obey. Hana wished desperately to be pregnant and was not. Baruch's prayers were ineffectual and he did not know why.

All the cosmos was appointed against him. There was a knot in the universe, a knot of evil. A man could move it from here to there, but he could not remove it entirely. Was HaShem also powerless against this evil? No, that made no sense. A man could believe many kinds of foolishness, but to believe that HaShem could not do a thing — that was beyond foolishness.

Why then did HaShem allow it? Because Baruch had sinned? And Hana? Yes, perhaps. But what sin had the boy committed? No, it was not possible that he had sinned.

Finally, the *Amidah* ended. Baruch sighed. He had failed to enter into the prayers. Today would be a day of sadness, of evil.

Warm laughter washed over the room. Men's heads turned. Baruch felt his heart leap within him. He nudged Ari. "Is that the voice of . . . ?" He dared not hope.

Ari stood on his toes and craned his neck, and his eyes widened. A smile leaped across his face. "Blessed be HaShem. Brother Shmuel has returned. Come along, Brother Baruch." He pushed forward.

A crowd had gathered already, and Baruch could not see over their heads. He waited impatiently, listening to the sounds of greeting, of men kissing each other in joy, of excited questions. More men crowded around. Baruch wanted to push through, but other men also wished to see. He waited, listening to the familiar voice, his heart sparking with new joy.

Finally, the men before him moved aside. Yaakov the *tsaddik* stood there, his eyes shining, his hand on the shoulder of a tall man with thick

black hair which hung to his waist. Brother Shmuel the prophet. Holy bold-
ness shone in his eyes. Baruch saw that he was no longer the retiring youth
who had gone out to the desert. Surely he had met HaShem there, for he
was a changed man.

A smile burned on Brother Shmuel's lips. "Brother Baruch! Brother
Ari!" He flung his arms around them and kissed them both. "You are troubled, Brother Baruch."

Baruch nodded. How could he explain all that had happened in the
many months since he had last seen Brother Shmuel? "I have suffered
much attack . . . by a wicked man."

Brother Shmuel looked into him. "The king of Amalek has done you
great injury."

Baruch did not understand this metaphor, but Brother Shmuel was a
deep and complex man. One did not always understand clearly the words
of a prophet. "Do you have a word from HaShem for me on this matter?"

"We will speak of it another time," Brother Shmuel said. "HaShem will
bring you healing when the king of Amalek is truly dead."

Baruch took in Brother Shmuel's deeply tanned face and his glowing
smile. "Your time in the desert has treated you well."

Brother Shmuel nodded. "HaShem appeared to me in the desert and
taught me many things." He held up his left hand. "HaShem came in great
power."

Baruch stared at the smallest finger of Brother Shmuel's hand. Baruch
had prayed for this finger many times, to no effect. It was now straight and
strong. Joy rushed into Baruch's heart. "Blessed be HaShem! You must tell
us all of this wonder."

Brother Shmuel smiled. "I will speak of it to all the men, but not today."

"On *Shabbat*, then."

"On the day when HaShem reveals to me that I will speak of this, and
many other things, then I will speak of them. A time of trouble lies ahead
for our people. Trouble such as the Rabban spoke of. The birthpangs are
upon us." Brother Shmuel cocked his head to one side, listening.

Baruch heard nothing.

Brother Shmuel nodded. "Yes, I will speak of it no more until HaShem
gives me leave. Now I must seek a quiet place to pray. Watch and be ready
for the birthpangs, and beware the king of Amalek!"

TWENTY-FIVE

Rivka

I'm all out, Racheleh." Rivka lifted her daughter away. "Still hungry?"

Rachel nodded. "Milk."

Rivka set her on the floor. "Go ask Aunt Hana if she's got any." Which was a little weird, but Rivka had gotten used to a lot of things after three years in Jerusalem.

Rachel toddled over to Hana's rocking chair. Dov sat in Hana's lap, nursing lazily. Rachel pointed a chubby finger at Hana. "Milk." Hana pulled her up beside Dov and cuddled both of them. Dov put a pudgy paw on Rachel's head, patting her with all the love of a two year old.

Rivka rocked in her chair. Lucky for her that Hana seemed to have an unlimited supply. Rachel still liked nursing, but Rivka just didn't have much anymore. Which was fine with her. She liked being a mother, but she'd had enough of this nursing business to last her a lifetime.

Not that she had much else to do. She hired help to deal with most of the housework. Rivka rocked her chair. What she wanted was to get involved in the city. Warn people about what was coming. Make a difference. But fat chance of that until —

"Rachel play!" Dov slid off Hana's lap and held out his arms. "Rachel play!"

Rachel pushed away from Hana and bounced down onto the floor. Dov wrapped her in a great big teddy bear hug and lifted her right off the floor. Rivka could not get over how *strong* he was. Dov tottered around the room, dangling Rachel's feet above the floor while she shrieked in perfect glee. "Rachel love me!" he bellowed, his face pink with joy. Dov seemed to love everybody, whether they deserved it or not — even Baruch.

Finally he set her down and planted a sloppy kiss on her cheek. Rachel took his hands in hers and danced around him. "Dov!"

The two children played together for a while. Rivka closed her eyes and listened to the sounds of pure and exquisite joy. This was her whole life. Rivka Meyers, homebody, woman of Ari the Kazan.

Witch woman, suspected of keeping a familiar spirit, viewed with dark eyes by her neighbors, known to all Jerusalem. Not every merchant would sell her vegetables in the market. Some women would turn and scurry up the street if they saw her coming. And if a man dared to talk to her — good grief, the guy would probably be burned at the stake. Brother Baruch stood up for her. Ari's friend Gamaliel also. And Yaakov the *tsaddik*.

But even Yaakov could not make the women of The Way accept Rivka. Women who had been her friends before the rumors began. Women she had helped through childbirth. Now she was an outcast. She had only Hana, dear Hana, obsessed with getting pregnant again. Midwife Marta came by occasionally, though she was busier than ever.

Nobody ever asked for the witch woman to serve as a midwife. There were babies born every day, women who died of infection because some idiot didn't wash her hands before attending the birth. Rivka wanted to shriek, but who would listen?

"Rivkaleh, we should go to the market," Hana said. "Baruch was much pleased with those Syrian figs we bought yesterday."

Rivka cracked her eyes open, wishing she could just stay inside all day. Right, that made sense. Poor pitiful Rivka. Sit here and rot because people thought . . . things. Since when did she care what people thought?

She pushed herself out of her chair. "Racheleh! Dov! Market!"

The toddlers grabbed her hands. "Market! Market!"

Hana stood up too and took Dov's other little fist. "Come, little bear. We must buy figs for *Abba*."

"*Abba!*" Dov shrieked. A grin split his cheeks. "Figs for *Abba!*"

The heat of the day had begun to fade when they arrived at the upper market. To the west, across the broad plaza, Herod's Palace gleamed in the late afternoon sunshine. It was not the palace where Agrippa and his sister stayed, the Hasmonean Palace near the Temple. Nobody lived in Herod's Palace, although the governor of Judea stayed there when he visited Jerusalem.

Rivka saw movement near the palace. Red feathers atop iron helmets. Her heart twisted. Governor Festus must have arrived today for the coming festivals, which would last for three weeks — first the new year, then Yom Kippur, then *Sukkot*. She wished the governor would just stay in Caesarea. He came to Jerusalem for the feasts to maintain order, but his presence here was part of what stirred up disorder.

"Fifteen *lepta!*" Hana shrieked at a fig merchant. "Fool! Who would pay so much? They look rotten."

Rivka turned to look. It still bothered her that you couldn't just buy something—you had to bargain for it, which generally meant a five-minute screaming match. But at least merchants would talk to a woman. Sheerly out of necessity, of course.

The tall Syrian merchant looked down his long nose at Hana and curled his fingers at the sleeves of his dyed-blue tunic. "If they are rotten, then do not buy."

"Six *lepta*. It would be a crime to pay more." Hana counted out six of the tiny copper coins in her palm.

The Syrian sneered. "It is you who attempt to rob me." He turned to Rivka. "Perhaps you wish to buy something?"

Rivka shook her head. "I'm with her." She clutched the children's sweaty paws. "You two could settle this quickly. Hana, give him ten *lepta* and be done with it."

Hana shook her head. "For ten, I could buy the whole cart!"

"This is foolishness!" The Syrian crossed his arms and glared at Rivka. "For ten *lepta*, I would starve to death. Go! Go!" He brushed at Rivka with his hands. "I will not listen to such idle chatter."

"Please, Sister Rivka." Hana pointed toward the square. "Take the children and leave the bargaining to me."

Rivka ambled through the market with the toddlers, teaching them new words. "Silk!" "Cucumbers!" "Ivory!" "Cheese!" "Jade!" "Linen!"

And on and on, past vendors roasting goat meat over open fires, men ladling beer from a barrel into stone cups, stalls piled high with beautiful red-glazed pottery—the *terra sigillata* she had studied in graduate school. They stopped to admire a handwoven woolen blanket. Dov sneezed three times. Rachel put her arms around him and laughed. "Dov sneeze!"

They wandered slowly, and by the time they reached the square, Rivka heard Hana calling her name. She turned and waited. Hana hurried up, her basket of figs clutched beneath her arms. "Ten *lepta!*" she said triumphantly. "The fool finally wore down and gave them to me for ten *lepta!*"

Rivka managed a thin smile. "Congratulations." She let go the hands of the children. "Run and play a little!"

Dov raced away. Rachel scampered after him, her arms poking straight ahead like one of those cartoon characters Rivka used to watch on TV, a billion light-years away.

Rivka turned to Hana. "I'm looking forward to the — "

Angry shouts from the direction of Herod's Palace.

A large cloud of dust rose up from the palace gates. Rivka saw — good grief, those were *rocks* flying at the Roman soldiers. Jewish men poured into the courtyard, and some of them had *clubs*.

Rivka began running. "Rachel! Dov!" She heard screaming from somewhere. A woman with a squalling infant in her arms came from nowhere and nearly bowled Rivka over.

"Sorry!" Rivka kept running. *Please, God, let me find Rachel and Dov.* The hot summer dust choked her. "Rachel! Dov!" Rivka's heart slammed into overdrive. Where were —

There! Dov was halfway to Herod's Palace, his hands in the air, having the time of his life. Rachel had fallen behind him in the dirt. Rivka raced toward her. A man tripped and fell right in front of Rivka. She jumped over him and kept running. When she reached Rachel, she scooped her up, tucked her under her arm, and staggered on. "Dov, get back here right now!"

He shrieked, and dashed on toward the palace. For him, this must be a grand game. Rivka hugged Rachel to her chest and sprinted. Ahead, the dust cloud in the palace courts mushroomed up. Men raced out of the palace courts. Toward Dov.

Rivka stretched out her arms. "Dov, come here now!"

He laughed and turned away from her. Then he saw the men, many men running toward him with shouts. Dov spun around and scampered back toward Rivka, his fat legs churning like pistons, fear twisting his face. Rivka ran.

When she reached Dov, she hauled him up and stumbled toward the row of market stalls along the south edge of the plaza. A stone slammed into her back. She lurched forward. *God help me!*

Dust, thick in her throat.

She reached the first stall. A gray-bearded, thick-armed merchant beckoned her in and hustled her to the back of the tentlike structure. "You will stay here!" He grabbed a club and stepped to the entrance of the stall. Rivka lay on the floor panting, squeezing Rachel and Dov tight. She heard shouting outside.

"Kill the *goyim!*" "Break their stalls!" "Burn them down!"

Rivka closed her eyes, terror washing through her. Screams outside. Rachel whimpered. Dov clutched at Rivka's chest. "Milk."

"Not now, Dov, please. Just stay calm."

"*Abba.* I want *Abba.*"

She stroked his head. "We'll find your *abba* soon. And your *imma.*"

The merchant stepped out into the street, roaring something Rivka couldn't understand. She saw the flash of his club, heard the grunt of wood on flesh. More screaming. Then he reappeared. Blood streamed down his dark arm.

Rivka closed her eyes and prayed.

Some time later — Rivka guessed a quarter of an hour — the riot died down. She heard the tramp of iron cleats outside the tent. The merchant slumped back inside and gave her a grim smile. One of his front teeth had gone missing. "It is over, child. The soldiers have restored order."

Rivka peered outside. Dust hung like a cloud above the square. Smoke rose from the row of tents where the Gentile merchants sold their wares. A few women scurried along the edge of the square carrying baskets.

A scream from the far side of the plaza. A woman appeared, clutching her ripped tunic, limping across the plaza. A bruise purpled her left eye. Hana.

"Dov!" she screamed

"*Imma!*" Dov struggled out of Rivka's arms and raced toward Hana, shrieking. Rivka followed, walking as fast as she could with Rachel welded to her hip.

Dov leaped into Hana's arms. She rocked him, crying. Rivka reached her a moment later. "Hana, are you all right?"

"Dov! My Dov!" Hana hugged her son. "I was so ... afraid." She put out a hand to Rivka. "You were brave, Sister Rivka. Somebody knocked me down, and then my hip hurt to run, but I saw you ... chasing Dov." Tears streamed from her eyes. "Thank you."

Rivka wrapped an arm around her. Hana had lost her figs, but that didn't matter right now. "Let's get you home. What happened to your clothes?"

Hana shook her head. "Please, not now."

They stumbled toward home. Ahead, smoke coiled up toward heaven. A row of tents had been burned.

Rivka turned Rachel's head away from the scene. "Close your eyes, Racheleh. Dov, don't look."

They reached the stall of the fig-seller. Hana gasped. Rivka peered in, then turned her head, revulsion welling up in her throat. A man in a blue tunic lay face down on the ground, his arm bent at an impossible angle behind him.

Unmoving.

At home, Rivka huddled in her chair holding Rachel, rocking, rocking, rocking.

Ari paced back and forth. "It is the fault of Caesar. Word came today from Caesarea that Caesar has rescinded the rights of all Jews there," Ari said. "They are no longer citizens of their own city."

Rivka sighed. "And that was worth causing a riot? Burning the market? Killing people?"

"I did not say it was right." Ari glared at her. "I would have stopped them, had somebody told me they would attack Herod's Palace, but I was at a job site in the New City."

"It's going to get worse." Rivka looked down at Rachel. She was sleeping. "This is the start of something new. In Caesarea. Here. Everywhere."

"We must find a way to stop it." Ari clutched his beard.

Rivka said nothing. When she said things like that, he told her she could change nothing. Apparently, it was possible when the shoe was on the other foot. He had to be really hurting, to even think of interfering with what was to come.

"What is to happen next?"

Rivka sighed. "I don't know! I know maybe one or two things that will happen in the next year. But in what order? What causes what? I'm flying blind. There isn't any more in the New Testament about Jerusalem. And Josephus is really skimpy here. There's going to be a to-do over King Agrippa's new dining room."

Ari came and knelt down in front of her. "What do you know?" His face was a web of anxiety. "Tell me."

Rivka studied him. "What will you do if I tell you?"

"I do not know." Ari stroked Rachel's head gently. Pain burned in his eyes. "Perhaps it is foolishness to do anything. What will happen will happen. But it is better to know what comes next than to not know, yes?"

Tears blurred Rivka's eyes. She clamped them shut tight. "I don't know anymore. A year ago, I'd have said yes. Now I'd rather not know. Ari, I don't want to be a prophet. I hate being the seer woman. The witch woman — that's what I've become. Because I tried to help out once. Just once, and I made a mistake, and they all think I have a familiar spirit!"

He touched her face with his warm fingers. "Just . . . be who you are, Rivkaleh. That is all I ask. Please. Tell me what is to come."

Rivka sighed. "If I do, will you do me a favor?"

"Anything, Rivkaleh."

"I want you to talk to Baruch. He's . . . hurting Hana, the way he treats Dov. Pretty soon, Dov is going to start asking why his *abba* never holds him, never hugs him. What are we supposed to tell him? It's not fair."

"Please, Rivka. Anything but that."

"You said anything. Ari, this is important. Listen, this city is going to burn. You keep telling me the future is inevitable, there's nothing I can do to change your phase space single-valued whatever-you-call-them. But we can try to make a future that's worth living. And that means building relationships. Baruch and Hana and Dov — their relationship is broken. Baruch is doing wrong by his son, and I can't stand it anymore. Now you just go talk to him and —"

"It is not so simple," Ari said. "Baruch is not a lever or a pulley, that I can apply force to him. What do you expect me to do?"

"Just . . . be who you are, Ari. That's the magic secret, according to you."

"Sarcasm is not your best point."

"I'm . . . sorry." Rivka shook her head. "Listen, you asked what I wanted. That's it. Talk to Baruch and then I'll tell you what comes next."

"It will do no good."

Rivka smiled. He had not said he would not do it. Only that it would not work. "So it's a deal?"

Ari sighed. "Yes, a deal. Tomorrow morning, I will speak to him."

TWENTY-SIX

Ari

Ari stepped out into the early morning chill. He did not wish to meddle in Baruch's affairs. He had meddled once, long ago, before Baruch and Hana were married, and see what happened. The matter with the boy. He should not have meddled. If he had it to do over, he would not.

Ari walked to Baruch's house and waited, unwilling to hasten the moment by knocking. Finally, Baruch's door opened and he came out. "Good morning, Brother Ari! You are early today."

Ari nodded. "Is Sister Hana well?"

"She is afraid," Baruch said. "Her bruises will mend, and she has no broken bones, but . . . I fear for her heart. She does not wish to go to the market without me."

More silence. Ari tried again. "And . . . the boy? Is he well? Rivka says that he cried for you yesterday during the riot."

Baruch said nothing.

"The boy loves my Racheleh," Ari said. "He is a good boy. And he speaks often of you."

Baruch coughed twice. "It is good that Brother Shmuel has returned. I wish to know about the matter of his finger." He began walking toward the synagogue.

Ari hurried after him. They walked in tense silence. Ari felt trapped. Baruch did not wish to talk about the matter. But . . . he had promised Rivka. Promised to try, anyway. "Baruch, it is not fair to the boy, what you are doing."

Baruch stopped. Ari turned to look at his friend. Baruch's face knotted with emotion, and his breath came in quick gasps. He leaned against the stone wall of a building.

"Baruch, I — "

"No!" Baruch shook his head. "Go, Ari. I will not talk about this matter with you."

"Please, I meant no —"

"Go. I do not wish for your help. You have no right —"

"I am your friend. A friend has the right —"

Baruch's eyes flashed with rage. "You will speak of it no more, forever! You are not my friend." He spun around and strode away.

Ari sighed. Most excellent. Now he had meddled and ruined things. Just as he knew he would. Just as he always did. He looked toward the synagogue of The Way, then turned back toward home with quick, angry steps.

Ari slammed the door and stalked upstairs, furious.

Rivka sat in the rocking chair, holding Rachel. Her mouth opened wide. "Ari, is something wrong? Was there another riot?"

"You wished for me to speak with Baruch." Ari crossed his arms and glowered at her. "I have done so. Baruch now informs me that we are no longer friends and he will not speak to me."

"He's angry. So he's either hurt or afraid. You have to —"

"Rivka, I do not have to do what you ask. There is nothing more to be done. Baruch is angry with me, and he will not speak to me."

"So how long are you going to wait?" Rivka jutted her jaw at Ari in that infuriating way she had when she was wrong yet felt certain she was right. "Baruch can stay angry a long time. He's doing wrong to Dov. Think how you would want to be treated if you —"

"This is exactly the difference between a Christian and a Jew," Ari said. "This notion of how to treat others. Your Jesus taught that you should do to others as you would wish to be treated. Whereas Rabbi Hillel taught the inverse — that you should not do to others as you would not wish to be treated. The Christian seeks to impose his own idea of goodness on others. The Jew respects the right of others to be let alone."

Rivka stood up. "So I'm wrong, just because I'm a Christian, is that it?"

"No, you are wrong because you are wrong."

"You're a passivist."

Ari flinched. "You are an activist, and an insufferable one. I have done as you asked, and now the matter is worse. Baruch will not listen to me at all."

"He wasn't listening to you before, because you weren't talking."

"He and I have talked of many things."

Rivka shook her head. "You weren't talking about anything that would have done any good. You weren't confronting him about what he was doing wrong. And he won't change until he's confronted."

"Yes, now he has changed. Now he hates me."

"It's always about you, isn't it? Ari the Teflon Kazan, getting along with everybody, never making enemies, never getting blamed."

Ari stepped back, more stung than if she had slapped him. He felt the rage pulse through him, wanting to . . . No, he would never hit Rivkaleh. He turned, staggered down the stairs, yanked open the door, stomped out. He had nowhere to go, nobody to see, but if he stayed here . . . no, he could not stay one more second listening to his woman dishonor him.

Ari walked.

He stalked north through the upper city, through the gates in the first wall, then turned right and immediately entered the gate through the second wall into the northern part of the city. He followed the avenue north until he reached the New City. Here, a wide boulevard carved a broad path diagonally northwest to the gate leading to Lud and Caesarea. At this hour, just after sunrise, the streets were mostly deserted. He ignored passersby and walked his rage.

He did not belong in this city. No, that was incorrect. He had learned to fit in here — mostly. It was Rivka who did not fit in. She was the one they called the witch woman. She was a woman shamed, while he had become a man of honor. He should not have married her. No, he had to marry her. He loved her. And she loved him. He could not have married a woman of this century. A woman such as Hana, for example. Hana was intelligent in her own way, not an empty head, and yet she had no concept of life outside this box called Jerusalem. No, there was no woman of this city for him other than Rivka. And yet she infuriated him, and he her. HaShem was making a joke of them.

Ari reached the northwestern gate and continued out of the city. Fifty meters beyond the gate, a crossroad led south along the western edge of the city. He followed this road for a kilometer, descending toward the Hinnom Valley while his thoughts turned black and cold. He turned east at the corner of the city and the pits of burning came into view. The day Dov was born, he had found Baruch here, and they had mourned together. Today, there was no Baruch. He had lost his friend, and for what?

He turned left again on the road leading up to the Essene Gate. He had walked the edge off of his anger, and now he felt depressed. He reentered the city, wandered the streets, aimless, not wishing to go home, but having nowhere else to go.

After some time, he heard shouts in the direction of the Hasmonean Palace. Fear tightened his throat. He should go home. No, he must investigate. If there were another riot—people might get hurt. A merchant had protected Rivka yesterday. Today, Ari might pass along this favor to some other innocent. He strode into the plaza in front of the palace. He had once taught his friends the meaning of democracy here.

But today, there was no democracy—only two gangs of ruffians throwing rocks at each other from opposite sides of the plaza. Ari shook his head, disgusted. Again, the partisans of Hanan ben Hanan and Ishmael ben Phiabi, making battle in public. This was a nuisance, and the king should stop it.

Hanan's men made a mad rush toward Ishmael's men, throwing stones, screaming insults. Ishmael's men held steady and returned a volley of rocks. Hanan's men slowed their assault, then wavered, then broke back. As they ran, a stone hit one in the head. He staggered. Windmilled his arms. Fell on his face.

A moment later, he lay alone in the plaza. Hanan's men took turns running forward a few paces, throwing a stone, and then retreating. Ishmael's men did the same. The man lay on the ground, screaming. Blood oozed from his head.

Ari wanted to help the man, to do something, to . . . meddle. But it was too dangerous. Anyone *meshugah* enough to walk into that no-man's-land risked being hit with stones. These battles could go on for hours. King Agrippa would do nothing.

The man would die.

Ari took a step forward, then stopped. No, he could do nothing for the man.

More shouts from Ishmael's partisans. They made a dash forward, waving clubs, volleying stones.

Ari's heart skipped a beat. They would try to kill the hurt man.

Hanan's partisans responded with a vicious shower of stones. Ishmael's men stopped, then backpedaled out of range.

Somebody pushed past Ari and strode toward the center of the plaza. A large man with black dreadlocks streaming behind him. Ari caught his breath. Brother Shmuel the prophet! What was he doing here? He would be injured in this battle. Ari started to follow, then thought better of it. He could not help.

Brother Shmuel strode boldly forward, his head high, both arms raised like shields against the stones. He turned his head to the left and to the right, and Ari saw a holy anger burning in his eyes — the righteous wrath of HaShem shining forth through his servant Shmuel. But this was *meshugah!* Wrath of HaShem or not, one could not stop stones with bare hands.

Ari raised his hands to his mouth. "Brother Shmuel! Come back!"

Brother Shmuel continued walking. Then a miracle happened.

Hanan's men and Ishmael's men stopped throwing stones. Slowly the cloud of dust began clearing. Brother Shmuel knelt beside the injured man. A vast silence fell like a blanket over the hundreds of onlookers. Brother Shmuel shook an angry fist at the partisans on both sides. "Fools, go home!" His voice boomed against the walls of the Hasmonean Palace. Ari could not believe one man could be so loud.

"Go home!" Ari shouted.

Others took up the chant. "Go home! Go home!"

The partisans on both sides dropped their stones. Stepped back. Slunk away.

Ari hurried forward. Brother Shmuel had done a great thing, but he would need help carrying the injured man. Others crowded around. The man lay on the ground in a puddle of blood.

Brother Shmuel looked up and pointed a finger at Ari. "You! Help me. And you!" He pointed to somebody behind Ari.

Ari stepped forward and knelt across from Brother Shmuel. "Will he live?"

Brother Shmuel looked pensive. "We must pray. Lay your hands on him, Brother Ari. And you also, Brother Baruch."

Ari's heart flip-flopped. He turned to look. Brother Baruch knelt beside him, tense, silent, not acknowledging Ari's presence. Ari put his hands on the bloody head. Baruch put his on Ari's. Brother Shmuel put his own massive mitts on Baruch's and began praying with great intensity. Ari looked at him in wonder. He had often heard of the wrath of HaShem. Now he saw that wrath in the shape of a man. A man enraged at the evil of one man against another. A stream of words poured out of Brother Shmuel's mouth. It was either a language Ari did not understand or it was mere nonsense syllables.

Soon Ari's hands felt warm. The heat crept up his arms into his chest, his heart, his head. His arms trembled, and he felt something like electricity in his body. He was shaking now, sweating. Baruch also began shaking. Shmuel's voice rose in volume, the words a ragged, raging rush of sound. Sound without meaning. Was this the Spirit Baruch spoke of?

Heat. The taste of electricity in Ari's mouth. A flash of light.

"Auggghh!" All six hands exploded away from the injured man's head. A gasp went up from the onlookers.

The man on the ground opened his eyes. Blinked. Shook his head. Pushed himself to all fours. Shook his head once more, as if testing that it was still attached to his body. He looked up at Shmuel, then at Ari, then Baruch. He stood up.

Ari stared at him. The man was healed. Fully healed.

"Go home," Brother Shmuel said. "Go home and be well."

The man took a tentative step. Then another. He reached the circle of watchers. They parted in a wave of astonishment. Murmurs ran through the crowd.

Ari felt a hand on his arm. "Brother Ari, are you well?"

His mouth fell open. "Yes . . . Brother Baruch, I am well. Are you well?"

"Come with me, Brother Ari." Baruch helped Ari to his feet. His huge eyes pooled with wonder. "Brother Shmuel, we must talk later. But first, Brother Ari and I will go home. There is a thing there to be seen."

Baruch

Baruch's heart glowed with the heat of what he had seen, heard, felt. The power of HaShem. The wrath of HaShem. The . . . healing of HaShem. Blessed be HaShem!

"Brother Baruch, please explain." Brother Ari gripped his arm.

Baruch shook his head. "I . . . cannot explain, but . . . did you feel the Spirit?"

"Yes."

And that too was a miracle, because Brother Ari had never yet felt the Spirit. Baruch wanted to sing for joy. "I felt the heat of the Spirit, Brother Ari. The wrath and the power of HaShem burned through my heart, and then . . ." Baruch could find no words to explain it.

"Yes?"

"It is gone, Brother Ari. The wall in my heart is destroyed."

"What wall?"

But Baruch could say no more. He strode through the streets, eager to reach his home, to see . . . Baruch did not dare to hope what he would see.

At the corner, they turned left. "Brother Baruch, what wall?"

Baruch shook his head. Now he was running. He reached the door of his home. Pulled the latch. Pushed open the door. Ran upstairs.

Hana's mouth flew open.

Dov sat on the floor, playing with a small wooden ball. "*Abba! Abba*, up!"

"Dov!" Hana cried. "Not now."

Yes, now. Baruch held out his arms. Dov ran to him. Baruch leaned down and pulled him up.

"*Abba!*" Dov shrieked. "*Abba*, love me!"

Baruch clutched the boy to his heart. Held him tight. Kissed the soft smooth cheeks of his son, his Dov. His lips did not burn. Baruch buried his face in the pale shining hair of his son, his only son, Dov ben Baruch, the son born of evil, now turned to righteousness by the power of the wrath of HaShem.

Hana's face was shining.

Berenike

Berenike stood at the large window of her new dining room and looked down into the square. The new room designed by Ari the Kazan was the highest in the palace, and beautifully placed for the best possible view of the Temple.

In the plaza directly below, two groups of men waged a pitched battle. Agrippa stepped up beside her, his arm grazing hers. She stepped away from him. Fool! Did he want people whispering about them? He must never, ever touch her again in public or in private. She still felt furious over the dream of last night. In the nightmare, he had killed her daughter again. This time, no longer an infant — now she was two years old. The dreams had not gone away. They were a message from HaShem that Agrippa was a murderer. She did not want him touching her.

"Hanan's men are winning," Agrippa said.

"You should stop them. Jews are fighting Jews."

"We have enough Jews."

She shot him a savage look, but he was enjoying the sport too much to notice. "We should send out the Germans to stop them."

"No, we do not have enough Germans."

Berenike could not believe his foolishness. "If we do nothing, the governor will send soldiers and there will be violence."

"There is already violence. We lack the power to stop it and the Romans have the power. Let them do the work, and then if there is trouble, they will also take the blame."

"The seer woman told us true — about Caesar's order in Caesarea. The people are enraged, and the sight of Romans in the streets enflames them. We must use our own people."

"We do not have enough Germans to stop two mobs." Agrippa folded his arms across his chest. "I received a letter from King Polemon yesterday."

Her heart quickened. Here at last was her chance to escape this wretched kingdom. "And?"

"And he will think on it. He has heard of your beauty, and he wishes to marry you, but he does not wish to be circumcised."

"Then let him simmer. Find me another king."

"*What* other king? The seer woman said Polemon." Agrippa sounded impatient.

Berenike's heart quivered. She must have a husband, but . . . she was afraid that this pursuit would fail. "Write a letter to Polemon inviting him to visit us next spring for *Pesach*. When he sees the wares, perhaps he will be more eager to pay the price."

Down in the street, one of Hanan's men fell in the middle of the battle-ground. Berenike gasped and leaned forward. "I knew this would happen."

"It will teach them sense," Agrippa said. "If he is hurt, the rest will think twice before fighting again."

"If he dies, the rest will seek revenge. The streets are already too dangerous. This will make them worse." Berenike stepped away from the window and plopped onto a dining couch. "We should stay indoors for the feast. The people are angry."

"We have to go to the Temple," Agrippa said. "It is expected of us."

She trembled. "No."

"We have bodyguards."

"Not enough. You already admitted we do not have enough."

"Not enough to end a street battle, but enough to protect ourselves."

"If there is a riot against us, we do not have enough."

Agrippa began pacing. "We always go to the Temple for the feast."

"You can go. I will not."

"You must."

Berenike scowled at him. "I will decide what I *must* do. I am not going."

"Then at least for The Fast?" Agrippa stared out the window toward the Temple. "There is a special sacrifice on my behalf on The Fast. The high priest makes atonement for the people and for the king. If we are not there ..."

"Go if you wish." Berenike stepped up beside him. "The people are angry and I refuse to make myself a target for the assassins. I will watch the sacrifices from here."

"What is happening down there?" Agrippa pointed toward the plaza. Below them, the battle had ended. Three men knelt around a man who lay in blood on the ground.

Berenike turned away. She did not wish to watch more. The man down there was dead, or dying. What was happening to her city? She felt her heart thumping.

The seer woman had been right. The violence would grow and grow until the Romans came and took away their city. Agrippa was too indecisive to stop it.

She would not go down in the streets when the people were in this ugly mood. That would be suicide, and she did not wish to die. Agrippa could go by himself if he chose, but she would not risk a disturbance by going to the Temple for The Fast.

It would be so much better to bring the Temple to herself.

TWENTY-SEVEN

Rivka

And he got up and walked away?" Rivka stood up and began pacing. "Brother Shmuel healed him just like that?"

Ari nodded. "I have never seen anything like it. Well . . . once. The time Baruch healed me. But this was different. More power. And Baruch was changed also in his heart. He returned home and kissed Dov and called him his son."

Rivka blinked. "You're kidding! Ari, that's wonderful! Why didn't you tell me that first?"

"I wished to save the best for last." Ari stepped closer, and his eyes were wet. "Rivkaleh, I am sorry for getting angry at you this morning. Please . . . forgive me. I also felt the fire when Brother Shmuel prayed. Like . . . lightning through my soul. For a moment, I feared for my life, so great was the power."

She caught his arm. "You felt the Spirit?"

"I did."

Deep gladness washed over Rivka. It was just a matter of time now. She was sure of it. "Blessed be HaShem." She nestled against him, feeling happier than she had since she had come to this city. Things were changing at last. For her. For Ari. For Baruch. Thank God.

But one thing didn't make sense. "Tell me, what's different about Brother Shmuel, anyway? He wasn't like that two and half years ago when he went into the desert. Back then, he was timid as a rabbit. He'd never walk into a battle zone. Or try to heal someone."

"I also am wondering." Ari stroked Rivka's head. His forehead creased in deep thought. "Power burns hot within him. Is there nothing about Shmuel in any of the books?"

Rivka tried to think. "No Shmuels, no Samuels, no Sams. I don't think Josephus mentions a single person by that name."

"That is most strange." Ari shook his head. "I suppose it means he will do nothing important."

"I suppose."

Ari

That day, Brother Shmuel disappeared. Rumors swirled through the city. He had gone back to the desert. He had hidden somewhere in Jerusalem. He was praying in the Temple. But nobody knew details. *Shabbat* came, and Brother Shmuel did not appear at the synagogue of The Way. Ari felt a knife-edge of worry in his soul, but the weather was fine as the last golden days of summer passed into the first of autumn. He resolved to be patient. Brother Shmuel would return when he returned. He was certainly getting most excellent publicity by staying away. All Jerusalem glowed with expectation for the soon return of the man with the wild black hair, the man under the vow of the *Nazir*. The prophet of power.

Two days after *Shabbat* came Rosh HaShanah. The brothers of The Way celebrated the New Year as always, with prayers and Torah reading and feasting. Rumors in the street multiplied. Brother Shmuel was the prophet Eliyahu, who would announce the coming of *Mashiach*. Ari did his best to quell this foolishness, but one might as well spit on a forest fire.

All Jerusalem held its breath, watching for Brother Shmuel the prophet. On the ninth day of the new year, a rumor raced through the streets that he would appear the next day, the most solemn day of the year, the day called The Fast, because no righteous Jew would eat or drink from sundown until sundown. Yom Kippur.

Late in the afternoon of the ninth day, Ari and Rivka enjoyed a large meal and prepared themselves for The Fast and wondered what would happen tomorrow. Ari went to the evening prayers, while Rivka stayed home with Rachel. Brother Shmuel did not come to the evening prayers.

Very early in the morning, Ari awoke and dressed in a fine linen tunic — a priestly garment. Even an *issah* priest had the right to watch the sacrifices in the Court of Priests. He put on his cloak but left his sandals at the door. Nobody wore shoes on The Fast, not even a king or a high priest.

Ari slipped out into the street, feeling excitement rise up in his heart like a flame. Something important would happen today. This he knew in his bones and in his soul. He would be ready.

Ari the Kazan!" Gamaliel waved his hands from the top of the steps before the Nicanor Gate. "Come up here with us!"

Ari bounded up the stairs. It was still an hour before dawn. Torches lit up the walls around the Court of Women, which buzzed with excitement. More men arrived every minute.

Gamaliel pounded Ari's shoulders. "I am glad you have decided to join us. Brother Eleazar asked especially about you."

Ari smiled. "It is good to stand with you today." He and Gamaliel joined the other Sons of Righteous Priests. Ari greeted Brother Yoseph and the others.

"We have an excellent spot, very close to where the king will stand." Gamaliel pointed toward a square of white silk at the center of the long and narrow Court of *Yisrael*.

Ari raised his eyebrows. "King Agrippa will stand here? But he cannot bring his bodyguards with him."

"He will be quite safe. No priest would allow danger to come near the king," Gamaliel said. "You may speak with him if you wish. Think how excited your woman will be to hear you have met the king!"

Ari did not tell Gamaliel that his woman had once almost punched the king. That would remain a secret for as long as she wished to keep it. The Court of Priests filled rapidly. Ari craned his neck and scanned the court. Two men were walking on the treadwheels of his pump, raising water to the tank where it could flow down under pressure to a dozen points around the court. Several priests led in the animals to be sacrificed today. Ari could not see the high priest anywhere. He poked Gamaliel's arm. "Where is Ishmael ben Phiabi?"

"In the high priest's chambers expounding on the prophet Daniel."

Ari wanted to laugh out loud. Daniel? That made no sense at all. "What does Daniel have to do with Yom Kippur?"

Gamaliel gave him the look one gives a small child. "The high priest is not permitted to sleep on the night before Yom Kippur. A matter of ritual purity. It is the custom for him to stay awake all night expounding the prophet Daniel with two young priests."

Ari shrugged. He would never understand this world. But no matter. HaShem had not called him to understand, but to perform the commandments.

On the right-hand side, four priests led a ram to the wooden slaughtering poles. They lashed its horns to the bronze rings. One of them held a silver pitcher while the other set a flint knife to its throat.

Ari held his breath.

A quick slice. Blood spurted from the ram's neck into the pitcher. In his teenage years, Ari had seen kosher slaughter and thought it barbaric. Yet he had often gone to McDonald's and bought a hamburger made of an animal slaughtered far more cruelly, thinking nothing of eating the flesh of that animal, and giving no thanks to HaShem who had created all life. In his former life, animal life had little value except as it made life more convenient for himself. Now he acknowledged that the life of an animal was sacred, that it was incumbent on man to take life without cruelty, and to give thanks to HaShem. Like all men of this age, Ari ate meat rarely, but he ate it with proper respect for the created order.

The ram sank to its knees as its lifeblood emptied into the pitcher. The priests unbound its horns and carried it reverently to a marble table. Two of them quickly skinned the carcass and cut it into pieces. Finally, the first pink of dawn appeared in the sky.

Ishmael ben Phiabi emerged from a stairway leading up from the bowels of the Temple Mount. A collective gasp rose from the ranks of the priests. Ari gaped at the high priest, feeling his jaw tighten. Ishmael wore linen garments similar to those Ari wore, but glittering with jewels. It was ... extravagant. Bad taste. One should not flaunt wealth in the face of the poor. Ari felt the air crackle with an undercurrent of anger. The rage of the oppressed against the oppressor, the starving poor against the shameless rich.

The packed Court of Priests rumbled with murmurs. Ishmael reached the stone table of sacrifice and picked up one of the hindquarters. He walked across to the stone altar, which towered above them all. Swinging his arm back like a bowler, Ishmael slung the hindquarter forward and up in a quick underhand motion. It rotated twice in the air and landed on the altar.

King Agrippa had still not arrived. When Ishmael crossed back to the stone table for the next piece of the sacrifice, he passed the gap where the king should have stood. Ari heard a deep, dense murmur behind him. He looked back and saw that the entire Court of Women was packed, elbow to elbow, with men.

Ishmael came back with another piece of the ram and tossed it up onto the altar. Again and again he went back. With each trip, the rising light of day caused his glittering priestly garments to sparkle more brightly. The rumble behind them grew and grew.

Finally, the first real ray of the sun peeked over the Mount of Olives and down onto the city. The golden roof of the Temple lit up like the faces of many ten thousand seraphim. Behind the Temple, the shadow of the Mount rolled down the western face of the upper city, and the morning light gleamed on a thousand walls of white stone. The facade of the Hasmonean Palace flickered to whiteness across the narrow valley.

Ari blinked. No, that was not possible. He looked again. Three hundred meters away, he could clearly see the new dining room he had helped design for King Agrippa. Today, the purple curtains were flung back, the wooden shutters hung fully open. Inside, several tiny figures lay on dining couches, watching the sacrifices here in the Temple.

Eating.

On The Fast, they were eating! Ari felt disgusted. The king could not be bothered to come stand barefoot here in the predawn chill. He preferred to stay home in comfort, eating and drinking and watching the proceedings as if it were a . . . rodeo. Ari trembled with fury at this insult to the altar of the living God. He nudged Gamaliel. "Look!"

Gamaliel stared at the palace, then poked Brother Eleazar and pointed. Soon, a whole row of priests were whispering, pointing, staring. Nobody was paying attention to the high priest, his extravagant garments. Ishmael came back with the last foreleg and tossed it up onto the altar. He saw the priests pointing and went around the left side of the altar to look.

His face darkened with rage and he spun to face the priests. "Abomination! Some of you young men . . . do something! You!" He pointed at Ari. "And you, Eleazar! Find some tall men and go stand on the inner wall and *block* the king's view!"

Ari had no idea what Ishmael was talking about. Brother Eleazar grabbed his arm. "Come along, Ari the Kazan, Brother Yoseph! You are too short, Brother Gamaliel — stay here and tell us where we must stand." Eleazar led the way to a narrow stone staircase along the side wall of the inner court. Ari followed him up the stairs and onto the top of the wall. They walked along, single file. The wall was wider than it looked from below — perhaps a meter, and sturdy enough to hold many men.

Brother Eleazar stopped. "Ari the Kazan, stand here beside me. Brother Yoseph, on my other side. Brother Levi, beside Ari the Kazan. Fill in the gaps."

Down below in the Court of Priests, Gamaliel waved up at them, signaling success. Ari turned to look up at the Hasmonean Palace. King Agrippa stood at the window, his arms folded across his chest. At this distance, it was difficult to tell, but he might have been scowling.

Hanan ben Hanan

At nightfall, Hanan broke his fast and then summoned his bodyguards. They strode quickly through the streets of Jerusalem to Agrippa's palace. When he told his business to the guard at the gate, the man admitted him quickly, but required him to leave his bodyguards outside.

Inside the palace, Agrippa's chief of staff met him.

"Hanan ben Hanan to see King Agrippa on Temple business."

The chief of staff looked him over and frowned. "This is an awkward hour to visit the king."

"This was an awkward day for the king to make a fool of himself. You will show me to the king at once."

The chief of staff raised his eyebrows. "I will — "

"The high priest has ordered me to deliver a message to the king today, and I will not leave until I have given it."

"Follow me." The chief of staff turned and led him upstairs into a small receiving room. "Wait here."

Hanan tried to find a place where he could not see the frescoes painted on the stucco walls. The palace felt entirely too Greek. He felt soiled, standing here, but since he held no office in the Temple, it hardly mattered if he became ritually impure. Hardly mattered to Ishmael ben Phiabi. Hanan seethed. Ishmael had forced him to do this unclean task because he had no office. Ishmael would pay for his insolence.

Presently, King Agrippa arrived. Hanan hid his feelings. "King Agrippa, I am sent by Ishmael ben Phiabi the high priest to inform you that he is most displeased with your new dining room and demands that it be demolished at once."

"Demands?" Agrippa gave a short laugh. "He *demands?*"

Hanan scratched his nose with his left hand. Ishmael had not chosen quite this word. "Yes, he demands it. It is an act of impiety for you to observe the sacrifices from your palace — it violates the customs of the fathers, and Ishmael directs me to tell you that he will not tolerate it."

"And he will compensate me for mutilating my palace? This new room cost me more than three silver talents. I had the services of Ari the Kazan in its design."

Hanan stood in silence for a long moment. "Ishmael said nothing of compensation. Shall I ask him?"

"Immediately."

He laughed at your request." Hanan ran his hand over his still-damp hair. He had gone home for a ritual immersion after entering Agrippa's palace. "And he demands full compensation for the costs of construction."

Ishmael scowled. "That is absurd. How much?"

"Nearly four silver talents."

"I could have hired Temple workmen to do it for half a talent."

Hanan coughed. "Undoubtedly."

"Ask if he will consider dividing the cost."

Hanan turned to leave.

"And you will immerse again before returning here with his answer."

"Of course."

Hanan nodded his head. "Yes, he offers one quarter of a talent — the rest of the cost to be borne by you."

Agrippa's eyes smoldered. "What? He *offers*? No *demand* this time?"

Hanan said nothing, but lowered his head.

"So he did demand it?"

"Your highness, he offers one quarter of a silver talent."

"It is unacceptable. The room stays until he offers fair compensation."

He demands full compensation," Hanan said.

Ishmael's eyes narrowed to slits. "I will not negotiate with a rogue."

"What then should I offer him?"

"Offer him nothing. We will not pay a *dinar*. The room must go."

Ishmael withdraws his previous offer. He will not pay a single *dinar*. He demands that you destroy the room."

Agrippa glowered at Hanan. "No. I will not remove the room under any circumstances."

"But . . . Ishmael demands it."

"Tell him never. I will not touch a single stone."

"I can ask him to reinstate his offer of a quarter of a talent."

"I spit on his offer. Tell him that."

He spits on you and the Temple."

"Did you immerse again before coming here?" Ishmael looked at Hanan's hair suspiciously.

"Of course. The king is being unreasonable. I suggest we take up the matter with the governor."

"There is another way." Ishmael smiled. "It will cost very little."

"What other way?"

"Go home. You have done all that a man could."

"What way?"

"You are dismissed."

"A pleasure to serve you." Hanan bowed slightly and backed toward the door. Yes, he had done all that a man could. But still he would like to know what foolish scheme Ishmael would try next.

TWENTY-EIGHT

Ari

Two days after The Fast, Ari went to the Temple with a grinning Gamaliel, who refused to tell him anything other than, "You must see what Ishmael has done."

They found most of the Sons of Righteous Priests standing in the Court of Priests, looking up at the top of the wall where Ari and Eleazar and the others had blocked the king's view. A new wall of white stone stood atop the old one, three meters high, running the full width of the western side of the inner Temple.

A broad smile covered Brother Eleazar's face. "Brother Ari! You would have been proud to see it! We used one of your cranes to lift all the stones. Ishmael hired fifty masons to work through the night. This morning, when Agrippa looked out his window, behold! His view was blocked!"

"What about wind?" Ari said. "The new wall is high and not thick."

"Come inspect it with me." Eleazar led the way to the staircase.

Ari followed him up onto the southern wall of the inner court. They walked along it until they reached the new wall. It was about fifty centimeters thick, Ari guessed. He did not like such a small ratio of thickness to height. A free-standing wall without corners or buttresses could blow over in a high wind.

"It must be reinforced," Ari said. "You should have consulted me."

Eleazar shrugged. "This was Ishmael's project. I was only called in last night to oversee the laborers. I will speak to him about reinforcements."

Ari walked along the wall to the northern end. Thirty meters away, a number of Roman soldiers stood on the roof of the porticoes of the outer court of the Temple Mount. He had seen them there many times. He had not realized until now how close they were to the back side of the Temple. They stood on a level just slightly lower than Ari's, looking up at him, scowling. Ari shrugged. Romans were always scowling.

Brother Eleazar took his arm. "Pay no attention to the dogs, Ari the Kazan. Soon enough they will be sent running into the sea. Look at Agrippa's palace."

Ari followed Eleazar's pointing arm to the new dining room of the Hasmonean Palace. The curtains were closed.

"He opened his windows and peeked out this morning," Eleazar said. "Then he closed them again so that none should see his dishonor. Ishmael has bested him."

"For the moment. Agrippa could depose him."

Eleazar laughed. "Then Agrippa would never live down the dishonor. He is not fool enough to use force on one who has outfoxed him."

"What is going on in the plaza?" Ari pointed toward the square in front of Agrippa's palace. Another rock fight? No, it could not be. The gathering looked peaceful. And in the middle of the crowd stood a tall figure with long black dreadlocks. Ari sucked in his breath. "It is Brother Shmuel."

"You know this man?" Eleazar's voice sounded tight. "My father is much concerned about him. All the Sanhedrin is worried."

"I know him," Ari said.

"This wall will take care of itself for the present." Eleazar took Ari's arm. "Come with me. We must see this man who has all Jerusalem talking."

Gamaliel and Brother Yoseph also insisted on going to see Shmuel the prophet. On the way, Ari told them what he knew of Shmuel. He was a follower of Rabban Yeshua. Ari had known him a few years ago. Then Brother Shmuel went out to the desert to seek HaShem. A strange, quiet man, much given to his prayers, quick to help a brother, quick to rage at injustice. A *Nazir* for the last ten years. Now he was back, a bolder man, with power to heal. Ari had felt this power.

Also Brother Shmuel had removed the strange rift between Baruch and his son.

Yoseph nodded gravely at all this. "He turns the hearts of the sons to the fathers, and the fathers to the sons."

Ari thought that was a strange way to put it, but yes, that was what Brother Shmuel had done for Baruch.

"Are you looking for *Mashiach* yet, my friend?" Eleazar asked.

No. Yes? Ari was no longer sure. He looked into Eleazar's gleaming black eyes. "Perhaps."

Gamaliel looked satisfied. "*Mashiach* is coming, and then your *perhaps* will become *yes* and you will give aid to him."

They arrived at the plaza. Brother Shmuel stood praying over a man with a crippled arm. Ari saw that the left arm was much smaller than the right. A genetic defect, maybe. Such things were hopeless. Even Brother Baruch had no skill to heal such things. Silence hung over the crowd like a fog, an intense expectant silence.

Ari stood watching for many minutes. The powerful voice of Brother Shmuel rolled over the crowd, an endless stream of syllables in a language Ari did not know. Nothing happened.

Finally Ari looked at Eleazar and Gamaliel and Yoseph.

Eleazar shrugged. They all turned away.

Ari raised his eyebrows. "So . . . will he give us *Mashiach?*"

"No." A thin smile curled Eleazar's lips. "But the birthpangs are upon us. *Mashiach* is nearer than you know, Ari the Kazan. Watch and be ready."

"I have agreed to consult with a builder in the upper city after midday," Ari said. "That is the only thing I am ready for today."

"Be well, Ari the Kazan." Eleazar turned and strode back toward the Temple, his great frame taking long strides across the plaza, Gamaliel and Yoseph scurrying to keep up. For a moment, Ari imagined Eleazar with armor, a sword, a great spear, striding across the earth like Hercules.

Something fluttered in his heart. Such a man . . . who would not follow him? Ari turned up the hill toward home. He must ask Rivka's opinion on this matter.

Rivka

Eleazar said what?" Rivka rocked faster in her chair. They had eaten a quiet lunch together and then she fed Rachel while Ari talked.

Ari pursed his lips. "That *Mashiach* is nearer than I know. As he walked away, I thought . . . he is such a man as the people look to for *Mashiach.*"

Rivka sighed deeply. Messianic fever. She had known it would be like this. She just hadn't known it would be . . . like this. She wished Ari would have nothing to do with that man. "You know what Eleazar is going to do to this city. Why must you — "

"Rivka."

She opened her eyes, startled by his sharp tone.

Deep sadness pooled in Ari's eyes. "Yes, I know that he will ignite the revolt. Yes, I know that he will cause untold suffering, destruction, death. Centuries of exile. But he is my friend. You likewise know the church will put our people to flame and sword, and yet you are not ashamed to call yourself a Christian. Why?"

"I'm just a follower of Yeshua. That's all." Rivka leaned forward. "You *know* he's *Mashiach* ben Yoseph, don't you? The Servant?"

Ari said nothing.

Rivka swallowed hard. He was close, so close. "If you would just . . . join with us, you could help me. The church doesn't have to become evil, Jew-hating. We could change the course of things, if you'd only help."

Ari knelt beside her, kissed her cheek. "If you believe this, Rivkaleh, then you should require me to befriend Brother Eleazar. He also is not evil yet, and you should urge me to do all in my power to keep him from becoming so."

Rivka felt very tired. "You don't believe you can prevent him."

"No." Ari tickled Rachel's cheek and stood up. "I believe that all is determined, and you and I can change nothing, however much we meddle. Now I am expected at the building site already. Be well."

She squeezed his hand. "Be well, Ari."

He stopped at the door. "You are certain Brother Shmuel is not mentioned in the books, Rivkaleh?"

"I'm not certain. But I will think on it again."

For ten minutes after he left, Rivka sat rocking gently, paging through Josephus in her mind, looking for a Shmuel. What was she missing? A healer. A prayer warrior. A man of God. A man to turn Baruch's heart to Dov.

A man who turns the hearts of the children to the fathers, and the hearts of the fathers to the children.

Mashiach.

Rivka's heart began racing. There *was* a vaguely messianic figure in Josephus for this year. But that made zero sense. Brother Shmuel was a good man. A gracious man, full of warmth. A follower of Yeshua. None of that described the "impostor" mentioned in Josephus. None of it. But Josephus did not name the impostor. Was it possible . . . ?

Rivka rocked Rachel in her arms, checking to see that she was still asleep. She slipped on her sandals and covered her hair, then headed downstairs. Rachel slept on.

Rivka left Rachel with Hana and scurried toward the great square in front of the Hasmonean Palace. When she arrived, a large crowd had gathered. It always amazed her how silently a large crowd could listen when they wanted to. It was a cultural thing. Without microphones, a speaker could not be heard unless his listeners cooperated. In America, this would have been taken as the right to shout down any speaker, and nothing would ever get said. In Jerusalem, nobody would think of doing such a thing. It was simply not legitimate for one individual to violate the rights of the many to hear. The whole crowd could decide corporately to shout down a speaker, but nobody would think of individually making that decision for the others.

Rivka could not see Brother Shmuel, but she could hear him. He had a kind voice, deep and gentle and resonant.

"My brothers, you are troubled. Why are you troubled? Because the rich and the powerful take advantage of you. The chief priests steal your tithes, and their servants beat the people with sticks, and there is none to bring justice. The king and the queen consort together, laughing on their bed of fornication, eating and drinking during The Fast. They care nothing for you and your hardship, nor will they give justice. Caesar treats our brothers in Caesarea as dogs. He cares nothing for the commandments and he does not love HaShem. His governor is an evil man who causes his men to kill our brothers without reason. You cry out to HaShem to reveal his wrath against all unrighteousness. And HaShem has heard your cry, my brothers.

"I have spent much time praying in the desert, my brothers. The word of HaShem came to me and he said, 'Tell my people to come out of the stone city, to leave the Temple made with hands, to leave the rich and the men of violence, to escape from the dogs of Amalek. Come to the desert and there you will find peace.' In the desert, our fathers received the commandments through the hand of Moshe, servant of HaShem. Now you also return to the desert, and there you will receive a new commandment. There you will be safe from the men of violence. Rest tomorrow on *Shabbat* according to the commandment, and on the third day, be ready to go to the desert."

The words of Brother Shmuel woke something inside Rivka. For the first time, she understood the deep injustice of this city. The social structure was fundamentally . . . broken. Not merely flawed. Evil. Deep anger burned in her heart, a fire in her bones. Righteous anger, the wrath of HaShem. A longing for justice. Evil men ruled here, and nothing short of revolution would stop it. Rivka felt a powerful ache in her heart to . . . follow this man.

Which was foolishness. She couldn't believe it, but her heart screamed that she should go into the desert with this good, simple, honest man. She felt sick to death of being jerked around by the chief priests, the king, the governor, Caesar. Dogs, all of them. Evil.

Rivka backed away from the crowd and began running. Tears murked her eyes, and she could not see and she staggered down the street, drunk with fear and anger and desperation. She had to *hurry*. Now she understood why Yeshua had warned so much about false prophets — because they looked so much like true prophets. The biggest lies were the closest to the truth.

Her hunch was right. Dear sweet Brother Shmuel the prophet was going to get hundreds of people killed. Maybe thousands. Josephus didn't say, but he wouldn't have mentioned it unless it was big. All those people would die unless she did some serious meddling. Fast.

Yaakov

Yaakov sat on the stone bench in front of his small home, praying. The Spirit was strong today, and he felt at peace and yet wary, both at the same time. The sun warmed him, but a shadow lay on his heart.

Brother Shmuel had promised to speak to him of what HaShem had shown him in the desert. That was more than a week ago, and he had not fulfilled his promise. It was not like Brother Shmuel to fail in a promise. Brother Shmuel was a good man. An innocent man. Gifted in prophecy, and lately gifted in healing also. A man like Rabban Yeshua, a man who burned with righteous anger against injustice. He was not yet wise like the Rabban, but wisdom would come with years.

What had Brother Shmuel learned in the desert? From where did his new power come? Yaakov had asked himself these questions many times, but he had not been able to ask Brother Shmuel. Many rumors filled the streets, and Yaakov felt uneasy. If only —

"*Abba*, may I sit with you?"

Yaakov opened his eyes and his heart leaped with joy. "Of course, my child." Sister Rivka — of all his flock, perhaps the most strange, the most delightful. He moved over to make room on the bench. Like Brother Shmuel, Sister Rivka was a good woman, and innocent. Like Brother Shmuel, righteous anger ran deep in her heart, far below the surface. She was a woman with much knowledge, but she had not yet learned that knowledge is always incomplete, that a little wisdom is better than much knowledge. She had yet to learn wisdom. One did not expect wisdom in a woman, of course, but neither did one expect knowledge. Therefore, she was a paradox, a fascination, a delight.

"What troubles you, my daughter?"

Sister Rivka spoke many words very quickly. Yaakov listened with care. Yes, he had heard that HaShem had given Brother Shmuel some new power for healing. No, he had not spoken with Brother Shmuel. Yes, he had heard that Brother Shmuel was speaking to the people. No, he did not know that Brother Shmuel urged the people to follow him into the desert.

Finally Rivka finished. "It has been given to me by HaShem to know a little of the future. HaShem has shown me that Brother Shmuel will lead many hundred to their deaths."

Yaakov pondered this in silence. Here was a difficult matter, and he felt his own lack sorely. HaShem had given him to know the hearts of men, of women. But HaShem had not given him to judge between prophets.

Sister Rivka was a prophet with a pure heart. Likewise Brother Shmuel. Many held that Sister Rivka was a false prophet. A few held that she was true, including Brother Baruch, a good man of honest character. None held Brother Shmuel to be a false prophet. None except Sister Rivka. This called for wisdom, discernment.

"My daughter, have you prayed on this matter?"

Sister Rivka shook her head.

"Have you spoken with your husband on this matter?"

Tears filled her eyes. "No."

"I must seek wisdom." Yaakov sighed. "I will pray to HaShem over *Shabbat* and he will give me wisdom. And you will speak to Brother Ari."

"But . . ." Sister Rivka's voice became tight. "My husband has not been given by HaShem to know the future."

"Knowledge is not wisdom, my child. Your husband is a deep river, a gift to you from HaShem."

Sister Rivka stood up to leave.

"You will speak with him on the matter?"

"Yes, *Abba*." Yaakov heard anger in her voice, and pain, and sorrow.

"Child, you love to run fast. Faster than your own husband." He stood up and held out his arms and felt his heart crack.

She sighed deeply and came to him and hugged him with wooden arms, a hug that was not a hug.

"Be well, my daughter. Do not be found running faster than HaShem."

"Be well, *Abba*." Sister Rivka turned and hurried away.

The quick, angry patter of her feet bruised Yaakov like stones upon his heart.

TWENTY-NINE

Rivka

That night, Rivka discussed the matter with Ari. She had no choice. Yaakov could prevent Shmuel from disaster, but he would not act without a word from Ari. She spoke for a long time, rocking with Rachel in her chair while Ari paced.

When she finished, Ari pulled up a short wooden stool in front of her. "Let me review your case, just to be sure that I understand. There is a man, whom we shall call Brother X, a good man, an observer of the commandments. Yes?"

Rivka nodded.

"Brother X is considered by many to be a prophet and he has some skill in healing. He has publicly performed healings that can have no rational explanation except that they are miracles. Brother X ascribes his skill in healing to HaShem."

Rivka rocked faster. "Ari, I don't see where you're going with this."

He tugged at his beard. "Finally, Brother X makes an appeal for those seeking relief from their woes to follow him. This appeal is not based on rationality, it is based on his own intrinsic authority. Yes?"

"Yes, do you have a point?"

Ari showed no reaction to her impatience. "The rational conclusion is that one should follow Brother X and obey whatever he says, yes?"

"No."

"Very good, then." Ari put his chin on Rivka's knee. "Against Brother X, there is only one piece of evidence. One book, written many hundred years ago, tells that Brother X is in fact a fraud. Perhaps a pious fraud, but he is to be the cause of death of many. He is not sent from HaShem. So says this one book."

Rivka took Ari's hands in hers. "We have to trust Josephus. He says that Festus sent out men and killed a certain impostor who promised relief from misery to the people."

Ari's eyes narrowed to slits. "Ah. We *must* trust Josephus? A man who gloried in his lies, who abandoned his people to aid and abet the enemy, a man whose various writings contradict each other, and a man who wrote *how much* about Brother X?"

"Two sentences."

"Yes, two sentences. You trust two sentences? How do you know to trust these two sentences?"

Rivka opened her eyes and looked down at Rachel. An angel. "I trust Josephus because he has no reason to lie. His very next paragraph tells about the incident with Agrippa's new dining room. This is the time! Do you see another prophet calling people to go into the desert? I know it's Brother Shmuel."

"And yet you were surprised." Ari caressed Rachel's cheek. "You were astounded when you found that this impostor was our Brother Shmuel the prophet, a member of The Way, a follower of Rabban Yeshua, a man gifted in healing."

Rivka sighed. They'd been over this already. Why was he being so dense? "There are always surprises in history. Little facts somebody forgot to mention that change the picture completely."

Ari sat up straight, as if had won a point. "Completely. So an additional fact might appear which changes Brother Shmuel from villain back to saint?"

Rivka bit her lip, frustrated. "Don't you believe me? He's going to lead a whole bunch of our people out into the desert. Festus will send out troops and blow them all away! Don't you care about that? Or do you only care when I *don't* warn you in advance, so you can blame me for not telling you? What is your problem here?"

Ari took her hand in his. "Rivkaleh, yes, I believe you. That is my problem. Brother Shmuel is going to lead our people to destruction and that is a tragedy. But my case against Brother X goes much deeper than that."

She stared at him. "What *are* you talking about?"

"The case which I have made against Brother X is precisely the case against your Rabban Yeshua, whom you wish so desperately that I should follow."

Ice seeped into Rivka's stomach. "Ari —"

"Please, hear my logic, Rivkaleh. I have heard yours. Rabban Yeshua is a man accounted righteous by all. A *tsaddik*, a healer, a prophet, an observer of the commandments. He ascribes his gifts of healing to HaShem, and he makes an authoritative claim to speak for HaShem, based on his miraculous skills. He calls men to follow him, and all men must choose."

Rivka sighed. "Ari, yes, I see the parallels. But there's a humongous difference. After Yeshua died at the hands of our leaders, he — "

"With respect, Rivka, it was Romans who killed him. This is another point against your Yeshua, that the legends of his death tell many details that cannot possibly be true. Why, therefore, should I believe the details of his life? You have read the Mishnah, yes?"

"Of course."

"Specifically, you have read tractate Sanhedrin. And therefore you know that the accounts of the trial of Yeshua must be fabrications. A capital trial at night? This is not allowed, Rivkaleh, and you know this. Furthermore — "

"Ari, the Mishnah won't be written for another century — after the Sadducees are dead and gone. They're the ones who ran the kangaroo court on Yeshua. The Mishnah records the Pharisees' version of how to run a court. You're comparing this year's apples to next century's oranges."

"It is a conservative culture, Rivkaleh. Customs change slowly."

Rivka wanted to shriek. "Customs change pretty fast when a whole culture gets destroyed overnight. Which is going to happen in about ten years. But just let me finish what I was saying, will you? Yeshua died and his followers continued in his teachings for two thousand years. Brother Shmuel is going to die and nobody will continue in his teachings for another ten seconds."

Ari nodded. "Those who follow Yeshua will commit murder against many Jews. The case, in fact, is many times stronger against Rabban Yeshua than against Brother Shmuel. You have two sentences of Josephus and the blood of hundreds against Shmuel. I have the whole weight of the rabbinic writings and the blood of millions against Yeshua."

Rivka felt deep heaviness in her heart. "Ari, you can't be serious! Yeshua can't be blamed for what his followers do."

"Really?" Ari raised an eyebrow. "Why then is he given credit for their good deeds, if he is not also answerable for their crimes? Why do you consider it a point in his favor that his followers will continue for two thousand years, if he is not in some way responsible for that fact?"

"Are you telling me you're going to just stand by and do nothing while Shmuel leads a pack of fools out there to be slaughtered? That's ... ridiculous!"

Ari patted her hands. "Perhaps not. I do not believe we can change this evil fate. Nor do I understand how such a good man as he could be the cause of many deaths. And yet . . . because I love you, I will help you oppose Brother Shmuel. I will speak to Yaakov the *tsaddik* in the morning. Perhaps our meddling will accomplish something."

Rivka stared at him. "You mean . . . you've been agreeing with me the whole time? Why did you go through all that rigamarole?"

Ari stood up. "I believe you know the answer to your own question, Rivkaleh. Please think on it. Now let us sleep."

Rivka lay awake far into the night, wondering how she was ever going to crack the hard nut of Ari's logic. If something didn't come along to . . . shake him up, he wasn't ever going to follow Rabban Yeshua, and that would just break her heart.

Please, HaShem, shake him up. Do whatever it takes, but shake him up good.

Ari

Come this way, *Abba*." Ari guided Yaakov the *tsaddik* through the crowd. Many people sat in the hot sun on the great flagstones in front of Agrippa's palace. Brother Shmuel stood praying over a boy with an ulcerated neck.

Ari felt his flesh crawling. Brother Shmuel was a better man than he, to be willing to look at that, to touch it.

Brother Shmuel finished with the boy and began speaking to the people. It was the same as Rivka had heard yesterday. The rich were oppressing them and the Romans were cruel. Therefore, they should follow him to the desert where he had found peace from HaShem. The message resonated in Ari's soul. Against his will, his heart tugged at him to go with this man. Brother Shmuel was a good man. He would never lie. But he must be lying, or else deceived, or mad.

He did not appear to be mad. Ari could not believe he was lying. Therefore, something or someone had deceived him. But who? HaShem? That made no sense.

Brother Shmuel finished his speech and then began scanning the crowd.

Ari walked forward with Yaakov. "Brother Shmuel, the *tsaddik* wishes to speak with you."

Brother Shmuel's face shone with pleasure. He hurried to Ari and Yaakov and kissed them both. Then he bent his head down to listen.

Too polite to embarrass Shmuel in front of the people, Yaakov spoke to Brother Shmuel in whispers. "Brother Shmuel, I command you to stop this at once. You may heal the people, but you are not permitted to tell them that they must go with you to the desert."

Brother Shmuel nodded slowly. "Yes, my father. But I may go to the desert myself?"

Yaakov hesitated and looked to Ari. Ari did not know what to say. Rivka had said nothing of this possibility.

"The desert speaks to me of HaShem," Brother Shmuel said. "*Abba*, please do not tell me I can no longer go where the voice of HaShem speaks."

Ari did not see what harm it would do for Shmuel to go alone to the desert. You could walk out half a mile from Jerusalem and you would be in the desert.

"You may go, but you must go alone," Yaakov said. "The Romans will kill you if you take the people with you."

Brother Shmuel looked at Yaakov with keen eyes. "You know this to be true?"

"It is a word from HaShem," Yaakov said. "Yes, Brother Ari?"

Ari nodded. "It is certain, yes."

"Yeshua warned us not to seek signs in the desert," Yaakov said. "He warned us to watch and pray."

Brother Shmuel thought about this for some time. At last, he nodded. "I will do as you have spoken, *Abba*. Bless me."

Yaakov put his hands on Brother Shmuel's massive shoulders. "Blessed are you, Shmuel, named for the prophet. Live in peace until the coming of the holy one, blessed be he, to reign as *Mashiach*."

Shmuel nodded and smiled, then kissed Yaakov and Ari again. "*Shabbat shalom*."

Ari wondered what to do now. He had come expecting resistance, expecting to fail. Now he did not know what to do with success. "*Shabbat shalom*."

Brother Shmuel turned back to the people and selected the next person to be healed. It was the man with the withered arm — the one he had prayed for yesterday.

Brother Shmuel laid hands on the arm and began praying. Ari listened for some time, but his mind could make no sense of the words.

Nothing happened.

After a very long time, Ari turned to look at Yaakov the *tsaddik*. Yaakov raised an eyebrow. "Yes, my son?"

"Perhaps we are finished here."

Yaakov nodded and turned to leave. "Yes, we have done what we could."

As they walked back through the crowd, Ari felt a strange sensation in his belly. He did not understand what had happened. It was not possible that his meddling could change the future. But how well did he know that future? Rivka knew two sentences from Josephus. Perhaps she was mistaken in the matter? Yes, that was the only possibility. Brother Shmuel would not be killed, and therefore, Josephus could not have reported him killed. Rivka was wrong, and Ari had changed nothing.

It was all a mistake, nothing more.

Hanan ben Hanan

Hanan squinted across the full width of the plaza, watching Kazan and the man Yaakov leave the impostor. He had suspected as much. This impostor was a puppet in the hand of his master, Yaakov the so-called *tsaddik*, who was in league with Kazan.

To what purpose? Hanan could not guess, but no doubt they planned some rebellion against the prevailing order. Perhaps against Rome, perhaps against the Temple.

He saw it all clearly now. This Yaakov was not the harmless holy man he appeared to be. He was, in his own way, as dangerous as the *apikoros* Saul. And together with Kazan, Yaakov was more dangerous than Renegade Saul.

Hanan waited still longer. At last the impostor decided that he had wasted enough time praying for the man with the withered arm. He sent the man away and turned to speak to the people. Hanan leaned forward.

"My brothers, you are troubled. Why are you troubled? Because the rich and the powerful conspire against you. The chief priests steal your tithes, and their servants beat the people with sticks, and there is none to bring justice. The king and the queen commit fornication together, mocking the law of HaShem. Caesar treats us as dogs. He does not love HaShem. His governor is an evil man who intends to kill us without cause. You cry out to HaShem to reveal his wrath against all unrighteousness. And HaShem has heard your cry, my brothers.

"I have spent much time praying in the desert, my brothers, and there I have heard the voice of HaShem. The word of HaShem came to me and he said, 'Tell my people to come out of the stone city, to leave the Temple made with hands, to leave the rich and the men of violence, to escape from the king of Amalek, from the dogs. Come to the desert and there you will find peace.' In the desert, our fathers received the commandments through the hand of Moshe, servant of HaShem. Now you also must return to the desert, and there you will receive a new commandment. There you will be safe from the men of violence. Tomorrow morning, at the rising of the sun, I am leaving for the desert and you will come with me, all who long for peace. We will gather at the Pool of Siloam. Wicked men conspire to kill me, but have I not received the blessing of the righteous one? Yaakov the *tsaddik* bids me go at once, and so I will go. Now go to your homes and prepare. The hour is short. I have spoken."

At once, the people began buzzing. Hanan scowled. Idle fools! His heart still burned at the insult the man had made to the Temple. *Made with hands!* Yes, the impostor said the Temple was made with hands, as if it were an idol. Hanan had heard this many times from the messianics. They did not love the Temple. Would they gather an army in the desert, awaiting their opportunity, then return to attack the Temple? Such things had happened before.

But he would not tolerate it. Tomorrow at the rising of the sun, the impostor would lead his flock of fools out. But they would go nowhere, because Temple guards would arrest the impostor. He must be killed. His followers would go free, but the impostor must be killed so that the Temple could live.

Tonight, after the going-out of *Shabbat*, Hanan would meet with Ishmael ben Phiabi and see to it.

THIRTY

Shmuel the Prophet

At midnight, Shmuel heard the voice of HaShem and he felt glad. Already, many dozen men had gathered at the Pool of Siloam. They lay bundled in their cloaks, asleep on the stone pavement. Shmuel had stayed awake to pray, to call up HaShem in his hour of need. And HaShem spoke to him in the *bat kol*, the audible voice from heaven, telling him that he must leave now, before the men of violence came.

Shmuel heard the word of HaShem with his own ears, though he knew that other men could not hear in this way. Other men had not lived in the desert for many months, crying out to HaShem for the suffering of the people, for the wrath of HaShem to be revealed against unrighteousness. Other men did not live under the vow of the *Nazir*. If other men lied or stole or killed, it was credited to their account as sin. If Shmuel the prophet did these things at the word of HaShem, for the glory of HaShem, in the wrath of HaShem, it was credited to his account as righteousness.

Shmuel felt righteous anger rising in his heart. The men of violence would come soon, as they had come once for Rabban Yeshua. That was many years ago, even before the birth of Shmuel. The murder of Rabban Yeshua was but the first of many. Shmuel had seen some of these with his own eyes.

Twelve years ago, in the uprising, his own family was also murdered. That was the day when Shmuel took the vow of the *Nazir*, on the day when they crucified his father and his mother and his older brothers, naked on crosses made with hands. They did not crucify Shmuel, because he was then only ten years old, a boy not responsible for the crimes of his elders. On that day, Shmuel vowed to someday fight in the armies of *Mashiach* for the avenging of the blood of his family. He was glad when his uncle took him in and taught him about the wrath to come.

Very soon, the wrath of HaShem would fall on the earth. On that day, Shmuel the prophet, the anointed one of *Yisrael*, would arise and take up his sword and destroy Amalek. He would cut off the head of the king of Amalek with his own hands. Then all *Yisrael* would know that Shmuel the prophet was the holy one of *Yisrael*, the wrath of HaShem, the anointed king.

Mashiach ben David.

Rage welled again in Shmuel's heart. Rage, his servant, his master, his power. Holy rage, the wrath of HaShem.

Shmuel arose and moved quickly among his people, rousing them from slumber, explaining that they would not wait for the rising of the sun, but they would go forth now. His hour had come. His men were few, but they would go forth to the desert to purify themselves, to draw strength from the desert, and to hear the word of HaShem. Then, like the army of Gideon, they would return to this city made with hands and destroy Amalek.

With rage.

Hanan ben Hanan

Shortly before sunrise on the day after *Shabbat,* Hanan was called to the palace of the high priest, Ishmael ben Phiabi, who informed him that the false prophet had gone out with many men.

"Gone?" Hanan stared at Ishmael. "How is this possible? I told you they would leave at the rising of the sun."

Ishmael drew his cloak tighter in the early morning chill. "Perhaps your information was incorrect. At midnight, they attacked the watchman at the gate and unlocked it. They are gone to the desert."

Hanan fought to conceal his disappointment. This could not happen. The impostor must have been warned. "Who did you send to arrest him?"

"The most trustworthy man among the guards," Ishmael said. "Eleazar ben Hananyah and his men."

"Fool!" Ice shot through Hanan's veins. "They are friends of Kazan. They warned him, and Kazan and the other messianics will have gone out with the impostor."

Ishmael scowled. "It is impossible. I sequestered Eleazar and his men until the appointed hour. They could not have told anyone."

"I saw Kazan and the *apikoros* Yaakov with the impostor —"

Ishmael waved him to silence. "I am irritated by your obsession with these people. This man Yaakov is a harmless fool. Kazan's pump has done great good for the Temple."

"We must find the impostor and arrest him and Kazan and the *apiko-ros*. Did the watchman note which road they took?"

"Toward Qumran. You will go to the governor and ask his assistance in the matter. The Romans have horses."

Hanan shook his head. "It is the eve of *Sukkot*. I will not soil myself by meeting a Roman."

"Agrippa then. You will go to Agrippa and ask him to speak to the governor."

"You could go yourself."

Ishmael narrowed his eyes. "I will have nothing to do with that filth. I have heard rumors of him and his sister — "

"Rumors begun by the impostor."

"Still, the people believe them. In any event, he will refuse to see me, because of the matter of the wall. I will not soil my feet on Agrippa's flagstones."

"And therefore, you expect me to soil mine?"

"You will immerse before you report back to me."

Hanan delivered the message to the king shortly after sunrise. "Ishmael demands that you speak to the governor about the troublemaker."

Agrippa scowled. "Why does he not make his demands in person?"

"It is the eve of the feast."

Fury widened Agrippa's eyes. "So I am unclean? Is that it?"

"I did not say so. Ishmael is the high priest and he has many duties. Your highness is aware that the people hold this impostor to be a prophet and a healer. The city is full of visitors from every land, pious men who would welcome *Mashiach* if he should enter the city. It has happened before, and great trouble came of it."

Agrippa looked troubled. "Your father should have left that man Yeshua alone. He was less trouble alive than dead."

"I did not suggest that the governor kill the impostor. Let them hold him over for trial, at least until after the feast. The streets are angry."

"I will think on it."

"Shall I tell Ishmael ben Phiabi you will speak to the governor?"

"Tell Ishmael I spit on his wall."

Ishmael's eyes lingered on Hanan's hair. "Did you immerse yourself before coming here?"

"Agrippa says that he spits on you and the Temple."

"Did you immerse?"

"Yes."

"Did that dog agree to speak to the governor?"

"He will think on it."

"When will we know?"

"When you see soldiers of Rome ride out of the gates."

Shmuel the Prophet

In the heat of the noonday sun, Shmuel fingered the short dagger hidden in his belt and watched the cloud of dust on the road coming from Jerusalem. Fifty men behind him muttered with fear. He turned to them.

"My brothers, you are troubled. Why are you troubled? Because the men of violence ride against you. Fear not! They are dogs, the vile scum of Amalek. The voice of HaShem speaks to me even now. The war of the sons of light against the sons of darkness has begun. We will destroy Amalek. Stand aside while the wrath of HaShem falls on Amalek."

Shmuel turned to face the host of the king of Amalek. The horsemen slowed as they approached. Shmuel saw that they were afraid of him, afraid of the wrath of HaShem. They would flee when they saw his rage.

The host of Amalek halted before Shmuel, prophet of the living God. One man rode forward and dared to speak to Shmuel in Greek, the language of dogs, a language Shmuel did not understand.

Shmuel did not flinch to hear the language of dogs. "Take me to the king of Amalek."

The man on horseback spoke again in the language of dogs. Shmuel shook his head, restraining his rage. Not yet, not yet would he reveal the wrath of HaShem. "Take me to the king of Amalek."

The man on horseback turned and shouted a great shout to the host of Amalek. Another man rode forward and spoke to Shmuel in Aramaic. His voice came slow and halting, the voice of a foreigner, a dog, an Amaleki. "The governor orders you to return in peace to Jerusalem."

Shmuel felt the rage burning now, the wrath of HaShem, a holy flame within his heart. Still he held it back, awaiting the word of HaShem. "Take me to the king of Amalek."

This man turned and motioned with his hand to the king of Amalek. The king of Amalek rode forward, and the pride of wickedness shone in his eyes. He was Agag, and folly reigned in his heart. He thought that the time for death was past, and he did not know that this hour he would die at the hand of Shmuel the prophet.

The king of Amalek stopped before Shmuel. He spoke to his servant in the language of dogs. The servant pointed to Shmuel. "What would you say to the tribune?"

Shmuel the prophet closed his eyes and called up the wrath of HaShem in his heart. Rage built within him, the rage he had learned to call on in the desert, the rage by which he lived and breathed and healed. The rage by which he would avenge himself on the king of Amalek.

Shmuel reached into his belt and gripped his dagger, waiting, waiting. The rage rose within his heart, a flood, a flame.

The word of HaShem came. *Slay the king of Amalek.*

Shmuel leaped with a great leap, and his dagger flashed like fire in his hand, and his blade entered the throat of the king of Amalek, and the blood of the king of Amalek gushed out like a drink offering before HaShem.

Shmuel the prophet shouted a great shout. *"Mashiach!"*

Baruch

Baruch had spent the morning playing with the children.

"Again!" Dov cried. "Rachel run again!" He seized Baruch's right hand. Little Rachel took his left.

"Run, Racheleh!" Brother Ari said. "Run in circles with Uncle Baruch!"

Sister Rivka knelt on the floor to watch. "Racheleh, catch Dov!"

Behind them, Hana beamed.

The two children began running in circles around Baruch while he turned. They shrieked in glee as they chased each other around and around and —

A flash of white rage burned through Baruch. He fell to the floor, clutching his head, moaning.

"Baruch!" Brother Ari sprang toward him. "Are you well?"

A spasm ran through Baruch's body. "The king of Amalek is dead."

"Please?" Sister Rivka said. "What did you say?"

Baruch shook his head. "I do not know. It came into my heart and I said it."

"*Abba*, come run in circles!" Dov shouted. "Play, *Abba!*"

Baruch shut his eyes, feeling the horror rise inside him. Stone upon stone, layer upon layer, a wall rebuilt itself in his heart. *Please, no,*

HaShem. His right hand felt scorched by fire. Not his left hand, but his right hand only.

"What does this mean, the king of Amalek?" Brother Ari asked.

Sister Rivka cleared her throat. "I . . . This is *meshugah*, but . . . King Saul captured the king of Amalek and kept him alive until the prophet Shmuel killed him."

"He is dead." Baruch put his hands over his eyes and wept.

"Who?" Brother Ari said. "This is ancient history, Brother Baruch."

Baruch shook his head. "No, Brother Ari. It is now." He stole a look at Dov. "Brother Shmuel the prophet is dead and all the works of his hands are destroyed."

"How do you know?"

Baruch felt the throbbing fire in his right hand. "I know."

Rivka

Rivka's heart lurched at Baruch's words. *No. Brother Shmuel could not be dead.* Ari and Yaakov had warned him just yesterday. He could not have gone out into the desert. He *promised* not to go out. She stood up and jammed on her sandals.

Ari leaped up and threw on his cloak. "Rivka, Hana, please stay with the children. Baruch and I will — "

Rivka grabbed Ari's arm. "I'm going with you."

"I am sorry, Rivkaleh." Ari put on his own sandals. "Of course you may come." He turned and headed downstairs. Baruch followed him.

Rivka knelt and hugged Rachel. "I'll be back soon, Racheleh. Play with Dov." She mussed up Dov's mophead. "Hana, we won't be long."

Hana waved her off. "Go! Go! I do not wish to see . . . what you will see."

Rivka hurried downstairs and joined the two men in the street. "Where shall we go?"

Ari sniffed the bright autumn air. "I suggest . . . that we go to the Temple and see which way the rumors take us."

There were no rumors when they got to the Temple, but the questions Ari asked created a buzz of gossip.

Baruch pointed toward the southeastern corner of the city. "If a man wishes to go to the desert, he will go to the gate near the Pool of Siloam."

Ari shrugged and smiled at Rivka. "I suppose we know the way."

Ten minutes later, they arrived at the gate. Rivka peered through, but saw nothing out of the ordinary. This was the first gate she had entered after wandering into this century through that horrible wormhole. The past — no, the future — seemed like a vague and distant world, a movie about somebody else's life. She was stuck in this century, and it was stuck with her. Had she done something terrible . . . by meddling?

"We should walk out a little way," Baruch said. "We can ask the news."

They walked down the road. It split into several branches. One bent away north through the tent city in the Kidron Valley. Another road led west, wending through the burning-pits of the Hinnom Valley. Another way led south to Bethlehem. The fourth led southeast, toward the Dead Sea.

Dust rising to the southeast. "Ari . . ." Rivka clutched his arm and pointed.

Ari put his arm around her. The dust rose in a ribbon. At last, a tiny column of horsemen appeared. Romans on horseback. Rivka gasped. The lead horseman held aloft a standard — a long pole with an image of the god of the legion at the top. This was . . . an abomination. An insult to the Jews, especially with the feast of *Sukkot* starting tomorrow. The city was packed with hotheads. So why would the Romans come riding into the city with their standards exposed? It was asking for trouble. What were they —

No. Rivka closed her eyes. An instant later, she tasted bile. That was not the image of a Roman god on the pole.

It was the head of a man . . . with black dreadlocks three feet long.

THIRTY-ONE

Hana

Hana read their faces when the three returned.

Sister Rivka was weeping. Therefore, Brother Shmuel was dead. Brother Ari's face was black with rage. Therefore, evil men had done this thing. And Baruch's eyes . . . were hidden behind a wall again. He came to her, yes, and hugged her. But he would not look at his son.

"Abba!" Dov shouted. "Run in circles!" He grabbed at Baruch's fingers.

Baruch jerked his hands away as if Dov's touch were fire.

"Play, Abba!"

Deep sadness twisted Baruch's face. Hana knew what this meant. Shmuel was dead, and his works were unmade. Therefore, they were not the works of HaShem, and never had been.

"We must . . . go to the synagogue," Baruch said, and his voice was the voice of a man strangled. "Some of our brothers may have gone with Shmuel, and we must learn who is dead."

Anger smote Hana like a stick. This was a weak excuse. "Go!" She waved him and Brother Ari out the door.

"Abba!" Dov shouted. He tugged on Hana's sleeve. "I want Abba!"

"Play!" Hana screamed. "Play with Racheleh!" She shooed them up the stairs and turned to Rivka and wept.

Rivka threw her arms around Hana. "What have I done?"

Hana patted her on the back. "Rivkaleh, you have done nothing."

"That's just . . . the point." Rivka shuddered. "I could have done something. Could have . . . stopped it if only I moved a little faster. Brother Shmuel didn't deserve to die."

Hana sighed deeply. "I see it now. He had a spirit of rage."

Rivka pulled away and stared at Hana. "Are you sure?"

Hana sat down on the stairs. Why had she not understood? "Rivka, do you know why Brother Shmuel could heal some and not others?"

Rivka looked puzzled. "Nobody heals everybody. Even Baruch —"

"Baruch heals by the Spirit of HaShem." Hana felt deep pain, thinking on Baruch. "Shmuel healed by a spirit of rage."

"You don't know that. You can't know that." Rivka sat beside Hana and put an arm around her.

"I know." Hana felt cold. "Who did Shmuel heal? The wounded man in the square. Rage had a hold on him, and therefore Shmuel could heal him. Likewise, Baruch hates the wicked man. He crossed over to rage, and so Shmuel could heal him."

"But . . . what about Shmuel's finger?" Rivka held up her own little finger, crooking it. "How was that healed?"

Hana bit her lip. "Through his own spirit of rage, I am sure. And now he is dead, and all the works of his hands are undone." She put her face in her hands. "Rivka, now all will be as before." Hot anger rushed through her. She had known joy these past weeks, and now . . . ? Now it was all taken away. She could not live like this, torn forever between her man and her son.

Rivka held her tight. "Hana, you won't give rage a hold in your heart, will you?"

Hana shook her head. No, never. Only a fool would give rage a hold.

Ari

When Ari and Baruch reached the synagogue, others were already there, their eyes red with weeping. Already, there was news. The total dead were fifty, not many hundreds. Sister Rivka had been wrong again, blessed be HaShem.

Brother Yosi and his son had gone out with Brother Shmuel, and they were dead. Also a new brother who had joined the community of Rabban Yeshua only a month ago. All told, six from the congregation were dead.

Ari's heart was stone within him. Could he have prevented this? What if he had listened to Rivka sooner? What if he had kept a closer watch on Shmuel? Ari thought of the many things he could have done, and had not.

Brother Yohanan arrived, whose brother was a Temple guard. All the men gathered around him. His face twitched with raw anger. "The Temple guards went out early in the morning to the Pool of Siloam," Yohanan said. "They knew Brother Shmuel was sleeping there with many men. But Shmuel had already gone, and the guards returned empty."

Yohanan twisted a strand of his beard, his face anguished. "Then the chief priests sent to King Agrippa, and he asked the governor to send out soldiers, and they went out and killed our brothers."

Yohanan's voice cracked. "It was Hanan ben Hanan who went to the king. He told Agrippa that Brother Shmuel had gone out with . . ." He looked around the circle, and his eye fell on Ari. ". . . with Ari the Kazan."

Ari felt a giant fist seize his insides. He could not breathe. The air felt very hot, and the walls swayed. He put a hand on Baruch's shoulder to steady himself.

For a moment, silence hung over the synagogue. Then everybody began talking at once. Ari heard only fragments. ". . . wanted to kill Brother Ari." ". . . pray to HaShem against the House of Hanan." ". . . set fire to his palace."

Ari felt shocked. Angry. This was outrage. Hanan had meant to kill him because he was with Shmuel. A sick feeling hit him in the gut. What if . . . Shmuel was not the target? What if Hanan had meant to kill Shmuel only because he was with Kazan?

Why should Hanan want Shmuel dead, after all? Hanan did not know Brother Shmuel. Therefore, he could not hate him, nor the others who had gone out of the city. Hanan hated Ari, and on his account he had killed Shmuel and fifty other men.

Ari slumped to his knees, nauseous with anger.

"Brother Ari, are you well?" Baruch knelt beside him. "Bring a drink!"

Ari clutched Baruch. Yaakov the *tsaddik* brought a small wineskin and held it to Ari's lips. Ari drank. He saw that even Yaakov burned now, burned with a righteous anger at the House of Hanan. Ari looked around the circle at these men who loved him, though he did not follow the Rabban. He must tell them the truth. They would hate him for it. "Hanan ben Hanan has made me his enemy," he said. "On my account, he killed our brothers."

Ari closed his eyes, unable to meet their gaze.

Hands gripped him, all around. Ari flinched. Whatever they did to him, he deserved.

"We curse you," someone said in a tight voice that froze Ari's blood. "We curse you, Hanan ben Hanan, who tried to kill our Brother Ari."

THIRTY-TWO

Hanan ben Hanan

A week later, when the feast of *Sukkot* ended, the Sanhedrin agreed to meet with Governor Festus to discuss the matter of the wall Ishmael ben Phiabi had built. The governor looked impatient, Hanan thought. He was learning that Jews were not easy men to rule.

"The matter is very simple," Festus said. "You must remove the wall which you have added atop your Temple. It is blocking the view of my soldiers who stand guard on the portico roofs."

Hanan translated this into Aramaic.

Ishmael ben Phiabi shook his head. "Let King Agrippa demolish his new dining room and then we will think on it."

Hanan repeated this in Greek.

Festus folded his arms across his chest. "I have no time for the feud between you priests and Agrippa. My men require to have a view of the entire outer courts of the Temple Mount. You have taken this away by building that wall. I demand that the wall come down."

Hanan translated.

A dozen chief priests began talking at once. Ishmael raised his hands and bellowed for silence. He glowered at the governor. "Excellency, you have authority over many things in this province — the building of roads and the extortion of taxes and the keeping of peace. But the Temple is our domain and Caesar gives us absolute rights to see to its maintenance. Now this wall in dispute is a part of our Temple, and therefore a part of our religion. It would be unbearable to us to dismantle any part of our Temple, and by Caesar's order, we may refuse any request to do so. In our view, the matter lies between us and Agrippa, not between you and us. We refuse your order."

Hanan translated to Greek. Festus listened in fuming silence. He turned to the three councillors he had brought along and they debated in heated whispers. Finally, Festus turned back to face the Sanhedrin. "You must take down the wall. I am ordered by Caesar to protect the peace within your Temple, and this I cannot do while that wall stands. Your religious observances never required this wall until now. I demand that you dismantle it at once."

Hanan translated this.

Ishmael made a secret hand signal to Hanan.

Hanan took a step toward the governor. "Excellency, perhaps I might make a suggestion."

"Speak."

"The source of the provocation is King Agrippa. We have no authority over him, and unfortunately, neither do you, since his territories lie outside your jurisdiction."

"Caesar appointed Agrippa king," Festus said.

"And that is my point," Hanan said. "Caesar has authority over him. If you would permit us to send an embassy to Caesar, the matter might be resolved quickly. We believe that Caesar will rule in our favor, forcing Agrippa to dismantle his dining room. Then we will take down our wall. But we are an obstinate people, and every one of us would die rather than permit an offense to the Temple."

Festus looked skeptical. "Ishmael is high priest, not you. Do you have authority to discuss this with me?"

"I could persuade Ishmael if you give him a certain inducement."

"And that would be what?"

"Ishmael would insist on leading the delegation to Caesar. It would raise his honor to confront Caesar himself."

"I suppose you also wish to go?"

Hanan shook his head. "Ishmael would never permit me to go. I come from a more honored family, and he sees me as a threat."

"Ask him for the names of the delegation and I will consider the matter."

Hanan nodded. "Very good, Excellency." He turned and strode to Ishmael.

Ishmael leaned forward. "What does he think of our proposal?"

Hanan sighed deeply. "The governor is a harsh negotiator. He thinks that this is only a delaying tactic. He refuses to consider it unless you yourself lead the delegation."

Ishmael scowled. "You told him I spit on Rome and will never soil my feet there?"

"He is unyielding on the matter."

"You could go in my place."

Hanan had gone to Rome once with his brother Yonatan on just such an embassy. While there, he developed a stomach illness, and in the end Felix was named governor. Altogether an evil result. "Festus refuses to accept any man without position in the Temple."

"I could reinstate you as *sagan*." Ishmael looked ill at his own suggestion.

Hanan did not wish to be *sagan* in Rome. "You could also make a dog your chief treasurer. Festus would consider it an insult, that you make such an appointment in order to circumvent his will. I can not take such a proposal to him."

"What does he want?"

"He wants the ten most eminent men in the Temple."

Ishmael scowled. "Then who will run the Temple? We might be gone for a whole year! Tell him I must leave at least my *sagan* here." Ishmael leaned back. "I refuse to consider it unless he agrees at least to this."

Hanan did not want the *sagan* to remain, but he saw that Ishmael would not yield. Finally he nodded. "I will ask him."

He went back to the governor. "Ishmael agrees. He insists that he must lead the delegation. His captain of the Temple, Yoseph Kabi, will remain. The remainder of the party will consist of the senior men in the Temple . . ." Hanan named the ten men who would go.

Festus gave a curt nod. "Agreed. See to it that they sail before the seaports close for the winter."

Berenike

The fall and winter passed in peace. The city held its breath, waiting to hear the end of the matter of the wall. On the new moon before *Pesach*, the first mail ship arrived in Caesarea, and two letters came at last to the Hasmonean Palace in Jerusalem. Berenike's spies told her and she hurried to join Agrippa as he opened the letters.

Agrippa slit the wax seals on the two letters with a small knife. "Which one shall I read first?"

Berenike was dying to see the one from King Polemon, but she knew Agrippa desperately wanted to see the other one. "Read the one from Caesar."

Agrippa unrolled it and laid out marble weights on the parchment. He read it aloud.

"Nero Claudius Caesar Augustus, Imperator, to Marcus Julius Agrippa, greetings. Whereas certain priests of the Jewish religion have appeared before me requesting that I settle a dispute between them and you, I make known to you my decision. You are not required to demolish any part of your palace. As for the wall on the Jewish temple, at which daily sacrifices are offered on my behalf, neither are the Jews required to take down any part of it. I am sending a letter to Porcius Festus, governor of Judea, with instructions to make no further demands on the temple hierarchy. My wife Poppea is much interested in your religion and has required that your high priest, Ishmael the son of Phiabi, shall be retained here in Rome indefinitely. As the Judean province has been restless of late, I will keep this Ishmael as a token of the good behavior of the Jewish people. Accordingly, you will appoint a new high priest."

Berenike stepped to the window and looked out. Caesar had settled the matter quickly. They had lost on the matter of the wall and won on the matter of the dining room. And they were rid of Ishmael.

Agrippa began pacing. "Excellent! I will notify the chief priestly houses privately that I am now accepting gifts for consideration for the high priesthood."

Berenike tensed. "What of your promise to the seer woman? Hanan ben Hanan is hungry. He will give the biggest gift."

Agrippa shrugged. "What if he does? How will he know whose is biggest? How will anyone?"

"So you will keep your promise?"

A slight hesitation. "A man of honor keeps his word," Agrippa said. "The seer woman has not been wrong in her predictions. I will choose Yoseph Kabi, whatever Hanan pays."

Berenike hoped the seer woman's next prediction would come true. "Perhaps we should consult the letter from Polemon."

Agrippa smiled. "You are most patient." He returned to the table and rolled open the parchment.

"Polemon, King of Pontus and Cilicia, to Marcus Julius Agrippa, grace and peace. In view of the generous offer you have made to me on behalf of your sister Berenike, be it known that I agree to your terms in full ..."

Agrippa continued reading, but Berenike did not need to hear any more. The seer woman had been right. Polemon, a man the age of Papa, had agreed to marry her in exchange for more silver talents than any man had a right to even look at. And he agreed to the terms Papa had laid down long ago — that any man who married a daughter of the House of Herod would be circumcised. Whether he followed any other commandments was up to him, but he would be a Jew.

And she would be a queen. Not a widow queen, but a real one, married to a real man. The only one to lose in this business was Agrippa, who would have to pay the silver and would no longer have her aid in matters politic.

"... greet your sister Berenike for me." Agrippa set down the parchment, his face tight. He shook his head. "Who would have believed Polemon would submit to the knife at his age? How did the seer woman know?"

Berenike headed toward the door. "You can ask her tomorrow. I am going to invite her over to thank her for her help."

"What help? I did this myself."

Berenike wanted to laugh. *With me holding a knife to your throat, you did it yourself.* "All true, but we never would have considered Polemon without her suggestion."

"Of course we would have." Agrippa looked offended. "I had been considering him in my mind for some time before she suggested it."

"No doubt." Berenike went out, fuming. Either Agrippa was lying or telling the truth. She could not decide which of those alternatives disturbed her more.

Hanan ben Hanan

Hanan gave Agrippa a thin smile. "I congratulate you on the announcement of your sister's wedding." He hesitated. There had been vile rumors about Agrippa and his sister for months. Hanan rarely listened to such idle gossip.

Except that Agrippa was yet unmarried and already a man in his thirties. Such a man should have married long ago. And his sister, though a woman of astonishing beauty, likewise had remained a widow a long time. It was obvious that this marriage was intended to end the rumors. "I understand you will be making a rather large gift to King Polemon, and I should like to contribute something toward that end. Five silver talents."

And if you consider it a bribe, that is merely your own interpretation.

Agrippa's eyebrows shifted upward. "I thank you for your ... generosity on behalf of my sister."

Hanan inclined his head modestly. Generosity was the wrong word. He had servants who knew servants in the houses of the other chief priests. And he knew for a fact that Yoseph Kabi had offered four talents. An outrageous amount. Even Hananyah ben Nadavayah had never paid so much. Hanan had borrowed money from his brothers in order to raise the cash on short notice. He would pay them back when he was high priest, but he would not tolerate losing again. Kazan's woman had cheated him last time. Now she was in disgrace, cursed as a "witch woman" by the whole city. Agrippa must use a more rational method of selection this time.

Agrippa's chief of staff entered and discreetly whispered in his ear. Agrippa nodded. "Tell her I will speak with her guest shortly." He turned back to Hanan. "As I was saying, your generosity comes at an opportune moment. King Polemon asked much in exchange for becoming a Jew."

"I wish your sister long life and many sons." Hanan bowed slightly and backed toward the door.

"Andreas will show you out." Agrippa nodded to his chief of staff.

Andreas opened the door and Hanan stepped through. His palms were sweating, but his heart felt light. Five talents! It was far too much, but nobody would exceed it.

Andreas led him down the hall to a marble stairway. They descended in silence.

A woman's laughter, off to the right.

Hanan craned his neck to look. The queen stood at a fountain, her arm extended, tickling the spray. She wore no veil, not even a hair covering. Hanan wanted to look away, disgusted by this vile display of her beauty.

But he could not break his eyes away. Beside the queen stood a slight young woman, her hair modestly wrapped in a silk head-covering. She was unveiled, and she stood in profile to Hanan, laughing at something, her hand also in the spray of the fountain.

Kazan's woman! Hanan felt vinegar in his belly. Why had she come? She was in disgrace. What reason could she have for talking with the queen? For *laughing* with the queen?

Berenike said something. Kazan's woman turned toward Hanan and their eyes locked.

He read fear in her eyes. Fear and anger and disdain. She dared to dishonor him! Dared to look him in the eye, as if she were a common woman of the street, as if he were a man who looked at such women. Hanan stopped himself from spitting in her direction only just in time. Not in Agrippa's palace. Not today, while his gift to Agrippa had yet to buy the king's favor.

He broke her gaze and marched down the stairs, feeling the hot blood in his face, his heart beating with fury. As Kazan's woman, so Kazan. And so all the messianics. When Hanan came into his rightful office, such vile scum would be dealt with. He would teach them to give honor to those for whom honor was due.

Rivka

Rivka's heart pounded. Hanan was stomping down the stairs like he owned the place. Why was he here? She turned to Berenike. "Your brother promised me something once regarding Hanan ben Hanan."

Berenike put a hand on her shoulder. "He will keep his word. I asked him specifically about his promise."

"And ...?"

Berenike laughed. "He said a man of honor keeps his word."

He had not answered the question. Rivka wanted to ask if Berenike thought Agrippa was a man of honor, but she already knew the answer.

A cold fist grabbed her insides and twisted very hard.

PART FOUR

PREMONITION

Fall, a.d. 62

Anyone who ponders these things will find that God does care for people, and by all sorts of ways shows his people the means of salvation, while it is to folly and evils of their own choosing that they owe their destruction.... For all that, it is impossible for people to escape their fate, even if they see it coming.

— Josephus, *The Jewish War*,
VI (310, 314), translated by Gaalya Cornfeld

THIRTY-THREE

Rivka

On a hot summer day three years after Governor Festus took office, Rivka heard an angry knocking at her door. She left Rachel playing with her wooden blocks and hurried downstairs.

Hana stood outside, clutching Dov's hand. Her blotchy face and red eyes told Rivka everything. Another fight with Baruch. "Rivka, we must talk."

"Racheleh!" Dov raced inside past Rivka and up the stairs in search of his best friend in the universe.

Rivka could only wish she were four again — that had to be the best year of anyone's life. She gave Hana a hug. "We'll go for a walk. Your neighbor Yohana can watch the children." *The one woman in this city who doesn't call me a witch woman.*

Dov and Rachel marched down the stairs, holding hands, singing, happy as kittens.

Ten minutes later, Rivka and Hana strolled in silence down the hill, past the Hasmonean Palace, through the public square, and past the shopping district. Hana said nothing and Rivka was content to wait. She knew Hana felt increasingly desperate to get pregnant again. And it wasn't happening. Maybe . . . Baruch was infertile? But Rivka would never say so. In this culture, it was the woman who was barren.

They turned south into the open plaza south of the Temple Mount. Stone benches invited them to sit and rest from the heat of the early afternoon sun. Rivka chose one and they sat down.

Hana gave a deep sigh, like a sob. "I have decided to leave him."

Rivka put a hand on her arm. "No! You can't. How will you . . . live?"

Hana set her face in stone. "I was alive before I met him."

"Hana! That . . . that was a hard life."

"It is an impossible life now. He says he loves me, but he does not love my son. Dov cries for his *abba*, but Baruch will not touch him, not speak to him, not look at him. It is killing my son. Therefore it is killing me. I would rather be a *zonah* again than continue like this."

"Have you told him?"

"Just now. He went out in a rage."

Rivka's heart lurched. Baruch was usually on such an even keel. Unless you brought up his . . . problem. Then he lapsed into sullen silence, or walked out. There was no talking to him on the subject.

Rivka leaned close to Hana and just held her. "I'm sorry, Hana. I wish I knew what to do. But you'll never have to live on the streets. If you must leave him for a while, come stay with us."

"No."

"Hana!"

"It would dishonor Baruch. Ari the Kazan would not allow it."

Rivka put her hands on her hips. "He'd better allow it. If he doesn't, I'll — "

A scream cut across the square. Rivka turned to look. From around the corner of the Temple Mount, a man came running — a Roman soldier with half his gear torn off, running as fast as Rivka had ever seen a man run. His iron-cleated leather boots sparked on the stone square, his arms and legs churned, and the red feathers in his helmet splayed flat in the wind of his speed.

Behind him rolled a mighty river of young men, shouting, waving fists, jeering.

The soldier sprinted toward Rivka and Hana. Halfway across the square, his foot skidded on something, a loose rock maybe. Arms windmilling, he staggered, fell, smashed against the pavement. He rolled forward and up onto his feet and stumbled forward, his eyes white, sweat slicking his face. Blood streamed from his left knee, and he limped as he ran. The young men behind were catching up.

Rivka grabbed Hana's hand and yanked her away.

Again the soldier stumbled and fell. Before he could rise, the young men were on him. Kicking, shouting, spitting, screaming. Four of them pinned his arms and legs. More men arrived with sticks, stones, clubs. One kicked the soldier in the face. Rivka hid her eyes. She had seen violence on TV long ago. Stunt men, fake blood, sound effects. Phony violence. This was real. They were killing a human being. The soldier screamed like a woman.

Rivka couldn't take it any longer. She didn't care what he had done, she was not going to put up with this. She marched up to the circle of men. "Stop it!" She pounded on the back of one of the men with her fists.

He turned around.

"Stop it!" She pointed at the soldier on the ground. "Leave him alone!"

"Rivka!" Hana grabbed her arms. "You will come with me now."

"No! Stop it, you cowards! How dare you kick a man when he's down?"

The man pushed hard on Rivka's chest. "Go away, witch woman."

"Don't you touch me!" Rivka clawed at his face.

Hana tugged her away. "Rivkaleh, come back now!"

Rivka strained forward. "You can't—"

Several hands grabbed her. Rivka staggered, desperate to keep her balance. Somebody yanked her hair far back. She closed her eyes against the brightness of the sun. "Witch woman!" somebody hissed.

The soldier on the ground screamed again and again.

"Kill him!" somebody shouted. An old woman began ululating in a high, cold chant. "Kill the *goy!* Kill the *goy!*"

Rivka couldn't believe it. Flash-printed on her retinas was the image of the Roman, lying on the ground, blood streaming from his mouth. His screams went on and on. More women picked up the chant. The air filled with the smell of sweating men. Long after the soldier fell silent, Rivka heard the thuds of club and foot on his broken body, the hooting laughter of the men, the horrible chanting of the women. Rivka was crying now, her eyes a smear of tears and sweat.

Finally, many hands released her. Rivka spun around, ready to tell off whatever *creeps* had been—

Half a dozen girls, maybe ten years old, scowled up at her. "You're the witch woman, aren't you?" said one. Another spit at her feet. They all turned and ran away.

Rivka was hyperventilating. *Little girls? Calling her a witch woman?*

"Rivkaleh." Hana took her arm. "Come, they are children."

Rivka collapsed into her arms and wept.

Rivka, there was nothing we could do." Hana shook her head. "They were mad with joy because the governor is dead."

"Governor Festus?" Blind panic swept through Rivka. *No, please, no.* She had been hoping she had another year.

"I do not know the name, but he was the governor from Caesar. He died two days ago and the people are happy."

"I'd hate to see them when they're upset."

"They had a spirit of rage."

Rivka couldn't argue with that. This was evil, plain and simple. More would follow. In the year Governor Festus died, evil would roar through this city like a flood.

And nobody knew it but the witch woman.

Baruch

Baruch stumbled blindly toward the Temple Mount, his eyes wet with tears. Hana must not leave him. Brother Ari must speak to Sister Rivka and she would speak to Hana about this foolishness.

It was all on account of the boy. Baruch did not hate the boy. Only what the boy represented—the evil man who had dishonored him, violated his woman. To see the boy was to see the evil man. To feel the boy's touch was fire. And this pain beyond pain was all the worse because he had once been free of it, before Brother Shmuel was lost.

Baruch hurried through the Huldah Gates and up the many dozen steps in the stony darkness of the tunnel leading through the heart of the Temple Mount. At last he emerged, blinking in the bright sunlight.

Brother Ari would be in the inner Temple, consulting on improvements to his water pump. Baruch must speak to him now. He would die if he could not speak to him. His heart burned with righteous anger. Brother Ari would help him.

Baruch hurried through the partition, then up the steps, through the Court of Women, past the Nicanor Gate, into the Court of Yisrael, and there he stopped. He was not a priest and he could go no further.

Brother Ari stood in the Court of Priests, talking to several men.

"Brother Ari!" Baruch shouted and waved his arms.

Brother Ari hurried to greet him. "Brother Baruch, are you well?"

Baruch shook his head. "It is a catastrophe. Hana has decided to leave me. You must speak to Sister Rivka."

Brother Ari tugged at his beard. "It is over the matter of the boy?"

Baruch nodded. "She does not understand."

"Brother Baruch, with respect, I do not understand either."

Despair flooded Baruch's heart. Brother Ari would not speak to Sister Rivka.

Brother Ari put a hand on Baruch's arm. "Go to Yaakov the *tsaddik* for help. Ask for his wisdom. Perhaps he can help you."

Baruch shook his head. "I cannot. Even to speak of the matter is dishonor."

"Then you will lose your woman, and I cannot help you." Brother Ari's voice sounded hard. "Brother Baruch, I think you worry yourself overmuch with honor."

Footsteps behind Baruch. An enormous young priest pushed past him and raced into the Court of Priests, shouting, "He is dead! The governor is dead!"

Ari

Ari's heart stuttered. Rivka had told him that after Governor Festus died, chaos would fall. But Brother Eleazar seemed to think it the best news in the world. He danced in a circle, leaping, shouting. "The dog is dead! The dog is dead!"

Yoseph Kabi, the high priest, rushed over, his face alight with joy. He kissed Brother Eleazar and leaped in the air. "Give praise to the living God! The prince of the world is dead!"

Ari gaped at them. Governor Festus had ruled wisely. Did they hate him only because he was a Roman? "My brothers, please!"

Yoseph Kabi threw his arms around Ari and kissed him too. "Rejoice! Today, our enemy is dead! He who dishonored us is no more, forever!" He spun Ari in a circle, then turned back to Brother Eleazar and slapped hands with him.

A stone settled into Ari's belly. This reeked of the disgusting way American football players behaved after a goal. It was most unseemly for a high priest.

More priests poured up the steps from the lower levels of the Temple Mount. Brother Eleazar greeted them with upraised arms. "Celebrate and be glad! Governor Festus is dead!" A great cheer rang through the court. The echo of it came back from the facade of the sanctuary.

Ari stared up at the tall gold-faced edifice. Very soon, Rome would come and destroy this sanctuary. Because of Eleazar and men like him. The horror of it cut through Ari's heart. He loved this city of the living God, this Temple, this people. Soon it would vanish in smoke and tears.

Somebody slapped Ari on the back. "Ari the Kazan! Dance with us!"

Ari turned and saw his friends, Gamaliel and Yoseph. The priests had formed into a circle and were dancing. Gamaliel seized Ari's hand. "Rejoice and be glad. The wicked man is dead!" He dragged Ari into the circle.

Ari did not know how to make this dance, and he did not wish to learn. He shook free and backed up against the altar of the living God. The circle of priests bobbed and leaped and laughed and shouted, all the while turning, turning, turning, a burning wheel of fire.

Ari turned to look for Brother Baruch. He was gone.

THIRTY-FOUR

Berenike

When Berenike returned to Jerusalem after a wretched year of life in Pontus, one of her first visitors was the seer woman. The woman listened quietly for three parts of an hour while Berenike talked.

"It was terrible, just terrible!" Berenike said. "King Polemon is an old man living in a drafty, cold palace. He showed no interest in me. He married me only for my money. I could take no more, so I left him. He has the money, I have my title. Both of us have what we really wanted." But that was a lie. She was out of the game again.

The seer woman looked at her in deep silence.

Berenike flinched. "What? I dislike when you look at me like that."

"I'm sorry," the seer woman said. "It didn't turn out well for you, and — "

"I told you I got what I wanted."

"If you say so."

Irritated, Berenike stood up from the bench.

"Please sit down. I have something to tell you."

Something in the seer woman's voice made Berenike sit. "Yes?" She hated that her voice came out breathy and expectant, but she *had* to know. "You have another word for me?"

"For your brother." The seer woman put a hand on Berenike's arm, and her touch felt hot and dry. Her voice quivered with emotion. "You will tell him, please, that he is to remember his promise in the matter of Hanan ben Hanan."

Berenike laughed. "A man of honor keeps his word."

"It's very important. Will you ask him?"

"He is unhappy with me right now."

"Because you left Polemon?"

Berenike nodded. "He paid many talents to arrange the marriage." *And the marriage ended many rumors that embarrassed him.*

The seer woman seemed to look inside Berenike's heart. "So now his investment is wasted and people will again whisper about you. Your beauty is a curse to you. I am sorry."

Berenike frowned. Beauty was no curse. It was a tool, a weapon. A woman's only advantage in the game of power. She would never regret her great beauty.

"Please, will you ask Agrippa?" the seer woman said.

"It is not a good time. Perhaps next month."

"Please do it today. Now."

Berenike felt weary of this. She saw Agrippa's chief of staff hurrying across the courtyard. "Andreas!"

He stopped as if shot with an arrow. "Your highness?"

"Where is Agrippa?"

"Receiving a visitor."

"Who?"

Andreas looked all around him. "It is not permitted to say."

"I will see my brother as soon as this mysterious visitor is gone."

"Yes, your highness." Andreas backed away, his head lowered. As he slipped into the shadow of the portico, he dared to look at her, then turned and scuttled away. But not before Berenike read the look of desire on his face.

Berenike laughed. It was such *fun* to torment men.

Half an hour later, Berenike saw the weasel-faced high priest, Yoseph Kabi, slinking out of the palace, a storm in his eyes.

The seer woman tensed.

"You knew it was him?"

The seer woman nodded. "He is dismissed."

Berenike waited. Presently, Andreas entered the courtyard and crossed to Berenike. "Your highness, your brother the king will see you now."

I had to dismiss him," Agrippa said. "He made a spectacle in the Temple yesterday, dancing on the grave of Governor Festus. There was a riot in the upper market and a mob murdered a soldier near the Ophel district. Yoseph Kabi incited it all, though he denies it. When Caesar hears of this, he will demand punishment."

"Of course." Berenike went to the window and looked out.

Agrippa came to join her, and his shoulder touched hers.

Berenike did not flinch. "The seer woman came to see me today."

Agrippa said nothing.

"You will uphold your promise?"

Agrippa folded his hands. "She has not upheld hers."

Berenike turned to look at him. "Oh?"

"She promised you Polemon."

"And I got him."

"And yet you are here." Agrippa's hands twitched, and he looked at her with heat in his eyes.

"She did not say I would stay with him, only that he would take me."

"It did not turn out as we expected. The seer woman is unreliable."

Unreliable. The word struck fear in Berenike's heart. "She predicted Festus long before he came to Judea."

"And she said Ishmael ben Phiabi was to be high priest. Ben Phiabi, who dishonored me before the people and Caesar."

"She did not promise otherwise."

"She did not warn me, and now I am certain she knew. Then she said Yoseph Kabi was to be high priest, and you see what he has done."

Berenike frowned. "She told you shards of what would be, but she did not claim to know all."

"The people say she is a witch woman."

"What are you telling me?"

Agrippa sighed and his shoulder pressed harder against hers. "Only this. The seer woman has failed to keep her word. She has not told me all she knew."

"And therefore, what?"

"And therefore, I am no longer obligated to keep my promise to her. I have notified the four houses that I am seeking to name a new high priest."

"And this time you will decide in favor of the highest bidder?"

Agrippa slipped an arm around her slim waist. "The treasury is depleted."

Berenike pushed him away and spun out of his grasp. "You swore an oath before the living God."

His eyes narrowed to dagger points. "She swore to tell all she knew."

Berenike stepped to the door. "I have not heard that one broken oath justifies another."

"You could persuade me to keep my oath."

Vile man! "If you do not fear to break an oath before the living God, you will not fear to break a promise to me." Berenike stormed out and went down to the courtyard.

The seer woman still waited, her face expectant and yet fearful.

Berenike stomped across the flagstones and stared into the fountain.

"What did he say?"

Berenike shook her head. "A man of honor keeps his oath."

"Is he a man of honor?"

"You know what kind of man he is, seer woman."

Yaakov

Yaakov sat on the stone bench in front of his house praying. It was late afternoon, and joy flooded his heart. HaShem was good. HaShem provided the sunlight and the rain in their seasons. Those who trusted in HaShem could never fear.

Footsteps stopped in front of him. "*Abba,* may I sit with you?"

Yaakov opened his eyes, and delight filled his soul. "Sister Rivka, my child!" He stood and hugged her, and she clung to him like a child, weeping, her whole body quivering.

"Rivkaleh, please. You will sit with me and tell me what troubles you."

Sister Rivka sat beside him. A sob gurgled in her throat.

Yaakov waited. Two things one could not hurry — the coming of the Spirit, and the weeping of a woman. Finally she began to calm.

"Now you will tell me what troubles you, my child."

"*Abba* . . . you are in danger." Sister Rivka peered up at him through teary eyes. "HaShem has given me to know the future, and . . . you are in terrible danger."

Yaakov smiled. Again her nameless fears. "I am old, child. If HaShem calls me home tomorrow, I will go with gladness."

"No . . . please, *Abba,* listen. King Agrippa has deposed Yoseph Kabi as high priest. He has not announced a successor yet, but I know it will be Hanan ben Hanan."

Something tingled in Yaakov's heart. "Hanan is an angry man."

"He hates me," Sister Rivka said. "And he hates Ari the Kazan. But he hates you most, *Abba!* I know it, and he intends — "

"Child, a man of Hanan's station does not know I exist."

Sister Rivka took his hand in both of hers. "*Abba*, I wish that were true, but it isn't. He knows you. And he intends to kill you."

"Child, surely that is impossible. The governor is dead, and it is not permitted for the Sanhedrin to execute a man without the governor's word."

"No!" Sister Rivka's voice shook. "*Abba*, hear my words. The governor is dead, and Hanan thinks to take advantage of his absence to kill you."

"You know this for a certainty?"

"Yes, it will all happen very soon. Within a few days, *Abba!*" Tears streamed down her face. "Please, go away for a time. Find some safe place to hide. Don't come back until you hear that Governor Albinus has arrived in Caesarea."

Yaakov sighed. Sister Rivka's words must again be an exaggeration. "Child, have you warned your husband about this matter? It is not I who am in danger, it is Ari the Kazan. Hanan ben Hanan is an evil man, and your husband is his enemy."

"I . . ." Sister Rivka sighed. "*Abba*, I have not spoken with him."

"You will speak with him on this matter, please."

"Yes, *Abba*." Sister Rivka clung to his hand. "I'm . . . so afraid for you, *Abba*."

"Nothing happens except HaShem allows it."

"But still some things grieve the heart of HaShem." Sister Rivka stood up and hurried away.

Yaakov sighed deeply. He was an old man and did not fear death. Therefore he did not fear Hanan ben Hanan. An evil man, yes, but Sister Rivka must surely be mistaken. It was often so. She was given a little knowledge by HaShem, a dim reflection of what would be. Like the image in a bronze mirror, hazy, indistinct.

Yes, Sister Rivka was mistaken in the matter. Why should Hanan hate him? He had done nothing to Hanan, had not spoken against the Temple. Indeed, he often went there to pray. HaShem's presence filled the Temple, and a man must be blind not to see it.

It was a paradox that such a good place was ruled by evil men. Men who beat the people with sticks for the sake of a few tithes. HaShem should not allow such things, and yet he did. This was a mystery.

HaShem had allowed Rabban Yeshua to suffer. HaShem had allowed evil men to stone Stephanos. Men of the House of Hanan had flogged Shimon and Yohanan, leaders of The Way. King Agrippa's father had once beheaded the other Yaakov, the son of Zavdai. Renegade Saul had suffered floggings many times. All these things, HaShem allowed.

And HaShem had allowed Hanan to send out men to kill Brother Shmuel the prophet, a good man who fell into terrible error and took many innocent men with him. Hanan had done this thing only because he hated Ari the Kazan. Hanan ben Hanan was an evil man, a wretched man. HaShem should punish such men. Rabban Yeshua would have spoken against such evil. Would have called on HaShem to bring forth justice on the earth. To bring forth wrath.

Anger welled in Yaakov's heart. Righteous anger. One must stand against injustice, against the evil men. It was not enough to say that all was in the hands of HaShem. Sometimes a man must call on HaShem, must beg him for justice.

For wrath.

Yaakov rose from his bench and went into his house and fell on his face to pray. Righteous anger wrapped itself around him like a shroud.

THIRTY-FIVE

Baruch

Baruch knocked on the door of Yaakov the *tsaddik*. Fear gnawed at his heart. He found it unbearable to tell Yaakov about the matter of the boy. But if he did not, Hana would leave him. Last night, she had agreed to stay on condition that he speak to Yaakov.

No answer. Baruch waited, uncertain, then knocked again. If he went home without talking to Yaakov, Hana would . . .

No, he must not fail. Hana was the joy of his life. The boy was the curse. He must not fail. He pounded on the door once more. "Brother Yaakov, are you there?"

Again, no answer. Despair fell on him. Baruch turned away. Yaakov could not be at the Temple. It was not yet the hour for afternoon sacrifices. Perhaps —

The door clicked open. Baruch spun around. Yaakov stood in the doorway, his face gray with dust. "Yes, my son?"

"*Abba*, I must . . ." Baruch could not say more. Sorrow welled in his heart. "Please, *Abba*, may I come in? We must talk."

Yaakov opened the door and Baruch went in. Yaakov's home was small, one room with a barrel-vaulted stone ceiling. Tall vertical window slits let in some light. A stone table stood against the wall. Two stools sat on either side of the table. A thin bedroll stood in the corner.

Baruch sat on one of the stools. Yaakov sat across from him. "Tell me your troubles, my son."

Baruch told him. There was little enough to tell, and Yaakov knew most of it anyway. ". . . and when I saw the boy, rage entered my heart."

Yaakov leaned forward. "Rage against the boy?"

"No, against the wicked man," Baruch said. "It is the wrath of HaShem I feel — righteous anger. He did a wicked thing."

Yaakov nodded. "Such a thing has happened many times since sin entered the world. You have forgiven the man, of course."

Baruch said nothing.

Yaakov put his hands on Baruch's. "Sister Hana has forgiven the man?"

Baruch nodded. He did not understand how, but Hana had forgiven the wicked man. "He did not dishonor her. He dishonored me."

"Baruch, my son."

Tears formed in Baruch's eyes. "Yes, *Abba?*"

"Of what price honor?"

Baruch did not know how to answer. Honor was all. One could not put a price on honor. Without honor, a man was nothing. A dog.

"The Rabban said that he who would have the highest honor must be as he who has the lowest honor. Have you heard this saying? That the first shall be last, and the last first?"

Baruch quivered. "It is a hard word. I do not understand this saying."

"Do you know why the Rabban made this hard saying?"

Baruch shook his head. "*Abba*, I do not like this saying."

Yaakov sighed. "My son, the currency of this world is a man's honor. But the currency of the World to Come is forgiveness. And a man cannot forgive unless he gives up his right to honor."

A knot formed in Baruch's stomach. "*Abba*, this is not possible. Without honor, a man is nothing."

"So if you would forgive, you must become nothing in this world. If you do not forgive, you will be nothing in the World to Come. Which do you prefer?"

"I . . . do forgive," Baruch said. "I forgive the wrongs of my woman and Ari the Kazan and — "

"You forgive the wrongs done without malice by those who love you." Yaakov shook his head. "My son, this is an easy thing, and it is not what the Rabban commanded. The Rabban commanded us to forgive our *enemies*. This is a hard — "

Baruch stood up, knocking the stool backward. "It is an impossible thing. You do not know what you ask."

"I know what I ask." Yaakov also stood up. "My son, do you see this dust in my beard?"

Baruch would never have dishonored Yaakov by mentioning it.

"I see that you do." Yaakov's eyes filled with pain. "My son, I had words with Sister Rivka yesterday which grieved me deeply. I learned a thing that has put me on my face in prayer since this time yesterday. I learned that there is anger in my heart."

Baruch's eyes widened. Yaakov the *tsaddik* had anger in his heart?

"Anger against the House of Hanan," Yaakov said. "They are evil men. They killed the Rabban without cause, and he forgave them, but I did not forgive the House of Hanan. HaShem raised Yeshua to new life, and still I did not forgive. The Rabban revealed himself to me and then he ascended to HaShem, and still I did not."

"You should never forgive them," Baruch said. "It is righteous anger."

"There is a time to put on anger, and a time to put it off. When righteous anger eats at your heart, the time has come to put it off. And yet I cannot. I feel hate against the House of Hanan."

"They are evil men."

"Yes, they are evil. HaShem will judge them. The Rabban did not say that HaShem will forgive them, but still he commanded that I should do so. This is a hard thing, my son. It means that I must do something which even HaShem will not do."

"Then it is impossible as I said. A metaphor."

"No. The Rabban spoke many metaphors, but not so here."

"How?" Baruch tasted bile in his throat. "If HaShem will not forgive, then how can a man?"

Yaakov sat again on his stool. "The Rabban did not tell us how."

Baruch began pacing. "I will never forgive the wicked man."

Yaakov sighed. "You must find a way."

Baruch sat across from him at the table. "Yet you have not forgiven the House of Hanan."

"It is a hard thing." Yaakov brushed at the dust in his beard. "I have not yet found the way, my son. I have spent the last day before HaShem, asking how it is possible. Such things do not come easily. They are wicked men, full of hate. Sister Rivka told me that Hanan ben Hanan will be named high priest and that he will kill me."

Fear burned in Baruch's heart. "She told you that today?"

Yaakov shook his head. "Yesterday. I have been on my face in the dust since then, seeking a way to forgive the son of Hanan."

Baruch closed his eyes, and he brushed at them madly, but still tears formed at the corners and ran down into his beard. "Then you have not heard that King Agrippa named Hanan ben Hanan high priest this morning?"

Yaakov recoiled as if Baruch had spit in his face. "May HaShem protect us all."

"You must hide," Baruch said. "Find one of the brothers and stay in their house. When did Sister Rivka say Hanan would try to kill you?"

"Within days." Yaakov's voice was a thin whisper. "My son, it shames me to say that I hate this man."

"All men hate Hanan. He is a wicked man."

"The Rabban did not hate the House of Hanan. He forgave those who dishonored him and those who killed him. He commands us to do likewise."

"It is impossible."

"It must be possible." Yaakov's face filled with despair. "The Rabban would not have commanded it if it were not possible. I must find a way. You, also, must find a way, or the evil which the wicked man did will gnaw at your heart all your days, and you will never be reconciled to your son."

"I have no son."

"You must forgive the wicked man. Each of us must find a way — "

Fire filled Baruch's veins and he could no longer stand to be in this house. He strode to the door and yanked it open. "When you find a way, tell me. It is impossible." Baruch stepped out and slammed the door. This was foolishness. The Rabban would not have commanded him to forgive this evil deed. All other deeds, perhaps, but not this. Never, ever, ever. Even the Rabban would not forgive such a thing.

Baruch stumbled toward his home, sick with rage. He had done as Hana asked, and it was folly. Even Yaakov the *tsaddik* could not forgive such great evil. If not him, then how could an ordinary man? The Rabban was wrong to command it.

He would not obey such a command. Not now, and not in the World to Come.

Hanan ben Hanan

Hanan watched the young men file into the Chamber of Hewn Stone. Some seemed awed by this place of story and legend — the chamber of meeting for the Sanhedrin. Hanan had come here many times, both as a boy and as a man. His father had presided here, and his brother-in-law and each of his brothers. Now his turn had come at last, when he was an old man, well past fifty, wise with years.

Last of all, the young giant Eleazar ben Hananyah entered the room. He pulled shut the great oaken door and sat in the place of highest honor.

Hanan studied the group. The Temple had many Temple guards, Levites. Forty were true priests — these young men who called themselves the Sons of Righteous Priests. A few were sons of aristocrats, men born to Sadducean families, men whose hearts the Pharisees had stolen. Hanan had long hoped to win them back. If the price of their hearts was power, he would give them power. In turn, they must give him loyalty. Absolute loyalty.

"Peace to you all, my sons," Hanan said. "Some of you know why King Agrippa deposed Yoseph Kabi yesterday. Two days ago, he engaged in disgraceful conduct in the Temple, dancing for joy over the death of Governor Festus."

Wariness crept into the young men's eyes. Some of these fools had also danced. They must never do so again.

"My sons, we are at a critical hour. The governor is dead, and we will have no law from Caesar for some months — perhaps not until next spring. We must be our own law, as it was in days of old, before the Roman dogs came to rule over us."

Eleazar ben Hananyah leaned forward. Hanan read in his eyes that he understood. The time had come to right past wrongs, while the dogs had no representative.

"The province is overrun with bandits," Hanan said. "Festus failed in capturing these because he failed to ask our help. If any of these bandits venture to Jerusalem, we will take them."

"And do what with them?" Eleazar jutted his beard forward.

"We will try them by our own laws." Hanan let a smile creep across his face. "Caesar is not our king. The living God is our king, and we will live by his Torah."

Eleazar bent to whisper something to his friend Yoseph. Hanan knew this young man Yoseph, the brilliant son of a fine Sadducean family, mentored by the best Sadducean minds. His mind had been poisoned by the Pharisees, but Hanan would win him back.

"Whose Torah?" Eleazar said.

Hanan had expected this challenge. When the Pharisees spoke of Torah, they meant the written Torah *as interpreted by the sages*. And the Pharisee fools could interpret it any way they liked. Such Torah was no Torah at all, it was abomination. To say this bluntly would alienate these young men. Hanan smiled. "We will live by the Torah of those who hold power in the Temple."

A low rumble of discontent filled the room, as Hanan had expected. Therefore, he had prepared a surprise. "My sons, it is unwise to quibble over things on which we disagree, when there are many points on which we agree. In a few years, some of you in this room will hold power in the Temple."

The young men quieted quickly. Eleazar leaned forward, his face tight. Hanan saw that for him, a few years would be too long. Excellent.

"And for one of you, power will come very much sooner." Hanan stopped to survey the room, allowing the tension to build. "I have decided to appoint Eleazar ben Hananyah as *sagan* of the Temple, effective —"

Cheers shook the chamber. The Sons of Righteous Priests leaped to their feet, hands in the air, shouting, stamping, bellowing, crowding around Eleazar, pounding him on the shoulders, kissing each other.

Hanan waited, knowing the celebration would end soon enough. It took the fourth part of an hour for the young men to settle down. The surly looks on their faces were wiped away. Each sat forward in his chair, eager to hear what Hanan would say next. Eager to cooperate. They had tasted their first draft of power, and its heady wine left them dizzy, wanting more.

"More appointments may come soon. I am indebted to certain families for the offices in the treasury, but it is possible that some of you" — Hanan gave a pointed look at Yoseph — "will have an opportunity to serve in that role in the future. I ask only your cooperation in certain matters from time to time."

The room became very quiet. "What sort of matters?" Yoseph asked.

"Matters of Temple security." Hanan twirled a small piece of his beard with his left hand.

"I have not heard that the Temple was threatened," Eleazar said.

Hanan hesitated. "Perhaps not today. But there are men who do not love the Temple, who speak against the Temple. It may be that such men will cause disturbances. We will not tolerate such men."

One young man near the back stood up. He was a short man, with a large head and large hands and thick black hair. He folded his arms across his chest and glared at Hanan. "Which men do you speak of?"

Men such as your uncle the apikoros. *Followers of fools and false prophets and messianic pretenders.* "Men who hate the Temple."

"*Goyim?*"

"No, we do not concern ourselves with dogs. I spoke of Jews."

Murmurs again. The young men leaned back in their chairs, arms across their chests.

"Jews in particular?" said the young man. "Do you have any names in mind?"

I do, but you will never know them, you fool. Hanan shook his head. "No, I have no names in mind. If men arise who hate the Temple, then I and the Temple leadership will make decisions at that time. I expect that you will cooperate in protecting the Temple. You are Temple guards, and that is your sworn duty, am I correct?"

The young man gave a short nod and sat down.

"I have nothing more to say," Hanan said. "Eleazar, you will report for duty tomorrow. You are free to appoint any lieutenants you may need. All of you are dismissed."

The young men filed out, talking in excited whispers. When the room was empty, Hanan paced back and forth. He had now neutralized Eleazar and Yoseph, friends of Kazan. They would not help Hanan, but now he had a lever to prevent them from hindering him.

Of the others . . . some would help, some hinder. He must meet with each individually, to sound them out, to learn which were true men who loved the Temple, and which were false men. This would take time, but he would find them. The Sons of Righteous Priests were more than forty men, and not all of them were the nephew of Renegade Saul.

He had also two hundred Levite Temple guards at his disposal. He would sift them for the right men, but slowly, slowly. Caesar could not possibly send a replacement before the New Year, only two months away. After that, passenger ships would not sail until spring. Hanan had many months to purify the city of the living God from those who did not love the Temple.

Ari

That is correct, *Abba*." Ari put an arm on the shoulders of Yaakov the *tsaddik*. "I am convinced Rivka speaks a true word from HaShem. She is adamant that Hanan will move against you quickly — certainly in the next weeks. My friend Gamaliel also warns me of danger. Can you not leave the city for a month or two? It is no dishonor to hide when wicked men seek to kill you. The prophet Eliyahu hid for three years in the days of King Ahav, and HaShem protected him."

"I have friends in Bethany," Yaakov said. "I could stay with them."

"Then go, *Abba!*" Ari felt surprise at the urgency in his voice. He was meddling now, just like Rivka. But . . . he had to. Hanan was a wicked man. Even if this were doomed to failure, Ari could not idly stand by and let a *tsaddik* be murdered. If he sat in Hitler's council room at Wolfsschanze now, he would detonate the bomb, even though he knew that history said the plot would fail — that Hitler would live and the bomber would die. A man must always battle evil, whether he had hope of success or not.

Yaakov slowly nodded his head. "There is wisdom in your words, Ari the Kazan. I . . . will go."

"Stay at least until the New Year," Ari said. "Then it will be safe."

"Two whole months?" Yaakov looked doubtful.

"Eliyahu was gone three years, and HaShem taught him many things."

"You are a good man, Ari the Kazan. I wish you were also a follower of Rabban Yeshua."

Ari allowed himself to smile. "And you are a righteous man, *Abba*. Go in peace, and go before nightfall."

Yaakov nodded. "Tell no one of my destination."

"Of course. Shall I watch over you on the way?"

Yaakov shook his head. "I will be quite safe. Kiss Sister Rivka and little Racheleh for me. And pray for Brother Baruch on the matter of the boy."

"Yes, *Abba*." Ari watched the old man stroll down the street and disappear at the corner. Hope raced through his heart. Most excellent! He had beaten Hanan. Defied the wicked man. Changed history.

But how? Physics said this was not possible. What fact was he missing? Had he entered some alternate universe in which Yaakov would not die? And how would that affect all history? Would the followers of Rabban Yeshua remain strong here in Jerusalem, even after the war to come? Would they hold at bay the gentilizing influences pushing to turn the church from her Jewish roots? Would there be no Constantine, no Crusades, no Inquisition, no . . . Holocaust? If so, then . . . why not follow the Rabban?

Ari walked slowly home. He must think on this thing. And pray. Yes, here was a mystery that only HaShem could unravel.

THIRTY-SIX

Rivka

For eight weeks, nothing happened while Rivka worried. The long hot summer drew to an end without violence, though Jerusalem seemed ready to explode. No governor from Rome arrived. Yaakov the *tsaddik* stayed safely in Bethany. Hanan made no move.

Rivka's fears grew. What had she forgotten? What had she never learned? What had Josephus failed to record? She felt that the few pitiful bits of knowledge she had were nothing, broken shards that stabbed at her the more she grasped them.

The New Year arrived late that year — two days after the fall equinox. With it, Yaakov the *tsaddik* returned to Jerusalem. Rivka bit her nails through Rosh HaShanah.

And nothing out of the ordinary happened.

There followed the ten Days of Awe, those days leading up to Yom Kippur, when every Jew examined his life, found himself wanting, asked forgiveness of the brothers he had wronged, and prepared for The Fast.

And still nothing happened.

Hanan ben Hanan presided as high priest over The Fast with all due dignity, ably assisted by his *sagan*, Eleazar ben Hananyah.

Still nothing.

On the fifteenth day of the year, *Sukkot* began. Ari and Rivka built a small booth atop their house and slept in it at night with Rachel. Baruch and Hana and Dov did likewise. Rivka got a full report every day of the growing tension between them. She offered to let Dov sleep over during the feast, but Hana refused. Ari and Baruch went to the Temple every day for the afternoon services, keeping a close eye on Yaakov, who insisted on attending.

Nothing.

Rivka was dying inside. She had told everyone of the danger to Yaakov the *tsaddik*. Had seen the look in their eyes. *Poor Sister Rivka is making another wrong prophecy.*

With all her might, Rivka wished they were right. With all her heart, she feared they were wrong. On the last day of the feast, she left Rachel with Hana and went to the Temple with the men for the afternoon services. Yaakov found them all a place to stand toward the front of the Court of Women, near the musicians.

The court was packed with worshipers, sweating together in the warmth of the late summer day. A deep quiet filled the entire court. Rivka scanned the rows of Levite singers on the steps leading up to the Court of Priests. Two priests with silver trumpets stood on the top row. Another priest held his bronze cymbals ready. A row of harpists set fingers to the strings of their twelve-string wooden harps, waiting. Rivka felt so tense, she thought her heart would explode.

Nothing happened during the burnt offering.

Nothing happened during the drink offering.

Nothing happened during the sin offering.

The musicians began the psalm for this fifth day of the week, the eighty-first psalm.

"Sing with joy to God our strength; shout to the God of Yaakov!"

"Woe!" shouted a voice.

Rivka's head spun to look. What was going on?

The singers continued. "Make music and strike the tambourine —"

"Woe!" the voice shouted again, with more power. A short man, standing in front of Baruch. Rivka could hardly believe one man could be so loud.

The musicians faltered and stopped. The priest leading the music turned and scowled at the offender.

"Woe!" the man bellowed.

Rivka's heart skipped a beat. This was strangely familiar. But what —

"A voice from the east! A voice from the west! A voice from the four winds! A voice against Jerusalem and the sanctuary! A voice against the bridegroom and the bride! A voice against the whole people!"

Rivka remembered, and cold shivered through her. Josephus had written of this episode, but he had put it out of place — more than five years further on in the story — that was why she had not thought of it. But he dated it to this year, this feast, this place. A crazy man in the Temple. And —

"Woe to the city! Woe to the people! Woe to the Temple!"

Rivka wanted to grab Yaakov and run, but they were trapped by this crowd. And anyway, she had a terrible, sick feeling it was useless. Something to do with phase space and all that nonsense.

Hanan ben Hanan

Hanan had no required role in today's sacrifices, but as high priest he could take part on any day he wished. Therefore, he did so today. He had waited all his life for this office, and he would not allow another man to take the honor that was rightfully his.

When the musicians struck up their psalm of praise, he walked to the Nicanor Gate to look out at the vast throng.

"Sing with joy to God our strength; shout to the God of Yaakov!"

And then . . .

"Woe!" shouted someone near the front.

Hanan's heart skipped. Who dared to dishonor the worship of the living God?

"Make music and strike the tambourine — "

"Woe!" the man roared again.

Hanan saw him now, a short man in the third row. People around him made shushing movements. And behind the man stood . . . Kazan and Yaakov called *tsaddik* and a third man.

"Woe!" In the silence that followed, the short man spoke a false prophecy, cursing the people, the Temple, the whole city of the living God.

Hanan strode through the Nicanor Gate. This . . . abomination must stop! The musicians parted before him.

Halfway down the steps, Hanan remembered that the dagger-men had murdered his own brother eight years ago at the foot of these very stairs while the singers sang the daily psalm to the living God. This might be a trap. He backed up the stairs and shouted into the Court of Priests for Temple guards. These messianics must not be permitted to curse the Temple.

Ari

A spirit!" somebody hissed behind Ari. "He has an evil spirit!"

Ari had no fear of evil spirits. Phase space was real, and Riemannian manifolds, and fiber bundles. Evil spirits were not.

But all around him, frightened faces backed away from the man. Ari's hands felt clammy. Rivka clutched at his arm.

Yaakov the *tsaddik* moved forward. "My son — "

"A voice from the four winds! A voice against Jerusalem and the sanctuary! A voice against the bridegroom and the bride! A voice against the whole people!"

Yaakov raised his hands. "Silence! I command you — "

"Woe to the city! Woe to the people! Woe to the Temple!"

" — I command you to tell me your name!" Yaakov put his hand on the peasant's head.

The peasant turned and his eyes were vacant, two black holes in an empty mind. "My name is called Yeshua!" His voice seemed to shake the Temple. "I speak in the name of Yeshua!"

Anger welled in Ari's heart. How dare this man insult Rabban Yeshua so?

Yaakov put his hand on the man's shoulder and spoke in a voice so quiet Ari could barely hear him. "I command you to be silent in the name of Rabban Yeshua the *Mashiach*."

The man was unmoved, his face slack and impassive. "A voice against Jerusalem and against the sanctuary!" he roared. "A voice against the bridegroom and the bride!"

Now Ari and Rivka and Yaakov and Baruch stood alone in the eye of the storm. This crazy man would not be silenced, even by the name of Rabban Yeshua. Ari shivered.

"You will come with me," Yaakov said. "Brother Ari, Brother Baruch, compel him to come with us. We must pray for him in a quiet place."

Ari took one of the man's arms. Baruch took the other. The man did not fight them. Yaakov led the way toward the nearest gate.

The people divided before them, terror on their faces. Ari and Baruch guided the man toward the gate as if Moshe held his staff over them, parting the waters.

All around him, Ari heard people hissing with fear. "An evil spirit!"

Which was ridiculous. The man was merely insane. He needed psychiatric help.

"Yeshua!" the man bellowed.

"Hush, you fool! You are causing much trouble." Ari pressed forward through the gate and down the steps to the level of the outer courts.

But the man refused to be quiet. Ari's heart pounded as they escorted him, shrieking, across the bridge into the upper city.

"Rivka, go home," Ari said, when he looked back and found that she was following them.

For once, she did not argue with him.

Ari and Baruch and Yaakov hurried the man through the streets to Yaakov's house. It was the only place they could go. Nobody tried to stop them. Ari kept a tight grip, but the man seemed strangely passive, unwilling or unable to fight. But neither would he be silenced. "Woe!" he shouted. "Woe!"

Yaakov led the way, praying aloud. When they reached Yaakov's home, they trundled the man in and set him on the floor. He stopped shouting.

Ari backed up against the door, but the man showed no sign of wanting to fight his way out. Baruch knelt beside him. "Friend, what is your name?"

"My name is called Yeshua ben Hananyah." The man spoke in a normal voice.

"From where do you come?" Yaakov asked.

"Migdal."

Ari wondered how they would send this man all the way home to his people in Galilee.

Baruch put a hand on him. "Do you wish to be free of your evil spirit?"

"Oh, it is you, Baruch!" The man's voice became deep and powerful and mocking in tone. "How very nice to see you again. You will leave him alone. He is ours, just as you once were. Do you wish to rejoin us?"

Baruch leaned back, sweating. "In the name of Yeshua *Mashiach*, I command you to . . ." His voice faltered.

"*You* command *us*?" said the deep voice. "What foolishness! We are very sorry, Baruch, but you have lost your power over us. You who do not love even your own son. How pathetic! Soon we shall have you back, and the boy and woman too."

"Enough!" Yaakov said. "Baruch, you will not speak to them more. You spirits, I command you in the name of Yeshua *Mashiach* to be silent."

"How delightful!" said the deep voice. "Friends, Yaakov the *tsaddik* commands us to be silent."

"Try again!" shouted a breathy female voice. "Frighten us!"

"Prophesy if you can!" said another voice, the one the man had used in the Temple. "But you are least in the kingdom of HaShem, Yaakov! A little warning — be wary of left-handed men, if you value your life!"

Yaakov stumbled back, his face ashen. "Enough!" he said. "I refuse to hear more."

Ari felt sweat all over his body. He took a step away from the door. "Perhaps we should . . . let the man go."

"And now we have the bold and courageous Ari the Kazan," said the deep voice. "Excellent! Who wishes to speak with this great lion of faith?"

"Be silent," Ari said. Which was ridiculous, but—

"Silence! Kazan orders us to be silent! Shall we tell your fortune, Ari?"

"No!" Ari backed away.

"Oh, he has no need of us! His woman can tell his fortune. And she so excels at it too! We promise not to bother you if you do not bother us, Kazan! But keep a sharp eye on your little witch woman. Is she home all alone with that delightful daughter of yours? It would be a tragedy if something happened to them, do you agree? Remember what we did to Baruch's woman! Do you want a son also, Kazan? Something can be arranged! And you also, Baruch, guard your woman! You have failed to give her what her heart desires, but we can! Would you like a daughter this time?"

Ari felt for the door, then jerked it open and stepped outside, breathing heavily. It took all his willpower to keep from bolting for home. Brother Baruch followed him out, then Yaakov.

"My sons, go home to your families." Yaakov kissed them both. "Protect your women, your children. And pray. We are all in deep need of repentance. It is our own sin that unfits us."

"You must not stay here tonight," Ari said. "Let the man go. Find some of the elders and . . . pray. There is a mighty . . . spirit of evil on this man." He could not believe he had said it, but what else could he say?

Yaakov nodded. "Go in peace, my sons."

Ari turned and ran. In a few minutes, the sun would be down. The coming darkness chilled his soul.

THIRTY-SEVEN

Hana

Hana's heart felt heavy all during the evening meal. Baruch said little, though she asked many questions. Was the service in the Temple good today? Yes, it was good. Was Yaakov the *tsaddik* still safe? Yes, he was safe. Was Brother Ari well? Yes, he was well.

Dov jabbered about the fine time he had spent with Racheleh today, and could he sleep in her booth tonight? And who made the fine wooden chairs for Racheleh's mother? And was it true that Ari the Kazan had strong magic from a far country? Baruch sat silent. Tonight, he had a dark spirit — yes, a spirit of fear.

And that was why Hana's heart felt sick. If only Baruch could be happy, then she too would be happy. Yaakov the *tsaddik* had not helped him. Hana did not know what to do. She would have to leave him after all. She could not live like this.

"Will I marry Racheleh when I grow up?" Dov reached for his stone cup of water mixed with beer, but silly little bear, he knocked it over. The beer poured over the small stone table, soaking Baruch's bread.

Baruch sprang up. "Fool!"

Dov burst into tears.

"Baruch!" Hana seized a rag and mopped up the mess.

Baruch stalked out of the kitchen, his face tight with a spirit of rage.

"*Imma*, I am sorry!" Dov clung to Hana. "Tell *Abba* I am sorry. Ask him to not be angry anymore, forever!"

Hana wiped up the mess and threw the rag in a stone jar. She hugged Dov. "Little bear!"

He buried his face in her chest and wept. Baruch came back into the kitchen and stood in the doorway and his face was stone.

Tears came to Hana's eyes. He was a good man, a kind man, except in the matter of the boy. He could not love the boy, and therefore he could not love her, because the boy was a part of her. She had done as Rivka asked — to wait and see. Now see. Every day, the boy cried for his *Abba*.

No more. She glared up at him. *No more will I live with you like this.* His eyes told her that he understood and that even so, he would not change. He would say that he could not change, but that was a lie. A man could change, if he would. But Baruch would not. Therefore, she must go. She and the boy. There was no joy in this house, and she could not live like this.

A knock at the door.

Baruch flinched as if he had been slapped. He stepped to the door and silently lowered the heavy wooden bar across it. The wood scraped as it fell into place. He turned and put a finger to his lips.

Hana felt the hot blood drain out of her face. "Who is it?" she whispered.

He mouthed one word. "Bandits."

More pounding. "Baruch! An urgent message from Ari the Kazan!"

"Ari the Kazan!" Dov shouted, his voice full of joy. "Open the door, *Abba!* A message from Ari the Kazan!"

Baruch crossed to Dov in two steps and slapped him full across the mouth. "Silence!"

Dov began screaming. Baruch raced upstairs.

Hana knelt by Dov, furious at Baruch, terrified by the pounding. "Shh-hhh, little bear!"

Baruch returned with a dagger. Something crashed against the door.

Hana shuddered, remembering the night the bandits had taken Rivka for ransom. Tonight, they had come for Baruch.

Another crash. Iron against wood. The door splintered.

Dov wailed and hid his face in Hana's heart. She patted his back and looked to Baruch. He stood like stone, waiting for the bandits.

Another crash, then another and another. Pieces of the door flew in. An iron bar poked through, hooked the wooden bar, lifted it off the brackets. The next instant, the whole door broke apart. Baruch sprang forward and swung his dagger. It caught on the doorframe, smashing the *mezuzah*.

Strong hands grabbed the dagger and wrenched it from his grasp. Two bandits lunged in and grabbed Baruch's arms. He fought like a tiger, but one of the bandits hit him in the face and the belly. The others bound his arms behind his back and tied a rag across his mouth, cinching it down hard so it wedged between his teeth.

Hana flung herself at the bandits. "Leave him alone! Take me and do with me as you will, but leave him!"

One of them laughed and slapped her hard. "Our business is with him tonight. Tomorrow, make us an offer!"

"Bandits!" Hana screamed. The neighbors must hear. They must come to help. "Bandits! Help us!"

"Fool!" The leader spat in Hana's face. "We are Temple guards, and this man is arrested by order of Hanan ben Hanan." He shoved at Hana's chest with both hands.

She staggered back, slammed into the wall. Dizziness took her.

"*Abba!*" Dov shouted.

Baruch

Baruch's head spun to look at the boy.

Dov rushed to throw his arms around Baruch's waist, then shook his tiny fist at the Temple guards. "You . . . you bad men! Go away. You must not touch my *abba*. He will not talk to you. He cannot talk to you. You must not bother him."

Acid heat burned through Baruch's body. Dov was repeating words Hana must have told him for years. *Do not touch Abba. He will not talk to you. He cannot talk to you. You must not bother him.*

One of the men tore Dov away from Baruch, set him down, and punched him hard in the belly. Dov fell to the floor, screaming. "*Abba!*"

The men seized Baruch's arms. "Walk!" The leader took a fistful of Baruch's beard and yanked forward.

Baruch walked.

Behind him, he could hear Hana's muffled sobs, Dov screaming. "*Abba! Abba!* Come back! *Abba*, I love you!"

Shame pierced Baruch's heart. For all Dov's life, he had rejected the boy, ignored him, refused him. Yet still the boy loved him as a father.

Baruch knew he was not worthy of such love. Could never be worthy of such love. The door of his heart shattered inward. Repentance crushed his soul.

He wept.

THIRTY-EIGHT

Ari

Ari spent the evening meal discussing the events of the afternoon with Rivka in tense whispers while Racheleh gabbled on, unaware.

"Josephus tells about Yeshua ben Hananyah," Rivka said. "He began lamenting the doom of the city at this feast and kept it up for more than seven years. He was harmless — never hurt a fly — even when the governor examined him by flaying."

"Flaying?" Ari's stomach tightened into a knot of fear.

Rivka looked down at Racheleh. "You don't want to know."

"What happened to him?" Ari whispered.

Rivka put her hand on Ari's arm. "I'll tell you sometime when we're not eating. I'm terrified about Yaakov. Make him leave the city again! I saw Hanan's face this afternoon. He had a spirit of rage. Where did Yaakov go after you left him?"

Ari patted her arm. "He will be safe tonight. He is praying with the elders."

"Where?"

"I do not know. I will warn him tomorrow at the morning prayers."

Rivka stood and began clearing the table. "I'm so sorry I forgot about Yeshua ben Hananyah."

"Yeshua!" Rachel sang out. "Rabban Yeshua!"

Ari kissed Rachel's forehead and stood up. In the morning, he must find Yaakov and . . . protect him until he could go into hiding.

The gun. Yes, it was time to take the gun out of hiding. The weapon was precious. Damien West had brought a gun through the wormhole, had died with three bullets loaded. Ari still had the gun and the bullets, and he had been reserving them for true emergencies.

This was a true emergency.

Tomorrow, he would clean the gun and go stand watch over Yaakov. He should have thought of that earlier, but he had believed Rivka — that the danger was over already weeks ago. Ari went upstairs to check that the gun was still in its deeply buried hiding place. If Rivka knew the gun was in the house, she would, as the Americans said, give birth to a cow. He had told her it was with "a friend," but he had not told her that the only friend he would entrust it to was himself.

A knock downstairs.

Ari froze. He heard Rivka's steps. "Who is it?" she called through the door.

A pause, then a muffled voice from the street.

"Ari!" Rivka shouted up the stairs. "Your friend Yoseph is outside! All he will say is that he brings word from Eleazar!"

Blessed be HaShem. Yoseph was a Temple guard. Perhaps he or Eleazar had heard some rumor. Ari raced down the stairs and stopped in front of the door. "This may be Temple business. It would be better if you go upstairs."

Rivka nodded. "I don't want to talk to Yoseph anyway. He's way too snooty to talk to a mere woman."

Ari waited until she had gone upstairs with Rachel, then unlatched the door and pulled it open.

A fist hit him in the stomach.

Ari crumpled, fighting for air. The man who had hit him was not Brother Yoseph. Ari caught a glimpse of the white linen tunic of a Temple guard. Then something slammed into his face.

"Ari!" Rivka screamed from upstairs.

Ari lunged for the man who had hit him, but his fingers would not close into a fist, his lungs would not draw breath.

Two of the men grabbed Ari's arms and twisted. An agony shot through his shoulders. They stepped behind him and drew his arms up tight, lashing them together.

Steps from above. "What are you creeps doing? Get away from my—"

The sound of flesh on flesh.

Rivka screamed.

A hand grabbed Ari's beard and yanked it down. "You will come with us, Kazan. Order your woman to stay here. We will set a watch, and if she leaves, we will take both her and the child."

Terror kicked Ari in the heart. Racheleh. If they touched Racheleh, he would die. "Rivka," he said through clenched teeth. "You will stay here with Racheleh, is that understood?"

"Yes . . . my master."

Master. That must be code, but Ari could not decipher it.

"Come with us, Kazan." The man holding Ari's beard tugged it forward.

Ari followed, while hot tears formed in his eyes. The gun. If he had gotten the gun, they could not have done this. If Rivka could find it and come rescue ... No, she did not know it was in the house. She would do something foolish, but she would not do the one thing that could save him. Because she did not know.

Rivka

Rage roared in Rivka's heart. Who were those men? She had not seen Yoseph among them, but they *did* look like Temple guards. She needed help. Yoseph, or better yet, that awful man Eleazar. He was *sagan* now. He could make them stop.

But ... since Eleazar was *sagan*, those men were under his command. Was he behind this — arresting an innocent man in the middle of the night? Why?

With a rush of fear, she knew. Yaakov the *tsaddik.* What had Josephus said? She'd been so focused on protecting him, she'd forgotten to *think.* Josephus said Hanan arrested *James, and some others.* "Please, HaShem, no!" Rivka fell on the floor. Did those "others" include ... Ari? He wasn't even a believer.

Rivka crawled to the open door and peered out onto the street. The men said they would post a watch. A bluff? She would have to risk it. If she did nothing, Ari would be killed, and Yaakov, and more. She had to get help or they would all die. Baruch and Hana lived only two streets over. Two minutes' walk. Baruch would help her.

Rivka pushed herself to her feet and raced upstairs. "Rachel, come now! We're going ... to see Dov! Do you want to see Dov?" Her voice sounded shrill in her own ears.

Rachel was hiding upstairs, crying. "Why were you shouting at *Abba?*"

"Not *Abba.* Some bad men. Now come! We'll go see Dov." Rivka found a dark cloak for Rachel. "It's a surprise, yes, Racheleh? You must go very quietly and obey me."

"A surprise!" Rachel shrieked. "Goodie!"

Rivka threw a cloak over her own shoulders. "I'm going to carry you, Racheleh."

"I want to walk!"

Rivka bent low and gave Rachel her fiercest look. "Rachel, I will carry you, or you will not go! And you must be very quiet!"

Rachel's eyes filled with tears. "Don't be angry on me, *Imma!* I'll be good! I promise!"

Rivka scooped her up. "Let's go, sweetheart. Shhhhhh! Surprise Dov."

Rachel nodded her head, already keeping her promise.

Rivka tiptoed down the stairs and grabbed a lighted olive oil lamp. She added more olive oil from a jug, then dusted the surface of the oil liberally with cinnamon powder. The soothing aroma of the burning spice calmed her senses. Rachel clung to her.

Rivka slipped out into the night, pulling the door locked behind her. *Please, HaShem, let there be nobody watching.* She moved quietly down the street, her ears poised for any sound. Nothing. She walked half a block, then dared to look back.

A dark shape moved behind her.

Rivka's heart stopped. *We will set a watch, and if she leaves, we will take both her and the child.* She was going to be killed. And Rachel too.

The shape came rapidly nearer. A man, dressed as a Temple guard. He carried a club in his right hand. A leering white smile cut a hideous hole in his beard.

Rivka knew she could not run away — not carrying Rachel. She could scream, but who would come to the aid of the witch woman? If the neighbors had not helped Ari, they would not help her.

She lowered Rachel to the ground. "Stand right here, sweetie, and look that way while I talk to this man. If I tell you to run, don't look back. Just run as fast as you can to Dov's house."

Rachel stared at her, eyes wide and fearful.

Rivka turned and took a few steps toward the approaching Temple guard. His eyes caressed her body greedily.

Rivka waited, her heart beating a ragged rhythm in her chest. One way or another, this was going to be an extremely short conversation.

He came closer. Closer. Switched his club to his left hand and reached for her with his right.

Rivka tossed a lampful of spiced oil into his face.

He screamed, clawed at his eyes.

Rivka twisted around and kicked backward with her heel, straight into his stomach.

He buckled in the middle.

She spun back and yanked his club away. Gripped it like a softball bat. She hadn't done this in years, but . . . She swung.

The club connected with his head. Not a home run, just a little bloop single.

The man staggered and fell to his knees.

Rivka whacked him again in the face. He pitched forward onto the ground, screaming. *It's you or my daughter, buddy. Sorry, but that's no choice at all.* She hit him again, this time in the kidneys. Then she grabbed Rachel and ran.

By the first corner, she was staggering, winded. She pressed on. If she could find Baruch, together they could try to save Ari. At the second corner, her breath was coming in great ragged gasps.

Rivka felt like she would faint. Rachel was so . . . heavy, and she was so frightened, and Baruch had to help her, and . . .

And the door of Baruch's house was shattered. Rivka lurched to the entry and peered in. Hana huddled on the floor with Dov, wailing. The doors of all the neighboring homes were shut against the terror by night. "Hana!" Rivka shouted.

Hana looked up, her eyes bleary and red, her face twisted with anguish.

"The men in white tunics took *Abba!*" Dov shouted.

"Temple guards?" Rivka said.

Hana nodded.

Rivka grabbed her hand. "Get up! We've got to do something!"

Hana shook her head. "I do not know where they are taken. And what can two women do?"

"More than you think," Rivka said. "I just made mashed potatoes out of one of those guards. We're going to Hanan's palace and we're going to . . ."

She stopped. Going to *what?* Was she a raving lunatic? Sure, she had caught one guard by surprise and punched his lights out. But a whole palace of Temple guards?

She wasn't Superman. Wasn't even Clark Kent. She was just an angry mama with two four-year-olds and a weepy girlfriend who had already thrown in the towel.

If Hanan wanted to kill Ari and Baruch and Yaakov and . . . whoever else, there was *nothing* she could do about it. She hadn't prevented anything by her meddling — she had made things worse.

Rivka slumped onto the floor. If Josephus was any guide at all, Hanan was going to win.

Bigger than she had imagined.

THIRTY-NINE

Hanan ben Hanan

Hanan's body twitched with anticipation. "Lead the prisoners in."

A Temple guard went out. Shortly, he returned leading fifteen men, their feet bare, their hands bound behind them. Two of them were bloodied about the head. All looked frightened, except Kazan. Rage twisted his face. He would learn fear soon enough.

Hanan looked to his right. His protege, Yeshua ben Gamaliel, looked fierce and eager.

On Hanan's left, his nephew Mattityahu ben Theophilus leaned back in his chair, his eyes half-closed. Hanan knew Mattityahu was not asleep — he was listening, and he would forget none of what he heard.

"We are met tonight to consider the case against you men," Hanan said. "We have a quorum of three judges — me, Rabbi Yeshua ben Gamaliel, and my distinguished nephew Mattityahu ben Theophilus. You are accused—"

"This is an illegal proceeding." Kazan looked agitated. "You are not permitted to try men at night. We demand to be tried in daylight before the full Sanhedrin."

Hanan glared at him. "Kazan, you will not speak out of turn. I have called this Sanhedrin of three judges, which is the minimum number required—"

"The minimum is seventy-one!" Kazan's face had turned a deep red.

Hanan pointed to a guard, who slapped Kazan with the back of his hand. A trickle of blood formed at the corner of Kazan's mouth. Two guards grabbed Kazan's arms and yanked them back. Another tugged a gag between his teeth. Kazan struggled. Another guard hit him in the stomach. He doubled over.

Hanan judged that Kazan would cause no more trouble. "You are accused of being followers of Yeshua, a false *mashiach* who spoke against the Temple and has caused riots here in Jerusalem. You are accused of inciting a man to disturb the worship of the living God today in the Temple. This man spoke against the Temple and repeatedly shouted the name of your false *mashiach*, Yeshua. You then aided him in his escape. All of this is clear violation of Torah."

Hanan paused. The fifteen men before him were sweating. The oldest, Yaakov called *tsaddik*, glared back at Hanan, his face strong with anger.

Hanan turned toward the guards. "I call the first witness, Shimon ben Levi."

Shimon came forward.

"Your name and office?"

"My name is called Shimon ben Levi, and I am a Temple guard."

Hanan smiled. Shimon was a man who loved the Temple. Not like those unreliable men who called themselves Sons of Righteous Priests. Hanan had given their leaders important work tonight in the Temple. "Shimon, swear an oath that you will bear no false witness, according to the commandment."

"I swear by the living God and by his holy Temple that I will tell all the truth before this court."

"Tell the court what you saw today in the Temple."

"A man disrupted the music by shouting out insults and provocations against the city and the people and the Temple. He repeatedly called on the name of Yeshua and he specifically cursed the sanctuary of the living God. He and some others then escaped. I was prevented from arresting him because of the crowd."

"Is that man here tonight?"

"No, but three who were with him are here." Shimon pointed first to Kazan, then to Yaakov, then to a man of medium height with a black beard and angry eyes.

"You!" Hanan said to the third man. "What is your name?"

"My name is called Baruch ben Yehudah."

Hanan pointed to Yaakov. "Are you the leader of that sect called The Way?"

"I am."

Hanan turned to Kazan. "I do not require an introduction to the third malefactor. I have long been acquainted with Ari called Kazan."

Kazan's eyes smoldered with a great rage.

Hanan waved away the first witness. "Enough from you! I call the second witness, Yohanan ben Yoseph."

A second guard came forward.

"What is your name and office?"

Yohanan gave his name and office, swore not to bear false witness, and then gave the same testimony as Shimon.

Hanan had now met the requirements for testimony, as required by all right-thinking men. The Pharisees held a different opinion, but they were not right-thinking men.

Hanan pointed a finger at Yaakov. "You will be permitted to speak, each of you in your own defense, as is your right according to Torah. You may call witnesses on your behalf, so long as they are present. You may not bear false witness, and you may not speak out against this court. After each of you speaks, I will pronounce your guilt or innocence and your sentence.

"The charges against you are these: First, that you are followers of Yeshua called *mashiach*, a seditious man who spoke against Caesar and the Temple. The penalty for this charge is death by stoning. This charge I make against all of you. The second charge applies only to three of you, namely Yaakov ben Yoseph, Baruch ben Yehudah, and Ari called Kazan. You three are charged with inciting a man to speak out against the Temple today. The penalty for this charge is death by stoning. The third charge applies also to you three alone, namely that you aided the same man in his escape. The penalty for this is a flogging."

Sweat shone on the faces of the prisoners.

Hanan smiled. He pointed to Yaakov called *tsaddik*. "We will begin with the eldest. How do you answer to the charges against you? Are you a follower of Yeshua called *mashiach*?"

Yaakov

Yaakov did not wish to speak to this wicked man at all. This House of Hanan were dogs! Evil men! HaShem would judge them on the last day.

Hanan asked again, "Are you a follower of Yeshua called *mashiach*?"

Yaakov said nothing.

One of the guards stepped forward and slapped him. "You will answer the high priest!"

"Are you a follower of Yeshua called *mashiach*?" Hanan asked.

Still Yaakov said nothing.

The guard hit him again, much harder this time.

Yaakov coughed, tasting blood. His face felt numb and his tongue thick and he knew he must answer or they would beat him until he spoke. "I follow Yeshua, who is *Mashiach*, captain of the hosts of heaven, leader of the divine council, Son of the living God."

Hanan leaned forward. "And you hold this Yeshua to be king?"

Yaakov coughed again. "He is king of the World to Come."

"And therefore he is greater than Caesar?"

"As you say."

"I spit on this Yeshua." Hanan drew his two councillors together and began whispering.

Rage seeped through Yaakov's body. A frozen numbness welled in his belly. These men were evil! They had no right to dishonor Yeshua in this way. His own dishonor, Yaakov could stand, but to see Rabban Yeshua dishonored — that was vile.

"We find you guilty of sedition against Rome and the Temple." Hanan gave him a thin smile. "Since the penalty for this is death, we waive an examination of the other charges."

Yaakov raised his chin. "I have something more to say."

Hanan narrowed his eyes. "You may speak, so long as you do not attack this court or the Temple."

Yaakov glowered at him. "I am innocent of any wrongdoing. Yeshua the *Mashiach* will judge you himself on the last day for your evil deeds, you dog." He spat at Hanan's feet.

Two guards hit Yaakov in the face. The olive oil lamps in the room flickered and then dimmed. He slumped to the floor, and dizziness swept over him.

Pain cut through Yaakov's soul like a sword. He had spoken out for the honor of Yeshua and . . .

What good had it done?

FORTY

Rivka

Rivka wanted to scream. Was this what she had come back to this century for? To have a baby and then watch Ari get murdered by some ... *creep?* HaShem wasn't playing fair. She'd stayed here so she could save Saul, and this was the thanks she got? To be left a widow with a war coming?

No! She was going to fight back. If Hanan wanted to kill her, he could go ahead and try. She'd scratch his eyes out. Rivka grabbed Hana's arm. "Come on, we've got to do something."

Hana huddled on the floor and hugged Dov. "There is nothing we can do."

"Then we'll get help. Rabbi Yohanan could raise quite a stink."

Hope flickered in Hana's eyes. "You know Rabbi Yohanan?"

"Of course! He's an old friend of mine."

Hana slowly stood up. "Will he listen to two women?"

"He'd better!" Rivka took Rachel's hand. "Racheleh, let's take a walk. We're going ..." Despair cut through her. "Hana, I don't know where he lives."

"But Ari the Kazan has many friends, yes?"

Hope flamed in Rivka's heart. Why hadn't she thought of that? She hefted the club in her hands. "Ari has a lot of friends." Rivka pulled Hana to the door. "I'll bet you anything Gamaliel can get us inside the palace of Hanan ben Hanan."

"Two women with one club are no match for many men."

"I know, but forty Sons of Righteous Priests could make a whale of a fight, don't you think?"

Light streamed through the window slits of Gamaliel's house. Rivka pounded on the door. "*Savta!* Gamaliel! I need your help!"

After about a thousand years, the door opened. Midwife Marta peered out. "Child! What brings you here so late? And with little Racheleh and your friend! Come in, child!"

"*Savta*, they've arrested Ari the Kazan and the husband of my friend Hana."

"At night?" Marta looked scandalized. "Who arrested them?"

"Temple guards. Men from Hanan ben Hanan."

Marta's face went pale. "Child, Hanan will not dare —"

"He will kill them," Rivka said. "Kill them and others unless we do something now. Is Gamaliel home? I need his help."

"Come with me." Marta led the way back to the sitting room. "Gamaliel! Rivka the Kazan needs your help."

Gamaliel jumped up from his wooden couch. Rivka sketched out the situation. Gamaliel asked a few questions. With each answer, his face tightened another notch.

"I have only one hope," Rivka said. "You must speak to Brother Eleazar and Brother Yoseph and the other Sons of Righteous Priests. Hanan means to murder Ari, and he will do it tonight."

Gamaliel nodded. "You will stay here with *Savta*. I will do what I can do."

"No." Rivka put Rachel's hand in Marta's wrinkled paw. "*Savta* can watch the children. Hana and I are coming with you."

"It . . . it is unseemly for women to go out alone with a man at night." Gamaliel's face turned a brilliant red.

"It was seemly enough five years ago when I helped you limp to the Fortress Antonia so you could save your uncle Saul."

Gamaliel's eyes widened. "That was you?"

"It was me — in red silk and a veil. I ask you now to let us come with you. We may be able to do things you cannot. If we delay, the life of Ari and many others will be forfeit."

"Gamaliel, you must take her," Marta said. "Whether it is seemly or not."

Gamaliel turned and disappeared up a long hallway.

Rivka's heart did a double back-flip and then belly flopped. Tears formed in her eyes. Her mind raced, but she could not think what to do. She still had the club she had used to beat up the Temple guard. It was hopeless, but she would have to try. "*Savta*, will you keep the children? Hana and I must do . . . something."

"Just let me have a word with that young fool." Marta hobbled toward the hallway. When she finally reached the far end, she stopped and gave a little shriek.

Gamaliel rushed past her and came tearing down the hallway, wearing the white linen uniform of a Temple guard. A huge grin covered his face. "Wearing this, I will find a way into the palace of Hanan ben Hanan," he said. "We need also Brother Eleazar. Run with me, Rivka the Kazan! Run!"

He is not here tonight," said the steward at the palace of Brother Eleazar's father. "He had business for Hanan ben Hanan tonight."

Rivka gasped. Then a little ray of light awoke in her heart. Brother Eleazar must be at the trial. He would never allow anything to happen to Ari or Baruch.

Gamaliel turned to face her and Hana, his face downcast. "We must try Brother Yoseph."

"Is it far from here?" Rivka looked up at the sky. The moon wouldn't be up for hours yet.

"It is past your house." Gamaliel strode rapidly, his steps almost a run. "The palace of Mattityahu the priest is near to the palace of Hanan ben Hanan."

Something clicked in Rivka's brain. "Mattityahu? Is that . . . one of Brother Yoseph's relatives?"

"His father," Gamaliel said. "You will hurry, please."

Rivka was gasping for breath now, but she had to know. "And does Brother Yoseph have an older brother also named Mattityahu? Are they Pharisees?"

"Yes and no." Gamaliel gave her a strange look. "Has Ari the Kazan told you nothing of Brother Yoseph's family?"

Rivka shook her head.

"They are Sadducees." Gamaliel spat the words. "A prominent family, allies with the family of Yeshua ben Gamaliel. Their men are named Mattityahu or Yoseph for many generations. Yes, Yoseph's older brother is named for his father. No, they are not Pharisees. They nearly disinherited Brother Yoseph when he became a Pharisee. He is a pariah in his own family, like Brother Eleazar. The Sons of Righteous Priests have sacrificed much for the truth. Here is the palace. You will wait here."

Gamaliel went to the gate and spoke briefly to a guard inside. A side door swung open and he disappeared inside.

Rivka's mind was churning. Once again, something she had *known* to be true was false. Josephus had a father and brother named Mattityahu.

And his name in Hebrew was Yoseph. According to his memoirs, published some years from now, his family was close to Yeshua ben Gamaliel. And they were supposedly *Pharisees*.

In other words, Josephus had lied through his teeth. Probably because, after the war, the Sadducees would disappear and the Pharisees would rise to prominence. Josephus would someday rewrite history to suit himself.

And she was basing all her plans on him? What kind of moron was she?

"Rivkaleh, you are pale." Hana touched Rivka's face.

"I think I'm going to throw up." Rivka brushed tears out of her eyes. "I just realized that most of what I know is . . . smoke and mirrors."

"I do not understand what this means, smoke and mirrors."

"It means I don't know anything anymore. I'm not a seer woman. Everything I know, I learned from a pathological liar."

"Rivkaleh, does this mean Ari and Baruch are safe?"

The door clicked open. Gamaliel came out. Alone. He strode toward them, his face tense. "Brother Yoseph went to the Temple with Brother Eleazar early this evening on a matter of importance for Hanan ben Hanan."

"To . . . the Temple?" Rivka felt horribly tired. *They aren't at the trial. They can't help Ari.* "Can we go to the Temple and find them?"

Gamaliel frowned and pointed up the street. "There is the palace of Hanan. If we go to the Temple and return to Hanan's palace, we will lose yet another hour."

"There isn't time! Who else can help us?" Rivka said. "Gamaliel, which other Sons of Righteous Priests live around here?"

He shook his head. "Most of us come of Pharisee families and live in the New City. There are no other Sons of Righteous Priests in this neighborhood."

Rivka's brain buzzed with . . . what? Fear. Uncertainty. Indecision. Hanan was going to kill somebody tomorrow morning. At least Yaakov the *tsaddik*. Probably several others. She had it on the word of a liar.

Hey, Rivka, go ahead and bumble right on in. You're awfully good at this prediction game. Maybe you can get them all killed.

Gamaliel shifted his weight. "You must decide, Rivka the Kazan. Where should we go?"

"I don't know!" Rivka said. "Just let me think for a minute. I need to ask HaShem what to do."

"And . . . will he tell you?" Gamaliel asked.

Rivka swallowed. *How should I know? I've been too busy reading Josephus to ask HaShem anything lately.*

"Rivkaleh." Hana put a hand on Rivka's arm. "I know what we must do."

"How do you know?"

Hana smiled. "Because I heard the voice of HaShem."

Ari

Ari's pulse roared in his temples. This was the vaunted Jewish justice his stepfather had boasted of? The Mishnah said a court could not hear a capital case at night. Nor could it make a decision on the same day charges were brought. The full Sanhedrin must sit on a capital case, not three biased judges.

So said the Mishnah, written by Pharisees a hundred years from now. But in this hour, Sadducee justice prevailed. Justice like the harsh Islamic law Ari had despised in his youth. His whole world was crumbling, the pillars of his temple falling around him, crushing him.

Hanan pointed to the next man, whose name was Taddai. "How do you answer the charges against you? Are you a follower of that Yeshua called *mashiach?*"

Taddai spit at Hanan. "I am." All of the accused had spit at the high priest.

A Temple guard hit Taddai in the face. Hanan conferred with his two councillors for a few seconds. "We find you guilty of law breaking and sentence you to death by stoning."

Ari's tongue felt bloated, his lips dry as papyrus. Hanan was going down the line by age. Ari would be next, then Baruch, then two others. And then . . . they would all die.

Hanan pointed at Ari and spoke to one of the guards. "Unbind his mouth."

The guard yanked off the gag. Ari felt one of his teeth loosen.

"You, Kazan, how do you answer the charges against you? Are you a follower of that Yeshua called *mashiach?*"

Ari shook his head. It would do him little good, but he must tell the truth here. "No," he rasped in a brittle voice.

Shock rippled across Hanan's face. He leaned forward. "Kazan, I adjure you by the living God to speak the truth. Are you a follower of Yeshua called *mashiach?*"

"I am not."

"Swear it."

Ari raised his face toward heaven. "I swear by the living God and by his Temple and by my lifeblood that I am not now a follower of Yeshua called *Mashiach*, nor have I ever been his follower, nor will I ever be." It would grieve Rivka to hear such words, but he must speak the truth.

Hanan turned to his councillors and whispered furiously for several minutes. Finally, he broke the conference and pointed to Yaakov. "You, Yaakov called *tsaddik!* Does Kazan speak the truth?"

Yaakov nodded. "It grieves me that Brother Ari does not follow Rabban Yeshua."

Hanan's face darkened. He pointed at the next man and the next and the next, asking each if Kazan spoke true. Each affirmed that he did.

Hanan huddled again with his councillors. Finally they seemed to come to an agreement. Hanan straightened in his seat, and his beard bristled with rage. "This court finds you, Kazan, not guilty of following Yeshua called *mashiach*. However, there are yet two charges against you."

Ari nodded, astounded that he had gotten off the hook in what the Americans called a kangaroo court. Hanan must be very confident of the other charges.

"You, Kazan, were you in the Temple today with these others, Yaakov called *tsaddik* and Baruch ben Yehudah and the man who cursed the Temple?"

"Yes, but I did not know the man who—"

"Do you admit that he disturbed the peace and spoke words of violence against the people and the Temple and Caesar?"

Ari nodded. This was hopeless. "Yes, he did those things."

"Do you admit that you incited the man?"

"No, I do not admit such a thing. I never saw the man before, nor did I speak to him until after he shouted his words."

Hanan's face turned purple. "Two witnesses have testified that you incited the man to speak."

A base lie. Ari could not listen in silence to foolishness. "With respect, the witnesses did not testify that we incited the man. They testified only that we were present. It is true that Yaakov tried to calm him, but this was not incitement. You have the witnesses. Ask them if we incited the man."

Hanan leaned forward. "Kazan, you lie — "

One of the judges touched Hanan's arm and leaned close, whispering something in his ear. Hanan shook his head several times, but the judge kept talking. Finally, Hanan said, "The witnesses will come forward."

Both witnesses came forward and held a long whispered conference with Hanan. When he dismissed them, his eyes glinted red in the light of the olive oil lamps that dotted the walls.

"This court finds Kazan not guilty of inciting the evildoer today in the Temple."

A bolt of joy raced through Ari's veins. Then he thought better of it. Hanan must have some other trick to play. He would never allow Ari to walk away from this.

Hanan fixed both eyes on Ari. "And did you leave the Temple with the evildoer?"

"Yes," Ari said. "We . . . Yaakov and Baruch and I wished to help him. Yaakov believed him to be possessed by an evil spirit."

"And did you also believe this?" Hanan gave him a sarcastic smile.

"I . . . did not believe in evil spirits," Ari said. "He seemed to have a sickness of the heart, speaking much nonsense."

"Nonsense? You helped this man escape so you could listen to nonsense?" Hanan glared at him. "What sort of nonsense would enlighten the famous magician Kazan?"

Ari tried to remember. He closed his eyes, desperate for something. Anything. "The man . . . warned Yaakov the *tsaddik* that he should beware of left-handed men."

A collective hiss ran around the room.

Ari opened his eyes.

Hanan sat frozen in his seat, a long strand of beard twirling in his hand. His left hand. "Very amusing, Kazan. It is well-known that I am left-handed. What other nonsense did you learn?"

But Ari's mind had gone blank. He said nothing.

"You admit you helped the man escape from the Temple."

Ari nodded. It was the truth, and what could he say?

Hanan turned to his two fellow judges and whispered to them for several minutes. He shook his head violently several times. Finally, he slammed his palm on his knee and turned back to face Ari.

"This court finds you guilty of aiding the escape of the evildoer. The penalty for this crime will be a flogging. Forty lashes, less one." Hanan pointed to four of the Temple guards. "See to it."

Baruch

Baruch had heard little of the proceedings. His ears still rang with the cries of little Dov. *I love you, Abba!*

The boy loved him. For no reason, he loved him. Baruch did not love the boy. Even now, he did not love the boy. Because of honor. The boy was the sign of his dishonor. And yet the boy loved Baruch as a boy should love his father, with a pure, bright, shining love.

Shame burned Baruch. He did not deserve such love, nor had he any impulse to return it.

But he wished to have such an impulse. The boy deserved a father. Baruch had been no father to him. And now he never would. Tonight he would die. Perhaps Hana would find another husband who could be a true father to the boy.

Now Hanan ben Hanan turned to Brother Ari. Hanan questioned Brother Ari closely. Brother Ari told the truth. Brother Ari was an honorable man. Of course he could not say he followed Yeshua the *Mashiach*. He did not follow Rabban Yeshua, so how could he say otherwise?

Hanan pronounced Brother Ari innocent twice before he found a charge on which Brother Ari was guilty. Two guards led Brother Ari out to be flogged.

Hope tore at Baruch's heart. Brother Ari would be flogged, but a man could survive a flogging at the hands of Jews. Jews used a whip of leather only, not like the cruel whips used by the Romans. A man could not survive thirty-nine lashes with a Roman whip, but a Jewish one, yes. Brother Ari would live.

Hanan pointed to Baruch. "You, Baruch ben Yehudah. How do you answer the charges against you? Are you a follower of Yeshua called *mashiach?*"

Baruch wobbled on his feet, and dizziness filled his head. He could save his life. He could be restored to Hanaleh. And he could try again, somehow, to be a true father to the boy. To return the love so freely given. All he must do was lie.

He could swear falsely that he did not follow Yeshua the *Mashiach*. The others would take that as proof that he was an *apikoros*. They would then swear truthfully that he had once followed Yeshua, but no longer. Then Hanan could not kill him for sedition. Also, Hanan could not kill him for inciting the man with the evil spirit to sedition. It was established that none of them had incited the man.

If Baruch renounced Rabban Yeshua, he would receive the same forty lashes less one as Brother Ari. He could survive. He could be restored to the boy. Did not Yeshua command his followers to love? But if he dishonored Yeshua here, Yeshua would dishonor him in the World to Come. Sweat poured down Baruch's sides.

Hanan's voice cut through the silence. "You, Baruch ben Yehudah. Are you a follower of Yeshua called *mashiach?* Answer yes or no."

Baruch's eyes blurred with tears. For his own honor, he had spent these past years denying love to the boy. Now, he would spit on that honor if he could have a second chance. But to do so, he must spit on the honor of Rabban Yeshua. Could he deny love to the boy yet again — this time for the sake of Rabban Yeshua's honor?

"You, Baruch ben Yehudah. Are you a follower of Yeshua called *mashiach?* Guards, strike him until he answers."

Panic filled Baruch's soul. He must choose between doing right and doing right, and which was the greater?

A fist slugged him in the belly. Baruch doubled over, gasping for breath. Two hands seized his beard and pulled it upward. "Answer the high priest!"

Baruch licked his cracked lips. Blinked twice so that he could see Hanan ben Hanan. Refused to look to the side, to meet the hot eyes of Yaakov the *tsaddik.*

"I . . ." Baruch coughed, and a fit of choking seized him. Finally he straightened. He looked Hanan in the face. "I . . . follow Rabban Yeshua."

"This court finds you guilty of sedition and sentences you to death by stoning."

Righteous rage filled Baruch's heart. He spit at Hanan. "I curse you with this curse — that HaShem will punish you at the hands of Esau."

The guard hit Baruch very hard in the face.

FORTY-ONE

Ari

Four Temple guards forced Ari outside, down some steps, into a large walled courtyard. The chill night air refreshed him after the stale heat of Hanan's palace. Fear and hope fought for control.

Two guards stood behind him, each holding an arm. A third stood in front of Ari with an iron club. "You will not move or it will go worse for you."

Ari felt his hands being untied behind him. He must choose now — fight, or submit? If he fought, he *might* escape. More likely they would catch him and club him to death. If he submitted, he would be flogged. Thirty-nine lashes would not kill a man.

Ari's hands came loose and the two guards pulled his arms out to either side. Ari did not resist. He would take what they gave him and survive. For Rivka and Racheleh he must submit.

The third guard slit the back of Ari's tunic from top to bottom. Then he cut open the sleeves. The tunic dropped to Ari's feet in front of him. The man with the club kicked it away. Ari shivered. Now he wore nothing but a loincloth, and the night air chilled his sweating skin. It struck him that the stories Rivka had told him about Rabban Yeshua's trial had happened here — in the courtyard of the palace of Hanan.

The men duck-walked Ari to the stone wall surrounding the palace. An old iron ring was set into the wall at the height of a man's head. The guards lashed Ari's wrists to this ring and tied ropes to his ankles. "Put your hands against the wall and step back, Kazan."

Ari set his hands to the wall and shuffled his feet back until he was stretched out at an angle to the wall. He heard the sound of a stake being pounded into the hard dirt behind him. Then he felt his ankle ropes being tied snug to the stake.

The guard with the club prodded Ari in the ribs with the cold iron.

Ari flinched, but he could not move.

The guard laughed. He grabbed Ari's loincloth and yanked it off.

Ari gasped. This final indignity ripped away the last shreds of his honor. He was naked to the world, as unprotected as a newborn child.

"Give me the whip," said the guard.

Ari stared at the ground, cringing. He could not turn his head, could not know when the first blow would fall until he would hear the whip singing through the air. He waited.

The guard held the whip under Ari. "See Kazan, here is your new friend."

Ari gasped. The weapon was not the one he had seen often — the humane Jewish whip, leather only. It was a Roman *flagrum* — a short wooden handle with several leather thongs, each tipped at the end with pieces of ragged bone or small balls of rusted iron. Sweat stood out all over Ari's body, and a huge puddle of molten fear grew in his belly. This was evil, pure and simple, and he had no defense. A man could not survive thirty-nine lashes with a *flagrum*.

The guard laughed and pulled the *flagrum* away. "So, Kazan, you were expecting something else? Hanan is terribly sorry, but we seem to have misplaced the usual whip."

Ari waited.

He heard the guard give a little grunt, then the whine of the whip, and then . . . The leather bit into his back, wrapping full around his body so that the sharpened chunks in the ends sank into his chest like the stings of a dozen hornets. Ari screamed. The pain so overwhelmed him that he lost control of his bowels and bladder. His knees buckled and his weight sagged against the ropes tying his wrists.

The man laughed and jerked hard on the *flagrum*. The ends ripped out and dragged around his body. Ari screamed again.

"One!" shouted the four guards in unison.

Ari could not see. His hearing dimmed. The only reality now was the burning rivers of fire across his back and chest.

The man with the whip grunted again. The whip sang. Pain like lightning seared through Ari's soul. Again the man jerked on the whip, and the ends tore loose again.

"Two!"

After the third stroke, Ari's mind began losing grip. There was no past, no future — just an eternally raging present. Lash after lash. Ten. Eleven. Twelve.

Then Ari heard shouting. The thirteenth blow did not fall. He waited. Blood cooled on his lacerated skin. His ears could barely hear the words.

"Fools! Unloose him!"

Ari's heart leaped.

"He is to be taken with the others to be stoned! They are gone already. You there, help me with Kazan. You three others, Hanan orders you to go quickly to the stoning pits. There will be much work to be done before morning."

Ari felt his ankles and wrists unbound and he collapsed in the filth of the courtyard. Strong arms seized his arms and hoisted him up. From a thousand kilometers away, words battered his ears. "You, Kazan, you law-breaker! The Court has changed its mind. You are to die after all."

Baruch

Baruch lay on the floor, gasping. He heard the last two men affirm that they too were followers of Rabban Yeshua. They too spit at Hanan. Baruch heard the guards beat them.

For a moment, there was silence. Then Hanan said, "You fourteen have shown yourselves worthy of death. We will execute the sentence now. Guards, you will gag them and take them out by the back door to the Essene Gate."

Rough hands yanked Baruch to his feet. A hand clamped over his nose. He opened his mouth to breathe and a coarse cloth was wedged inside, then tied behind his neck. He blinked many times and his vision cleared.

Fear darkened the faces of the other men. Baruch looked to Yaakov the *tsaddik* for courage. Yaakov was crying.

"Move!" A guard poked Baruch in the back. Baruch moved.

They went out single file into the courtyard. A scream ascended into the night sky. Baruch felt his insides crawling. They rounded the corner of the palace. There was Brother Ari, tied to the wall and staked to the ground, his back striped with many lashes. A *flagrum!* Baruch turned his head so he would not vomit. *Be merciful to him, HaShem. Give him death quickly.*

The whip whined and struck again. Brother Ari screamed. "Six!" shouted his tormentors. Acid fury burned in Baruch's belly. Brother Ari was right, had been right all along. Evil ruled this world, and there could be no reason for it. Perhaps HaShem himself could give no answer.

A guard unlocked a small iron door at the back of the courtyard. The line of prisoners shuffled out. Baruch knew that this slow pace would lengthen the pain and fear, but he did not wish to hurry. Yes, the resurrection was coming, and that was a comfort, and yet . . .

And yet he did not wish to die. HaShem had created life to be lived. Therefore, even a life of pain and fear was better than no life at all. Baruch wanted one more day of life in this world, to walk under the sun, to lie down with his woman, to hear the laughter of . . .

Of the boy. Yes, the laughter of the boy. He would give much to see the boy, even if his touch burned like the lash of the whip.

Brother Ari screamed again. His floggers shouted, "Seven!"

Hot tears blurred Baruch's vision and he stumbled. He would not live another hour, would not see the sun or his woman or the boy again.

And he deserved death. Not for the reason given by Hanan — for his trust in Rabban Yeshua. No, he deserved death because he had failed to follow Rabban Yeshua's commandments. It was a hard thing to love one's enemies, and perhaps not possible to do so. That must have been a metaphor only. Rabban Yeshua did not really expect him to love Hanan ben Hanan, or the wicked man.

But surely Rabban Yeshua expected him to love the boy. The boy was the son of Hana, and deserving of respect and love. And Baruch had failed. Failed because he could not put aside his honor. Brother Ari was right — honor was not so important as the men of this world deemed it. Yaakov the *tsaddik* was a man who often put aside his own honor, and yet all loved him. All loved him precisely *because* he would put aside his own honor for the sake of the honor of Rabban Yeshua. Brother Ari, who did not follow Rabban Yeshua, had yet a better understanding of the Rabban than Baruch did.

If Baruch did not have a rag in his mouth, he would have raised up his voice to wail. Instead, he could do nothing but shuffle along. Far up the street, he saw the black outline of the Essene Gate against the starlit sky.

He stumbled and fell to his knees, then wavered off-balance. The guards could have caught him now, could have kept him from pitching forward onto his face.

But they did not and he fell. Two of them laughed aloud, jeering him for his clumsiness. They kicked him many times while the other prisoners shuffled by. Finally, they pulled him to his feet.

"Hurry!" One of them cuffed him across the ear. "Hanan wishes this business done before the third watch of the night begins."

Baruch hurried.

Rivka

Rivka huddled in the shadows of the wall in front of Hanan's palace, clinging to Hana, clutching her club. Gamaliel had gone in a quarter of an hour ago. Would he come out? Or would he —

Iron hinges creaked. Rivka pulled back into the shadows, terrified of who might come out. The main gate swung inward. A Temple guard stepped out. Then Gamaliel.

Between them hung a man. Ari. More dead than alive. Blood streamed from his face, his chest, his back. He wore nothing, and his feet dragged in the dirt.

"We must hurry," Gamaliel said.

"Move, Kazan!" The other guard slapped Ari in the face.

Ari's head flopped limply to one side.

Rivka put her hand to her mouth to keep from screaming. Hana pulled her back deeper into shadow. The three men staggered down the street toward them.

Hana backed around the corner of the palace into a dark alley, jerking Rivka with her. "Give me the club."

Rivka's nerveless hand let go of the weapon. She leaned against the wall and tried not to vomit.

Voices approaching. Rivka heard Hana take a deep breath.

The men passed by them in the street. Hana stepped out behind them and clubbed the strange guard in the back of the head. He collapsed without a sound.

Ari and Gamaliel fell with him. Rivka and Hana helped lift Ari. Rivka slipped in underneath Ari's right arm. Gamaliel did the same under the left. "I am sorry, Rivka the Kazan," he said. "They were flogging him when I found him."

"We've got to find somewhere safe to clean his wounds!" Rivka said. "If he gets infected, he won't . . . ." She couldn't think.

Gamaliel pointed. "Back that way to the palace of Brother Yoseph's father. I will speak to the guard at the gate — his brother is a follower of your Rabban Yeshua."

They hobbled back up the street as fast as they could carry Ari. Rivka could not see through her tears. She heard Hana sobbing behind them.

At the palace of Brother Yoseph's father, Gamaliel had quick words with the gatekeeper. In minutes, they placed Ari on a clean bed in the palace. "I need vinegar!" Rivka said. "Clean linen! Water! Olive oil!"

Ari moaned something.

"What of Baruch and Yaakov the *tsaddik*?" Hana said. "What will Hanan do with them?"

Rivka's heart ached. "Oh, Hana, I'm so sorry. Hanan is going to take them out to be stoned in the morning. We'll have to round up some help before then to go and stop — "

"No." Gamaliel made a strangled sound in his throat. "Tomorrow morning will be too late. Hanan ben Hanan means to stone them tonight."

"Tonight?" Rivka turned to stare at Gamaliel. "But . . . I thought he was going to do it in public." Josephus hadn't said so, but Hegesippus did. In full view of the people. They *must* wait till morning. "Even Hanan ben Hanan wouldn't murder those men in the middle of the night."

"Yes, tonight." Gamaliel's face filled with grief. "They had already gone out the back gate when I arrived. I could do nothing for them. Fourteen men — all to be stoned in the Hinnom Valley."

Hana screamed and grabbed Gamaliel's arm. "Which way did they go?"

Gamaliel pointed south. "Toward the Essene Gate."

Hana bolted away, wailing.

"No!" Gamaliel shouted. "It is useless!" He turned to Rivka. "The woman is a fool."

"She knew what to do to save Ari the Kazan," Rivka said. "She is a woman of great courage. Perhaps more courage than you."

Gamaliel flinched. "I . . . there is nothing I can do."

"You could at least prevent her from being killed."

Indecision flitted across Gamaliel's face.

"Would you allow a woman more honor than yourself?" Rivka held out the club. "Hana does not flee before injustice, even if a man does."

Gamaliel hesitated a moment, his face a mix of fear and anger and . . . honor. Then he snatched the club and ran.

FORTY-TWO

Yaakov

Yaakov stumbled along the street, his heart sick with grief. What had he done? What had he done? He had thought to demonstrate his love for Rabban Yeshua. His honor for Rabban Yeshua. His righteous anger on behalf of Rabban Yeshua. That was why he had spit at Hanan ben Hanan.

The Rabban would not have done so. The Rabban went to his death with a prayer on his lips. A prayer for his enemies. With love for his enemies.

Yaakov caught his breath. Had he been asleep these many years? The words of the Rabban burned in his heart.

You will love your enemies. You will pray for those who persecute you.

A man could not choose to love or hate his enemies. And yet a man could choose to pray for his enemies. Such a prayer would be bitter as bile. And yet . . . And yet, was it possible that the Rabban taught a deep thing here?

You will pray for your enemies, and by doing so, you will come to love them.

Yaakov's heart pounded a harsh rhythm in his chest. No, it could not be so simple. Words were not action. He had argued many times with those who believed that mere words constituted trust in HaShem. Words were nothing. By a man's actions, you saw his heart.

And yet words were a form of action. By words, men's heart were set aflame or pacified. By words, men persuaded, insulted, built, destroyed, loved, hated. By words, HaShem had created the world.

Words were something, and it was a lie from the enemy to say words were nothing. Words were something, because words led to actions. As a man thinks, so he is. As he speaks, so he becomes.

And if a man went to the grave with hate in his heart, even hate for an enemy, an evil man, then how could he face HaShem in the World to Come? Rabban Yeshua had commanded a hard thing, but not one beyond a man's grasp. Or if beyond a man's grasp, not beyond his thought. If a man could think it, he could attempt it. If attempt it, by the grace of HaShem, he might achieve it.

It was better to die trying than not trying. Better to meet HaShem in the Spirit of Yeshua than in a spirit of rage.

Yaakov shook his head furiously, hoping to dislodge the rag that stole his voice. He must say the words. A true prayer was one said aloud. But he could not shake loose the cloth. The best he could do was think the words.

Blessed are you, Lord our God, King of the Universe. Grant peace to us and to all Yisrael. And grant peace to . . .

Sweat poured down Yaakov's face. It was more difficult than he had imagined to bless his enemy. His heart felt frozen with hate. With rage.

And grant peace to . . .

Again, he could not do it.

HaShem, you who hears our prayers, grant now my request. That I may have strength to pray for my enemy. To forgive my enemy. In the same power as your servant, Rabban Yeshua the Mashiach. And let all Yisrael say amen.

Hana

Hana ran, lashed by a spirit of fear. Hanan was evil. He meant to kill Baruch. If he killed Baruch, then her life also would be over. She had been angry at Baruch, had meant to leave him. But that was foolishness. He was a good man. Her man. Even if he hated Dov, she must find some way to bear the grief.

She turned at the corner of the palace of Hanan and ran down the long dark street toward the Essene Gate. Had the men left the city yet? She must run faster!

Footsteps behind her.

Hana refused to look. If it was one of the evil men, he would kill her and her suffering would be over. Otherwise, she had nothing to fear. She ran.

The footsteps pounded closer. "Woman!" The voice of the man Gamaliel.

Still she would not look. There was no time. If he tried to stop her, she would fight him, scratch his eyes out, kick him in the tender regions. She would not allow him to prevent her.

Gamaliel drew alongside her. "Woman!" He was not breathing hard, a good runner for a man so short. "Woman, I will help you, but you must let me do the fighting."

Her breath came now in ragged gasps. "Can you save my Baruch?"

"Y–yes."

"You are lying."

"I will *try*. There is a chance, but I can save only one man, not all of them. And you must not help me. If you try, they will kill him and you also. Let me try."

"No." Hana's heart was bursting with panic. If Gamaliel failed, then she would never be able to live with herself, knowing that she had done nothing while they killed her husband. She would rather be dead.

"Woman, you are a fool. You have no chance to save him."

"Then I wish to die with him."

"Very well, then your son will be left an orphan."

Pain knifed through Hana. *Dov*. If she and Baruch both died, he would be an orphan. Rivka would take him in. Rivka and . . .

Rivka and Ari? Ari might be already dead. He had bled much from his wounds. If he died, then Rivka would be alone with two children. Poor, helpless Rivka, who could neither sew nor carry water, who was too proud to work as a *zonah*, too beautiful to beg. She would starve, and the children with her. Yaakov the *tsaddik* would not live to give alms to the poor.

Hana's heart felt torn. If she tried to save Baruch and failed, they would both die and Dov would starve. If she wished to save Dov, she must live herself, and so Baruch must die.

They reached the Essene Gate. Gamaliel studied the small iron door beside the gate. He released the inside latch and pulled it open on protesting hinges. "I have no key to return," he said. "I will try to save Baruch, but you must stay here. When you hear my voice, open the door. If you disobey in this, you and I and Baruch will all be caught outside and Hanan will kill us."

Hana could not think what to do. Gamaliel would try to save Baruch, but she did not think he would try as hard as she would. Yet he was a strong man and she was not.

"Please," Gamaliel said. "I beg you."

Hana had not heard a man beg her for anything, ever. She knew it was foolishness, but . . . somehow this act of humility caught her heart. She stepped back from the door. "Go."

"Do not follow after me." Gamaliel slipped through. "Wait here. Hanan has a key. If you hear voices of many men returning, then run! I will have failed and all will be lost."

She heard his footsteps padding away into the night. Hana counted fifty beats of her heart. Then she slipped through the door. Before she could block it open, it slammed shut. She turned and hurried down, down into the blackness of the Hinnom Valley. She would let Gamaliel try, but if he failed, then she could not endure to live.

Baruch

Baruch stumbled along the dark path. Ahead, the others shuffled slowly, but still Baruch could not keep up. His knee throbbed where he had fallen in the street. A guard clutched his arm, hurrying him down the steep path toward the stoning pits, but he could go no faster. He was last in line — just as he would be last in the World to Come.

Burning shame flushed Baruch's face. For the sake of honor, he had despised an innocent boy. That was foolishness. For that, he would be least in the kingdom. Rabban Yeshua would not throw him out of the kingdom, but he would give him no honor. He would be like a man who escapes naked from a burning building, saving his life, but nothing else.

Something caught between Baruch's feet. He stumbled and fell hard to his knees. Blinding pain shot up his thighs, and then he fell forward to the ground, unable to break his fall.

"Fool!" said a voice behind him.

"Who goes there?" said the guard beside him.

"Yoseph ben Mattityahu," said the same voice. "Eleazar ben Hananyah and some others are just behind me. Hanan ben Hanan sent for us. Where is he?"

"He is leading the way."

"Go and inform him that Eleazar the *sagan* is coming. We will deal with this slow-mover."

Strong hands yanked Baruch to his knees. "Sluggard! Do you think you will escape your just reward by dallying?" A hand slapped Baruch hard across the face.

The other guard laughed and hurried on ahead.

"Baruch!" It was a hiss in his ear, a whisper. Hands fumbled at Baruch's face, and then the cloth rag was gone.

Baruch turned his head with much pain. "You!" It was Gamaliel.

Gamaliel grinned. "I am alone. Stand and go back with me to the city."

Baruch stared at him. "The door will be locked."

"Your woman waits inside to let us back in."

Baruch tried to stand. His right knee collapsed with the effort.

"Stand!" Gamaliel said. "If they send men back to look for us . . ." Sweat stood out on his forehead. "Both our lives are forfeit if they find us here."

Baruch tried again, pushing up with his left leg.

Gamaliel helped hoist him up and then put his head under Baruch's right arm. "Can you walk?"

Baruch took a step. His right knee would bear no weight. On level ground, he could limp along with support from Gamaliel. But he could not climb the dark and stony path. "It is impossible."

A white form appeared just ahead of them. Hana.

She rushed into Baruch's arms. He held her, his eyes filling with tears. His woman loved him — enough to risk her life to follow him. He was unworthy of such love, and yet —

"Woman!" Gamaliel's whisper was a hiss of panic. "I told you to stay! We cannot reenter the city."

Baruch shook his head. "I could not climb back to the gate anyway. We must hide."

Gamaliel pointed toward a stand of trees beside the path. "Can you make it that far?"

Hana slid under Baruch's other arm. "Yes, he can. We will carry him if we must."

The three of them staggered off the path and into the trees. Baruch wanted to collapse. "Here. Stop here."

"Farther," Gamaliel said.

A little farther and again Baruch asked to stop.

Gamaliel refused.

They passed all the way through the trees and into a clump of bushes. Baruch collapsed. "I cannot go any further."

"Shhhh!" Gamaliel put a hand to Baruch's mouth. They had come to rest at the head of a ravine. He pointed down its length.

Torches flickered at the bottom of the Hinnom Valley. Thirteen bound men stood in a small cluster. Around them stood many Temple guards, listening to Hanan ben Hanan.

Faint and clear and far away, every sound funneled up the ravine.

"That is impossible." Rage filled the voice of Hanan ben Hanan.

FORTY-THREE

Hanan ben Hanan

Furious, Hanan jabbed a finger at the guard. "That is impossible! Yoseph and Eleazar knew nothing! Nothing! I set them a task in the Temple that would take all night."

The guard looked bewildered. "The man said his name was Yoseph and that Eleazar and others were coming."

"Who said this?" Hanan roared.

The guard searched the faces of the other guards. "He is not here."

"What did he look like?"

"It was dark. He wore the garb of a Temple guard and he spoke with authority and he told me he would escort my prisoner and that I must run ahead to — "

"One of the prisoners!" Hanan grabbed the guard's tunic. "Which prisoner?"

The guard's eyes whitened with fear. "One of them. I do not know the names of the prisoners."

Hanan counted the heads of the prisoners again by torchlight. *Thirteen!* "One of them is missing." But which one? They all looked much alike. Before today, he had known Yaakov and Kazan by sight, but the others were strangers.

Hanan paced back and forth, rage gnawing at his belly. Precious time passed while the guards studied the prisoners' faces. Finally, one of them said, "The man called Baruch. The friend of Kazan, he is missing."

Hanan remembered. Yes, that was the one. The man with the fiery eyes. "In the morning, you will search the city for this man Baruch, who dared to curse me. Take prisoner his woman and children. Use them to lure him in."

Three of the guards came to report. "The stoning pit is ready."

Hanan went to inspect it. The pit was deep, more than three times the height of a man. A natural limestone platform provided good footing along the north edge. Men with torches stood on the other three sides to light the pit. Hanan nodded. "It will serve. Prepare the prisoners."

They went back to the condemned men. All had their arms bound behind them. One guard went to the prisoners and yanked Yaakov away from the others. He took out a short knife and slit Yaakov's tunic down the front. He did the same on the sleeves and pulled away the sliced garment. Then he tore away Yaakov's loincloth. Finally, he went behind Yaakov and unknotted the cloth that had bound his mouth.

He went around in front of Yaakov and grabbed his beard. "This way, old man!"

"Bless you, my son," Yaakov said.

The guard stared at him, then pulled Yaakov toward the men holding torches. "Stand there without moving or they will light up your beard and hair!"

The old man stood naked and shivering in the torchlight. Hanan felt grim satisfaction. It was dishonor to be seen naked. That was part of the punishment of stoning.

The guard stripped the next man, and the next, and the next. Each went to stand by Yaakov. Hanan heard the prisoners talking together, and gladness filled his heart. They were arguing.

With anger in their voices.

Yaakov

Here at the end, Yaakov knew despair. He had failed. He had shown righteous anger toward Hanan, but the fruit of that anger was not righteousness.

Because of Yaakov's failings, Ari the Kazan would never follow Rabban Yeshua. Baruch would never be reconciled to his son. And his men would go to the grave with a curse on their lips. They did not believe Yaakov's words.

"You *must* pray for these men." He looked at the other men, skinny, naked, shivering in the night breeze. "Rabban Yeshua would have it so."

The youngest of the men shook his head, and fire lit up his eyes. "They are evil. HaShem will punish them."

"Then you should pity them," Yaakov said. "Rabban Yeshua commanded us to love our enemies, to pray for those who persecute us."

"It is foolishness." Several of the men shook their heads. "We will not do it."

"I command you in the name of Rabban — "

"No," said one of the men.

"I will not do it," said another.

"You have no authority to command such a thing," said a third. "It is impossible."

Yaakov knew it was impossible. He had no right to ask. Rabban Yeshua had done so, but he was a man without sin. An ordinary man could not love his enemies, could not pray for them.

The last prisoner joined them and now Hanan approached. He wore an evil smile.

Yaakov knew that his time had come to die, time to say the *Sh'ma* for the last time. He raised his voice to the heavens. *"Sh'ma, Yisrael! Adonai, Eloheinu! Adonai Echad!"* Hear, O Israel! The Lord is our God! The Lord is One! Every Jew wished to die with this prayer on his lips.

The other men joined him. *"Baruch, Shem K'vod, Malchuto, le'olam va'ed."* Blessed be his Name of glory whose kingdom shall be forever and ever.

Hanan waited. Yaakov knew that even the Gentiles allowed a Jew to pray the *Sh'ma* before dying. Hanan would surely allow it — all of it.

Yaakov and his men continued. "And you shall love the Lord your God with your whole heart and with your whole life and with your whole might. And it shall be that these words which I command you today shall be on your heart and you shall teach them to your sons and you shall speak on them when you sit in your house and when you walk in the way and when you lie down and when you rise up. You shall bind these words as a symbol on your hand and you shall bind them between your eyes and you shall write them on the *mezuzah* of your house and on your gates."

The prayer ended and Yaakov's men fell silent. Hanan pointed to two of the guards. They approached the prisoners. Yaakov saw a spirit of fear fall on them, heavy as a woolen blanket dipped in water. They huddled together. A cold hand squeezed Yaakov's heart until he felt he would faint.

The guards seized the youngest man by the beard and yanked it downward. He bent over at the waist with his arms tied behind him, powerless to fight.

"No!" he screamed. "You pigs! You dogs! You sons of *zonot!*"

The guards forced him to walk, bent over, to the limestone shelf beside the pit, and turned him around with his back to the pit. His bowels and bladder loosed their contents. "You dogs!" he shouted. "I curse you with — "

They pushed him backward hard. He tumbled into the pit, screaming. "Dogs!" Then silence.

Several of the guards picked up rocks the size of a man's head and dropped them over the side. One of them signaled to Hanan. Hanan turned and pointed to the next man to die.

Yaakov wanted to retch. No! This was all wrong! How could one enter the presence of HaShem with a curse on his lips? And yet the men would not listen to him. One by one, they would die and he could do nothing, only watch them die in torment. In rage.

The guards came for the next prisoner. Yaakov stepped in front of the man and faced the guards. "Bless you, my sons. And blessed be your mothers who bore you and your fathers. Blessed be your sons and daughters to the fourth generation."

One of them slapped him and pushed him aside. They seized the beard of the next man and yanked him forward, bent double.

"Dogs!" the man shouted. "Pigs! Gentiles!"

One of the guards hit him in the face. They forced him back to the edge. He too soiled himself. "I curse your —"

They pushed him back.

His scream filled Yaakov's heart with grief. His men would not listen to him. They would die with a curse in their hearts. No, he could not allow it.

The men around the pit threw in more stones to ensure that the second man was dead.

Hanan pointed to the third man who was to die. The guards came for him.

Yaakov walked to the edge of the pit and turned around, his back to the abyss. If his men would not listen, they must see.

The guards fought with the third man. He screamed, shouted, kicked, writhed, spit, snapped at them. They dragged him to the limestone shelf and stopped. Yaakov blocked their way. They could not kill their prisoner without pushing Yaakov over first, and this they dared not do.

"Come away, old man!" said one guard. "Your turn will come soon enough."

Yaakov's lips felt like iron. He could not say the words. He must say the words. "Bless you, my son. May your sons dwell in the peace of HaShem for a hundred generations."

The guard looked at Yaakov and fear glinted in his eyes.

The other guard glared at him. "Enough of your tricks, old fox! Step away, or throw yourself in!" He stepped forward and spit in Yaakov's face.

Rage filled Yaakov. This was foolishness. His men were right. A man could not find it in his heart to love his enemies.

But he could find it in his mind. He could say the words.

Tears sprang onto Yaakov's cheeks. "Bless . . ." Anger forced the words back. Righteous anger burned in his heart. But even righteous anger could be wrong, if it prevented a greater right. Yaakov tried again. "Bless you, my . . . my son. HaShem, who sees all, loves you with an everlasting love. May he bless you and keep you and . . . bear you up, lest you strike your foot against a stone."

Something broke in Yaakov's heart. He felt a gush of hot joy in his soul. And love.

Yes, he did love this fool, who was ordered by an evil man to carry out judgment against law-breakers. This man was wrong, but he was a man, the son of a mother and father. Loved by HaShem.

And now by Yaakov.

Yaakov felt a smile on his lips. "Bless you, my son."

The guard stood there frozen, disbelief in his eyes. He turned his face away, but not before Yaakov read his shame.

Hanan ben Hanan strode up to them. "Push the old man in, fools! We have little time."

The two guards refused to look at Hanan.

"Push him!" Hanan shouted. His eyes glowed red in the circle of torches.

The men shook their heads.

Yaakov closed his eyes. "Blessed are you, Lord our God, who created the heavens and the earth and . . ." Yaakov's throat felt that it would strangle. ". . . and the House of Hanan." His voice became stronger. "I . . . I bless you, Hanan ben Hanan. I bless your house and your sons and daughters, your servants, your animals."

The words came like a mighty river now. "*Abba*, forgive him. Grant him grace and peace and — "

Two hands pressed against Yaakov's chest and pushed hard. Yaakov felt himself falling, weightless, unbound from the earth.

Joy unspeakable filled his soul.

Hanan ben Hanan

Hanan watched Yaakov fall. His head smashed against a rock and his neck broke. His body lay still. Hanan signaled the guards to throw in more stones.

Nobody moved.

Rage flared in his heart. "Throw in the stones!"

They backed away from the pit on all sides.

"Fools!" Hanan went around and lifted a large stone. He carried it to the edge and dropped it in. It crushed Yaakov's rib cage. Hanan spit into the pit and stalked away. He had finally completed what Father had begun, many years ago. The last of the messianics were dead. He had won.

Rage smote his heart like a fist.

Baruch

Baruch stuffed the sleeve of his tunic into his mouth to keep from crying out. Yaakov the *tsaddik* was dead. Baruch had prayed to HaShem, had begged for a miracle. And he had seen one, but it was not the miracle he asked for.

Yaakov, who hated the House of Hanan, had blessed it. Had died with joy on his face.

With love for his enemy.

Torchlight flickered on the faces of the men around the pit. The guards now brought the next man, backing him up to the edge of the pit. They moved like dead men, their joints stiff, their movements sluggish. The condemned man laughed for joy and blessed them.

They pushed him in.

Screams filled the whole Hinnom Valley. Baruch shut his eyes against the horror. It happened sometimes that a man did not die when pushed into a stoning pit. Several guards around the edges hurried forward and dropped in large stones.

The screaming ended.

Baruch breathed again. Beside him, Hana wept silently. Gamaliel's labored breathing rasped in Baruch's ears.

The next man to die said a prayer to HaShem and did not soil himself and died with peace on his face.

The next blessed those who killed him.

One by one, the men of The Way went to their deaths. Baruch wept to see it. These were good men. Elders in the synagogue. Men who had prayed with him, cast out demons with him, healed the sick with him, taught him the way of Rabban Yeshua.

And yet they were ordinary men, men who on an ordinary day feared death and hated injustice and raged at the House of Hanan. They were not the sort of men who would die with joy in their hearts.

But this was no ordinary day. Baruch had seen a miracle. No, it was not the miracle he would have chosen, but perhaps it was a greater one.

He buried his face in the dirt and prayed, but not for the House of Hanan.

FORTY-FOUR

Rivka

When daylight broke, Ari lay near death. Rivka had done her best, but he had lost much blood. Also, it was impossible to sterilize his whole body. His entire back and chest was one raw mass of wounds. If an infection set in . . .

Footsteps outside. Brother Eleazar and Brother Yoseph burst in with a short little old man. Rabbi Yohanan ben Zakkai. The old rabbi knelt beside Ari. "Will he live, my daughter?"

Rivka shook her head. "I don't know. Where's Gamaliel?"

"He took us to the stoning pits and we saw the evidence with our own eyes. It is an outrage. When the Sanhedrin learns of this, Hanan ben Hanan will not last one hour longer as high priest."

Rivka put a hand on Ari's hot forehead. "I need Baruch."

Rabbi Yohanan sighed. "The young man Baruch is in hiding outside the city. Gamaliel and several of his friends are protecting him, but he may not enter the city. It would endanger them all, so long as Hanan is high priest."

"When are you going to talk to Agrippa?" Rivka said. "He'll depose Hanan."

"I have sent messages to all the Pharisees on the Sanhedrin. When they see with their eyes, then we will go to Agrippa."

"You'd better make it soon. It's the eve of *Shabbat*."

"My daughter, patience is not your strongest point."

"My husband is on the edge of death and you're lecturing me about patience?"

Rabbi Yohanan shook his head. "Ari the Kazan will live or he will die. His life is in the hands of HaShem. Not mine. Not yours. Until *Mashiach* comes, there will be evils in this world. The wise man battles evil, but he recognizes that evil sometimes wins. The universe is not unmade because of a little evil — or of much. But on the day that HaShem ceases to be King of the Universe, on that day it will be unmade. When you have learned that, you will be wise." He turned and went out.

Rivka followed him out and put her hands on her hips, glaring after him. *Fine, so I'm a dummy. Will it hurt for you to hurry things up a little bit? Because if you won't, I will.*

Rivka checked Ari. No change in his condition. If she waited for the Sanhedrin, she'd be waiting a long time. Rabbi Yohanan was wrong. The whole system was stacked against her — had been stacked against her ever since she got here. Because she was a woman. She had learned a long time ago how to deal with that kind of attitude.

If she wanted something, she had to get angry and make it happen.

Now.

Berenike

Berenike watched the two dozen rabbis walk out through the courtyard into the square. She spun on Agrippa. "What do you mean, you do not have to do anything? Hanan murdered those men! What more proof do you want?"

Agrippa frowned. "Hanan was a bit hasty, but he did pay me a rather large gift before I appointed him and I think it only fair to hear his side of the story. These Pharisees are furious today, but how will they be in two weeks? I will not change the high priest so soon, just on account of a few dead men of no consequence."

Berenike stamped her foot. He could be infuriating when he put his back against the wall. A typical Herod. If he deposed Hanan, it would be an admission that he had made a mistake in appointing him. So he would drag his feet. For weeks. Months.

"You idiot," she said. "Do you wish to hear what the seer woman told me while you were talking to the rabbis?"

"No."

"She said that you would refuse."

"I told you I do not wish to — "

"I am telling you anyway. The seer woman says that you will be stubborn until Governor Albinus sends a letter ordering you to depose him."

"Who is this Albinus? I have not heard of him. When this Albinus appears on my doorstep, I will believe the seer woman. She is unreliable."

"You could depose Hanan now — make a fool of the seer woman."

"I refuse to be manipulated by a . . ." Agrippa curled his lips in distaste.

"A woman? She is not just any woman. She hears from HaShem."

"I was not speaking of the seer woman."

Of . . . me then. The realization stabbed through Berenike. Agrippa would not take her good counsel because she was a woman. Because of his honor. Which meant that all her machinations over the years were nothing. She had lost the great game before she ever entered it — solely because she was a woman. She was a fool. She had imagined all her life that somehow, by playing the game well enough, she could overcome that accident of birth that made her a woman and Agrippa a man.

She was wrong. At last she knew this truth, and it was bitter as wormwood, black as rage. Agrippa could have chosen to be a great man like Papa, but he preferred to wallow in his own incompetence rather than accept help from her, a mere woman.

Berenike turned and strode to the door. "The seer woman asked me to tell you one more thing."

"I do not wish to hear it."

Berenike walked out, knowing that he would later demand to know the seer woman's words. Would beg for them.

And she would never tell him.

The world will remember Agrippa as a weak man who could have done right but chose to do nothing.

It was, Berenike thought, exactly right.

Rivka

Late that night, Rivka could not sleep. A fever raged in Ari's system. Rachel and Dov slept in another part of the palace. Yoseph — yes, the same Yoseph she had hated and feared, the man who would someday be Josephus — assured her that she and Hana would be quite safe in the palace. His father would never give up Ari the Kazan to Hanan ben Hanan.

Baruch was somewhere outside the city, hidden in a cave, closely guarded by Gamaliel and Brother Eleazar. Still under a death sentence, Baruch could not enter the city. Nor could Ari be moved.

Rivka dug her nails into her hands. Ari was dying and there was not one single blessed thing she could do about it. She paced back and forth beside Ari's bed. He needed antibiotics. Now.

It was all so *wrong!* Senseless. Hanan had no reason to hate Ari or the others. No reason but that they got in his way, they dishonored him, they threatened his Temple somehow. The guy was . . . evil. Josephus had called him a bold and insolent man. Well, old Joe sure wasn't going to get convicted of exaggeration, was he?

A step at the door.

Rivka whirled around, her heart racing. "Oh! Hana, you scared me!"

Hana hurried to Ari's bed and felt his forehead. "The fever is worse."

Rivka's eyes blurred with tears. "He has an infection."

"I do not understand this word *infection*."

"It's caused by . . . little bugs. Very tiny. They're in his bloodstream and his body is fighting them. I need antibiotics — more little bugs that fight the bad ones."

Hana's face was serene. "He is in the hands of HaShem."

Rivka slumped to the floor. "Hana, I don't want him to be in the hands of HaShem. I want him to be — "

She stopped, shocked. How could she have said that? It was like she was . . . fighting HaShem to make him do the right thing.

Rivka put her face in her hands, weary beyond words, sick to death of fighting.

Ever since she came here, she had been fighting, fighting, fighting. Fighting an unfair patriarchal system that shamed her for being a woman. Fighting a superstitious people who saw evil spirits under every rock and called her a witch woman. Fighting to make HaShem get his act together.

Rivka felt shamed to her core. What was it Saul had told her? *You must not run faster than HaShem will lead you.* Was that why she felt so exhausted all the time? Because she was trying to outrun HaShem?

She was a good fighter. Adaptable. Quick. Persistent. But when was the last time she asked HaShem for advice, rather than dishing it out to him?

She had been so sure she knew what needed doing, but . . . the truth was, she didn't know diddly. Everything she thought she knew had turned out to be just a little wrong. Not a lot, but enough to put a wrench in things. She saw the future, but it was distorted, like a reflection in a brass mirror. Her knowledge wasn't a blessing, it was a curse, just like Berenike's beauty.

She saw the future, but she couldn't change it.

Evil was coming. Unthinkable evil. Perpetrated by ordinary people.

People who thought they had to do wrong things to make things right. People like Berenike, who would poison her own body to protect her family honor. People like Hanan ben Hanan, who would kill "renegades" to save his stupid Temple. People like the Christians of coming centuries, who would torture Jews to make them confess Christ.

And maybe . . . people like the seer woman, who would manipulate others to do what she wanted, who would try to change the unchangeable, who would even fight HaShem, because she was so bent on mending the shards of this shivered, shattered world?

Rivka trembled. Something shifted deep at the foundation of her soul.

Arms encircled her. "Rivkaleh." Hana's voice, soft and gentle. "The safest place for Brother Ari is in the hands of HaShem. Worse things may happen to a man than to die."

"I'm sorry, Hana, I've been so horrible. I'm wrong. I do want Ari to be in HaShem's hands. It's just that . . . I want him to live. I want Racheleh to have a father."

"Then pray for him, Sister Rivka. And listen to the voice of HaShem." Hana kissed her forehead softly. "Now I must find a quiet place to speak with HaShem. Perhaps he will speak to me." Her footsteps padded out of the room.

Rivka closed her eyes and wept.

Hours later, Rivka woke up. Her body felt tight, twisted like a pretzel. Hana was still gone. Rivka felt cold and worn out. Painfully, she pushed herself off the floor and checked Ari.

His fever had gone higher.

Rivka went outside to look at the night sky. *Shabbat* morning would soon be dawning. The children would be up. Rachel would cry for Ari, and Dov for Baruch. Then both of them would go outside and forget their sorrows in a game of chase.

Rivka turned to come back in, but torchlight in the street caught her eye. Three men in the uniform of Temple guards stood outside the gate of the palace. They spoke to the guard, who let them pass. A woman in a veil followed them in.

Rivka saw by her walk that the woman was Hana. The short guard was Gamaliel, while the enormous one was Brother Eleazar. And the guard in the middle was . . .

Baruch.

Rivka ran down the steps toward them. Joy flooded her heart.

Baruch smiled. "Sister Rivkaleh."

Forgetting propriety, Rivka ran into his arms and hugged him. "Brother Baruch, I'm so glad you've come."

"Evidently. Please take me to Brother Ari."

FORTY-FIVE

Ari

Ari the Kazan stood before the judgment seat of HaShem. Heat unimaginable radiated from the throne of the living God, the King of Kings, the Eternal One, blessed be he. Sweat poured from Ari's face, but still he approached the throne.

"Your name?" The voice was like the power of galaxies.

"My name is called Ari the Kazan."

"I have watched you long, Ari the Kazan. All your life, I have held you in my hand, and yet you have struggled against me. Do you wish to make a debate with me?"

Ari lowered his head. "No."

Silence.

Ari dared to look up. "Yes."

"Speak, then." The sound of HaShem was like thunder, like music, like the smell of a woman's hair, like the laughter of children, like the voices of men at prayer.

Ari did not know where to begin. Before the throne of HaShem, all the world seemed small.

"You wish to discuss the Problem of Evil with me, is that not correct?"

Ari nodded.

"Say on. I have had words with men on the matter before. But perhaps you have something new."

Ari shook his head. "I have nothing to add." He dared to look into the brightness of HaShem. "But have you something new? The Problem of Evil is not solved."

Long silence.

"Are you familiar with Gödel's Theorem, Ari the Kazan?"

"You know that I am."

"Then you will appreciate that the Problem of Evil can be solved, but not in the language of men. There is a line in front of you. Do you see it?"

Ari saw it.

"That is the last line you must cross, my son. When you have crossed that line, you will no longer remember the language of men, but you will know the language of the World to Come. Then you will have words to speak with me more on this matter, and then you will understand. Do you wish to cross?"

Astonished, Ari raised his eyebrows. "I am permitted to choose?"

HaShem sighed. "Not in the ordinary course of things, Ari the Kazan. However, you have a most persistent friend. My son Baruch has persuaded me to give you a choice. I will give you now a taste of the World to Come, and I will show you one other thing, and then you will choose, yes?"

"Yes."

"Close your eyes, Ari the Kazan. The glory of the World to Come would blind you otherwise."

Ari closed his eyes.

"Are you ready, Ari the Kazan?"

"Yes."

HaShem laughed.

An instant later, infinite joy pounded in Ari's heart. Liquid laughter pulsed through his veins. A brightness like a thousand galaxies filled his soul, a brightness of being. Ari could put it no better than that — a brightness of being. Now he understood why HaShem laughed, because no mortal man could ever be ready for his first taste of the World to Come.

And then it was gone.

"It was good, Ari the Kazan, yes?"

"It was very good."

"Now I will show you some things in the World That Is. You have seen these things all your life, and yet you have not seen them. You may open your eyes."

Ari looked. He saw a cosmic vastness, a shining thing of aching beauty, a painting of many dimensions. Swiftly, he zoomed in, past a million galaxies until he reached a delicate pinwheeling galaxy of two hundred billion stars. To the edge of this galaxy he spiraled in, growing smaller and smaller. A white-yellow star appeared, and as he approached, his heart pounded with the perfect, impossible symmetry of its system. A pale blue dot expanded in his eyes to fill all his vision.

And there was the land of *Yisrael*, the Sea of Galilee, the Jordan.

Jerusalem, city of God.

Rage pulsed in its streets.

He saw joy also. Beauty. Kindness. Love. Men praying. Women nursing. Children laughing. Green grass, blue skies, red sunsets. Roasting meat, sharp cheese, cold beer.

"Ari the Kazan."

The vision disappeared. Ari looked again into the face of HaShem.

"You are much disturbed by a world of senseless evil, yes?"

Ari nodded. "The Problem of Evil, yes."

"I invite you then to ponder the Problem of Good. Senseless joy. Irrational love. Mindless beauty. Look on it and despair, Ari the Kazan!"

"I do not understand why this should be a problem."

"Think on it, my friend."

Ari stood silent a long time.

"There is a line in front of you. If you cross that line, I will explain to you the answer to the Problem of Evil and the Problem of Good. If you do not cross, there is a thing I would have you do. Do you wish to cross?"

"I will think on it."

Rivka

For an hour, Rivka watched Baruch pray over Ari. Her heart felt full of fear, full of peace. HaShem would do what HaShem would do. Hana clung to Baruch and held Rivka's hand.

At last, Baruch took his hands from Ari's head and sighed deeply.

Rivka studied Baruch and Ari, hoping for a clue.

Hana massaged Baruch's neck. "Will he live?"

Baruch shrugged. "I do not know. I have done all I could, but . . . there is a line which I cannot approach, and he lingers there."

Rivka put her hand on Ari's forehead and her hopes sagged. "He is grown hotter."

"Only trust in HaShem and wait." Baruch stood up. "Hana, please, I must find Gamaliel. There is a matter I must discuss with him."

They went out, leaving Rivka alone with Ari. She knelt beside him and kissed his cheek. "I love you, Ari the Kazan."

Some time later, Ari's eyes flickered open, vague, unfocused. "No, I will not cross."

Rivka gasped and leaned close. "What did you say?"

Ari shook his head. Slowly his eyes lost their dreamy look. "Rivkaleh." He smiled. "It is good to be home. HaShem sends his greetings."

Rivka was afraid something had . . . happened to his mind. His fever had been so terribly high. "Ari, what are you talking about?"

Ari spent the fourth part of an hour telling her of his visit to the throne of HaShem.

Rivka clutched his hand. "Was it . . . real?"

He smiled. "It is the only thing that is real." His eyes probed her face. "You have something you wish to tell me."

Rivka laid her head next to his and just cried. "Ari, I've been such an idiot about . . . a lot of things. I've been so angry at you and HaShem and everybody else."

Ari said nothing, only listened while she talked. And cried. And talked some more. When she was cried out, Ari stroked her hair softly.

She looked at him through bleary eyes. "I'm going to try to do better. Try to learn to listen for HaShem's voice. Stop trying to save the universe. I've made such a mess of things so many times, trying to rush ahead of HaShem. Ahead of you. Can you forgive me for being such an . . . obnoxious know-it-all?"

"Of course, Rivkaleh. It is part of your charm. HaShem also forgives you. But here is a matter akin to Gödel's Theorem. Can Rivka forgive Rivka?"

Rivka stared at him, feeling strangely warmed, filled, cleansed. Ari had been to the throne. If HaShem said she was forgiven, then . . . who was she to say she was not? She held Ari's hand to her cheek. "You've changed, haven't you? You sound like a . . ." She wanted to say *tsaddik*, but he would call that foolishness.

Ari smiled as if he read her heart. "One does not return from the throne of HaShem unscathed. Yes, I am changed, but I have still far to walk, and the Problem of Evil is not solved."

Rivka sighed deeply. "Do you have any idea what he meant by the Problem of Good?"

Ari shook his head. "It is enough for now to know that such a problem exists. I will think on it."

"And I'll think on it with you. But what about . . . the thing he wants you to do?"

Ari's face twitched. "I will know it when I see it, and perhaps not before." He yawned. "Where are the children?"

"Still sleeping."

"I will sleep now also, but when the children wake, you will bring them to me, please. I wish to see them. And Baruch and Hana also — all of them together."

"Sleep well, Ari the Kazan."

He closed his eyes. "In the hands of HaShem."

Baruch

Baruch stood at the gate of the palace, aching with joy and fear. His heart would break if —

There! Far up the street, Gamaliel appeared, running as if Hanan ben Hanan himself were on his heels.

Sister Rivka called from the palace. "Brother Baruch! The children are up and they're waiting to see Ari!"

Baruch pretended he had not heard. Not yet, not yet.

Gamaliel raced nearer, and Baruch saw that he was smiling. He reached the palace gate, spoke to the guard, entered.

"Baruch!" Sister Rivka's voice took on a shrill note. "We're all waiting on you!"

Baruch strode to Gamaliel and kissed him. "I thank you, my brother."

Gamaliel slipped something into Baruch's belt. "Am I too late?"

"Almost." Heart pounding, Baruch turned and ran.

Sister Rivka looked at Baruch with suspicion in her eyes. "What took you so long? Ari wanted to see us all together, and you're holding us up."

Baruch nodded meekly. "I beg forgiveness, Sister Rivka."

They went into the palace. Hana stood outside Brother Ari's room, shaking her head. "The children already went in." She gave Baruch an accusing look. "Where have you been?"

Baruch merely shrugged. He had not told her his business with Gamaliel.

They all entered Brother Ari's room. The children lay on the bed, clutching him, laughing, shouting, squealing, bouncing. Baruch saw the life in Ari's face, and deep joy warmed his heart.

"*Abba!*" Rachel patted Brother Ari's beard. "I knew you would come back, *Abba!* I knew it!"

Brother Ari held her tight. "Yes, my Racheleh, you had much to do with the matter."

Sister Rivka knelt beside Brother Ari and kissed his forehead. "Blessed be HaShem."

Dov pounded on Brother Ari's chest for attention. "Uncle Ari! Rachel and I made a new game! Come play it with us!"

Brother Ari smiled. "Not just yet, my friend."

"Brother Ari . . ." Baruch stopped. He felt his honor rising up inside him yet again, a mighty fist strangling his voice. He must speak now, or his courage would fail. "Brother Ari, there is a . . . business matter to discuss."

Brother Ari's eyes narrowed. "Business? On *Shabbat?*"

Sister Rivka leaned back and stared at him. "Really, Baruch! At a time like this? Can't it wait until — "

Dizzy with fear, Baruch shook his head. "With respect, Sister Rivka, no, it cannot wait." He took a small packet out of his belt and began opening it. His hands trembled. He walked to the side of Ari's bed.

Dov stood up on the bed. "What is it, *Abba?* Is it for me?"

Baruch felt a great heat fill his heart. "Yes, it is on account of you."

The fist squeezed Baruch again, but now . . . it had no hold.

Baruch slowly shook out five coins into Ari's hand. "Ari the Priest, I choose . . . to redeem my son from you. Here are the five shekels for his redemption."

He held out both arms to Dov.

Joy filled Dov's shining eyes. He leaped into Baruch's arms. "*Abba!*"

"My son . . ." Baruch's voice cracked and he could not see because of his tears. He kissed Dov's cheek.

His son's skin felt cool to the touch.

Glossary

Abba: Papa.

Amidah: Literally, "standing." A traditional daily prayer of nineteen separate benedictions, chanted while standing. Often called "the Eighteen Benedictions."

Apikoros: Renegade. May be a Hebrew transliteration of "Epicurean."

Bat Kol: Literally, "daughter of a voice." An audible voice from heaven.

Cohen: Priest.

Consilium: A judicial advisory board in the Roman Empire.

Dinar: The "denarius" of the New Testament. Nominally a day's wage for a working man, enough to feed twelve people for a day.

Goy: Gentile. Plural, *goyim*.

HaDerech: Literally, "The Way." Name of the earliest Jesus movement in Jerusalem.

HaShem: Literally, "The Name." Used instead of "God" out of respect for his holiness.

Hanukkah: Feast of Hanukkah, usually in December.

Haredim: Literally, "Tremblers." Ultra-orthodox Jews in modern Israel.

Hasidism: A branch of Orthodox Judaism with a strong emphasis on emotion and mysticism.

Havurah: A fellowship of Pharisees in ancient *Yisrael*.

Imma: Mama.

Ishah: Woman, wife.

Issah: Literally, "mixture." Priestly families whose legitimacy was questioned. It was forbidden for a priest to marry a woman of an *issah* family.

Kadosh: Holy.

Koine: Literally, "common." The common Greek used in the New Testament.

Lepton: The smallest copper coin, the "widow's mite" of the New Testament. Plural: *lepta.* 128 *lepta* made one *dinar.*

Lubavitcher: A sect of modern Hasidic Jews centered around a family of holy men from Lubavitch, in Lithuania.

Mamzer: Bastard.

Mashiach: Messiah.

Matzah: Unleavened bread eaten at Passover.

Meshugah: Crazy.

Mezuzah: Literally, "doorpost." A small case attached to a doorframe, containing a tiny scroll with certain biblical passages inscribed.

Mikveh: Ritual bath.

Minyan: A quorum, ten men, the minimum required for daily prayers.

Nazir: Nazirite. One who takes a vow to abstain from the fruit of the grapevine and from cutting the hair. The vow could be either temporary or lifelong.

Pesach: Passover, usually falling in March or April.

Pidyon ha'ben: Ceremony of redemption of the firstborn son, as required in Exodus 13:11–15.

Rabban: Literally, "Our great one." Applied to a very few rabbis — Gamaliel, Shimon ben Gamaliel, Gamaliel II, and Yohanan ben Zakkai. In view of John 20:16, it is plausible that Jesus of Nazareth was called Rabban Yeshua.

Ro'ah: Seer woman.

Rosh HaShanah: The New Year, usually in September.

Sagan: Captain of the Temple guards, second only to the high priest in the Temple.

Sandak: Godfather.

Sandakit: Godmother.

Savta: Grandma.

Shabbat: Sabbath.

Shalom: "Peace." Used as a greeting and a goodbye.

Shavuot: The Feast of Pentecost, falling in May or June.

Sheol: In Jewish tradition, the shadowy world inhabited by the dead awaiting resurrection.

Shofar: A ram's horn, blown at festivals.

Sh'ma: Literally, "Hear!" Traditional daily prayer affirming the Oneness of God.

Sukkot: The Feast of Tabernacles, falling in September or October.

Talent: A unit of weight, variously estimated between about sixty and a hundred pounds. A silver talent was 10,000 *dinars*, a lifetime's wage for a working man.

Tallit: Prayer shawl. Worn draped over the head and shoulders during prayers.

Tefillin: Phylacteries. Small leather boxes containing Torah inscriptions, worn during daily prayers (and all day by the pious), but not on *Shabbat* or other holy days.

Tsaddik: Literally, "Righteous one." Used among modern Jews of exceptionally holy men.

Tunica: The standard tunic worn by a Roman woman.

Tzitzit: Ritual fringes, made with blue and white twisted thread.

Yisrael: Israel.

Zonah: Prostitute. Plural, *zonot.*

HISTORICAL CHARACTERS

The following characters are based on real historical persons. With some, I took a fair bit of literary license. Rivka's comments on each should be understood as the conventional judgment of history, when that differs from my presentation in the story. Spellings for each name have been chosen from Latin, Greek, Hebrew, or English as seemed appropriate.

Agrippa: Marcus Julius Agrippa, also called Herod Agrippa II, last Jewish scion of the Herod family. Born about A.D. 27.

Albinus: Lucceius Albinus, governor of Judea A.D. 62–64

Armilus: A "wicked king" who kills the Messiah ben Yoseph in some Jewish messianic legends.

Berenike: Agrippa's oldest sister. Born about A.D. 28. Rumors of incest dogged her and Agrippa. Intensely jealous of her young sister Drusilla.

Caesar Nero: The emperor Nero.

Eleazar ben Hananyah: Son of high priest Hananyah ben Nadavayah. Captain of the Temple in early sixties. Born to a Sadducean family, apparently became a Pharisee, sparked the Jewish revolt in A.D. 66.

Felix: Marcus Antonius Felix, governor of Judea approximately A.D. 52–59. Lured Agrippa's youngest sister Drusilla away from her husband.

Festus: Porcius Festus, governor of Judea approximately A.D. 59–62. Died in office, leaving Judea temporarily without a governor.

Hanan ben Hanan: "Annas, son of Annas." A Sadducee, youngest son of the "Annas" who presided over the trial of Jesus. Became high priest in A.D. 62 and promptly executed James son of Joseph brother of Jesus.

Hananyah ben Nadavayah: "Ananias, son of Nedebeus." A Sadducee, high priest circa A.D. 52–59. Widely hated for stealing tithes.

Ishmael ben Phiabi: A Sadducee, high priest approximately A.D. 59–61. Built a wall to block Agrippa's view of the sacrifices.

Josephus: See Yoseph ben Mattityahu.

Mattityahu ben Theophilus: A Sadducee, high priest A.D. 64–66, nephew of Hanan.

Moshe: Hebrew form of Moses.

Polemon: King of Pontus A.D. 38–64. Agreed to circumcision in order to marry Berenike, but the marriage soon failed.

Saul: Saul of Tarsus, the apostle Paul. Saul is the English form of the Hebrew "Sha'ul." Paul is the English form of his Greek name, "Paulos."

Seneca: Lucius Annaeus Seneca, a Roman philosopher who tutored Nero and later served as his court adviser. Nero forced him to commit suicide in A.D. 65.

Shlomo: Hebrew form of King Solomon.

Shmuel: "Samuel." I have vastly expanded Shmuel from two sentences in Josephus describing an unnamed "impostor" promising "relief from troubles" in the desert.

Yaakov ben Yoseph: "James, son of Joseph." Brother of Jesus, leader of The Way in Jerusalem, murdered in A.D. 62 by Hanan ben Hanan.

Yeshua ben Dannai: "Jesus, son of Damneus." A Sadducee, high priest A.D. 62–63.

Yeshua ben Gamaliel: "Jesus, son of Gamaliel." A Sadducee, high priest approximately A.D. 63–64. Friend of Josephus and protégé of Hanan.

Yeshua ben Yoseph: "Jesus, son of Joseph." Jesus of Nazareth.

Yeshua ben Hananyah: "Jesus, son of Ananias." Peasant who shouted obscure oracles in the Temple from A.D. 62–70.

Yohanan ben Zakkai: A Pharisee, one of the most influential Jews of all time, the traditional founder of rabbinic Judaism after the war.

Yoseph ben Mattityahu: "Joseph, son of Matthew." Born A.D. 37/38, aristocrat, priest, soldier, historian. Main historical source for this period.

Yoseph Kabi: "Joseph Kabi." A Sadducee, high priest approximately A.D. 61–62.

A Truncated Bibliography

I have read many books in my research for this book. A few have been especially helpful, including the following:

Nahman Avigad, *Discovering Jerusalem* (Nashville: Thomas Nelson, 1980).

Meir Ben-Dov, *In the Shadow of the Temple: The Discovery of Ancient Jerusalem* (Jerusalem: Keter Publishing House, 1982).

F. F. Bruce, *New Testament History* (Garden City, N.Y.: Doubleday, 1980).

F. F. Bruce, *Peter, Stephen, James & John: Studies in Non-Pauline Christianity* (Grand Rapids: Eerdmans, 1980).

Shaye J. D. Cohen, *From the Maccabees to the Mishnah* (Philadelphia: The Westminster Press, 1989).

Gaalya Cornfeld, *Josephus: The Jewish War* (Grand Rapids: Zondervan, 1982).

L. Sprague de Camp, *The Ancient Engineers* (New York: Ballantine Books, 1960).

Henri Daniel-Rops, *Daily Life in the Time of Jesus* (Ann Arbor, Mich.: Servant Books, 1961).

James D. G. Dunn, *Unity and Diversity in the New Testament: An Inquiry into the Character of Earliest Christianity* (Philadelphia: The Westminster Press, 1977).

Martin Hengel, *Acts and the History of Earliest Christianity* (Philadelphia: Fortress Press, 1979).

Martin Hengel, *Between Jesus and Paul* (Philadelphia: Fortress Press, 1983).

Joachim Jeremias, *Jerusalem in the Time of Jesus* (Philadelphia: Fortress Press, 1969).

J. G. Landels, *Engineering in the Ancient World* (Berkeley: University of California Press, 1978).

Bruce J. Malina, *The New Testament World: Insights from Cultural Anthropology* (Atlanta: John Knox Press, 1981).

Richard M. Mackowski, S.J., *Jerusalem, City of Jesus* (Grand Rapids: Eerdmans, 1978).

Jacob Neusner, *First Century Judaism in Crisis* (New York: KTAV Publishing House, Inc., 1975).

Jacob Neusner, *The Mishnah: A New Translation* (New Haven, Conn.: Yale University Press, 1988).

Raphael Patai, *The Messiah Texts: Jewish Legends of Three Thousand Years* (Detroit: Wayne State University Press, 1979).

Tessa Rajak, *Josephus: The Historian and His Society* (Philadelphia: Fortress Press, 1983).

David M. Rhoads, *Israel in Revolution 6–74 C.E.* (Philadelphia: Fortress Press, 1976).

Emil Schurer, *The History of the Jewish People in the Age of Jesus Christ*, Revised and edited by Geza Vermes, Fergus Millar and Matthew Black (Edinburgh: T&T Clark, Ltd., 1973).

A. N. Sherwin-White, *Roman Society and Roman Law in the New Testament* (Grand Rapids: Baker Book House, 1963).

We want to hear from you. Please send your comments about this book to us in care of zreview@zondervan.com. Thank you.

GRAND RAPIDS, MICHIGAN 49530 USA

WWW.ZONDERVAN.COM